HELEN DALE
KINGDOM OF THE WICKED

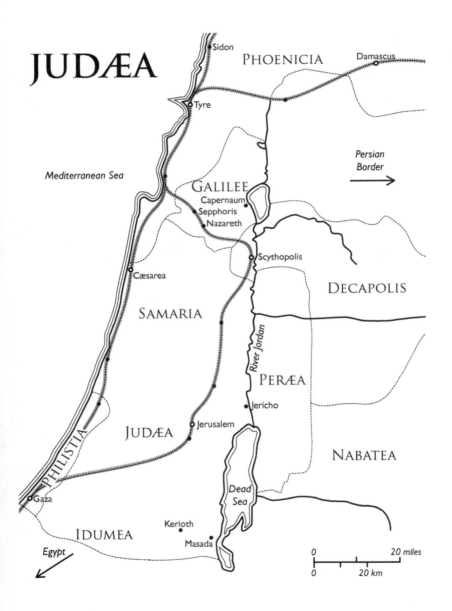

JUDÆA

Sidon

PHOENICIA

Damascus

Tyre

Persian
Border

Mediterranean Sea

GALILEE
Capernaum
Sepphoris
Nazareth

Scythopolis

Cæsarea

DECAPOLIS

SAMARIA

River Jordan

PERÆA

Jericho

Jerusalem

JUDÆA

NABATEA

PHILISTIA

Dead
Sea

Gaza

Kerioth

IDUMEA

Masada

Egypt

0   20 miles

0   20 km

JERUSALEM

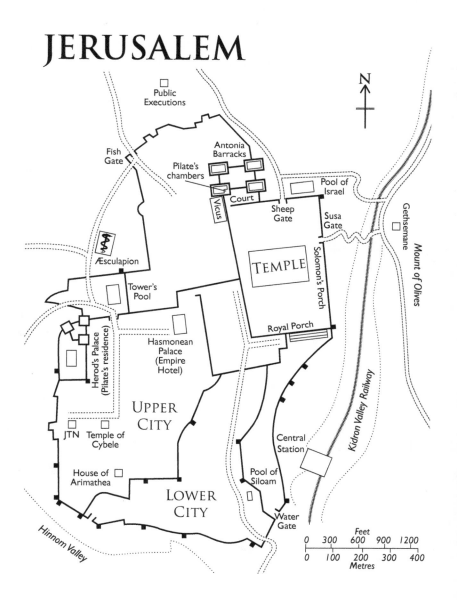

N

Public
Executions

Antonia
Barracks

Fish
Gate

Pilate's
chambers

Pool of
Israel

Vicus

Court

Sheep
Gate

Susa
Gate

Gethsemane

Æsculapion

TEMPLE

Solomon's Porch

Mount of Olives

Tower's
Pool

Herod's Palace
(Pilate's residence)

Hasmonean
Palace
(Empire
Hotel)

Royal Porch

UPPER
CITY

Kidron Valley Railway

JTN Temple of
Cybele

Central
Station

House of
Arimathea

Pool of
Siloam

LOWER
CITY

Water
Gate

Hinnom Valley

Feet

| 0 | 300 | 600 | 900 | 1200 |

| 0 | 100 | 200 | 300 | 400 |

Metres

BOOK TWO

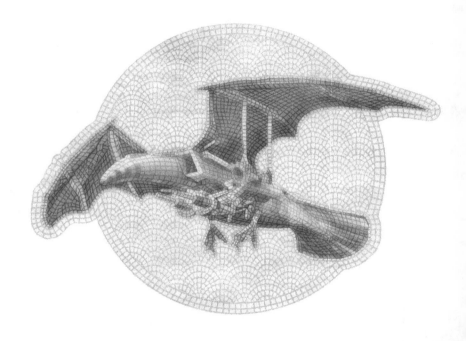

ORDER

Although we must endeavour to make society good in the sense that we shall like to live in it, we cannot make it good in the sense that it will behave morally.

—F. A. Hayek

PART VI

I made her no rash promise of return,
As some do use; I was sincere in that;
I said we sundered never to meet again

—Thomas Hardy, *Panthera*

*Long before Yehuda disappeared into Antonia's maw, it was Kelil
who had started to waver first, although for a long time Saul did
not know why. He and Yehuda were inseparable, and even when
he was called away for long periods, Yehuda always returned loyal
as before. Not so Kelil, who would lie awake at night, muttering to
himself. Sometimes he would seek Saul out and insist on engaging
in long and convoluted conversations about this or that target.
Matters came to a head when they hid a bomb in a culvert outside
a school. When it went off it didn't just get a Jewish collaborator
teaching the conqueror's language but three students as well, all of
them under sixteen. Kelil and Yehuda argued after that, and Kelil
swore he wouldn't be party to any more child-killing.*

'We killed the Latin teacher,' he said.

'Their language is filth,' Yehuda countered.

*'When we are free, we will need to trade to live, and we will need
their language in order to trade. And killing children is wrong. We've
got to stop it, Yehuda. Killing a child is like killing the prophets, and
you know as well as I do we've got a bad habit of doing that.'*

*This silenced Yehuda, albeit temporarily. Saul waited for the
young man to leave and took it upon himself to ask Yehuda what
Kelil's problem was.*

'He's too Greek,' Yehuda said.

Saul soon learnt this wasn't a reference to his sexual proclivities but to his associates. Kelil had Greek friends from school; they knew him as Stephanos and would call out and shake his hand in the street, asking after him and wanting to know what he was doing now. Kelil liked them and didn't want to reject them. One of them had a sister he fancied, too.

'You need to ask her and my parents soon, Stephanos,' her brother said. 'She likes Apollodoros, too, and if he asks first he'll get her, not you. So make up your bloody mind.'

Saul was disbelieving that this was the only reason, and said so.

'Both of you listen to that Ben Yusuf character too much,' he told Yehuda. 'It's all pie in the sky, you know. He hates the Romans but doesn't do anything about getting rid of them, just talks about the Kingdom of God.'

Yehuda went scarlet and tried to change the subject. Saul wasn't having it, dragging him back on point.

'Yeshua Ben Yusuf wants the Romans out of Judaea, and an end to their pernicious influence on our culture,' Yehuda said at length.

Saul shrugged, noticing only that Kelil could no longer be induced to lay charges or bury explosives or shoot to kill. The best they could get him to do was drive brothers to designated locations or repair vehicles. He would attack Roman troops when they were separate from Jewish civilians, but not otherwise. Two attempts to target Roman legionaries who had taken Jewish women came to nothing as a consequence.

In time, the non-compliance became too great to ignore and word came down that Kelil needed to have his loyalty tested.

'There's a problem with the Rabbi in Capernaum,' said Yehuda. 'He, ah, accommodates the conqueror too much.'

Kelil looked at the ground, his face flushing. 'What did he do?'

'One of the Roman filth took a boy from the town.'

Kelil did not understand, shaking his head and stroking his fine soft beard. Saul knew he was innocent, but not how innocent.

'As his pais, his padika,' *Yehuda said.* 'As his boy lover.'

Kelil nodded; that, he understood.

'He's the Commander of the Capernaum garrison, this Propertius,' *said Yehuda.* 'Now he bends one of our boys over his bed in his quarters every night and fucks him up the arse like a woman.'

Kelil covered his mouth, horrified. Saul spoke now, his voice soft.

'The Rabbi worked out a deal, you know. The Roman could have his boy so long as they didn't rub what they were in the locals' faces. You know, no kissing and handholding in the street, no canoodling. But the boy still gets on his belly every night for his Roman master. This isn't good enough, Kelil.'

Kelil, Yehuda told them, had to go and ask for an audience with the Capernaum Rabbi, explaining that he, too, had a Roman soldier who loved him. He was to walk down the cardo in the early morning light as the town woke from its slumbers and knock on the Rabbi's door, concealing a pistol in his clothes. When the Rabbi answered, he was to shoot him and flee. There would be so many Zealots stationed thereabouts he would get away clean, even if the Rabbi did not die straight away. The Romans in the castrum would not be able to respond fast enough to the emergency.

'They'll learn not to be so accommodating, the worthies of Capernaum,' *Yehuda said.*

'I don't want to do this,' *Kelil said.* 'I think it's wrong.'

'It's not about what you think, Kelil,' *Yehuda said.* 'It's about what we have to do to get the Roman filth out of our country.'

'It's their town,' *Kelil said.* 'He's their Rabbi. Those are their rules, what they've worked out among themselves.'

Yehuda had beaten him then, leaving him blubbering in the corner, his lip split open, his hands clutching his head.

'This Roman is fucking one of our boys,' *he said.* 'Imagine if it were you, Kelil.'

Saul was stationed in the safe house on the hill with a pair of binoculars, watching Kelil walk down the cardo to the Rabbi's house. The sun was rising and long shadows cut across the pale concrete streets the Romans had built for this lovely lakeside town. The light bounded off the Sea of Galilee and lit the fishing boats lining up along the shore as fishermen brought in the catch for the day's markets. Wake-up sounded from the castrum and as he watched, a dozen men ran around the perimeter, their cadence calls soaring upwards. This was one of the simpler ones, telling how much they loved working for the Senate and People of Rome. He remembered how—when he was a child—it had taken him some time to appreciate that most Roman army cadence calls were satirical, ironic, or vulgar. The running men assembled and proceeded to raise the Tenth's vexillum, the great-tusked wild boar pawing at the ground and snorting steam from both nostrils.

The men on security changed over now; all very efficient it was, as they saluted each other and marched everywhere double time. The castrum reeked of permanence and activity, with its stone and wire and paved streets and detachments of men all strutting off to appointed tasks.

He saw one soldier—a junior officer—step out of his quarters, his torso bare and his camouflage jacket tied around his waist. The woman he'd just used clung to him. The soldier kissed her, ruffling her hair, and made his way back inside. He dressed as he went, his helmet crooked on his head, the chinstrap swaying in front of his neck, his identity disk glinting in the sun. He returned with another officer of similar rank, this one bareheaded and bristle-skulled. Both had cups of coffee in hand. The second man kissed the woman as well, handing her coffee, and Saul realised what the three of them had spent the night doing. A loud burst of music came from within and the helmeted man dived inside to shut it off. Saul felt profound gratitude. He couldn't abide Roman popular music.

Kelil came into view now, walking in front of the barracks, his head huge and face distinct in Saul's binoculars. He turned the corner, crossing the street to stay in the sunshine; it was chilly in the shade. Saul watched as he stopped before the Rabbi's house and knocked. Saul waited as the Rabbi come to the door, tefillin wound around his arms and forehead, shawl over his head. The two of them spoke quietly for some time, but no shots were fired. The Rabbi leant against the doorframe, nodding, his beard flicking in the breeze. He was too far away for Saul to see the expression on his face. Eventually the Rabbi closed his door and Kelil made his way back along the cardo, towards Saul's position. Saul saw him stop in the street below. He banged on the door, his face pale in the dawn light. The man whose house it was admitted him, his expression quizzical. Kelil bounded up the stairs and opened the door. He stood so he was face to face with Saul.

'I quit,' he said. 'I quit now.'

THE FATHER

When Abdes Pantera first came to Bingium in Germania, local children stood on the station platform and stared at him and his Cohort, wondering how they came to be that colour. One bold child ran up to him and rubbed the skin on his forearm to see if the brown came off. The soldiers and the children laughed at this, although the little boy—for they saw, now, that the child was a boy of about eight—became frightened and hid behind a woman in her late teens with flowing golden hair. Her face was long and oval, her nose ramrod straight.

'Where do you come from?' she asked.

'We are from Sidon by the Sea and Mauretania, pretty lady, sent to keep the Germans from your door.'

'We are Germans, too,' she said.

The German children followed them as they marched to the Roman barracks along the town's neatly paved cardo. The sky above was cool and grey while the town itself was filled with sharp, pointed slate roofs. He'd never seen anything like it. He'd been told—as they all had—that the roofs were designed to slough off snow. He'd never seen snow, save in pictures. A few children followed those who Pantera dispatched outside the barracks to the *limes* and its fortifications and minefields. People walked out of their shops and houses into the street, curious but wary. It began to drizzle as fair faces came to top-floor windows to look out on these lean dark men from the south in their tan and sand camouflage, so unlike the dark green and brown of the north. They saw the Cohort commander squint up into the weather and curl his lip.

The rain got heavier, and Pantera began to curse Varus and his military adventurism and the order that had dragged his Cohort and twenty or so others from all over the Empire to make up the losses.

Could be worse, I suppose. Could be in Britannia.

He looked at the civilians on the footpath, standing under awnings leaning out into the street. Water poured down the canvas into the gutters and drained away. He could feel it running down the back of his neck; it was cold. He peered through the rain at the signage hanging over various shop fronts: there wasn't a word of Greek in sight. He suspected he'd spoken Greek outside his Cohort for the last time in his life, unless he somehow contrived to get himself posted south or east again. He noticed the Latin was often riddled with errors, or served only as an adjunct to a picture of the goods for sale. Sometimes there was a sign in what he suspected was the local tongue, but he could not puzzle out a single letter of the German script. He saw the golden-haired girl and the curious little boy from the station duck under an awning in front of a shop selling tools and agricultural machinery; it abutted a tavern and he caught a last glimpse of her as she vanished up a flight of stairs beside it.

As the timber-framed houses grew denser and more people came into the street, Pantera called his men to order and they began to sing a marching song. The German and Celtic civilians who lined the way liked this; they hadn't heard the song—it, too, probably came from the south—but it had a lively step to it. Some of them clapped and stamped along, admiring the way the Romans' rifles all pointed in the same direction over their shoulders as they marched. Some of the young women smiled now; the Romans looked so much nicer in their neat uniforms than the German guerrillas from over the *limes* with their mismatched military cast-offs and stolen weapons. Even so, if Pantera and his men had hoped to be welcomed with flowers, none were forthcoming. Instead, the flowers were in the window boxes, pink and orange mixed together. The combination made him squint.

Are Germans colourblind or something?

The girl with golden hair took her little brother by the hand and led him upstairs to the rooms above the tavern. The boy broke away from her and looked out the window at the marching soldiers.

'They are that colour naturally,' she said to her mother. 'Ansgar tried to rub it off.'

'It doesn't come off?'

'No, not like the coal miners.'

'They don't sing *When Marcus comes Marching Home* anymore.'

'No, mama; that's because this year, he didn't.'

'You'd better get some wine delivered, Gunda, and call in a few favours around town. They've come a long way.'

'And they'll want women and drink, I know.'

'And music and company, Gunda. There are worse things to want.'

Gunda seethed inwardly; her mother had taken up with a Roman soldier five years ago—a Lucius—and the man had worked his way into their lives, providing a father figure for Ansgar and encouraging Gunda at school, but he was of the XIXth and killed in the *Wald*. She remembered a legionary comrade of his—exhausted and filthy from fighting and his long flight across the Rhenus—scraping his camouflage helmet off as he stood on the threshold and told them of Lucius's death, and of the ill-starred battle.

'The Germans surrounded us,' he said, drawing a shallow bowl in the air with his hands. 'They knew everything; their leader (*spit*) pretended to be our ally. They'd tunnelled into the hills and buried their artillery so they could fire on us directly. Their positions were so well concealed under forestry we couldn't bring counter-fire. *Legatus* Varus went into his dugout and killed himself with a hand grenade, so many men were dying.'

He reached around his neck and worked a heavy chain—Gunda could see it was gold through the filth—over his head.

'Lucius left everything to you, and told me to give you this.'

He dropped the chain into her mother's outstretched hands.

'What will happen to the Nineteenth?' she'd asked, her voice wavering.

'There is no Nineteenth. They captured our Standard. They took some prisoners, but I don't think they'll live long. We saw them being marched further into the forest from where we were hiding, the women from our field brothels with them. One man fell from exhaustion and they shot him where he lay. They beat many of the others. We saw.'

Shock showed on her face. 'They *surrendered*?'

'No, captured; Romans don't surrender, you know that.'

'Lucius wasn't captured?'

'No. He died in front of me.' He indicated the top of his chest with one hand. 'A big piece of shell casing got him. It was quick.'

She held the chain up to her face, feeding it through her fingers.

'It had my name on it, that shell casing, but he took it instead.'

Later that year, there was a story in one of the newspapers that the Germans had reverse-engineered their batteries from a single captured Roman artillery piece. She didn't quite grasp what had happened—Romans published newspapers for other Romans, who shared their military obsessions. The Germans couldn't do proper indirect artillery fire, the paper said, they didn't have the mathematics to calculate elevation (*whatever that is*) and their copied weapons could not be calibrated finely enough—but in the end, it didn't matter. They had line of sight.

Gunda saw both her mother and the soldier were crying now. Her mother took the man by the hand and led him upstairs. She ran him a hot tub—they had a big copper bath and spacious if sparsely furnished rooms above the tavern—and bade him sit in it. Gunda watched through a gap in the wood as she cleaned his body and head with her own hands, dressed his wounds and led him into her room. Gunda heard their lovemaking in between crying from both of them.

For her part, she wanted nothing to do with Romans, not when they got killed like that. She was glad when Lucius's friend did not return, and when her mother showed no interest in taking up with another soldier, despite offers. She also—although she did not like to admit it—appreciated that Lucius's money let her mother buy both the tavern and the building of which it was part, including the agricultural supplies store with which it shared a common wall.

That night, Gunda watched one of the lean brown men walk the length of the bar on his hands, balancing a drink on his shoe. His confreres laughed at him as he bounced down to join them afterwards. The tavern had a radio—long tuned to *Roma Vocat* and regularly bathed with grease such that the dial was now stuck—but it seemed the southerners preferred to make their own music. One man played a fat-bellied instrument across his lap with a bow while other men danced across the flagstone floor. She'd never seen a horsehair bow before. The sound was strange but infectious.

Pantera asked her if it ever stopped raining.

'There's a reason it's so green here,' she said, 'although it stops raining in summer.'

He grinned at this and bought them a jug of ale to share.

'Not too much,' she said, 'Mama doesn't like it if I drink while I'm working.'

'It's only one,' he said, smiling at her.

The men from the south seemed less inclined to fight either each other or the locals than the northern Italians who'd hitherto made up the bulk of Roman troops in the district. Only one man had to be deposited on the footpath outside by means of a foot planted in the middle of his back; only two threw up. The latter, Gunda suspected, came of underestimating the alcoholic strength of German ale.

'Your men are very good,' she told him. 'Men from the Nineteenth would fight and whore whenever they got the chance. They broke windows, threw chairs and fucked girls up against the walls out back, even in winter. We couldn't get insurance.'

'I suspect my men will do that, too, in time,' he admitted. 'At the moment we're just glad of places to go where you can meet local people, local women.'

'Couldn't you do that where you come from?'

'Not in Judaea, no,' he said. 'There were places where Romans and Greeks went to socialise, and presumably places where Jews went to socialise, although I never saw the inside of one. You went with a whore, or you lived like a Vestal Virgin.'

'How long were you in Judaea?'

'Eleven years,' he said. 'Believe me, I'm willing to put up with a lot of rain just for the chance to sit here and talk with you like a normal human being.'

She laughed at this and stood up to help her mother, older brother, aunts and uncles with serving.

After the last brown southerner had left and they'd cleaned the beer and vomit off the floor and scrubbed the tabletops down, Gunda's mother sat beside her at one of the tables.

'The Cohort Commander likes you,' she said. 'He really

likes you.'

Gunda spun around and stared, colouring, blue eyes blazing. 'He told *you*? Why?'

'It's a sign of respect,' she went on. 'He asked me if he could court you.'

'Why would he do that?'

'I think he thought he had to. I said it was up to you.'

'If he likes *me* I want him to tell *me*, not my *mother*.'

When Pantera called on her for the tenth or maybe the eleventh time—she wasn't sure, he was taking his time with her—Gunda decided she had to know why he'd talked to her mother about his feelings before speaking to her. She liked him and didn't want to hurt him, but it'd been gnawing at her every time she saw him. She leant against the doorjamb at the top of the stairs above the tavern.

'We are Germans,' she said. 'We have our own minds. Everyone knows that.'

He fidgeted, looking down. 'I'm sorry,' he said. 'I was trying to do the right thing, the honourable thing.'

'My own father and brother crossed the *limes* to fight against Rome; soon after they left, my mother had a Roman in her bed.'

'I didn't want to take you for granted,' he said, at length. She could see his breath in the cold, clear air. 'And habit from Judaea, too,' he went on.

'I think we're getting closer to the real reason,' she said.

He smiled as she stood aside and invited him in, fetching bread, sausage and ale for both of them. He put the cherries and raspberries he'd bought at a local greenhouse on the table before her, tearing the paper around them open with his fingers. Ansgar stood behind her in the gloom, his face picked out on one side by the gaslight mounted on the opposing wall.

'When I grow up, I want to join the legions,' he said.

Gunda shuddered. 'He's been like that ever since Lucius. I don't want him to die.'

'I won't go down the pit.'

'Not every battle is like the *Clades Variana*, Gunda. Since the Civil War, we've generally been good at preserving the lives of our soldiers.'

'We call it *Teutobergerwald*, Roman,' she said, tartly.

'I'm not doing very well today, am I?'

She smiled, eating one of his cherries and flicking the pip adroitly into the bin at the back of the big kitchen where three of her mother's near relatives prepared food each evening.

'That's all right. I still like you.'

She leaned across the table and kissed him; he poured ale for both of them. She stood and unhooked the gas lamp from the kitchen wall and brought it over to the table, sitting it beside the plates of fruit. Ansgar climbed into Pantera's lap and asked to see his service pistol. He took it out, emptying the chamber and showing him the innards.

'Can you still shoot it?'

'Yes. It's called *dry firing*. It's bad for the firing pin, though.'

Ansgar ran his fingers along the barrel as Pantera ate some of Gunda's German sausage and dark bread; he was rapidly becoming addicted to both. She brought butter from the icebox and he cut off a chunk, leaving it to soften on the side of his plate.

'Sometimes you could buy this in Judaea,' he said. 'Not often, though. The Celts in *Legio* X *Fretensis* and *Legio* III *Gallica* would pine for it.'

She watched him eat, his face a picture of concentration. Now she'd become used to his colouring—not to mention his thick eyebrows and tightly coiled hair and black eyes—she found him very attractive. She'd watched him oil his brown skin—he went a rich, glossy mahogany—at the baths in Mogontiacum. She had to make herself scarce before she embarrassed herself; this involved hiding in the toilets until the urge to masturbate had passed.

She wondered why he hadn't pressed his claims further; she knew from holding him to her after he'd taken her to the theatre in Lugdunum and to the Temple of Isis in Mogontiacum that he wanted her. The two trips had involved overnight stays, and while he'd booked rooms for a couple in both cities, he'd merely kissed and cuddled her each night and then rolled over to sleep. This happened even when she conveyed to him through the intensity of her response to his kisses that she wanted him to finish what he'd started.

The latter trip in particular was fascinating and frustrating in equal measure; she watched him prostrate himself full length on the floor of the *cella*, hands outstretched above his head before the statue of an austere and beautiful Egyptian woman breastfeeding her baby. 'His name means "servant of Isis",' one of the priestesses told her. 'When you are scattered to the wind's four quarters, as he has been, the Queen of Heaven will make you whole again.' Afterwards he'd kissed her and touched her in such a way that she felt sure he would take her to him. He didn't.

'He won't have me,' she told her mother.

'That's a sign of respect, Gunda.'

'I want him to have me.'

'Well, tell him.'

She noticed he was watching her eat with particular intensity, so she sent Ansgar downstairs to their mother. The boy slid off Pantera's lap and went—instead of to his mother—to his room. He looked back at his sister with a mixture of curiosity and fear. His departure allowed Pantera to gaze at the blood-coloured juice from fat cherries and raspberries dribbling down her chin and neck as she ate. He stood and stepped around the table, crouching beside her. She leant forward, suspecting he'd crossed a threshold of sorts. He began to lick her throat. She felt him undo the fine cloth ties across her breasts with eager fingers; his tongue worked its way from the hollow in the base of her neck to the cleft between her breasts, following the sweet trail down to her navel. She kept eating and salivating, using her fingers to pop the tiny curls on the top of his head as he licked her.

'I want you to have me, Pantera,' she said, 'but be gentle.'

He paused and nodded, his black eyes shiny as he looked up at her. He began to stroke her breasts.

'I'm a virgin,' she went on, 'and I want to enjoy you.'

He stood, pulling her into his arms. His lips and chin were covered with red fruit stains. 'Where's your room?'

She took his hand and led him to a room behind the kitchen; she could smell roasted buckwheat, hops and savoury meats as they passed it. She pulled her heavy down bed covers back; he sat on the edge and took off his boots and trousers while she wriggled under the covers up to her chin. Pantera joined her and they goosed each other with cold fingers, giggling as they undressed, doing their best to stay underneath the down.

'Hold me,' he said, 'I'm cold.'

He wanted her to straddle him in the Roman way but she shook her head; it was too cold for that. He pulled her backwards into his chest, taking care to keep them both covered and burying his face in her hair. He inhaled deeply; he loved her scent. She watched him dip his fingers into a small tub of ointment he held in front of her face. It smelt good and she reached out so she could hold it under her nose. She was unprepared when he began to massage the slippery balm in between her legs. She smiled inwardly when she realised he must have brought it with him for just this purpose.

'That's nice,' she said.

'I'm glad,' he said.

That he had been restraining himself for some time became clear when he took her. 'This is mine,' he said over and over, 'just for my cock.' She always maintained that she conceived that night.

'You fuck in German,' he said afterwards.

She moved closer and he clinched her to him. The temperature outside was plummeting; she suspected the rain she could hear falling was beginning to freeze.

'It's Alemannic,' she said. 'That's my dialect.'

'What does *liebli* mean? You kept saying it.'

'Beloved,' she said, 'that's what it means.'

'Thank you,' he said.

She rested her head on his chest and he pulled the covers over both their heads.

'Why did you take so long?' she asked. 'I've been disappointing Roman soldiers for the last three years. That's the thing with Romans—you won't die wondering.'

He chuckled at this.

'I really wanted you, Pantera, but you made me chase.'

He buried his fingers in her hair, massaging her scalp.

'I have history,' he said, 'and I don't want to repeat it.'

'Tell me,' she said.

PANTERA'S STORY

'After I finished my basic, the Empire sent me to the Galilee, a part of Judaea province. It is beautiful but very poor. I don't know how far you've travelled outside Germania Superior but you need to imagine clear light and blue skies and dry ground the colour of old bones. The people who live there are resentful of Rome taking their liberty from them, more resentful even than you Germans. Originally there were no cities and everyone lived in villages, or on small farms, or fished in the lakes and rivers, growing just enough to live on— salad vegetables, some olives, apples and grapes—Jews and Samaritans side by side. As you know, Romans do not suffer a place to be without proper cities, so we built them. One city was Sepphoris, the Jewel of the Galilee, the bird on the hill. Many of the city's pieces had to be sent by rail and over the sea from Rome. The one I remember is the Temple of Roma, which came unassembled and had to be put together by local craftsmen. It had Ionic columns that they hadn't seen before. All of these were installed upside down, with the scrolled bit at the bottom. This was very funny when the *municipium* inaugurated it.

'Judaea is not a safe province, so even though there was this new fine city, it still needed to be garrisoned. We soldiers built a permanent *castrum*, and very good it was, too. Each day detachments would go forth to watch over the people of the Galilee in case they were revolting. They revolted a lot. Once they tried to revolt in Sepphoris itself, but that was before my time. Afterwards the revolting went north, into the wild hill country. At first the Galilean revolters were mistrustful of Sepphoris and it was mainly Greeks who moved in beside us Romans in our *castrum*. In time they became less wary and soon there was a lively trade going on in the forum. At first the customers were the men who built the city, but soon people came from outlying villages to buy and to sell. One day a man stood up in the forum and said that buying and selling in the marketplace like this was immoral, because the sellers looked only to their own concerns, not those of the people who bought from them. Maybe he had been cheated in commerce, because he was very bitter. One of the shopkeepers came out of his store and said that this was well and good for the man standing and speaking in the forum, because friends supported him. That is, they paid for him to catch the train between towns and harangue people about their immorality, while the immoral people made a living the best way they knew how and so made life better for everyone.

'The Galilee is full of signs and wonders, even I have seen some. In one village there was a woman four hundred years old who could tell the future. In another there was a man who could conjure something out of nothing, like the Egyptian priests in days gone by, and which we do not see so often in our time. Once I went to the old woman to have her cast me a horoscope and she forecast that I would not recognise my first-born son. She was frightened by this prediction and so was I, although I put it down to having Sagittarius who fires his arrows one way and runs the other as my rising sign. Soon after this our Cohort fought in a battle on the border and I captured a dozen Persian mercenaries with my own hands, for which I was awarded Roman citizenship. When I marched them back to the prison camp one of them looked at me and took an eye out of his face. He held it up above his head and used it to see much further than a normal man. Once he'd seen where I was taking him and his comrades he put the eye back in his head.

'I wanted to know where I might get an eye like that but he said they only existed in Persia, that we Romans made many good things but not magical things. Once we were in the *castrum* I determined to show that he was wrong and went to the Cohort's leading *architectus* and asked him to show the Persian in the cells our most powerful magic. He laughed at me and said there was no such thing anymore, that Lucretius was right and that everything could be explained by means of reason. I asked the *architectus* how the Persian could still see with his eye out of his head, to which the *architectus* replied, "Are you sure he can see?" I had to admit I was not sure.

'Not long after the battle on the border I saw a beautiful young woman selling clothes in the forum in Sepphoris. She was too poor to rent a shop so she just had a table in the place set aside for street stalls. As soon as I saw her I wanted to fuck her. She had glossy black hair that she styled up with fine silver bands. She'd decorated these with what looked like silver coins except that the discs were too small and too fine to be coins. Some of these hung over her forehead. Then there was her skin, as fair as you Germans but without the high colour of the north. At that moment a breeze swirled up and showed me her sweet shape as it coiled her clothing around her. In my mind's eye her naked body was already in my arms and I was kissing her breasts.

'So that I could find out her name and stand closer to her I bought one of her shirts. It had long sleeves with a button and was embroidered around the neck. Her name was Miriam and she did the embroidery herself, as well as making the shirts. When I was on leave I wore it and everyone complimented me on it, so I bought two more from her. I began to think how I might convince her to have sex with me. I thought

I had a good chance at her, mainly because she did not have male relatives around her all the time. Normally in the Galilee a woman does not leave the house without a man. Among them a woman who does go out alone is often called a harlot, even when she is no such thing. In Miriam's case her parents were both dead. She told me that her family had once been well off, her father trading in the fine things that his wife and daughters made. He had no sons, she told me, so he put his womenfolk to work.

'One year they caught the ferry to Cyprus for a holiday in the Roman manner: the man, the wife and the daughters. You may remember it, when the Master slept and forgot to close the bow doors and the ferry capsized in little more than a minute. Miriam and her oldest sister lived—the Imperial Navy fished them up out of the sea—but the rest of the family drowned. After she told me that I felt sorrow as well as lust for her, so I told how my people were all seafarers and fishermen until a Roman senator built a pulp and paper mill by the waterway that ran through our town. The mill leaked dye into the river and the sea, and the fish swam away from us. Even the seabirds went from our skies; no more did we wake to their screeching cries as they followed the catch into the bay. My father sold his boats; he didn't have the money for the great trawlers that go out beyond the Pillars of Hercules into the Atlantic seeking whales as well as fish. My brother and I joined the *auxilia*, while my sister took an apprenticeship as *hetaera* in Antioch. She got to visit our father more than we did. She said he steered his trawler in his sleep.

'Miriam and I were two people who sorrowed for each other. I'd been a soldier for, what is it, four years at most. Miriam had been alone in the world for something similar. On the day in question her sister was there with her behind the table in the forum; the sister was doing the selling while Miriam had eyes only for me. The two women had rented a small room off the forum to store bolts of cloth and reels of thread and buttons and decorations, not to mention the machines Miriam needed to make the things she did. I realised they were living there, cooking on a little gas stove in the corner, going to the public baths to keep clean and washing their dishes in the tiny sink. She took me into this room and we lay on her mattress on the floor in the middle of the beautiful things she had made to sell. She trembled as I undressed her, so shy like all the women of her people and yet ardent, too, as I stirred her up. She knew not how to be clever in the Roman way so I taught her over many more visits how to please a man and how to please herself.

'I was twenty-two and didn't want woman or child, and told her so. I wanted sex, and to find it willingly—given up without recourse to *hetaera* or other women who pleasure men—was a great delight. Miriam seemed to think something similar, because we kept going to the well and drinking from the same cup together. At first she insisted that we go to the little room off the forum only when her older sister was not there, but Elishiba was not deceived and at the end of one market day she walked in on us. I remember it was winter and cold—as cold as it gets in Judaea, at any rate—and Miriam was humiliated. She leaned forward and clung to me and I threw my army-issue coat over her. This covered her completely and allowed me to stroke her hair and back and soothe her. She said, "She's fourteen, Pantera. You might want to think about that."

'I said, "She likes it well enough."

'"So do you," she replied.

'A few months after this incident Miriam told me she was pregnant, and as I was her only man and I took her virginity I must be the father. At that stage the Æsculapion in Sepphoris was only half built so I offered to take her to Caesarea.'

'What for?' asked Gunda, her head still resting on Pantera's chest.

'For an abortion. I told her that the Æsculapion there was finished and that we could stay on for a few days if she liked. Caesarea's nice. But she told me that she didn't want an abortion. So I told her that I didn't want a baby. Then she pushed her hands against my chest and swore at me. I said to her, "I didn't want a woman or baby, Miriam. You've enjoyed this arrangement as much as me."

'"So you won't help me with it?" she asked. I told her that no, I wouldn't. Under our law, if a single man states clearly and explicitly beforehand that he does not want a child, the woman has no claim on him if she has one.

'Miriam then said, "And I suppose being Roman, you'll have that in writing." Which, of course, I did, with the legionary *Advocatus*. Miriam said that we truly were the wicked kingdom, we Romans. I offered again to take her to Caesarea. It's easy enough to get rid of it. Better to have an abortion, then she wouldn't be "shopsoiled". But Miriam didn't want an abortion; she said it was wrong.

'I shrugged my shoulders at this and told her to have it her way, then. I was sorry to lose her in those circumstances, but at least a line was drawn. Soon afterwards I was posted to Jerusalem, and I told her that I did not expect to see her again.

'Jerusalem was a city calculated to drain the hot blood from any healthy young man; the local women would not come across under any circumstances. At one point I hadn't had sex for six months and I began to regret leaving Miriam. I spent a lot of time standing in the sun on Temple perimeter duty or skulking around patrolling the countryside thereabouts, contemplating contacting her again and asking if she would have me back. This was presuming, of course, I could sit comfortably for long enough to get to Sepphoris on the train.

'My sister had moved to Alexandria after our father died—still sailing in his sleep, she said, the housekeeper found him on the floor with an old tiller in his hands—so I made plans to visit her when I had some leave. Just before I left I had cause to think of Miriam again. There were honour killings in the villages outside Jerusalem, and one particularly terrible incident where a girl had talked to a Roman soldier who'd innocently asked her for directions. Her family did not consider her dishonoured but the village elders did, and she was murdered on the way back from the well. Her parents were willing to give evidence, but no one else would and they started to get threatening letters shoved under their door. I led a detachment that helped them move into the city for their safety. While I was there helping them pack their belongings, I saw a photograph of the dead girl; she was Miriam's double. I wondered if Sepphoris had any village elders like that. Yes, it was beautiful and civilised, but it was also in the Galilee.

'I spent much of the train journey feeling shame about what I had done to Miriam and longing for her, such that when I arrived in Alexandria and saw my sister on the platform the first thing I told her after we exchanged greetings was what had happened in Sepphoris. She insisted I incubate in the Temple of Isis so that I might learn what I ought to do. After spending that night in the arms of one of my sister's close friends from the same House I resolved to attend to matters of the spirit.

'If there is magic still in our Empire of steam and speed it is in Egypt, and so on my sister's recommendation I presented myself to a priestess skilled in the interpretation of dreams. I cleansed myself according to her instructions and took heed of her words when I arrived at the Temple. She held a tonic to my lips and bade me drink. Once the tonic began to take effect, she led me by the hand to the place at the Goddess's feet where I would sleep that night. She touched my head, noting how soldiers have little hair to stroke away from the forehead in the traditional way.

'A falling dream came to me, picked out in great detail thanks to the drink she had prepared. I stood on the highest point of the Pharos, its great rotating ray of light cutting across me at regular intervals. It was night and I could see ships of all shapes and sizes scattered out across the water: ironclads and fishing trawlers and ships taking cargoes to Terra Nova and other far flung places. I knew I must step off from my place of safety and did so. I fell alongside the wall, arms outstretched, then fell through the lighthouse's concrete foundations and then the sea and the seabed. I was not afraid that I would hit the ground and die, although I became afraid when I passed through solid objects like a spirit. I saw a green sea serpent eating its own tail and heard it speak to me but not what it said. At length I crawled up out of the sea and out of my dream and told the priestess what I had seen. She warned me most solemnly that I must not go back to Miriam and told me that everything was already fixed. She also stressed to me that Isis looks out for the weak people and that I must never again take advantage of weakness like that. The priestesses of Isis are not given to hysterical warnings and so when I saw her worried face from my place beside the statue I knew she was concerned for me. I promised her I would abide by her instructions.

'I kept my promise for nearly nine years, requesting frontier duty and avoiding Sepphoris. I saw much action as a result and rose through the ranks, becoming Cohort Commander shortly before being posted here. It was when I heard about the terrible defeat in the *Wald* and then learned of my Cohort's imminent transfer to the *limes* that I broke my promise to the priestess. I remember the announcement over the radio in Antonia and how everyone stood to attention out of respect for our honoured dead. I wondered what had become of Miriam and her child and thought that it was safe to look in on her in the forum in Sepphoris.

'I made arrangements to meet Victor, a comrade of mine in the Sepphoris *castrum*, and caught the train from Jerusalem. Victor took me into the forum and I was pleased to see that Miriam was doing well. She now had a nice shop of her own and lived in an apartment above it. Victor told me an older tradesman, Joseph from Nazareth, did not mind that she was shopsoiled and took her in marriage; I saw two of his children by her standing near the entrance to the shop. Victor pointed out my son to me when he stepped outside to join the other two, although his dark colouring and height made it clear he had different paternity from them. I walked towards him but did not have the courage to cross the street and approach him directly. I just loitered there in front of the theatre opposite Miriam's store and hoped he would notice me. He was a good-looking little boy with my hair and his mother's fine features. He was wearing a brightly coloured kippah and great tufts of curly hair protruded from under it. He started to play a game of tag with the other two children and finished up beside me, in part because he had to keep stopping and holding onto his hat. I spoke to him and to my surprise he replied.

'"I am Yeshua," he said. "I'm going to be a carpenter when I grow up."

'I asked him, "Do you go to school?" And he told me that he did. "Here in Sepphoris, I can speak Greek. My father is *tekton*."

'I tried to detain him longer by making more small talk, but I've never been good at small talk and in time I could see he was becoming bored with me. He then asked if he could look at my beret, which I was pleased to show him as it was new and had my Cohort Commander's insignia on it. I handed it to him; he gazed at me. "You're my father, aren't you?"

'I did not know what Miriam had told him and so stood

rooted to the spot, unable to stay or go. "Yes, Yeshua, I'm your father," I said.

'He went on, "Your name is Pantera," looking closely at my shoulder flashes. "And you've been promoted."

'He handed me my beret, staring at me. He had enormous dark eyes and at that moment I could not turn away from him. Then, solemnly, he said, "You did the wrong thing."

'By then Victor had joined me in front of the theatre. He was eating an ice cream and handed one to me. He said, "I got you *chocolatl*, so you owe me because it's twice the price of the others." The boy heard and asked for an ice cream.

'Here was my chance to redeem myself in a small way; I led Yeshua to the gelateria and let him choose two flavours, whatever he wanted. He ordered strawberry and *chocolatl*. His two siblings, I noticed, had retreated to the other side of the street and were heading into their mother's shop.

'Yeshua tucked into his ice cream and smiled at me. "This is nice," he said.

'Then a voice behind me said, "You haven't changed, have you?" It was Miriam, standing behind me with her hands on her hips. She was round and fat with a baby but still very beautiful. "Bribery will get you everywhere."

'I told her he'd asked for an ice cream, so I bought him one.

'At that point Victor wriggled his eyebrows at me and stepped backwards, smiling. He said in Latin, "This is getting into awkward territory so I'll just go feed the ducks in the park next to the baths."

'With Victor gone I asked her if she wanted an ice cream too. The three of us stood on the footpath in the sunshine eating our ice creams, not speaking, watching the customers go in and out of Miriam's shop to be served by her sister and two other women. When I'd finished eating, I held out my hand for her to shake, but instead she called me a prize shit. Her tone was amused, not hostile. She took Yeshua's hand and walked him across the street to her shop.

'She didn't look back at me.'

Twenty-one years later, Gunda ran up the stairs past the shiny new *Eagle's Rest* sign to answer the *vocale* only to see her mother sitting in the rocking chair and taking to Carissa's hair with a brush. The little one tried to wriggle away from her grandmother and was on the point of tears.

'Mama! How many times have I told you not to brush it?'

Her mother put the brush down on the floor. 'It was a mess.'

'Well, she looks like a dandelion now. Only with a wide-tooth comb, when it's wet, and full of conditioner.'

'Yes, dear daughter.'

She heard Isidore answer the *vocale* and switch from German to Latin. She breathed a sigh of relief. Carissa ran to Gunda and hugged her.

'When your brother's finished, ask him to braid it for you.'

Isidore poked his head out of the tavern's office; he really was a handsome young man, light coffee, lean and muscular with soft fair curls. His father wanted him to join the army but he had his heart set on the priesthood.

That's eight years in Egypt, sonny... first medicine in Alexandria, then a learning residence at the Temple in Philae.

I don't fancy getting killed for the Empire's honour, Papa.

'Someone in Judaea wants to talk to Papa.'

'Who? You sure it isn't something to do with Ansgar?'

'*Avunculus* Ansgar's on the train, Mama. He'll get home on leave tomorrow.'

'Oh, that's right. Well, try to find your father and then braid your sister's hair. Someone tried to brush it again.'

Gunda's mother flushed. 'Sorry.'

Isidore looked at his littlest sibling. 'You have to promise me you'll sit still.'

Carissa skipped towards her big brother and took his out-stretched hand. 'I think Papa's still in Mogontiacum with Iri-na, picking up a truckload of booze.'

'For tonight and tomorrow?' asked Gunda's mother.

'We're going to have most of a Cohort in here over the next three days.'

As though to remind him of that point, a booming bass line reverberated through the floor beneath their feet as Ric—the next down in age from Isidore and his twin sister Irina—did a sound test.

'Well, tell whoever it is in Judaea to call back after *Megalesia*.'

'He can't, it's for a court case.'

'The courts are in recess,' said Gunda's mother.

'Not in Judaea, Mama,' Gunda said, a shadow crossing her face. 'Is the man from Judaea still on the line?'

'No, I hung up, but I took down his details.'

'Let me see.'

Isidore retrieved the scribbled on envelope and handed it to Gunda. As he did so she saw the trident-shaped contra-ceptive 'chip' in his left forearm—it was fresh, the skin still raised and red—and smiled to herself. He was a young man of robust good sense, something he'd taken from his father. 'You've got a good one there,' she remembered one of Pan-tera's subordinates telling her, years ago. 'He wouldn't go near the field brothel when we were fighting over the *limes*.'

She read the name and her son's comments on the paper and put her hand over her mouth.

'Well, that's to be expected, I suppose.'

Isidore cocked his head to one side. 'What, Mama?'

'Oh, never mind.'

Pantera propped beside the truck when Irina threw the keys at him. He caught them in front of his chest and climbed into the cab. She clambered in beside him, squinting heavenwards. She pulled off her mittens and blew into her hands.

'Looks like snow, Papa,' she said. 'April snow.'

'Now, *start* you fucker,' he said, wringing his left hand. This was missing two fingers, fingers that came back in cold weather and were trying to come back now. The starter motor turned over a couple of times and the truck's engine coughed into life. He eased the choke out slowly. 'Thank you.'

He nosed the vehicle into what was military traffic for the most part, getting honked at for his trouble by a half-track full of legionaries. He contemplated winding the window down and giving them the finger, but thought better of it. It was too bloody cold.

It's your booze, gentlemen; you'd better let me through or she'll be a dry bar tonight.

'I thought they'd all been decommissioned,' Irina said.

'They have. They've only dug that relic out for *Megalesia*. They're probably going to paint it for the parade.'

She laughed; she'd already seen a couple of decommissioned military vehicles decorated with some of the most exuberantly erotic artwork she'd ever encountered, artwork that became notably sloppier and less precise as one walked around the vehicle.

'They were sober when they painted that bit,' her father explained, 'and drunk when they painted that bit.'

'Crucial question,' she said, holding her hands in front of the truck's heater and spreading her fingers. 'Do we have enough piss for *Megalesia*?'

'We do now,' he said, grinning. 'There are lots of headaches in the back.'

Shortly after he'd left the legions, he'd argued with Gunda

over how much drink to lay in for Saturnalia; he found it impossible to believe that his erstwhile comrades could sink that much piss. Well, they could, and they did. And the tavern had run out of ale. It was not a good look. The Eagle's Rest now had a reputation for ordering in more booze for major Roman festivals than any other tavern along a decently long stretch of the *Limes Germanicus*.

'Is the Boy coming over this evening?' he asked.

'Yes,' she said, 'and I still have to do my hair for him.'

'Your hair looks fine.'

She started to unpick her cornrows, shaking her head and rolling her eyes. 'I like it fresh for my Boy.'

Pantera shook his head. He'd preserved his Roman army high and tight for the most part. There had been one point there when he'd celebrated being out of Caesar's clutches with a set of locks, but the novelty had soon worn off. He wondered at his daughter, remembering—as he always did at moments like this—when she and Isidore were born. One of the midwives in Mogontiacum had come and hauled him out of the men's room by the hand and run him down the corridor.

'*Soldier!*' she'd yelled at him. 'You have children like gods.'

He'd known there were twins on the way but even he hadn't quite been ready for the sight of Gunda in the baths the Æsculapion set aside for new mothers with a white baby on one breast and a black baby on the other.

'They're the most beautiful children I've ever seen,' the midwife said. Pantera remembered propping and kneeling at the water's edge, leaning forward and kissing Gunda with unbridled passion.

'We made lovely babies,' he'd said.

The dimorphism hadn't remained so stark, of course: in time Isidore's skin darkened and Irina's eyes went green.

Even so, turning up on the first day of school with a coffee-coloured blond boy and a mahogany-coloured, green-eyed girl had excited the usual frank appreciation of beauty from the Roman head-teacher. And she was from the *Caput Mundi* itself; she had her charges listen to CR's *Roma Vocat* every morning to 'improve their accents' and always ensured that some of her students appeared at local receptions for Imperial officials—senators, generals, the provincial governor and once the Emperor himself.

Pantera could remember both Irina and Isidore—inevitably chosen to present garlands to visiting dignitaries by the priests at the Temple of the Divine Julius—coming home with prime cuts of meat from sacrifices, unopened bottles of excellent wine (including, on one occasion, some Falernian) and baskets of seasonal fruits. Both were photographed with the Emperor and two different consuls. The images turned up in local newspapers and as soon as the pair turned sixteen, offers of marriage and concubinage started to turn up in the tavern's postbox. Boy the alchemist had been one of these; Irina had liked the look of him and Pantera had invited him to dine. He had dined, all right, on both food and—within the week—Irina herself.

'You just like him because he's red,' Pantera said to her.

She shook her head. 'I want him very much regardless, Pater. He will do the Celtic trial marriage, if you like.'

Boy had the contraceptive trident implanted in his forearm and handfasted with her for a year and a day in token of his good faith. In that time ESSENTIA Mutual hired him as research alchemist in Lugdunum and it became clear that he would make an excellent husband for her. He was fierce and brave, but also clever and disciplined. Irina told her father that in time—because the world had changed of late—she would have Boy's babies.

Irina's head was half unpicked by the time they'd followed

the train line along the banks of the Rhenus and arrived home; the loose side was vertical. She bolted up the stairs while Pantera yelled at staff to get the beer barrels stored away.

'Horizontally, you cockhead,' she heard him yell. 'Do that again and you'll be cleaning the lines until Saturnalia, you hear?'

'Pay a *denarius* to see the crazy-haired woman,' she said as she flung the door open, admiring the tableaux her all-the-colours-of-the-rainbow siblings presented.

Pantera tapped a barrel and sat down in the gloom of the still-closed bar to drink a glass. He had about an hour to rest up before people started arriving, and maybe another three or four hours after that before Boy arrived from Lugdunum and took Irina off his hands. He'd have liked her around for the whole evening, to be honest, but it was hard to expect her to work through when Boy was in town.

Pantera suspected the temperature had risen a little, just enough to let it snow. He'd noticed that about life on the *Limes Germanicus*: often, on the bitterest days, there was no snow. Gunda would tell him solemnly that it was too cold to snow. He watched through the tavern's front windows as flakes clumped together and turned the street white.

'Pantera?'

He turned; it was Gunda, looking pensive, with a scrap of paper in her hands. She joined him behind the bar; he poured her a drink as well and curled his arm around her. She stroked his head—salt and pepper now—and held his chopped down left hand in her own. He buried his nose and mouth in her golden hair and inhaled. He still loved her scent.

'How's the beautiful mother of my children?'

'You need to speak with this man in Judaea,' she said, sliding the envelope onto the bar. He picked it up, reading his son's neat Celtic script and scratching the back of his neck—a nervous gesture. She kissed his cheek as he read.

'In trouble with the law, by the looks.'

'It would seem so.'

'They've had a lot of problems, Gunda.'

'The terrorism.'

'Yes. I hope he wasn't tangled up in that.'

'Doesn't a military prosecutor mean it's a capital offence?'

He nodded and kissed her, then stood up, walking into the small office at the back of the bar, taking his ale with him. She heard him dialling the operator and speaking in Greek, before reverting to Latin. There was a pause before she heard him chuckle.

'No one's called me Tiberius Julius Abdes Pantera since my citizenship ceremony, sir. It's a bit of a shock.'

'Yes, I had the *Advocatus* draft a disavowal, *Aquilifer*.'

'Yes, he's mine, sir. I was born in Sidon but both my parents were Mauretanian by descent. It's reasonably difficult to miss. You won't need a test.'

'Not since he was about eight or nine. Just before I was posted here, in point of fact.'

'Is he one of the terrorists? I saw some of that footage on screen... it was, well, pretty shocking.'

'So not a terrorist then?'

'I see.'

Gunda heard her husband exchange pleasantries and hang up; she waited for him to step back into the bar. When he failed to emerge after five minutes or so, she collected her own drink and went into the office. He was sitting in the middle of piles of paper with his elbows propped on the table and his head in his hands; it was difficult to see if he were crying. She sat beside him, cuddling him and resting her head on his shoulder.

'It's done now, Pantera. You can't change it.'

CORNELIUS

Mirella woke slowly and looked to one side; Cornelius was oiling her body, his face a picture of concentration and intent as he worked, his eyes half closed in the grey light. When he saw she was awake he propped himself up on one elbow and kissed her. She slid her leg across him and mounted him. He chuckled and flicked her navel with one finger, not caring that she bled onto him. For her part, she was still tender, but she wanted him again. She felt his hands grab both cheeks of her backside as she leant over him.

'The next week is going to be, ahem, ordinary,' she said.

'Yes, very.'

'I can't come back until Sunday, can I?'

'You'd need to be registered here, and you're not, yet.'

She stretched her body out along his as she felt him dribble more oil—it was cool against her skin—on her back. He put the glass jar on his bedside table and pulled her to him, his fingers busy. Her voice was husky.

'At least I can still please my warrior.'

'Very much so.'

It had been a strange moment, last night, when he'd returned from the Empire and—she presumed—some sort of Cohort-wide debriefing. It was late, and he'd already been to the barracks baths. He crossed the room, kissed her and sat beside her on the bed, his arm around her. He then proceeded to describe the firefight. It became clear that he wasn't so much speaking to her as fixing the memory in his own mind. His voice was low; his gestures small and controlled. He used a great deal of technical vocabulary she did not understand. When he'd finished, he turned to face her and smiled lopsidedly.

'Thank you, Cornelius.' She kissed his forehead. 'Thank you for defending civilisation.'

She remembered how—she'd seen it as a child in Carthage—Romans from Italy proper would honour their military. They'd applaud and cheer on railway platforms as the men disembarked. They'd stand and give soldiers the best seats at the cages. Strangers would stop returning veterans in the street and buy them drinks. During parades for Caesar's birthday, older boys saluted them while younger boys ran alongside as they marched, holding onto their hats. Younger girls would offer them flowers, while older girls would signal sexual availability in a variety of subtle ways.

And there were always banners thanking them for defending civilisation. *If you can read this in Latin*, one went, *thank a soldier*. That saying was popular among the Roman upper crust in Carthage and was, she suspected, calculated to rub it in rather. As one teacher had told her at school, 'Clio, that capricious muse of history, is a right bitch sometimes.'

She'd expected that he'd want sex after his little disquisition, but instead he held her close to him and they fell asleep in each other's arms. For this, she was grateful: he was very big and she needed some respite. It was only in the morning that she awoke to feel his hands everywhere.

Wake-up sounded; he reached up and stroked her cheeks.

'Hands off cocks and onto socks, Mirella.'

She grimaced at him and licked her lips.

'I'm almost there, my lovely.'

After they'd finished, she dressed and filled in the registration forms he brought her, holding her identity card up in front of her face and copying relevant details across. He washed, dressed and laced his boots while he waited and then guided her out of Antonia. He took care to note identifying points so she could remember how to find his quarters.

'Once you've got keys,' he pointed out, 'the guards out front will expect you to know your way.'

She shielded her eyes when they reached the entrance hall and its security detail, squinting into the brightness, noticing how the guards seemed to be pacing more than usual. Several men were in the process of setting up the hall for a press conference; there was a podium with the Procurator's seal on it, several long tables, transducers and trailing cables. She watched as a military technician unspooled a great length of it across the floor. Light cut across the square as the sun came up; she curled her arms around his neck when they reached the steps.

'Thank you for a most enjoyable three days,' she said, wryly. 'I'm having difficulty walking.'

'Good,' he said. 'Just as it should be.'

'Cheeky, Cornelius.'

'If you find court interesting, you can watch me in action starting Wednesday.'

'The trial?'

'It's open to the public, and after yesterday's, ah, effort, there's likely to be a bit of interest.'

She could see a paperboy in front of Antonia, hawking copies of *Tempus* and a local Greek-language paper. 59 DEAD, MANY HURT IN JERUSALEM TERROR ran the banner headline.

'They're all connected?'

'I think so, yes,' he said. 'Of course, I have to convince the Procurator of that.'

'I'll see what my shifts look like,' she said. 'I'd like to see you lawyering.'

She stretched up and kissed him one last time and then turned to go. He watched as she stopped to buy a newspaper before crossing the square towards the taxi rank.

Cornelius made his way to the Law Room, expecting he'd have to apologise for his lateness to three subordinates, but only Saleh was waiting for him. The young medic's eyes were bloodshot.

'Morning, sir.'

'Morning, Saleh. Coffee?'

'Yes please, sir. I'll prepare it if you like.'

He held up a box of Phrygian filter coffee and waggled it.

'From the *vicus*?'

'Rachel's addicted to the stuff. She can drink it at night and just go off to sleep, but I'm afraid it makes me run like a dormouse on a wheel.'

Cornelius smiled as Saleh went into the small kitchen and set to work; coffee smells permeated the room by the time Cyler and Aristotle appeared at the door together. Aristotle looked distinctly uncomfortable; Cyler was rubbing his eyes. Cornelius's smile turned into a fierce smirk.

'I take it you wanted some more sleep, Lucullus?'

'Yes, sir, I did.'

Cornelius looked at the young man's face; he was reasonably sure Cyler had found something enjoyable to do with at least part of the night. He ordered the three men to sit and leant on Viera's desk, facing them and scratching his chin.

'I'm aware that yesterday was not a good day for two of you.'

'No, sir, it wasn't,' said Saleh, leaning forward and pouring coffee for everyone.

'You've lost comrades. You've been placed in a difficult position. You're worried that today could go the same way.'

Aristotle nodded at this.

'I don't want to finish up in the same room as *Advocatus* Crispus ever again, sir,' he said.

'The man with a broken moral compass,' said Saleh.

'I'm glad you gave me that pass, sir,' said Cyler.

'I can't make guarantees, Eugenides, but as I flagged yesterday, I'm not going to avail myself of my Form 23 powers with Ben Yusuf today.'

'Well, you need *Centurio* Lonuobo for that, sir.'

'Not necessarily, but in any case I think he'll be compliant, and I'm willing to interrogate him on that basis.'

'Isn't Iscariot one of his, ah, followers?'

'Yes,' said Cornelius. 'So was the principal terrorist at the Empire.'

Aristotle found this perplexing. 'Doesn't that mean that, ah, he's a terrorist too?'

'Maybe. At this stage I think he's more of a terrorist enabler, someone with a sense of his own importance, someone assured of his moral authority.'

'So just as dangerous, sir?' asked Saleh, frowning.

'Someone who gives the Zealots an excuse for what they do,' said Cyler.

'Yes,' said Cornelius.

Saleh's voice was soft. 'When I was a boy and first learning our secret, sacred rites in the Temple in Caesarea, I remember one of the visiting *Archgalli* impressing on me that there's nothing more dangerous than a man who thinks he's an instrument in his god's hands.'

Cornelius looked at Saleh.

'That power can be used for good or ill, of course,' Saleh added. 'Think of Homer's heroes, in the days when gods still walked on the land.'

'This is why I need you today; not as medic, but as interrogator.'

Saleh shook his head, his eyes growing wide.

'I've had no HUMINT training, sir—none at all. I'm just a medic, there to stop them from turning their toes up under interrogation.'

Cyler looked at him. 'But you know all this religious shit. You've forgotten more religious shit than the rest of us will ever know.'

Saleh chuckled at this. 'I can't play-act, though. I can't be *Domine* Sarcastic or whatever you call it. I can ask religious questions, I suppose.'

'You've also got Aramaic, yes?'

'Nabataean, sir. He'll think I've got a ridiculous accent, but we'll understand each other well enough.'

'Good. I do think he speaks with forked tongue sometimes, says one thing to his followers in Aramaic and something else in Greek when people like us are around.'

Saleh chewed on his bottom lip, nodding. 'That doesn't surprise me, sir.'

Aristotle looked at Saleh, scratching his head. 'There's something wrong with the religion here, isn't there? I mean, it shows in their weird sexual hang-ups and whatnot, doesn't it?'

Saleh nodded. 'I think so, Eugenides. I've got a bunch of theories that I've thrashed out with my mother, although they've never been tested.'

Cornelius sat back in his chair, watching the three men. Cyler leaned forward, his interest well and truly piqued.

'What's the problem with their religion, then?'

Saleh pressed his lips together. 'They fear their God too much, Lucullus. Their God scares the living shit out of them.'

'But you're supposed to fear the gods,' Cyler protested. 'That's what being brought up to right religion means.'

'Not fear like that, Lucullus. You revere the gods as you would your parents. The gods are good to us, more inclined to spare than to punish.'

'My old man could scare me good and proper.'

'So could my mother, and the high priestess in Damascus, but we both turned out all right.'

Cornelius lodged his chin in his hands, watching the bright but traditional Cyler struggle to grasp something almost, but not completely, beyond his ken.

'You mean what we call the *superstitio*, don't you?' he asked. 'A fear of the gods so great it paralyses you.'

'If you fear too much... you won't get out of bed in the morning. You won't try to better yourself. You won't build railways or aqueducts or anything good and useful.'

'Because you'd just be afraid?'

'Yes. And you'd want everyone else to be afraid, too. Fear loves company; it makes it easier to bear.'

Cyler shivered and rubbed his neck.

'That's creepy, sir... Look, I'm not initiated to anything. We always just honoured the old gods, watched the *Lares*... so it's all a bit over my head.'

Cornelius rapped his knuckles on the table.

'Let's not get diverted,' he said. 'I think it's clear why I need you, Saleh.'

'Yes, sir.'

'To that end, Eugenides, I'm going to relieve you of interrogation duty and substitute Saleh for you.'

Aristotle looked grateful.

Cornelius waited until Aristotle's footfalls had faded away before speaking again. 'I'm going to conduct this interrogation entirely *ex camera*, and I'm going to try to get to the bottom of what this man thinks.'

'Am I to be *Domine* Sarcasm, as usual?' asked Cyler.

'If you feel like it, Lucullus; I'm more inclined to just wing it and see what happens.'

CONSUL CRISPUS

Pilate gave his press conference under exploding flashes and tried to do a rough headcount as he sweated behind the podium and its official seal. Half-a-dozen husky soldiers flanked him while Marius stood beside him, passing him briefing documents from time to time but not speaking. It annoyed Pilate that the press pack was backlit from outside. It meant he struggled to recognise even familiar faces and felt uncomfortably spotlit, like he was on stage.

Do I deliver a soliloquy while I'm here?

Media types had converged on Jerusalem from all quarters, although he was amused to note that two senior CR people from Rome looked both dyspeptic and suntanned, as though they'd been dragged off a beach somewhere and had been enjoying *Megalesia* far too much. At one point, he saw the CR cameraman step outside to be sick, two legionaries looking on with ill-disguised contempt. He did wonder how they'd managed to get themselves to Jerusalem so quickly until he overheard one reporter mention she'd called in a favour and stepped off a Navy ground effects vehicle in Caesarea early that morning. She'd then caught the train to Jerusalem as the sun came up. She was now prevailing on sundry locals to find a place to stay in Jerusalem for the duration of the Ben Yusuf trial.

'Good luck with that,' Pilate heard someone with a JTN press pass hanging around his neck say. 'The biggest hotel in town is out of action, it's Passover and even if you offered to bonk a legionary officer every night, he's not allowed to let you stay in his quarters.'

Pilate smiled to himself as he answered the same question—rephrased, of course—for the fifth time. 'I'm not at liberty to disclose how we came by our intelligence. I think I've already made that point.'

'Procurator, can you at least tell us if it involved the use of torture?'

'Yes, it did. There was a Form 23 application by the senior legionary legal officer here, which I granted. That's a matter of public record.'

'Can we have access to that record, Procurator?'

Pilate could feel himself getting grouchy; he was fed up with journalists who seemed unwilling to do the most basic research. 'Look it up. I'm not going to do your archival work for you. You can't have the recorded interrogation as the matter is not currently before the courts, but you can certainly see the application.'

A slim, well-dressed man Pilate did not recognise stood up, waving his hand. Pilate pointed at him.

'Aristides Eiron, Athens Broadcasting Service, Procurator. Is it fair to say that torture saved hundreds of lives?'

Pilate looked at the Athenian. Marius had given him background briefings on the various networks, and ABS took a consistent anti-torture line.

'Yes.'

Eiron pounced. 'Does that mean you approve the use of torture in all similar circumstances?'

Pilate felt his lips curl and knew instinctively he would feature on the front page of half-a-dozen afternoon edition newspapers looking like he'd been sucking on lemons.

'I'm going to do what you press people accuse Imperial officials of never doing. I'm going to do some nuancing.'

There was general laughter at this comment.

'Ask me if torture saved hundreds of lives yesterday and

I'm forced to admit that, yes, it did. However, ask me if I think that torture is right in any circumstances, some circumstances or all circumstances and I'm also forced to admit that I don't know the answer.'

Aristides Eiron sat down, his expression quizzical.

'I'm now going to run a book on how many of you reproduce that comment in its entirety.'

This brought further laughter. He pointed at the woman from CR, who was waving her hand.

'This province is becoming more violent, not less, Procurator. Is there an end in sight?'

Pilate let her question sit for a moment; he knew he would have to answer it with great care—the answer would turn up in despatches.

'Judaean society is in transition. The violence, unfortunately, is a part of that. I think it's also worth pointing out that the violence we saw yesterday is emanating from a very small and deeply unrepresentative group of people.'

The press conference wound down slowly. Pilate knew that he'd be free to go to his office and make what was becoming an increasingly urgent call once he noticed camera crews shooting establishing footage around Antonia's interior and across the square. This was flooded with crowds of holidaying schoolchildren, pilgrims, and legionaries on high alert. He looked at Marius and made wind-up signals from behind the podium. Marius nodded and drew the conference to an official close.

Pilate bounded up the stairs two at a time, raced along the corridor and hauled Horace into his office.

'Have you fed the baby sharks?'

'Yes, Procurator.'

'Good, because I've just fed their older brothers. Get me a

secure line to this number.'

He handed the young man a business card. Horace saw the fine purple border indicating a senator around it. He then read the name and blanched. He went through the security codes allowing him to bypass the operator and gave the handset to Pilate once he obtained a dial tone. Pilate sat behind his desk and signalled for coffee.

It took time—and meant navigating his way through various flunkies and undersecretaries—but eventually he heard the resonant voice of *Consul* Gaius Crispus on the other end of the line. Horace knocked; Pilate buzzed him in and watched as the young man put an espresso in front of him. He nodded and smiled and indicated that Horace should leave with a wave of his hand.

Pilate announced himself. He heard Gaius sigh.

'What has my eldest son done *now*?'

Pilate outlined the previous day's events.

'Which amounts to what?'

'He's facing court martial, Consul, and dismissal. Unauthorised use of torture; illegally obtained evidence; bringing the legion into disrepute. It's a bit more serious than being a cad. You won't keep his name out of the papers this time around. There is a real risk of *infamia*.'

'I see.'

'I'm now also in the position where I'm forced to admit that intelligence obtained under torture contributed to yesterday's, ah, successes.'

'Do the press have any inkling of what really happened?'

'As yet, no, although tender-minded Greeks of various descriptions are on my case for what's already on the public record.'

'Yes, well, we know what Greeks are like. One of them had the hide to ask if he could marry my daughter last year. I don't care if he's *duumvir* of Corinth, a consul's daughter is simply out of the question.'

Pilate felt himself inhale, he hoped not audibly. He drew the line at Greek servants and non-citizens, but if a senior Greek official had courted Camilla and she had reciprocated his affections, he would not have opposed the match. That said, marriages between Roman women and Greek men tended to fail: Greeks often tried to order their wives about, and Romans wouldn't wear it. Still, he hoped Gaius's daughter's view of the Corinthian was the same as her father's.

'The real problem is that the record of interrogation we do have will be available to the press as soon as Iscariot comes to trial, and it will then be clear that it contains no advance warnings of yesterday's attacks.'

He swore he could hear the wheels whirring between Gaius's ears. 'What's my eldest son doing as of now?'

'He's been relieved of all duties and confined to his quarters.'

'Well, at least he's not been thrown in the stockade.'

'He will have to go in there in due course.'

'I see.'

'Consul, I'm not going to be able to help you or your son. In fact, I'll probably have to order removal of the matter to Syria due to conflicts of interest.'

'I see.'

'Consider your position. Retain good counsel.'

'Yes.'

'I'm very sorry, Consul.'

'I appreciate your candour, Procurator. Good day.'

The line went dead. Pilate realised that his coffee was both cold and untouched. He buzzed for Horace.

THE VISIT

Joseph Arimathea found himself admitted to Antonia at the tail end of a press conference; he watched the Procurator field questions, finding himself respecting the man's skill as he did so. The last few were easy enough, however, and the gathering broke up with mutual expressions of goodwill and good wishes for what he knew to be one of their festivals. *Io Cybele!* he heard Pilate say to a dark, sharp-faced woman with an access-all-areas press pass hanging around her neck. Joseph could see the letters *CR* on it in bold relief.

'You'll need to wait here while I send for someone from the cells, Rabbi,' a legionary on the security detail told him. 'Please take a seat.'

Joseph sat in the grey hewn stone waiting area and busied himself with a Latin-language newspaper. He noticed that it was *Acta Diurna*, the state-owned gazette. What it lacked in gruesome photography—it carried no images, save portraits of members of the Imperial Household or persons holding high public office—it more than made up for by pushing a relentless line. He found himself drawn to its account of the previous day's events. Once he got to the phrase 'a part of the larger battle between civilisation and barbarism' he very deliberately put it to one side.

'Rabbi?'

He looked up to see a handsome young soldier with eyes he'd only ever seen before on a woman: rich, dark and violet.

'I'm here to take you to the cells. Do you have your visitor's pass?'

The soldier held out his hand and introduced himself as Cassius; they made their way through the Antonia labyrinth. Joseph had visited on previous occasions and some of it was familiar to him, but the cells were not. He followed Cassius closely, not pausing to look at anything too long out of a strong desire not to get lost. They passed a lot of men, and for the first time Joseph became aware of what Passover leave cancellation meant for Roman troops in Jerusalem: Antonia was filled to absolute capacity. Cassius led Joseph into what he assumed to be an empty interview room—although there was a very young supervising guard in attendance—and told him to wait.

'I'll see what the availability of the two men is like, Rabbi.'

Joseph waited for what seemed like a very long time. There were no newspapers in this room and he fidgeted with boredom. He'd failed to bring any reading material of his own, not even a novel or some of the papers from a local *yeshiva* he was supposed to be marking. He looked at the guard and attempted to make small talk. The soldier gazed fixedly at him and apologised in wooden Greek.

'I am posted here from Gallia Aquitania, Rabbi, and my Greek is very bad.'

Joseph switched to Latin, watching the young man's face soften with gratitude. 'So Latin is your mother tongue?'

'Euskara is my mother tongue.'

Joseph shook his head; he'd never heard of it. Every day, it seemed, he was confronted with evidence of his own ignorance.

'I am *Vasco*.'

Joseph nodded this time, understanding that he had named his language in his own tongue, but given the Latin name for his people.

'Yesterday must have come as a bit of a shock.'

'I did not have to fight, Rabbi, so not too shocking for me.'

After a while conversation dried up; the soldier was no

more than eighteen and if it were possible to have less in common with an elderly member of the Sanhedrin, Joseph struggled to see how. After a while he sat down at his little desk and took out a magazine. Joseph saw the cover—a man with a long rifle crouched beside a short-coated, muscular dog with some sort of body armour over its chest—and surmised that the soldier was a keen hunter.

Cassius poked his head around the door. 'Rabbi, I'm sorry about this, but Ben Yusuf is under interrogation at this very moment and Iscariot is in the infirmary. I can't extract Ben Yusuf although I've been assured that the interrogation will be over in less than an hour.'

'I'll wait, Cassius.'

'You can see Iscariot, Rabbi. He's a bit druggy, but still *compos mentis*.'

'What happened to him?'

Cassius smiled guilelessly. 'He fell down the stairs, Rabbi.'

Joseph doubted Cassius believed his own lie; he could hear the young Vasco snickering behind his hunting magazine.

'Enneconis, take Rabbi Arimathea to the infirmary.'

Enneconis led Joseph past curtained, occupied beds. Iscariot was lying on his metal bunk at the far end of the Antonia infirmary, isolated from the wounded soldiers. The soldiers were exchanging jokes and banter with each other, even those wholly hidden behind their curtains. He could hear what sounded like kisses and two voices trading endearing diminutives coming from behind one set, followed by a woman's voice alone.

'Now you're not allowed to get yourself killed in the next week, you hear me?' she was saying. The soldier's nickname, it seemed, was Puppy.

'I'm not going *anywhere* for the next week, baby. It's called a bullet in the leg.'

The kisses started up once more.

'You need to stop, baby, you're making me want you and right now I can't perform.'

'Puppy, you are the sweetest.'

He listened as they bade their farewells and then watched the soldier's woman emerge from behind the curtains, her lipstick smeared and hair dishevelled. She brushed past him, starting at his prayer shawl, recovering and then moving on. The sad, singsong lilt to her Latin betrayed her origin as clearly as her shock at his presence. *And yet.* Her movements through the infirmary were so natural: uninhibited by history or faith.

'You've got a good one there,' one of the other men said when she'd gone.

'Oh yeah,' he heard Puppy say. 'I got lucky with her.'

Enneconis pulled the curtain back and motioned him inside. 'I have to stay to supervise, Rabbi.'

Iscariot's left arm was in a cast and rested across his chest. His beard had been neatly trimmed and a patch on one side of his head was shaven; the effect was to make him look moth-eaten. His eyes were shut but Joseph suspected he was no more than dozing.

'Hello, Yehuda.'

Iscariot's eyes snapped open; he stared at his visitor.

'You came.'

'Yes, even though you don't deserve it.'

Joseph realised that Enneconis did not understand what the two of them were saying to each other.

'What did I do?'

'Handed Ben Yusuf over to the law.'

'He has to show himself, Rabbi.'

'I don't know where you get this apocalyptic vision that says he has to die and it's your appointed task to make sure that happens, but I'm here to say it's bullshit.'

Iscariot propped himself up on one elbow.

'You and Simon—I presume you know the Romans shot him to atoms at the Empire Hotel—have almost certainly ensured an innocent man will die.'

'Simon's *dead*?'

Joseph ignored the interjection. 'Even the most just legal system is vulnerable to guilt by association, Yehuda. Yeshua gave you and Simon the benefit of the doubt. I told him not to, but his heart was filled with compassion at what had happened to both of you at Rome's hands. He thought he could make you better men.'

'He told us to arm ourselves!'

Joseph sighed. 'Yes, that is true.'

'He will either lead his people out of bondage or die in the attempt.'

'What's he going to do? Come down from on high with armies of angels and knock the Romans' guns out of their hands?'

'Yes.'

'That's a lot of dead angels, then.'

Iscariot's eyes grew wide. 'That's blasphemy, Rabbi. Man cannot raise his hand against God.'

Joseph sat on the little stool beside Iscariot's bunk and leaned over him. His voice was tinged with sadness.

'The world has changed, Yehuda. If anyone can, it is these people, these men of the West who... can do without God.'

A voice came from one of the wounded soldiers. It was distinctly testy. 'We've got our own gods, thanks.'

Joseph pulled the curtain aside and looked at the man who had spoken. He was holding his own curtain open, revealing a lean, dark face with a short but fuzzy aureole of hair.

'This conversation doesn't concern you,' Joseph said in Aramaic.

'I think it does, Rabbi,' the soldier responded in Latin, wriggling to face him and revealing a serious shoulder wound. 'You're calling us godless. That's not true.'

'What's going on here?'

The legionary medic—an older officer with a clipboard tucked under his arm—stepped into the midst of the debate and looked at each of the three men in turn. 'This place is an infirmary. Men are supposed to be convalescing, not debating finer points of religion. That includes you, Julianus.'

He pulled the curtains around Julianus's bunk closed, returned to his spot at the other end of the room and started to fiddle with the coffee machine.

Joseph leaned over Iscariot, speaking very softly.

'Before I came to see you, I went first of all to the Empire Hotel, where my daughter works. She—like hundreds of others—was held hostage for the best part of ten hours. She told me what she saw. Civilians were shot; civilians were raped; civilians were burnt; civilians were pushed off the roof to their deaths; there was a special focus on Jews with Roman citizenship, and they were most of them killed.'

'Oh God.'

'Of course, when real soldiers turned up to raise the siege, the fight was over in a twinkling. The Roman troops rescued everyone, too, not just their own people.'

'I didn't know about your daughter, Rabbi.'

'Don't lie to me, Yehuda. You've known since we met that she worked for a Roman company.'

'Not that she worked at the... Empire Hotel.'

The medic spoke up again. 'Keep it down in there!'

'Rivkah is staying with me for now; staff accommodation at the hotel is a smoking ruin. She is well but I dreamed last night—over and over—of her death.'

'I'm sorry.'

'No you're not. You apologised after trying to murder your sister. You apologised after you shot the medic at Dea Tacita. You apologised after the hand grenade—'

'Rabbi, I—'

'—and we believed you each time. Yeshua and I both knew about the hand grenade, how you cooked up that attack with Simon, but we said nothing. You have made us accessories after the fact to your acts of terror. Petros and Mary want nothing more to do with you. For once they agree with each other, and I agree with them.'

Joseph leaned forward so his face was inches above Iscariot's. 'Petros thinks you don't deserve to live. He's looking forward to your execution.'

'I'll save him the trouble of waiting, Rabbi.'

'Spare us the melodrama, Yehuda. I didn't think sentimental Roman cinema was to your taste.'

Enneconis poked his head around the curtain. He was smiling hugely. 'I made you all coffees.'

Joseph took the tiny cup gratefully. Enneconis sat the second coffee beside Iscariot's bed and beat a hasty retreat. Joseph heard an unfamiliar male voice talking with the medic. 'I'm not sure coffee was such a brilliant idea, sir,' it was saying. 'They'll all need a piss at about the same time, now.'

He heard the medic chuckle. 'Most of them can walk.'

'When you next feel like whining about how Rome has treated you, Yehuda, just remember that you're about to kill Ben Yusuf, an innocent man. Let that thought occupy your mind. I imagine they'll drag you both to the arena in Caesarea to provide some sport for a Roman crowd.'

'Not during *Megalesia*,' Julianus chipped in. 'There's never any killing for *Megalesia*.'

This time the medic was too preoccupied with talking to the nurse to notice that Julianus had stuck his oar in again.

'I didn't know that,' said Joseph, surprised.

'When Cybele first came to Rome during the War against Hannibal, her priestesses and the *galli* insisted she not be celebrated with blood. They even suspend racing for the duration of the festival. Of course, they'll get creative afterwards.'

'I've got a creative idea.'

Joseph felt himself startle; it was Cassius. The man moved like a cat; somehow he'd managed to pad into the infirmary without making a sound. He pulled the curtain to one side and glared with his impossible eyes. They were velvety purple now.

'If it were up to me, I'd cut your dick off, butter it with pig fat and make you choke on it. Extra, extra, read all about it: Terrorist croaks while giving himself a blasphemous blow-job.'

'That's enough, you lot.'

The medic turned up again, the nurse at his heels.

'Everyone, shut up; that's an order. Anyone not bedridden get the fuck out of my infirmary.'

Joseph looked sidelong at Cassius as they made their way back to the waiting room. The Roman was smiling grimly.

'We're not all like him, Cassius.'

Cassius stopped dead and turned to face him, his eyes wide. 'When you do nothing to stop them, you're *just* like them, Rabbi.'

'Take his hood off, Cyler Lucullus, we'll start from a position where everyone can see everyone else.'

Ben Yusuf heard someone hot-foot it towards him across the tiles; he felt the man's fingers fiddling with something around his neck. When it was lifted—and as his eyes adjusted to the light—he beheld the snaggle-toothed but otherwise handsome young man who'd fetched him a box of books and enthused about cinema holding the hood in his hands.

The rest of the room came slowly into focus, and he saw

a very tall red-headed soldier—presumably a Celt of some description—beside a young medic. Both were sitting at what looked like school desks. To his relief, the room was airy, well lit and not filled with torture equipment. He realised his back was to the door and the chair he was shackled to was bolted to the floor. There was a large map of the Empire—its borders picked out with fine purple lines—behind the redhead and the dark medic.

They had not kept him awake overnight, as he'd expected. He'd gone to bed and enjoyed sound and dreamless sleep. Before he slept, however, he'd seen Antonia's troops—through his accidentally open hatch—called out to battle in the afternoon and evening, and heard them whoop and cheer at their chance to kill the enemy. This was frankly terrifying; he'd seen fighting Romans in the Galilee—on horseback on the high hill behind Nazareth or marching through the streets of Sepphoris, singing—but never in a place they considered wholly their own. Antonia, however, was theirs, and they were trained to be warriors.

As they prepared to fight, someone played appropriate music through the barracks PA system, aggressive, patriotic and filthy by turns. One song celebrated—with undifferentiated joy—everything from their Constitution, to famous battles, to liberty, to the printing press, to slavery, to their sexually uninhibited festivals, to the major Roman political parties. Each celebratory line was topped and tailed with a vulgar chant. He saw Cassius of the violet eyes striding along the corridor shouting, 'Today I get to cut me a slice of prime sheep-shagger arsehole,' and showing the notches on the stock of his long rifle to a comrade. Some of them stood still and sang *Patria, Patria* at that point, making the cells ring with their fine young voices as they broke into parts, the high voices singing one line, the deep voices another. He felt himself swept up along with them as he watched them sing, their eyes half shut.

He'd seen them return, too, still cheering and singing. They played the chanting song a few more times, with other music—equally loud, but joyous rather than martial—following. They screamed that they were masters of war. They didn't just defeat their enemies; they *broke* them. Some dared others to complete various physical challenges. He saw a man run up the wall and flick his legs backwards and downwards over his head, landing in a neat crouch. Another man did back handsprings down the corridor and glanced a comrade upside the head, knocking his helmet off. A man with superficial wounds to his face and chest danced in the corridor before a nurse dragged him away to the infirmary. He saw the snaggle-toothed soldier now before him in earnest conversation with a blue-uniformed woman whose face was partly covered in elaborate silver swirls. The strangeness of her patterned face and head aside, she was beautiful. Then they played the music he'd come to associate with their religion, or perhaps the goddess whose festival it was this week. He gave thanks that he didn't speak their language well enough to understand it when it was sung. He watched the tattooed woman take the snaggle-toothed man by the hand and begin to lead him to another part of the barracks; she was grinning. He had trained himself over many years to be insensible to the charms of women, but when he saw the soldier push her against the wall opposite his cell, kiss her and then smooth back her hair, the intensity of their passion reached him.

'Hold me,' she said to him. 'I want you so much.' He swore he saw something lithe and sinuous uncoil itself from the side of her head and make its way down the inside of the man's uniform collar and along his bare back. He closed his eyes when he saw the soldier ruck her skirt up with one hand.

And just this afternoon, he was in the brothel.

An officer must have disturbed them; Ben Yusuf heard a voice chastise both and the woman apologise.

'Not here,' the officer went on. 'Take him to your quarters.'

The snaggle-toothed man spread long fingers over his scalp and forced his head back, ensuring he faced the Celt directly. He flinched.

'It's all right,' the redhead said in Greek. 'We're not going to hurt you.'

'Do you say that to everyone you interrogate before you beat them to a pulp?'

'If we're going to beat someone to a pulp, we just do it.'

The other two men chuckled at their superior's wit.

He noticed, then—and wondered why it had taken him so long to do so—the scales of justice on Cornelius's collar.

'How do I address you?'

'Politely, Ben Yusuf.'

'Why did you take my hood off? Why aren't you torturing me?'

Cornelius and Cyler laughed at this; Cornelius pressed the tips of his fingers together in front of his face and smirked.

'We can hood and torture you if you like, Ben Yusuf—there are men in this barracks who'd do a fine job of it, too.'

'Can you at least tell me why you didn't keep me awake all night with your smutty music?'

'That didn't take long,' said Cyler, sitting down on Cornelius's right and taking a sheet of folded paper out of his back pocket. 'I'm keeping a tally of how often Rome, Romans and Roman culture get called variations on the "smut" or "wicked" theme.'

Even the medic found this amusing.

Cornelius seemed to contemplate matters for a moment; he reached down and picked something up off the floor. It was a block of the same lined yellow paper Ben Yusuf had seen Linnaeus use, although Cornelius's was covered in flowing handwriting. He read through this document for some time before speaking.

'I don't see why you can't be told,' he said at length.

'I'm assuming there's some ulterior motive, that's all.'

'Oh, there's always an ulterior motive,' said Cyler, grinning. Ben Yusuf looked at the young man, considering him. After the cinematic conversation in his cell he'd been inclined—the soldier's unrepentant sexual immorality to one side—to like him. He now found himself reassessing that impression.

'The reason you weren't kept awake last night is because we were a bit busy.' Cornelius reached down beside his seat again and picked up a newspaper. He unfolded it and held it up in front of his face. Ben Yusuf read the headline and saw the Empire Hotel burning fiercely into the night sky. Cornelius turned the front page; there were photographs of corpses strewn over various footpaths. The exterior of what looked vaguely like a temple had been shot to pieces. Ben Yusuf looked down at his feet; Cyler vaulted the desk and used his long, graceful fingers to force his head up again.

'One of your conspirators—a man known to us only as Simon—led the attack on the Empire Hotel. That's where most of the casualties were concentrated.'

'Simon? My Simon? Where is he?'

'In the morgue with a label hanging off his left big toe. I should know, I put him there.'

Had his hands been free, Ben Yusuf would have put at least one of them over his mouth. He wanted to be sick and fought his leaping gag reflex down with everything he had. Cyler hadn't returned to his seat, and turned to face his superior.

'Lucullus, get him a bucket. I don't want to spend the day in an interrogation room that smells like vomit.'

Ben Yusuf shook his head. 'It's all right, I won't be sick. I just... I'm just shocked.'

'I'll get that bucket anyway, sir. You never know.'

The door slammed behind him as he went; Cornelius waited until he returned, pail in hand, before continuing.

'You seem to spend a lot of your time being shocked by the things your followers do, Ben Yusuf. I'd like to know whether that shock is real or not.'

'Yes.'

'To that end, I've made an executive decision that we'll get more out of you by addressing you like this, without a hood, without torture, without a climate of fear. You see, part of me suspects that you're not actually a terrorist—'

'Although,' Cyler chipped in, 'you know lots of them.'

'—While part of me suspects that you're the worst sort of terrorist. That is, you make the bullets and get whack-jobs like Iscariot and Simon to fire them.'

'That's not true.'

'Well, now's your chance to convince one part of me at the expense of the other.'

'Isn't this academic? You'll do me down for the riot in the Temple, surely.'

Cornelius smiled; his pen skittered over the yellow paper. 'I'm glad you're happy to go on the record with the word "riot", because that's what it was.'

'I don't like seeing people exploited,' Ben Yusuf said. 'The ritual baths cost, the doves cost, the matches cost, everything costs. The whole Temple has been turned into a market. The Sanhedrin and the merchants are being enriched at the expense of some of the poorest people in your Empire.'

'And what made you and your eleven friends think that precipitating a major riot in there would fix things? We're curious.'

'I am at liberty to cleanse my father's house,' Ben Yusuf said, his black eyes fixed on Cornelius's grey ones.

'And who is your father?'

'God is my father, lawyer of Rome.'

Cornelius's eyes had narrowed to slits.

'Really?' he asked, one fair eyebrow cocked.

Ben Yusuf looked at the three of them, at their fine young faces and clear, cloudless eyes—miracles wrought by a childhood in the sunshine on an ample diet, by modern medicine and plenty of exercise—and caught himself smiling at their shining optimism.

'You Romans really believe you can change the world by force of will, don't you?'

'We already have,' said Saleh.

'I'm not talking about little things, the bridges and aqueducts and railways,' he said. 'You think you can change people, make them into something new.'

'And we've done that, too,' said Saleh.

'As I discovered last night,' said Cyler, grinning.

'So that *was* you I saw persuading an aviatrix to join you in a mutual expression of affection.'

'Yes, sir, it was.'

Ben Yusuf could feel his flesh crawl—their scientists had taken God's human form and *warped* it. He could see Cornelius listening to the dialogue in frank fascination. His fingers described coiling spiral patterns in the air.

'And she did things with her...'

'Prehensile Communication Device, although no one calls them that; the *strix* women call them headtails.'

'I've heard about this,' Cornelius said. 'It's supposed to be pretty good.'

'Imagine a woman with two hands, two feet, one standard tongue and one five-foot... tentacle.'

'No wonder you looked wrecked this morning.'

'I did get *some* sleep, sir. She wore me out.'

Ben Yusuf—in a strained voice—asked for the bucket. Cyler brought it to him, and he was violently, shudderingly ill.

'And on that note, I suggest a brief adjournment.'

Cornelius ordered Cassius to take Ben Yusuf to the latrines and clean him up while he made his way to the monitor room. A fat envelope sat on the desk; he tore it open, emptied its contents across the table and began to rummage.

He separated Abdes Pantera's service record from various photographs and—what he was really looking for—a yellowing legal instrument dated thirty-three years earlier. In a clear hand the twenty-one-year-old Pantera had documented his relationship with a Miriam Bat Amram in Sepphoris. There he had made it explicit that he would not support any children from the union. The legionary *Advocatus* had witnessed his signature; the space where Miriam's signature should have been was blank. Cornelius peered at the scribble and poked at the wax seal. The lawyer was a member of *gens* Crispus, albeit 'first name illegible'. He found himself smiling.

Why does that not surprise me?

He put the legal instrument to one side and trawled through the photographs until he found a small, white-bordered snap of the two of them in front of Caesarea's then newly constructed pleasure pier. Cornelius felt himself startle not only at the remove of time—accentuated by the black-and-white image—but also at Miriam's youth. *Centurio* Pantera, he thought, was a grub and a deadbeat.

He rummaged some more and came up with a birth certificate, watermarked 'non-citizen' and headed PROVINCE OF IUDAEA. It was in both Latin and Aramaic, with a dividing line down the middle. The name recorded was Yeshua Ben Pantera, and in the column under PATER was the name Abdes Pantera, status 'Roman citizen'.

He took three copies of the birth certificate, relevant photographs and the legal disavowal, and stapled them into separate bundles, storing the originals back in the large envelope with its German postmark. He tried to work out whether he was amused, furious or sad, or a peculiar admixture of all three. That Ben Yusuf had some idea in his head that a god had sired him was almost too risible to contemplate. He picked up Pantera's enlistment photograph, taken before the army barber had sheared his burgeoning afro, then the official military photograph from after his promotion to Centurion. He was a good-looking, muscular man, no doubt about it. Cornelius could imagine him banging local women the length and breadth of the Empire.

It was while he was contemplating this fact that none other than Tiberius Julius Abdes Pantera materialised on the other end of the line. Cornelius was stunned; the young man he'd spoken to before he'd commenced the Ben Yusuf interrogation had actually bothered to pass the message on.

He gathered up the paperwork and made his way back to the interview room; he could smell coffee. Saleh and Cyler were already waiting. Cyler brought Cornelius some coffee and a plate of olives and cheese.

He handed both of them one of the stapled bundles. Saleh broke first, roaring with laughter. Cornelius watched Ben Yusuf stare at the chortling medic. Cyler just shook his head and giggled. He looked at Ben Yusuf.

'So your mother liked Roman cock.'

Cornelius stood and handed his final bundle to Ben Yusuf, who was now glaring at Cyler. He stood to his full height and folded his arms. Had Mirella been present, she would have seen the shadow of his great-grandfather—all he lacked were the face tattoos and the plaid.

'You may think your father is a god, but I've just spoken to
him. As you can see, he looks awfully like a big Mauretanian
legionary. Did your mother not mention this?'

'God is your father, too, lawyer of Rome.'

Cornelius sat down and stared at Ben Yusuf. 'Oh, that's
good, that's very good. I can see why you wowed the little old
ladies in the Sepphoris Forum.'

'I have long preached that much Jewish law is too harsh,
that it's used as an excuse to kill and break rather than save
and heal. I forgive sinners, and tell them to go and sin no more.
But you Romans, you do not even see what you do as sin.'

'Another one for the tally,' said Cyler. 'It's those smutty Romans again.'

Ben Yusuf turned on him. 'You,' he said softly. 'You spent
yesterday afternoon whoring, yesterday evening killing and
last night in the arms of a... *monster*.'

Cyler exposed his crooked teeth, leaning forward.

'Oh yah,' he cooed, 'and it felt *good*.'

Cornelius could feel the hair on the back of his neck
standing up. Ben Yusuf looked at him. 'You, lawyer of Rome,
returned after your fight to a woman you made yours during a
festival involving the active worship of human lust.'

'She's not mine,' Cornelius said softly. 'She belongs to herself.'

'And you, clever child of a demon temple, you had a woman beg you on her knees to take her so that she would not be
cast out on the streets with her baby.'

'And you people cast women like her out onto the streets,'
said Saleh, reddening.

Cornelius wanted to leave the room, *now*. He pressed his
fingertips down into the surface of his desk, inadvertently
pushing his block of yellow legal pad to one side as he leaned
forward. He wasn't sure his question was going to facilitate
anything, but now he was angry enough to ask it.

'Ben Yusuf, have you ever fucked? Woman? Man? Donkey? I'm not talking this'—he held up one hand and jerked it back and forth—'I'm talking mutuality.'

Ben Yusuf met his eyes, his gaze steady.

'No, lawyer of Rome.'

Cyler's mouth dropped open. 'That's terrible!'

Ben Yusuf looked at him, an expression in between pity and contempt on his face. 'Only to a Roman.'

Cyler glared at Ben Yusuf.

'You've made up all these stupid rules about sex because you've never had any—' He stood up to orient himself and then pointed. 'The Greek Quarter's that way. Go and get it out of your system, seriously. Hire a nice *hetaera* for the week. She'll teach you that it's not just to piss through.'

Ben Yusuf's expression—directed at Cyler—was now one of pure contempt. 'Your records will not show this, but Pantera tried to convince my mother to abort me. "That's the Roman way," he told her. And your law lets him refuse to pay for his own child.'

'That's to stop women from running around looking for a man to slap a paternity suit on. Romans take fatherhood very seriously. There's nothing more honourable, or more demanding.'

Cornelius smiled; this was Cyler in 'reasonable' mode.

'So the woman must murder her baby?'

Cornelius was about to break in, but instead Saleh spoke, his voice gentle. 'Ben Yusuf, it's always difficult to confront one's own non-existence, but a dead man cannot miss being alive. You fear death because you imagine it filled with the things—beautiful and terrible—you experienced when you were alive. But the non-existence before one's birth and the non-existence after one's death is identical in every respect.'

'That's very Roman. There is no afterlife. There is no judgment. You go through your days knowing that you will never have to atone for the evil that you do. When you die, you dissolve into atoms.'

Cornelius leaned forward. 'I don't think the soul dissolves into atoms, Ben Yusuf. In my rite, we carry on. We ascend to a place where soldiers may lay down their arms at last, and where we can behold the universe.'

'So even Roman soldiers dream of peace?'

'We want it most.'

'If you wish to live forever, Ben Yusuf, you have to do something with your life,' said Cyler, his voice soft. 'That's what Homer's heroes did. There are still shrines to Achilles and Helen and Ulysses all over Greece.'

'What of those who have not the courage or beauty or wit to earn undying fame?'

'People aren't equal,' said Cornelius.

'And there is no succour for the poor, the hopeless, the downtrodden, is there? The rich deserve their wealth, the brave deserve their plaudits and parades through the streets, the beautiful their admiration.'

'Life gets notably better for the poor and downtrodden whenever we conquer a place,' said Cyler. 'There's a rumour that the Dacians want to declare war on Rome so they don't have to build their own railways.'

'Very funny,' said Saleh.

'It's all going to be finished soon, men of Rome.'

Cornelius looked up from his paperwork. 'What?'

'There will be tribulation, and God will come in glory to judge the living and the dead.'

Cornelius wanted to leave the room *very* badly. 'Right. Could we have the time and date, please? Just for our records.'

Cyler snickered. Saleh spoke now; he held his hands up as he did so, the palms open. 'And your God will burn up the chaff with unquenchable fire, yes?'

'Yes.'

'For all time.'

'Yes.'

Cyler pulled a face. 'Who thinks this shit up?'

'The Jews, probably,' said Cornelius. 'No wonder they've got hang-ups.'

'No, sir,' said Saleh. 'That's not fair to the Jews.'

Cornelius raised both eyebrows at this. 'How so?'

'This eternal punishment in a burning pit is a Ben Yusuf innovation. Most of the Jews in this province don't have an afterlife at all. That includes the High Priest.'

Cornelius looked at Ben Yusuf. 'I'm starting to understand why Caiaphas thinks you're a shit.'

To Cornelius's relief, there was an impatient knock at the door. He stood up and opened it, admitting the legion's senior medic and surgeon, a man of advanced middle age.

'My apologies for this interruption, Getorex, but I've temporarily lost my nurse and need to attend to an urgent request. Can I borrow Saleh to supervise the infirmary?'

'Of course, Felix, be my guest.'

Saleh stood and moved towards the door and his commander. He turned to Ben Yusuf before he left, speaking with a serious tone Cornelius had never heard him use before.

'There are three deaths, Ben Yusuf, not one, and there is no endless torment. Only vicious gods torment, and I'm given to understand your god is kindly, not vicious.'

'So you say.'

'The first death is when the body stops working. The second death is when the body is burnt up in a show for its relatives and friends. The third death is that moment, some time in the future, when its name is spoken for the last time.'

The senior medic's eyes grew wide.

'He's only trying to convince us we're all going to burn in Hell,' Cyler said cheerfully, pointing at Ben Yusuf.

'What's Hell?' asked the older man.

'Never mind, sir,' said Saleh.

Cornelius looked at Cyler, undecided as to what to do next. Ben Yusuf watched the two of them, his face a mask.

'You've lost your religion expert,' he said.

'Shackle his hands, and then join me outside.'

'Yes, sir.'

Cornelius stepped into the corridor. He'd never been the smoking type, but right now he felt a powerful urge for a cigar or joint. Cyler soon joined him, pulling the door shut. Cornelius walked along the passageway until he was almost directly opposite the *Camera*. 'That room's not soundproof, and this one has sensitive ears.'

'You noticed, sir.'

'Yes.'

'He already knew about me, sir.'

Cyler confessed to his decision to enter Ben Yusuf's cell the previous day and—he admitted—'shoot the shit' with him.

'That probably wasn't wise, Cyler Lucullus. I'm concerned at how much personal information he has about members of this legion.'

'As I say, sir, he already knew about me.'

'Yes, but not Saleh and not me.'

'This province eats and breathes religion, Saleh,' said *Medicus* Felix as they made their way up the corridor. 'I've even had trouble with it in the infirmary.'

'How, sir?'

'We've got military personnel up one end, and we've got Iscariot shoved up the other end, after your botched torture session yesterday.'

'Ah, it wasn't my botched torture session, sir.'

'Well, he had a visitor from the Sanhedrin a short while ago and managed to get into this religious shit-fight with Julianus. I have no idea how it started but it got loud. There are men in here with serious injuries, including one who's now minus a foot. Then Cassius stuck his oar in.'

'And it all went downhill from there, sir?'

'It was already downhill. It then derailed.' He paused. 'Iscariot gives me the screaming heaves, to be honest. If I hadn't sworn the Hippocratic oath I'd have given him a lethal dose of morphine and be done with it.'

Saleh swivelled around with surprise; Felix had always been a scrupulous and ethical commander. 'Shocked you, did I? Maybe I'm just getting grouchy in my old age.'

Most of the sets of curtains were drawn, although Puppy had dragged his only part way and dozed off, the book he was reading splayed across his chest. Saleh could see lipstick smudged across his cheek.

'Looks like most of them are sleeping, which is a good thing.'

Felix sent the nurse on his way and left Saleh to it.

Saleh parked himself behind Felix's desk and rummaged through a large pile of back issues of the *Roman Medical Journal* in one drawer until he found something on recent developments in biomechanoid research and its military applications that—in light of Cyler's vivid account of his night in the sack with one of the beneficiaries—took his interest. He was soon engrossed in the article.

'*Medice*, can you do us a favour?'

It took Saleh a while to appreciate where the voice was coming from, and that it had been on the edge of his consciousness for a good ten minutes or so. It was Julianus.

'I'm sorry, soldier.'

He made his way down the ward and pushed Julianus's curtain to one side.

'Can you close that, please, sir?'

Saleh pulled the curtain to behind him just as he realised that Julianus was working his infirmary gown up one-handed. He knew what was coming, now. Julianus exposed the yellow discharge beading on the end of his penis and grimaced up at Saleh. 'It would be really nice to get rid of this, sir.'

'Without anything going on your military health record, I take it?'

Julianus smiled hugely. 'That would be even better, sir.'

'I'll get you a shot.'

'Will it hurt, sir?'

'Yes. One bad prick deserves another.'

Saleh let himself into the medical stores and poked around until he found an ampoule of what he wanted. While he was looking, he could have sworn he heard a bolt of material being dropped. He shook his head and dismissed it, making his way back into the infirmary and sweeping Julianus's curtain aside. He pulled it to behind him.

'On your good side, soldier, arse out.'

He drew up the shot and injected it into Julianus's right cheek. To his credit the man inhaled sharply but didn't yell.

Saleh heard the dull thump again—less insistent now—and this time was close enough to realise it was coming from the other end of the infirmary. He dumped the syringe and ampoule beside Julianus's bunk and bolted the length of the ward.

Iscariot had somehow contrived to lay his hands on a length of electrical cable and tie both it and his head to the metal bedhead, winding several loops around his neck. He'd then rolled himself out of his bunk in such a way that the cable pinned his neck like a chokehold in hand-to-hand combat. His eyes were already bugged and his lips blue; his mouth was open and his tongue was hanging out. Saleh could see a massive death erection through his gown.

There was a commotion in the corridor outside; Joseph could hear it. A voice he recognised as Ben Yusuf's was wailing disconsolately and he could hear Cassius and Enneconis swearing in Latin. They barged into the waiting room together.

'Ben Yusuf will be in the visit room in about twenty minutes, Rabbi,' said Cassius, 'but he's not in a particularly fit state.'

'Torture?'

Cassius snickered at this.

'Just upset and crying; there's been no torture.' He wriggled his eyebrows. 'We don't actually do it that often.'

Joseph stared at the young man with the cruel and vivid imagination, noting that his eyes were nowhere near as dark or angry now. Enneconis turned to Cassius.

'*Euskaraz badakizu?*'

'*Bai!*'

The two men turned to face each other, speaking rapidly in the strange tongue. It sounded like *nothing* he'd ever heard before, but was musical and beautiful, that much was obvious.

'What language are you speaking?'

Cassius turned to face him. 'Euskara, Rabbi, the language of Gallia Aquitania.'

'You are Vasco as well?'

'No, I am Gaul, but I grew up in Aquitania, and I speak good Euskara.'

He watched Cassius and Enneconis banter. He suspected that they were talking about him for part of it, but there was no way of knowing for certain. He began to appreciate what was passing between the two when Cassius touched the younger man's cheek. His hand lingered just for moment; he then let it drop to his side. Enneconis flushed and brushed his fingers against Cassius's chest. Joseph had no desire to watch them go any further and interrupted.

'Tell me, gentlemen, what do you make of Ben Yusuf?'

Both men turned to face him.

'I don't know him, Rabbi,' said Enneconis. 'I only bring him his meals. He doesn't talk to me very much.'

Cassius cocked his head back and to one side and folded his arms. 'I don't understand him very well,' he said, 'but he's always polite. Iscariot tried to bite people.'

'No one wanted to take him his food,' Enneconis added. 'He even bit the nurse who gave him painkilling shots. Ben Yusuf never does that.'

Joseph looked at them, at the coy way they were glancing at each other and smiling. 'Why don't you understand him?'

Cassius wrinkled his forehead; Joseph could see his attempt to think of an answer was genuine. No doubt told by the High Command he had to be courteous to members of the Sanhedrin, he met Joseph's gaze.

'I don't understand this whole province, Rabbi. I hope I get posted away soon, to Caesarea or the frontier.'

'Why is that?'

'I don't like being hated for what I am, Rabbi.'

Saleh scrubbed up after Theatre and sought permission to go to the *vicus*. Felix peeled off his gloves, stepped out of his gown and walked him out into the infirmary, expressing amazement at the Antioch surgeon's assertion that they could 'regrow' the soldier's missing foot. When Saleh hesitated as nurses wheeled the sleeping man in front of him, Felix beckoned to him. 'Julianus told me what you did.'

Saleh felt his face flush; he hoped his dark colouring concealed it. 'Will you report either of us, sir?'

'No, I won't, but that's only because he was honest with me. Without his honesty, you'd be on a charge with an official entry in your service record. It's not like you to be so careless. Strangulation makes a racket. Don't do it again.'

Cornelius informed Horace of the morning's events—Pilate, it seemed, was unreachable for the moment—and listened to the young man swear. He then returned to his quarters, changed into his training clothes and ran around the nearly empty playing fields Antonia shared with Jerusalem Academy. Most of Antonia's men, no doubt, were spread out over the city. He ran for nearly forty minutes, alternating fast sprints with slow jogs, doing his best to work the cumulative irritations out of his system. The thought that he should somehow pity Iscariot made him ill, but it was impossible to push it away. He ran until his chest hurt and he was forced to prop, crouched over, hawking and spitting. When running proved only partly successful he went to the *palaestra* beside the *frigidarium* and trained to failure across as many muscle groups as possible. He ran into Lonuobo and the two of them spotted for each other. Cornelius's shoulders and thighs began to tremble with the exertion.

'That's your one rep max, sir,' Lonuobo said. 'You need to back off. You've done two sets at ninety per cent.'

Cornelius looked at the Olympic bar above him and drove it away from him with an anguished growl. Lonuobo caught it before he crushed his chest. Cornelius rolled sideways off the bench press, grabbing at it and vomiting. Lonuobo crouched beside him and ordered an enlisted man to scrub the floor. Cornelius shook his head.

'Don't make him clean up after me. I'm a filthy bastard.'

Lonuobo ignored him, draping Cornelius's arm around his shoulders and walking him towards the baths. Cornelius turned and pressed his forehead against Lonuobo's. Lonuobo did not flinch away from his acrid breath.

'While I was fucking to beat the band... you were bleeding a man like a piece of meat... *on my watch*!'

Lonuobo did not answer. Cornelius grasped his shoulders like a wrestler would; Lonuobo braced himself in case

Cornelius tried to throw him. The two of them stood there for some time, not moving, in the midst of racked weights and grunting soldiers. Lonuobo realised Cornelius was hanging on to him in order to stay upright. People stepped round the two men, glancing sidelong but otherwise ignoring them.

For once, Cornelius ate in the mess at the same time as most of his brother officers. He scarfed down a large and hearty meal and then made his way to the Law Room. By midway through the afternoon he'd colonised the entire floor area with bundled statements, summaries written in his flowing hand and relevant documentation. He stood and admired his handiwork. He realised he was avoiding calling Irie Andrus, which annoyed him. At one point he rounded Cyler up—the latter was on his way to the baths, streaked with dust and sweat from patrol and training—and pointed out that he'd need him to act as auditor for Cornelius's opening address the following afternoon.

'I take it *Advocatus* Crispus won't be available, sir?'

'He's in the stockade, Cyler Lucullus.'

Cyler smiled, using his hand to wipe his forehead clear of the worst of the filth. 'That figures, sir.'

'Go and clean up for your woman, Lucullus, and remember how fortunate you are.'

'To have my woman in the barracks, sir?'

'Yes, Lucullus, the rest of us have to do without.'

Cyler laughed at this.

'I really like her, sir,' he said at length.

'Mind you treat her well,' Cornelius said softly. 'They don't have the easiest time of it.'

'I do, sir, I mean, I will, sir.'

It was after this conversation—and also after some awkward periphrasis—that Cyler asked if he could pay Cornelius for some olives, cheese, dates and wine from the officers' mess. Cornelius smiled at this.

'I'll treat you. You've clearly got your priorities right.'

Eventually, Cornelius grew sick of his own timidity and contacted Irie Andrus when he knew the man would be in the barracks in Sepphoris. There was some to and fro, but the Cohort Commander was located soon enough.

'I swore a statement, *Aquilifer*, and got my men to give statements.'

'You've been called by both sides, Andrus, and I think it's fair to say your statement is the most, ah, striking.'

'*Centurio* Propertius was the one who got his lover back. Call him, not me.'

'That's true, but *Centurio* Propertius is now in Britannia, and you outrank him.'

'Short of a direct order, *Aquilifer*, I'm not leaving my woman. She's about to give birth. I want to be *paterfamilias*.'

'So do we all, Andrus. And I'm happy to have you summonsed.'

Andrus swore.

Saleh walked out into a square congested with pilgrims and soldiers and locals. He'd read somewhere that Jerusalem swelled to five times its size during Passover. He could believe it after fighting his way through visitors burdened with boxes and bundles, and locals who swore at them because they didn't know where they were going. He waved the flies that seemed to follow them out of his face; the city reeked of sheep and sheep shit at this time of year. There were fire-eaters, a man who drew portraits, and lots of beggars. Some of Jerusalem's lepers had also come out into the sunshine to supplicate. He noticed that Greek and Roman passers-by would tell them to go to the Æsculapion, while Jews gave them money. For a moment he wondered what would happen if the Zealots let off a bomb in Passover week, at the point where the Temple walls met Antonia, where the crowd was at its densest. He shook his head to rid himself of the image; it didn't bear thinking about.

He doubled back on the fortress and walked in the lee of its northern wall, passing the north-western tower—where the aviatrices stayed; he could see a *strix* tail hanging over the roof's edge right at the outer limit of his vision—and turned immediately into the *vicus*. Sure of his way now, he negotiated the labyrinth, and ran up the stairs and along the concrete landing until he came to Rachel's flat. He took the key out of his pocket and let himself in.

As she'd said she would be, she was sitting at the table in the sun breastfeeding a very sleepy Marcus. He saw her as a painter might see her, bathed in butter-coloured light with motes of dust dancing around her head as she cradled the child. Marcus had just about had enough; as Saleh crossed the room, her nipple fell out of his mouth. She stood up and Saleh kissed her, then bent down and kissed Marcus's forehead. 'Is he bigger than he was yesterday?'

She smiled at his Aramaic, answering him in Latin.

'He's a fat baby already.'

'I brought some nice food from the mess,' he said. 'Some sausage, olives, cheese and good fresh bread, some very good oil—nicer than that stuff in the market—and some fresh figs for both of us.'

He began to set the table as she put Marcus in his cot. He yarkled once or twice, and then seemed to uncurl in her arms.

'All his bones are missing,' he said, chuckling. 'We've got a boneless baby.'

'Milk drunk,' she said, laying him down and covering him.

She joined him now, leaning into him, and began to eat; he

noticed that she'd left her shirt unbuttoned. He cupped one breast, then the other.

'Do you want wine?' she asked. 'Photis got some today—you can get anything at the moment, if you're willing to fight through the crowds—and it's pretty good.'

He shook his head. 'I've got an autopsy this afternoon.'

She wrinkled her nose and giggled. 'I'll have to start reading medical books, if you're going to start rolling out those expensive words.'

'There are more interesting things to read.'

'Maybe,' she said, smiling at him. 'Rufus got me into cabinet making. I know the difference between a dowel and a dovetail.'

Saleh had a sudden awareness of the beautiful furniture in the flat, and its provenance. The two of them ate in silence for a while. He hadn't realised how hungry he was. At one point she told him to slow down; he was bolting his food.

'So you have to go back?'

'Yes. I just wanted to see you.'

He dipped his bread into the oil and ate it, then cupped her breasts again. When he went to take his hands away, she caught his wrists and brought them back. 'I like that.'

He leant forward and kissed the tip of her nose.

'Do you know Yeshua Ben Yusuf?'

'The holy man? The one who's in the shit for terrorism?'

'If it's the same one.'

'He used to preach in the Galilee, before he got famous. He'd ride on the tops of trains in between towns, jump off in central station and start talking. Where there was no railway he would hitch rides in local farmers' carts and just turn up in the villages and talk to people. I've heard him speak. He knows a lot about our religion.'

'Have you ever met him?'

'No, just seen him speak. He got more popular as time went on. I thought he was a Zealot. My father was frightened and told my brothers to stay away from him; but that was before the fire... when Rufus saved me.'

He nodded, stroking her cheek and sliding his hand around her waist. 'Some of his followers *are* Zealots. I was in the infirmary this morning when one killed himself.'

'The one from the Empire Hotel? I thought men from the First Cohort killed him...' her voice trailed off.

'Another one, a different one; a *high value asset* as the spooky types like to say.'

He outlined the morning's events as they ate, including his own subterfuges. She wrapped both arms around him and rested her head on his chest.

'If a man wants to kill himself, he will find a way.'

'I did the wrong thing, Rachel. Some of it's so wrong I can't even tell you.'

She snapped her head to face him. 'Stop it, Saleh. You're a good man. You saved me; you saved my baby. You can't save everyone.'

Marcus started yarkling from his cot and the two of them went and stood over him. He was trying to eat one of his big toes and looked contented enough. Saleh reached in and started to draw circles on his belly with one forefinger. Rachel covered him with his blanket, tucking it firmly around him. This seemed to have a soporific effect, and he was soon sleeping again. She was very definite in her dealings with the child, always making sure that she and Saleh could fuck uninterrupted.

'He's happy,' she said, moving around the cot and standing before Saleh. He felt her hands unbuttoning his fly. 'Now, let me make you happy.'

CAPITO

'Your hat, my office,' said Capito, gesturing as the orderly swung the door open. Lonuobo saluted, touched the top of his head and patted his hair—a nervous gesture—and faced his Commander directly. He sat stiffly, his back not touching the chair at all, his beret on his knees. He'd only seen the inside of Capito's quarters once before, and found himself admiring the great mosaic of the city on the wall and the austere grey and white marble. Capito remained standing.

'We don't really know what to do with you. I've spent half the morning discussing matters with the Procurator when both of us have better things to do and we're still no closer to a resolution.'

'I'm sorry, sir.'

'Crispus is in the stockade. I've thought seriously about sending you to join him. He's also awaiting court martial.'

'Yes, sir.'

'I presume you're also aware that Iscariot somehow contrived to commit suicide this morning.'

Lonuobo felt as though he'd eaten something foul by mistake: a sweet with a rotten core. It explained Cornelius's behaviour in the *palaestra*.

'How, sir? He was in the infirmary.'

'While Saleh was distracted with another patient, he hung himself off his bedhead. Roman army Æsculapion bunks are sturdier than they appear. There's also some link with a visit by Joseph Arimathea. It seems the two argued beforehand.'

'This is a mess, sir.'

'It's a mess all right. There's no telling where it will end. It's good news for you and Crispus, though. No dirty laundry in public now that Iscariot won't come to trial. Crispus may even be able to retrieve his political career.'

This last line was spoken with a degree of sarcasm of which Lonuobo had not believed his Commander capable.

'If I ought to be flogged, sir, just give the order.'

'I won't do that, Lonuobo, unless it becomes militarily necessary. If you were a lawyer or an engineer or a medic I'd have flogged you without hesitation, but your identification as a sort of human Standard in this legion means your authority cannot be undermined before the men.'

'*Advocatus* Crispus wanted to go further, sir, but I could have refused to cut the wires, or at least lied and said I was incapable.'

'You don't need to assay your culpability, Lonuobo. The Procurator and I are well aware where his responsibility stops, and where yours starts.'

Capito shifted in his seat and tapped his fingers against the dark-red inlay in the top of his desk. He met Lonuobo's gaze.

'There are some things you do not appear to understand, even allowing for your frankness with me just now.'

'Sir?'

'Where do the provisions on torture in our Military Code come from, Lonuobo?'

'They were enacted by the Senate, sir, to stop what happened during the war against the *Marsi* in Germania—'

'—From being repeated, yes; this is exactly my point. We don't need villagers rounded up and shot into ditches or blown apart with grenades or tortured to death for sport, unless there are specific orders to that effect.'

'No, sir.'

'You may disagree with the provisions. I disagree with at

least one of them.'

'Yes, sir.'

'You may think the Senate uninformed, indecisive and incapable of understanding the military, especially when the *Populares* are in the ascendant.'

'Yes, sir.'

'The Senate is, however, elected by the Roman people. You are not. You cannot arrogate to yourself the right to bend the rules when it suits you. I don't care who you are, what's happened to you, or how much your men love you.'

'It won't happen again, sir.'

Lonuobo looked at his boots. He was ashamed.

'Eugenides also told us about *Medicus* Saleh's efforts to prevent you two from making the army look like a haven for butchers and hardheads who've learnt nothing from the Civil War.'

'He's a good man, sir.'

'You will, of course, be required to give evidence against Crispus, as will Saleh and Eugenides.'

'Yes, sir.'

'Until we work out what ought to be done with you, you are relieved of any further interrogation duties and will supervise fatigues in lieu.'

'Yes, sir.'

'I'm scheduling HUMINT training for Saleh in the interim, as the man speaks fluent Aramaic. Should he request any assistance from you, aid him to the best of your ability.'

Capito stood up.

'You are dismissed.'

Horace was sure he could smell burning coming from outside his office, and he went to investigate. The corridor was deserted, and he tried various doors along it—including the

War Room—noticing they were all locked. He turned to face
Pilate's corner office: the glass was blacked out. He bent down
outside the door; the smell seemed stronger there. Whatever
was burning—and it was a very unpleasant smell, not incense
or anything sweet—was coming from inside. Horace stood
and knocked, then waited for a minute or so, but there was
no response. There were two guards in an alcove at the end of
the passageway. He thought of fetching one for assistance, but
held back, undecided. He knocked again, and after a pause,
the buzzer sounded. He stepped inside.

'Yes, Horace?'

Pilate was sitting at his desk before a large and beautiful
ceramic bowl in the Athenian style—red figures on black—
decorated with what looked like dancing maenads. He held a
sheaf of papers in one hand and was burning them one by one
into the bowl, which was slowly filling with blackened debris.
They had large blue titles on a white field; he saw the suffix
'-ates' consumed by the flames. It dawned on him that Pilate
was destroying his correspondence—monthly newsletters, re-
quests for donations, candidate profiles and so on—from the
Parti Optimates, of which he was undoubtedly still a member.

'I could smell burning, Procurator.'

'Yes, Horace, indeed you can.'

Pilate had disabled the fire alarm above his head; Horace
could see the decorative bronze cover that screwed over the
top of it sitting next to the inkwell at top centre of his desk.
Pilate continued to focus on the task at hand before lighting a
cigar and sitting back in his chair.

'Would you like a cigar?' he asked, holding a metal tube towards Horace and motioning him to sit. Horace swallowed as
he took the tube and—under Pilate's watchful eye—showed
he knew how to cut it, light it and draw the flame to its end
as he rotated it in his fingers. Pilate smiled and pushed the

Athenian bowl towards Horace, so it was halfway between the two of them.

'If the *Parti Optimates* stuck to supporting the soldiery, increasing trade and commerce and teaching young men how to smoke cigars properly, then I would have no need to burn their papers.'

Horace cocked his head to one side and exhaled, smiling.

'I had cause to speak to our fine Consul, Crispus Senior, for a second time today. I informed him—as I felt duty bound to do—that Iscariot was dead, of the circumstances of his death, and that there would in consequence be no trial. He assumed that Gaius would thereby escape censure. I pointed out that his son was still subject to military discipline, and that there were three outstanding and reliable witnesses—two officers and one enlisted man—to his cruelty.'

Horace restrained himself from biting his bottom lip. He knew what was coming, and he knew his own father would do likewise. The thought made him uncomfortable.

'At that point, *Consul* Crispus sought to prevail on our friendship to release his son from both stockade and court martial.'

'Yes, Procurator.'

'I like my party, Horace. I think it's an important bulwark against opportunism and profligacy. I believe—with some justification—given too much power the *Populares* would extend the franchise and lower the property qualification such that the worst sort of people could dig their greedy paws into the *fiscus* and plunder the wealth of productive citizens.'

Pilate commenced blowing smoke rings towards the ceiling. His face was red, presumably with anger.

'However, when my party asks me to dishonour the law in favour of men, to protect wrongdoing... it tempts me to put a line through my ballot and write rude comments on the paper. Don't look so peevish, Horace—I haven't burnt my membership card yet—and this small act of desecration has made me feel rather better.'

Horace let his ash fall into the bowl and inhaled. He gathered up his courage and spoke.

'Was what Gaius did so very wrong, Procurator? My understanding is that his actions saved upwards of two hundred lives.'

'What he did remains wrong regardless of the effect it had, Horace. It may have been *necessary*, but that is a separate question from its rightness or wrongness, and Gaius *will* be called to account. That I had to explain this to his father just now makes me wonder at some of the people we elect to govern us.'

'I didn't have you pegged as a philosopher, Procurator.'

Pilate snorted at this.

'Don't accuse me of the second Greek vice, please.'

Horace chuckled. It was Pilate's turn to drop ash into the bowl. Horace hoped whatever the Procurator had burnt in there wasn't too hot; it really was a lovely piece of Athenian ceramic, 400 years old at least. Pilate smiled at last and shoved the few unburnt political papers at his side into one of the desk drawers.

'What are your plans for this evening, Horace? I'd rather hoped you'd be interested in joining my wife and me for supper.'

'That's very kind of you, Procurator, but I'm already dining with Capito in the mess tonight.'

'In that case I'll warn both of you that I require you at the residence on Thursday evening. I would like to discuss matters with my clerk after the trial concludes. You're most welcome to join us for supper.'

'Of course, Procurator.'

'Andreius Linnaeus is currently in my house'—Horace

blanched at this—'but he and his concubine will be dining separately. It's almost impossible to avoid talking about legal matters so contact is best avoided. In any case he's rather enamoured of his concubine, so you are unlikely to see much of him.'

'It would make me very uncomfortable if I did see him, Procurator.'

'I'm not happy with it myself, but after the debacle at the Empire, it's difficult to avoid. We can't have counsel sleeping in the streets.'

'That's true, Procurator. I didn't realise he was staying there.'

Pilate stood up and offered Horace scissors for the unsmoked portion of his cigar. Horace took them and set to work—it had already gone out.

'Well, now I've satisfied you I'm not burning the place down, I'd best let you prepare for an evening's enjoyment of the more pleasurable of the two Greek vices.'

Horace went scarlet, nodded to his superior and then left.

Ben David watched as Linnaeus joined Fotini on the platform. The two of them smooched agreeably until her train arrived. He suspected his view of Fotini had begun to change when he'd watched her and Linnaeus interact. As was his people's way, Linnaeus lusted after her—Ben David could not imagine a Roman of either sex pairing off without that—but there was something finer as well, and it showed when he saw her onto the train to Caesarea, the gentle way his hand rested on the small of her back, the way he spoke to her, the way he watched the train leave the station. Ben David stood beside his cab and waited, the weather—as it sometimes did during Passover week—reminding everyone that summer was coming and that sleeping on the roof under the stars was soon to become mandatory, at least in some parts of town. Linnaeus skipped his way lightly down the stairs; Ben David opened the car door for him.

'It's just occurred to me that I have a rather pressing problem,' Linnaeus said.

'What's that?'

'You've seen Ben Yusuf on screen. How did he look?'

'Always very sharp, *Domine*—a bit rustic, yes, but his hair was always braided or pinned back or shaven, and he wore good clothes.'

'Exactly. He needs court clothes; he can't turn up looking like he's just walked off a construction site.'

Linnaeus wanted to go to JTN's offices on the *cardo*.

'I have a suspicion I know where he's been sourcing his clothes.'

Nic Varro was preparing to walk home when Linnaeus accosted him outside JTN. Linnaeus noticed construction crews—presumably called in from Caesarea—were already hard at work at the Fleet Fox. He saw one of the priestesses directing operations in imperious tones. There was a vigorous exchange going on between her and a man leaning out of his crane box.

'Yes,' Nic said when Linnaeus outlined his suspicions. 'That was a bit of a sore point between Mary and me. She lent him my clothes without asking me.'

'Ah.'

'So I'd compliment him on his dress, only to realise he was wearing something of mine.'

Linnaeus noticed that Nic was withdrawing something from his briefcase, a series of pictures, printed on quality card.

'Mary's insisting that she doesn't want to see the ring before the big day and wants me to choose,' he said, 'so I've gone with matched gold and platinum puzzle rings—an Etruscan custom. But'—he paused—'I'd also like to get her something individual beforehand.'

Linnaeus looked at the pictures. They showed elaborate rings studded with rubies, sapphires, emeralds and diamonds.

'Those look like they'll cost more than your *coemptio* wedding, Nic.'

'It appears my Etruscan pride has been doing me out of sex for nearly twelve months. I looked at our accounts. I won't need to go near the bank.'

Nic's skin was glowing with happiness, and Linnaeus noticed for the first time the row of tiny bites down his throat and along his collarbones. He seemed to like showing them off, wearing his cream silk shirt open to the middle of his chest.

'You realise you sound like a sixteen-year-old, don't you?'

'I don't care. I wasn't even too perturbed when a few legionaries forced us to close up shop for five hours yesterday—'

'—Because it meant you could go home and resume fucking your wife?'

Nic smiled. 'First time I've ever put fucking above a major news story. Now,' he said, 'what do you think?'

He spun the pictures out like a fan. Linnaeus looked closely, thinking at the same time of something suitable for Fotini.

'Not emeralds, Nic, green's an envy colour. I think rubies, diamonds and dark-purple amethyst are the way to go. If you're going to go regal, go properly regal. Give her a rock ensemble that's visible from space.'

Ben David took both men to Nic and Mary's apartment on the boundary of the Greek and Roman Quarters. Linnaeus listened to Nic outlining wedding plans, and watched as Mary went through the clothes Nic no longer wore, complaining that they'd have to get married in Damascus because the Empire Hotel was no longer available.

'Damascus is a wonderful city, Mary,' Nic was saying. He winked at Linnaeus behind her back. 'And we could even go to the Temple of Baal and Astarte afterwards.'

'No, Niccy,' she said mildly. 'We won't be going to the Temple of Baal and Astarte afterwards.'

Nic chuckled.

She chose three gowns; one dark blue, one dove grey and one rich maroon, presenting them to Linnaeus and pointing out that Ben Yusuf's sinewy frame was a near match for Nic's.

'You may have to get him to watch the hem on those; he's about an inch shorter than me and all of those were cut for my height.'

'I'd get someone to trim his beard, too,' said Mary. 'I used to clip it myself every time he went on JTN; I don't think he touched it in between times.'

Linnaeus took the clothes out to the cab and folded them up. Ben David looked at him from the driver's seat.

'Where to now?'

'We will see a frightened man living in a warm stone tomb, David: to the Mount of Olives.'

Once they reached the Jewish cemetery—which seemed to cover an entire hillside—Ben David had to park his cab at the bottom. They made the rest of the way over the hewn white gravestones and tombs on foot. Linnaeus had a crumpled map that Ioanne had marked with a circle and a single, wriggling line.

Linnaeus felt rather impious stomping over people's graves, but Ben David picked his away through and over them without a second thought, following the path drawn out on the map with nimble expertise. Linnaeus found himself gasping for air about halfway up the slope. At one point he turned and faced the city, watching the sun set. He was covered in fine white dust. Ben David paused and turned as well. The Temple and Antonia dominated, but he could see the cut and dip in the midst of the city and then Herod's palace rising beyond. Shadows lengthened as he watched. He sat down on someone's tomb, admiring the Hebrew writing as he did so.

'I hope this is all right,' he said, 'it would be very rude in Rome.'

Ben David shrugged. 'There are worse things to do than rest your weary bones on a tomb.'

The light was dipping, but as it did so, it caught the stonework and bounded off it; pink and white dominated, but was leavened by the presence of butter yellows and golden browns. Even from this far, Linnaeus could see the great Temple courtyards, which were thronged with pilgrims and merchants, and what looked like dots along the top of its outer wall: Roman troops on perimeter duty. Far above the Temple, two *striges* circled and swooped, using thermals to conserve energy. From time to time the great wings would beat, taking them higher and letting them ride the heat once more. For the most part, their flight path took them over the Temple and the Jewish Quarter.

'It's beautiful,' he said. 'It's a beautiful city.'

This comment surprised Ben David, and he said so.

'No Roman is insensible to beauty, David. We are schooled to value it above all else, as you've seen.'

'Yes, but you seem to value...' He searched for the right words. 'To value *order* as much as anything. I've been to Caesarea. It's so very neat.'

Linnaeus smiled. 'Maybe I'm coming to appreciate chaos a little more these days.'

One of the *striges* banked sharply, its wings beating. It circled over them, swooping and dipping, raking the shadowed ground with a shaft of white light. Ben David clapped his hands over his head and cowered. It flew low enough for both of them to see the slavering Medusa head cut into its underbelly and its great claws extended. A man was trying to outrun it, taking shelter under trees and in between boulders and stonework.

'He'll never make the cemetery,' Linnaeus observed, his tone detached. 'He has to cross the road, and she'll have him.'

Ben David's hands were clenched together in front of his mouth, as though he dared not breathe. The runner did not emerge. The *strix* began to circle slowly around the spot. Ben David lowered his hands.

'Those things terrify me. They're not... not... natural.'

'Nor was the flight of Icarus and Daedalus, which inspired the man who developed them.'

'Flying like a bird of prey is only part of it, *Domine*. It's that... you take women... and make them killers.'

'That was hard for us, too, David. We have a custom that harm is men's business. Plato said that women could be harmworkers and guardians, but for a long time, no one believed him.'

'You have women gladiators and cage fighters.'

'Despised occupations, David, not honourable. To fly *strix* is a great honour.'

The dusk was deepening now, and lights began to wink on in the city below. There was a gap like a child's pulled tooth where the bulk of the Empire Hotel was supposed to be, but on the whole the city of Jerusalem threw plenty of light. The circling *strix*, they noticed, was blackened, visible only by the stars it obscured.

'We'd best find this Matthias before the night defeats us,' said Ben David. 'Not everyone who comes to Jerusalem during Passover is a pilgrim with honourable intentions.'

'Save yourselves the trouble, gentlemen,' said a clear voice from behind them. 'I've been watching you thumping around fit to wake the dead. It's a wonder that you didn't have half the people buried up here telling you to shut down the bloody racket.'

Linnaeus and Ben David turned to face the speaker. Torchlight picked out a man even leaner than Linnaeus, his beard neatly clipped and his hair trimmed Roman-civilian short. He was dressed in heavy cotton trousers and a grubby but fashionably cut twill shirt. It seemed he'd been sleeping on the Mount of Olives for some time.

'Matthias Levi?'

'That's me.'

There came a startled scream from behind them. All three men turned and stared. The runner had tried to sprint across the road into the olive grove, perhaps thinking that he stood a better chance of survival under cover of darkness.

'They see better at night,' Linnaeus said softly, 'like owls.'

The *strix* dropped like a stone, its great wings tucked in, one clawed talon extended. The aviatrices could retract the claws and scoop people up without harming them, but she had chosen not to: they could see the man skewered through the chest as the *strix* went into a climb, turning as it went.

'Sometimes the aviatrices pass out when they pull out of a dive like that,' said Linnaeus, a note of admiration in his voice. The man was no longer screaming; the *strix* made its way back over the city towards Antonia's north-west tower, its prey hanging limply against the city lights.

JULIA

'What is going on in here?' the Centurion was bellowing. 'If I find the man responsible for leaving bristles all over the sinks in my lovely clean latrine I *will* unscrew his head and shit down his neck!'

Centurio Friere objected to having his most capable intelligence officer relieved of duty and was struggling without him. He'd already had a bellow at Lonuobo in the Surveillance Room but the men he'd taken out for exercise were also coming in for their share. Cyler and the other seven men in his *contubernium* kept their heads down and made their way to the baths to clean up. Cyler scrubbed himself until his skin glowed pink and prayed that Friere would be out of the baths by the time he'd finished washing; he really wanted to shave, and dropping bristles—even when one planned to clean them up immediately afterwards—went with the territory. He dripped across the tiles and planted himself in front of the mirror. He oiled his skin, took out his straight edge and set to work. Friere seemed to have found other people to harass and was nowhere to be seen.

'Someone's being extra careful on the appearance front today,' said the youngest man in his *contubernium*. Cyler could see him in the mirror behind him as he worked.

'You smell like a perfumery, Cyler Lucullus,' said Cirullo, joining the young man. 'What's the story?'

'Bugger off, you two. I've got a woman.'

'During Passover? How'd you manage that?'

'Yeah, enquiring minds want to know, Lucullus,' added a

third voice.

'And don't you leave any bristles in my latrine, Lucullus.'
That was Friere, still hanging around.

'No, sir, I won't, sir.'

'I mean,' the young one continued, 'do we get to watch?'

'Ladies' man Lucullus finds other places to fuck,' said Cirullo. 'That's why he didn't put in an appearance last night.'

'I had a pass out. Now piss off.'

'Ooh, nasty,' the third voice chimed in again. 'He doesn't want to share.'

Cyler straightened up, checking to see that Friere was no longer in the baths, and looked at the three of them.

'Look, I'm sorry you haven't got what I got, but that's not my fault. Blame this shitty province.'

Cirullo nodded, and the three faces softened for a moment. The young fellow looked down, scratching the back of his neck.

'Who's the lucky girl?'

'One of the aviatrices,' he said, choosing not to reveal her name.

Cirullo whooped at this. 'Lucullus is into the kinky!' he shouted, loud enough for half-a-dozen other men to swivel around and stare at them. 'He's fucking a snake-woman.'

'Does she bite?' one of them wanted to know. 'I mean, do the snakes bite?'

Cyler sighed and folded his arms.

'They're not snakes,' he said, his tone resigned, 'despite what you might think.'

'You got onto her last night, didn't you?' said Cirullo. 'When *Optio* Macro put you up front on the way from the Empire.' Cirullo turned to the gathering audience. 'I saw him hanging around up on top of the tower waiting for her.'

Cyler saw no point in disputing this and nodded. He was starting to get irritated.

'Apart from the fact that *you're* not getting any, why is who

I fuck any concern of yours?'

'It's not *who*, Lucullus, it's *what*,' said Cirullo. 'They're not, you know, fully human.'

'Yeah, Lucullus, they're... whatchamacallit... *modified*.'

'Do you only look at one side of her face when you're fucking her?' Cirullo pointed at his cheek. 'They've got all that shit in there.'

Cyler weighed three days in the stockade for decking one of them against continuing to swallow shit. He raised his fist and took a step forward—which did look threatening, Cyler was a tall, strong man—and *Centurio* Friere took the opportunity to walk into the midst of the little knot of legionaries.

'This is getting a bit heated,' he said.

'He's fucking a snake-woman, sir,' said Cirullo.

Friere smiled at this. 'I've fucked the odd snake-woman in my time,' he said. 'They're good in the sack.'

Cyler hadn't had much time for Friere until now but he was grateful for this intercession. He looked at the officer, conveying thanks with his eyes.

Cirullo's head whipped around; he faced Cyler.

'Is that true?'

It was Cyler's turn to smile.

'Oh yes, Cirullo. Best sex I've ever had.'

Cyler stopped by the fridge in the Law Room. Cornelius had bought him fat Syrian dates, fine Gallic cheeses, stuffed vine leaves, and a selection of sausage and ham. He scrabbled around on top and retrieved a bottle of expensive red wine. Cornelius had written him a one-line note on a scrap of paper wrapped around the bottle with a rubber band.

Go forth and conquer!

He read the label and decided that he would die then and there for Cornelius Getorex, surely a god among men. Cyler removed the note and stuck it in his pocket. He strode towards the north-western tower and made his way up the stairs to the small section given over to the aviatrices. He'd been there before—and only last night, too—but he'd been focused on what was to come. This time he took in the elaborate double doors with their decorative roundel of the Medusa picked out in blues and greys, the way the black and red stucco of the Army shaded by degrees into the sky-blue and white of the Air Force. There were two women on duty outside, one with a dark and complex *perplexae*, one whose *perplexae* was finer and lighter, as though incomplete. He thought the latter woman looked younger, but it was hard to tell. The tattoo—if that's what it was—changed their skin such that it rendered them ageless. He also noticed that the two guards carried the *perplexae* on opposite sides of their faces.

'I've got permission to visit Julia Procula,' he said.

The 'darker' of the two guards curled her lip into a sour expression, and he was startled to see how similar it was to the face Cirullo pulled in the baths. He had visions of setting up a matchmaking service between *strix* aviatrices and men in his Cohort. *If the lads could just get over the* perplexae *and the headtails,* he thought, *the strix women are healthy and fit and sexy. And they can do... stuff.*

'She's expecting me.'

'I'm here,' she said.

Julia was at the entrance, standing and holding the great formal doors ajar, her *perplexae* rich and dark and flushed with blood. He could not see much of her pale skin underneath it: the silver threaded through with blue and gold dominated. He did not know what she had done with the great roiling complexity on her head but he knew it would be beautiful and alluring. She'd looked flushed like that last night when she'd alighted from the *strix* and told him he had to wait.

'Why's that?' he'd asked.

'Because I respond to a man I like in the way I respond to my *strix*,' she said. 'Well, the *perplexae* does. And the biology can get confused.'

'So you like me?'

'Yes, I like you. It's written on my body. Now you need to wait for a bit while it sorts itself out.'

He'd stood on the top of the tower for a good half an hour watching her master herself, her hand resting against the ribs of her machine. He could have sworn he saw it shudder at one point. She was tall and lean, leaner than he usually liked in women, like the caryatids that held up the front of some Greek temples. He suspected her own hair would have been light brown, but she had none, her scalp covered instead with corded silver headtails that she could bind together at will and lengthen into what he had taken to calling a tentacle. He saw her turn her head slowly to one side, observing the fine, clear distinction between the patterned side of her face and the rest.

'Come here,' she'd said at last. He'd approached the *strix* with caution; even though he'd been inside it, he found it un-nerving to watch Julia stroking it and smiling at it. He reached out to touch the machine; she swatted his hand away.

'You're allowed inside when we take you to battle,' she said, 'but you can't touch her unless I say so.'

He'd nodded, swallowing. *Whatever you say.*

Cyler stepped towards the formal entrance, the platter balanced across his forearms, the wine caught between his fingers. The two guards could see their sister's face and made no attempt to intervene. The more senior of the two smiled at him now.

'I brought you some nice food and wine,' he said to Julia. 'I thought you'd like to share it with me.'

'Yes, Cyler, I would like that.' She paused, her head cocked to one side. He realised she was staring at him, stunned and quizzical. 'I didn't think you would come.'

'Don't be daft, love,' he said, leaning forward and whispering into her ear, the platter lodged on his hip. 'I want to fuck you silly.'

She led him up the corridor—decorated in blue and white, even the walls, the ceiling and the tiled floors—and he followed, his offerings in hand. He watched her coiling headtails and neat bare feet and swaying backside. She opened the door to her quarters and beckoned to him, fingers pointed upwards. He felt his cock begin to stiffen. He put the platter down on the table beside her bed, noticing once more how similar her quarters were to, say, Saleh's quarters.

Except for the blue. They really do have a blue thing going on here.

She stepped forward and they kissed; he felt her hands on his bare back, sliding up under his fatigues. He pulled her hips into his.

'Sorry for slavering,' he said. 'I want to eat you.'

'I'll get some glasses and plates.'

He pulled a multi-tool from his pocket and set about opening the wine. For her part, she doled out olives, cheese and bread between the two of them.

'Can you hold off long enough to eat?' she asked. 'I'm hungry. I had duty tonight, and I had to kill a man on the Mount of Olives.'

'Oh yes,' he said, grinning, 'but I still want to fuck you silly afterwards. Last night was just the entrée.'

She smiled at this and began to eat, the *perplexae* darkening even further as she passed food to him. He watched the process, fascinated but also a little frightened. He took some of her bread and mixed it with the olives, ham and dark-green oil. She watched him and mimicked his gestures. The

darkness was bleeding across the side of her face such that
he had trouble picking out the finely delineated swirls and
spirals. He poured them a glass of wine each.

'That's impressive,' he said. 'You get a hard-on in your face.'

'Yes,' she said. 'We do. It comes up like this when we fight,
but also when we want a man.'

'Did it do it that much last night? I can't remember. I'd never seen one of your faces up that close before.'

'Some of the way, but not this much... what's making it so
dark now is that you came back. Lots of men don't come back,
so when they do, we light up like a baboon's bum.'

He found this funny, and started to giggle.

'So that means one of the guards on your door fancied me,
but the other one couldn't give a crap?'

'Could be, Cyler.'

'That's a man's wet dream, you know,' he said. 'That way
you'd only try to chat up the ones who have it... written on
their faces.'

'That was part of the idea.'

'Can you turn it off? I mean, not show what you feel on your
face? It's just I remember getting stiff ones on the high-diving
platform as a kid and it was, well, embarrassing.'

'Yes we can, but we have to concentrate, and of course right
now I don't want to. I want you to see it.'

He observed as she reached around the back of her head
and released her headtails. He watched the silver strands bind
together and begin to roil and dance. He was hungry too, but
he wanted her like a crazy man, and he said so.

'Will you come back again?' she asked.

'Yes, Julia, I will. I love good sex and I want a woman.'

Her eyes grew wide. 'So you really do mean it.'

'I wouldn't be here if I didn't.'

'You don't care that I outrank you? Or that I'm not... normal?'

He shook his head, refilling both glasses and poking two vine leaves into his mouth. He licked his fingers and then leaned across the table, stretching out one hand and tracing the intricate patterns on her cheek with his fingers, realising for the first time that it was implanted in her flesh like some sort of growth and likely made of the same material as the headtails. He ran his thumb over it where it was thickest, then circled one finger—very gently—around the indentation in her right temple.

'I *like* this,' he said, 'I think it's beautiful.'

The mass on her head resolved into a single thick lash and coiled around his forearm. The movement was sudden and he stumbled as she pulled him towards her, only just avoiding the table with its open wine bottle and full glasses. It was incredibly strong, and she was unafraid to show it off, now.

'Give me my hand back,' he said. 'I need two hands to take your clothes off.'

He felt it slide away and make its way down inside his trousers, gentle now, warm and tender around his balls. He undressed her with a desperate urgency, trying not to pull off the buttons down the front of her uniform. Her robe fell to her feet and she stepped into his arms. She used two headtails to drop his trousers around his ankles. He kissed her face over and over, noticing that the *perplexae* was almost black now, like wrought iron picked out with gold leaf and lapis lazuli.

'I draw the line at you fucking me in military issue footwear,' she said, combining all her headtails into one again and forcing him to sit on the edge of the bed. He bent over and unlaced his boots, kicking them away, then leaned back and smiled at the clothing strewn all over the floor as she wound her headtail around his cock and squeezed. He gasped and his eyes started to water. He hooked his hands under her armpits and stretched out, pulling her on top of him. She propped herself up on her hands and let her single lash uncurl and separate into its component parts, touching his chest and face with a score of them and flicking his nipples. Two or three then coiled around each of his wrists and guided his hands up to touch the outspread fan of her living mane: the individual strands were all alive. He felt others combine again to the thickness of a lead pencil and slide into his mouth; they tasted salty and he smiled, understanding that this was an act of extraordinary love and trust; she was making herself vulnerable to him, relying on him not to bite her. At this remove, they did look like snakes with blind, blunt heads and she like the Medusa, but with a face of staggering beauty. He caressed the living fibres with the pads of his fingers, watching how they combined and lengthened—then separated again—without any apparent joins or marks. Each filament was warm and dry and covered with tiny, soft vellus hairs.

He reached down and guided his cock into her.

All cock and a yard long, he thought.

'This first one might be a bit quick,' he said, 'I'm about to explode.'

He clasped his hands across her lower back and drove so hard that she could feel his balls slapping against her backside as he jerked, lifting both of them off the bed. He cackled and chortled and stroked her breasts and sides with both hands. She liked the smouldering, grinning joy on his face so much she let him flip her onto her back and pin her down with his weight. He licked her *perplexae* when she tugged him closer to her.

'Coming now,' he said, 'sorry baby.'

While they waited for his refractory period to pass, she amused him by using a medium-thickness headtail to retrieve his glass of wine and another to feed him dates. He watched with fascination as she recruited a third to pit the dates before his eyes and pop them into his mouth, all the while sitting cross-legged, propped against the wall, drinking her own wine. For his part, he could see from the flushed state of her *perplexae* that he still had work to do.

'I've had more sex in the last two days than I've had in the last six months,' he announced, 'and a good thing it is, too.'

She wriggled closer to him and smiled sadly. 'Last night was the first sex I've had since arriving in Judaea.'

He lifted his head and stared at her. 'When did you arrive in Judaea?'

'Eighteen months ago, Cyler.'

His mouth dropped open and he shook his head. 'No wonder you were a bit keen yesterday.'

'I suspect I did a female version of everyone's stereotype of the randy Roman.'

'Don't worry, I was randy too,' he said. 'I saw you looking at me on the roof at the Empire and I'd never had an aviatrix before,' he touched her *perplexae*, 'and I've always liked the look of these things.'

He leaned across her and kissed both breasts with great tenderness, one after the other. She stroked his hair as he did so, enjoying the shape of the bristles under her fingers.

'Didn't you think of going to one of the Houses?' he asked. 'There's some that look after the ladies these days.'

'I did do that in Damascus a few times, but not here. The only place I like being in Judaea is in my *strix*.'

'Fair enough.'

'All the things that you men go through, well, magnify them a hundred-fold for each of us. Children run away from you. People in cafés stand up and leave when you sit down, Jews and Greeks both. Men spit and women make signs to ward off the evil eye. The catcalls; the jeering taunts; *you monster; you freak; you demon.*'

'Yes.'

'Then your own countrymen think there's something wrong with you.'

'You must regret enlisting sometimes, even though flying one of those things would be *amazing*.' He began to think how he could angle for a joyride: spinning, diving, flying upside down and all.

'I didn't have much choice, Cyler.'

He propped himself up on one elbow and stared at her.

'What do you mean? Romans don't conscript.'

She smiled and rested her head on his chest; he played with her headtails and she curled them around his fingers as she spoke.

'No, instead they send clever people in smart blue uniforms to the poorest villages and farms and offer to pay a whole *denarius* to each village child who will do a special test. When I was little, they used to test both boys and girls. These days they've worked out that boys almost never pass, so they only test girls. They give you a hearty meal—the best meal you've ever had—and then inject you with some funny smelling blue stuff. Then they stick you in a long metal tube and take pictures of your brain while they play word games with you and make you do hard puzzles.'

'I've heard about this. It's to see who can learn languages best, isn't it?'

'It's to see who can do three or four things at once without performance degrading across any of them, but being able to deliver commands at the same time as flying the *strix* is a big part of it.'

'So you tell it to shoot by speaking?'

She shook her head. 'No, I use controls for that'—she mimed grasping a stick and pressing buttons with her hands—'but I control the flight dynamics and speed with this'—she tapped her temple—'and these.' She took his hand and laid it on her headtails.

'So that's how you do all those stunts at the airshows?'

She nodded, holding up one hand, tipping it back and forth. 'This is *pitch*,' she said, 'and this'—she rotated the same hand—'is *roll*.' He nodded, watching her move the hand from side to side through a horizontal plane. 'Last of all,' she said, 'this is *yaw*.'

She went on. 'When I think it, the *strix* responds instantly. There's no time delay. That's the foundation for all the stunts everyone loves so much.'

He hooked his hands around her backside and pulled her up onto his chest so he could look at her face directly and stroke her back.

'Can't you break it or crash it, though? I mean, we all imagine more than we can actually do.'

'Cyler, I am the machine,' she said softly. 'I become the *strix* mind, and it becomes my body. I could no more damage it or overreach with it than I could voluntarily saw off my right arm without anaesthetic.'

'I see.'

'They take the best girls away and turn them into *strix* aviatrices. It's easiest when you start young; you grow into the machine then. The *perplexae* and these things'—she grabbed a handful of her headtails—'take years to develop as you fuse.'

'Fuse with *what*?'

She chuckled at his discomfort. 'With our first *strix*, of course.'

'They're *alive*?'

'Yes, but it's only instinctual life, not conscious life; we share genetic material with them. You saw that last night, on the tower. I had to show her that I wasn't preferring you to her, that I just wanted a man.'

'Do you have to feed them?'

She roared laughing. 'Cyler, that's the best question any-one's ever asked me.'

He shook his head. 'I'm serious, Julia. I've never under-stood how they work, only that you can kill things very fast in them, and they look as scary as fuck, like an eagle crossed with a hornet... on steroids.'

'Yes, we do have to feed them, and yes, they're carnivores.'

He pulled a face. 'So how do they... *grow* them, and, ah, grow you?'

'Cyler, you want to know everything, don't you?'

'Well, it's just, I think other people are doing it too.'

She smiled, and he suspected she knew roughly what he was about to say.

'I went to a House in Heliopolis a couple of years ago, look-ing for something a bit different. I got a woman with feathers instead of hair on her head, and two tits on each side... nice tits, though, a nice shape. I thought she'd had surgery, but she said no, they could do it with *morphogenesis*.' He grinned. 'It was incredibly hot sex, anyway. Afterwards, on her day off, we went to the mime and there was this actor with voluntary control over his penis. He could make it bend round corners. She said it was done with a related technique. She did say the name, but I've forgotten it.'

'There's a complex of genes that control body part positions and shape,' she said. 'You can manipulate them into growing all sorts of weird shit. When they first started experimenting with insects, they'd give bugs legs where there were supposed to be antennae and whatnot. They experimented on animals, on slaves, and then after abolition on war captives.'

'No shit.'

'There are freelancers out there who know the techniques and who've got their own labs, happy to sell what they can do to the highest bidder. A couple of them are even ex-military.

That's why you get feathered, multi-breasted sex workers in certain parts of the Empire.'

'The ultimate, ah, *menagerie-à-trois*,' he said.

'You could say that.'

'What did your parents say when they took you away? Your father must have hoped you'd marry well. You're very pretty.'

She kissed him. 'They were angry, but they were also proud. I went home for Saturnalia at the end of first year, but I didn't like it. Home was nowhere as nice as the fabulous school I went to. The food was shit, and it was cold, and I'd forgotten lots of things about my family. My parents didn't like what was happening to me. My mother tried to cut one of these off—' She held up one thicker headtail. 'It was only when I started to bleed that she stopped. And at school I got to *fly*, and what child is immune to the wonder of flight?'

He kissed the top of her head and rubbed her back and backside. He thought she'd been ill used, but the matter-of-fact way she spoke about it seemed to belie any real anger.

'I never saw that as conscription, to be honest, but as a way out. All four of my grandparents were slaves, then *mezzadri* outside Capua. My paternal grandfather used to belong to the Procurator's wife's family.'

'Will you still be able to care for your parents when they're old?'

'The Air Force sends them money in my name for the length of my service. After that, I've got two brothers who can do their bit.'

He felt her move along his skin and watched her headtails flicker and wriggle. His cock stirred against her belly. She felt it too, and smiled at him.

'Wild,' he said, grinning, his hand sliding in between her legs. She wriggled forward, the *perplexae* darkening once more. He kissed her, salivating. She giggled like a schoolgirl and coiled her headtails into three or four cords, binding them around his back while he touched her. She stroked his scalp with her hands.

'You have clever fingers,' she said.

'This time, slow and steady,' he said, 'because I want you to come and come and *come*.'

'Procurator, *Medicus* Felix wants to know what to do with Iscariot's corpse.'

Horace stood before him as Pilate flicked through the autopsy report. He was pleased to note Felix had ensured Saleh's presence in the autopsy room was not noted anywhere in the paperwork. It was an exercise in arse-covering worthy of a lawyer. He looked up at Horace.

'What was that you were asking?'

'What to do with Iscariot's corpse, Procurator—'

'Tell Felix to take it to the north-west tower as normal, Horace. I don't see why we should deviate from our usual practices in that regard.'

'Yes, Procurator.'

'I'm sure the *striges* will appreciate a break from the cat food they usually get.'

'Yes, Procurator.'

'And once you've spoken to Felix and made me coffee, you'll need to bring Vitellius up on the Eye in here. He wants to speak with me.'

Horace inclined his head and left. Pilate sat back in his chair, his hands clasped across his belly. For the first time since arriving in Jerusalem, he felt like he was getting on top of the mountain of work the city had dumped in his lap. It annoyed him that so many cases that could more easily be disposed of in Caesarea were remaining in Jerusalem and snowing him under when he turned up once or twice a year. Now they were in the third week of their stay, he also knew it was only the presence of Linnaeus and Fotini that was stopping Claudia from engaging in her customary complaints about the Holy City. She'd been particularly happy to witness their contract of concubinage before the two of them went off to supper.

'You have no idea how pleased I am about this, Andreius,' she'd said. Linnaeus had nodded; Pilate thought he looked genuinely relieved. It was interesting to see a Linnaeus who—while still both driven and clever—seemed to have had all his anxiety melt away. He held Fotini to him and kissed her; Pilate was stunned to see a tear running down his cheek as he did so. Claudia had Aristocles bake the traditional round bread shared at weddings in the Campania and bade the two of them eat of it. Camilla and Antony stuck a floral wreath around Nero's ears; it slipped crookedly over one eye, although he made no attempt to shake it off, sitting at Fotini's feet, his head on his paws. His tail thumped the floor from time to time. Claudia brought out an orange silk scarf of her own and draped it over Fotini's head.

'You shouldn't wear so much white,' she said, 'it looks like you've just come from a funeral.'

Fotini nodded. 'In Greece, we wear white at weddings.'

'Romans wear orange and saffron. White is for funerals.'

Each fed the other, Fotini perhaps more impressed by the ritual than Linnaeus, who smiled as she popped pieces of bread into his mouth.

Fotini dipped a piece into some oil that Dana brought them. She smiled at Claudia as she ate, licking her fingers.

'You don't mind if we make use of one of your studies, do you?' Linnaeus asked.

'Not at all,' said Pilate.

'I'll need to impose and ask for one with a big mirror,' he went on. 'I hate it when I can't see myself to rehearse an address.'

Fotini giggled at this; Pilate had Zoë take the two of them to the largest of the spare studies.

Horace returned with coffee and set about activating the Eye. Vitellius was in Antioch reviewing building codes; great and beautiful it might be, but the city experienced earthquakes with monotonous regularity. His visage swam up out of an office with a view over the glittering Orontes. Pilate could see the famous walled island in the middle of the river, fishing boats and a dredge dumping sediment onto a nearby barge. For once, Vitellius did not look thunderous. Pilate saw an attractive woman walking around in the background; she appeared to be completing her dressing and collecting items of personal property. As she left, Pilate recognised her: it was Herodias, Vitellius's mistress and Herod Antipas's wife. Vitellius smiled amiably at her as she went.

'How many Zealots are you holding at present, Procurator?'

'We captured a dozen or so, *Legatus*,' he said. 'They're being held separately but beyond the most cursory examination, none have been formally interrogated.'

'Capito tells me there are two or three who were caught on CCTV committing egregious crimes.'

Pilate swore under his breath; he disliked the way Capito would go over his head on things like this, although he was aware that when he was in Caesarea, the procedure was normal.

'That's correct, *Legatus*. There's a nasty little rapist from the Empire Hotel and one only a bit older who shot out the frontage of the Fleet Fox and then murdered a civilian.'

Vitellius pulled a face. 'The Fleet Fox?'

'The Temple of Cybele, *Legatus*; it passes as a members' only entertainment establishment in order that Romans in the city might have somewhere to honour at least some of our gods.'

Vitellius shook his head. 'Strange people, with their prohibition on everyone else's gods and simultaneous demands that their God always and everywhere be accorded respect.'

Pilate cut to the point.

'Are you suggesting we do something with some of the Zealot prisoners? Do you want them transferred to Syria?'

'I want you to select two or three of limited intelligence value but against whom there is overwhelming evidence of guilt and have them executed before lunch on Friday. You need to teach these people a lesson while Sunday's terrorism is still fresh in everyone's mind.'

Pilate felt himself blanch; he was reasonably sure the colour draining out of his face was obvious to Vitellius.

'*Legatus*, you're asking me to engage in extrajudicial killing—'

'Convene a military tribunal today and ensure any issues are ventilated that way.'

Pilate formed a tent over his nose and mouth with his hands and gazed at his superior.

'I realise the procedure is irregular but something has to be done, Procurator.'

'What next, *Legatus*? Declare martial law and impose a curfew?'

'That won't be necessary, Procurator.'

'To jettison even the appearance of justice is to animate the spirit of the Proscriptions and the very worst of the Civil War. It just adds to Crispus and his fondness for the *parrilla*.'

Vitellius snorted. 'Don't be histrionic, Procurator; we're not talking about the most eminent leaders of the Republic, we're talking about terrorists who seem to think that rape and murder are a form of recreation, all in the name of their long-haired, smelly and vindictive god.'

'I'm not willing to do it, *Legatus*.'

Vitellius pulled a *don't-try-my-patience* face. 'If it helps, Procurator, I'll order you to form an ad hoc military tribunal today and select two or three of your Zealot captives for execution.'

'I'm a lawyer, not a butcher.'

Vitellius's eyes narrowed to slits.

'May I remind you that you now have a formal position within the chain of command, and this is an order.'

Pilate sighed. 'And just where am I supposed to find another lawyer? Gaius Crispus is in the stockade and Cornelius Getorex is preparing for tomorrow's matter.'

Vitellius smiled. 'I had a visit from *Advocatus* Viera yesterday, Procurator; he's finished his course in Rome. I understand he's on the Damascus–Jerusalem Express as we speak.'

Yaakov could hear movement outside his cell. Someone pulled the hatch in the door open and left it open. He'd only been fed an hour or so ago so it couldn't be more food. He hoped it wasn't the violet-eyed soldier. From the very first, when they'd brought him in from the city and roused him from his stupor with a bucket of ice water, he'd found that particular legionary terrifying. It was strange, because the violet-eyed man had done less to him than several of the others.

A much younger man who spoke no Greek roughed him up on the Sunday night. Yaakov expected to be beaten and dishonoured, and the young man did both, knocking him about with open palms and then bending him over his bunk and fucking him from behind. He was very strong; his handslaps alone sent Yaakov flying against the walls. Three or four of them gathered in the doorway watching the young soldier as he went about his work. The violet-eyed soldier joined them, standing with his arms folded. He did not partake when two other men queued up, but his laughter as he watched sliced the air like the whine of a dentist's drill.

'You're enjoying that, Enneconis, aren't you?'

Yaakov heard Enneconis say *ita, recte* from above him, one hand pinning his neck down as he spoke. 'You do realise it's forbidden under the Military Code, don't you?'

Enneconis said *ita, recte* again. The violet-eyed soldier sighed. 'I suppose it's to be expected, given the circumstances.'

'I want him next,' said a voice by the door.

Enneconis came and then pushed the boy's backside towards the new man, sliding down the wall, exhausted. Yaakov clung onto the metal frame of his bunk while this man went at it, trying to avoid collapsing on the floor. He suspected falling down would invite a group kicking, and he doubted he would survive that.

'Give over, lads,' the violet-eyed soldier said when all three had sated themselves and Enneconis was readying himself for another go. 'You've made your point; leave him be for now.'

They threw him onto his bunk when the last man finished; Yaakov could see Enneconis buttoning his fly, his expression sour. The violet-eyed one stood over him as he trembled and bled.

'Let that be a lesson to you,' he'd said in Aramaic, 'in responsible cock ownership.'

Most of the men who walked into his cell this time were officers, and while Enneconis was present, the violet-eyed soldier was nowhere to be seen. The most senior officer was in dress uniform, not fatigues, and snowy haired. Yaakov stood to attention beside his bunk, sweat beading his top lip.

'He looks about twelve,' said the snowy-haired officer.

'He turns sixteen in a fortnight, sir,' said Enneconis.

'Executing children never looks particularly good.'

'*Advocatus* Viera, he's of no use to us in terms of useful

intelligence,' said another officer, a man with dark, fiery features. He flicked papers up from a clipboard. 'We have a Gestas and a Bar Abba, as well.' He squinted at something. 'Another rapist and a murderer.'

Viera appraised Yaakov critically, pausing at one point to lodge his fingers under the boy's chin and look directly into his eyes. 'It can't be helped, I suspect,' he said, shrugging his shoulders and sighing. 'Bring him into the interview room. *Centurio* Friere, fetch *Centurio* Lonuobo and I'll convene our military tribunal.'

'Lonuobo has been relieved of interrogation duty, sir.'

'He's needed. Chase him up.'

Viera sighed again. For this piece of flotsam, and another couple he hadn't met yet, the Legate had hauled him away from his long-planned assignation with a Priestess of Aphrodite in Corinth. He'd been seeing her off and on for years—in a non-professional capacity, too. He was reasonably sure with careful effort he could make the pairing permanent, and he cursed Vitellius for throwing sand in the gears of his arrangements.

Enneconis shackled Yaakov's hands together and to his feet.

'Go,' he barked, shoving Yaakov into the corridor.

Lonuobo remained beside Yaakov as Viera passed formal sentences and had them recorded; the rest of the group went out soon after, leaving him alone to unshackle Yaakov's hands and guide him up the corridor to his cell. Yaakov was sweating and trembling at the thought of what this man would do to him, and he kept his head down as the soldier unlocked his cell door and led him inside.

Lonuobo's voice was soft. 'I won't hurt you,' he said. 'I know what Cassius and his friends did to you.'

Yaakov nodded, sitting on his bunk. He wiped away tears

with the back of one hand. 'I'm to die, yes?'

'Yes, on Friday. By rights you shouldn't, you're not of age yet, but you got recorded committing a capital crime.'

Yaakov nodded again, his terror receding. He'd never heard of a gentle Centurion. 'Riding your bike without a light's probably a capital crime to you Romans.'

Lonuobo chuckled. 'At least you won't be flogged, you're too young,' he said. 'And when you go, it'll be quick; the men in the First Cohort will shoot straight. Compared with how we used to kill, the firing squad's a mercy.'

'I'm sorry for what I did.'

Lonuobo bent down and clasped his shoulder, facing him. Yaakov could see him struggling with what he wanted to say.

'Ah, before what you did on Sunday, had you, eh'—he gazed up—'ever coupled with a woman?'

'No, never; Simon would have killed me and killed the woman, too.'

'Sex is fun, Yaakov, when you both want it. I think you should learn that before you die.'

Ben Yusuf watched through his incompletely closed hatch as Lonuobo walked down the corridor towards Yaakov's cell, an attractive woman in tow and a bottle of wine in hand. He was telling her that he'd put a bedroll on the floor and that the young man spoke no Greek, but that he was sure they would be all right. He handed her the bottle.

'He's a first timer,' Lonuobo went on, 'and Galilean. He'll have no idea what to do with it, so nothing too tasty.'

She nodded at this, chuckling and looking at the label.

'This is good wine,' she said.

'Help him relax; it's like a last meal for the condemned.'

Ben Yusuf had already listened with fascinated horror as they used sex to punish the boy for a sexual crime. The *lex*

talionis, they called it. This time around—soon after Lonuobo
shut the cell door behind him—there were giggles and kisses
and clinking glasses and then sounds of pleasure, a woman's
low moan and a man's soft grunts. Ben Yusuf watched as Lonuobo sat opposite Yaakov's cell, his back to the wall and his
hands clasped loosely around his knees. He took a knife out
of his pocket and began cleaning under his fingernails while
he waited. Ben Yusuf wanted to say something, but that would
reveal that he'd jammed a heel of hard bread into the slot
where his hatch moved back and forth and that it hadn't been
properly shut for days. The noises from Yaakov's cell became
more insistent, and Lonuobo gazed up at the ceiling, smiling.

This thing, they consider it compassion.

And the lex talionis, *too.*

A FLOGGING

Pilate looked out over the parade ground from his office, smoking while he ate a ham and cheese roll. Below, a *contubernium* was preparing for a flogging. As he watched, four legionaries frogmarched two men out from under the arches in ankle and wrist shackles while two others set out a heavy wooden table covered with implements made for inflicting pain. The soldiers forced their charges to sit on Antonia's clipped, velvety grass and face the whipping post. One of the shackled men was spouting a steady stream of invective in Greek, directed at his captors. Two soldiers stripped to the waist, handing their jackets to the men superintending the table.

He had not appreciated until his appointment as Procurator that flogging was hard, physical work, and that even fit young legionaries found themselves gasping for air afterwards. Pilate—like most civilian governors—confined physical chastisement to forty strokes. He knew that military governors sometimes went higher, but he also knew how dangerous that could be. A hundred strokes—given the right tool—would kill a man. The two shirtless men swung their arms around in circles and limbered up, their lean, v-shaped torsos pale in the sun. They stood over the table, choosing their implements, while the others stripped the first victim naked and chained him to the whipping post, his hands above his head. It wasn't the shouter, but his silent comrade. Pilate squinted as the two floggers riffled through the gear set out on the table. It looked like they'd gone for lengths of birch or rattan. They dragged them through the air, flicking their wrists, looking at each other and grinning at the singing sound they made.

An officer strode across the parade ground from the direction of the infirmary, stopping before the table. Pilate saw the caduceus on his collar as he turned and squinted up for a moment. He was a dark young man, his face mobile and gentle. Pilate saw him issuing instructions and imprecations. *Medicus Saleh*, he thought, *you've been busy this week.* Saleh spread medical items along the edge of the table: a silver stopwatch, bandages, bottles of smelling salts and antiseptic, a blood pressure cuff. He stood on the other side of the whipping post, facing the criminal—Pilate realised it was likely one of the Zealots Viera had dealt with that morning—and put something in between the man's teeth. The two floggers peeled off along diagonal lines, standing opposite each other, marking out two sides of an equilateral triangle with the post at its apex. It was then Pilate realised the two paths to the post were paler—almost blond in colour—than the surrounding grass. The post itself was marble and set in a dozen square slabs of apricot stone, attractively cut.

Pilate snorted at this. *We make beautiful things.*

Saleh counted down from five, folding in the fingers of one hand as he did so, then blew a whistle. 'Do the work!' yelled one of the men at the table. Pilate watched the first flogging, noting the Zealot's attempt during the first five or so blows to avoid screaming. The two floggers alternated, loping to the post, delivering a blow and then whirling on the spot and returning to the round blond patch of grass at the top of their runs. From above, their timed movements were metronomic and balanced, light like a dancer's steps. He noticed their torsos begin to glisten in the sun, and saw blood spatter the apricot stone below as well as one of Saleh's breast pockets. The medic pulled a face but did not flinch, stepping forward to revive the Zealot when he passed out at the twenty-seventh stroke. He held his palm up at the two soldiers; both of them were mouth breathing. Pilate guessed that he counted to thirty. He waved them in again. Pilate closed his eyes when the prisoner's screams became loud enough to penetrate the bulletproof glass of his office window.

Saleh was unhappy about the blood on his pocket, and he disliked the obvious relish with which the soldiers—especially Cassius, he of the violet eyes—carried out their duty. While he attended to the first man—with antiseptic and an antibiotic shot—they hooked the second prisoner to the pillar. Saleh looked around Antonia's parade ground, closed in by walls and its four squat towers. He saw an aviatrix poring over a map with a Centurion from the 1st Cohort. He was scratching his head; she was shaking hers. Four men hung a banner wishing everyone a 'Magnificent *Megalesia*' across the entrance hall. No one paid the flogging any mind, although a few turned their heads as they walked past. The aviatrix smiled at him as she walked by. He made his way to the post; the Zealot hanging there succeeded in marking his uniform with spittle.

'I'd stop with the abuse,' Saleh told the man, speaking in Aramaic. 'They don't have to keep using the birch. Piss them off enough and they'll trade up to the *flagellum* and you'll die of hypovolemic shock from loss of blood.'

The Zealot looked at him, perhaps shocked at his fluent Aramaic. 'I'm going to die anyway, Roman filth.'

'The bullet or the *flagellum*,' Saleh said. 'You choose.'

Yaakov was still fornicating with his bought woman—grunting, chattering and giggling, it sounded like she was teaching him the Greek words for different parts of the body—when Ben Yusuf heard the two men being brought back inside from the parade ground.

The scream was high and faint at first, difficult to pinpoint with any accuracy. As it came closer, it resolved into a screeching, inchoate cry of agony and a confused babble of voices. One—from the medic who'd been part of the group that interrogated him—was angry. He was remonstrating with what sounded like half-a-dozen men in Latin. Ben Yusuf heard heavy, booted footsteps beat up the corridor—they were dragging something, he heard it scrape the stone—and hands fling open the cell beside his. *Ah, Bar Abba.* He heard them dump Bar Abba on the floor, heard him land on his front with a soft *thump*, and heard the cell door slam. The two men retreated the way they had come; they were laughing. The medic was still expectorating. Ben Yusuf caught the phrases 'should be bloody banned' and 'we don't ask men in this legion to donate blood so it can go to fucking terrorists'.

The high thin wail came from the other man, Gestas; it was fading now. Ben Yusuf suspected his cell was further down the corridor, closer to the infirmary. He'd heard him abuse all the Romans who'd come to his cell, whether it was to bring him his food, or to take him to the baths, or outside for his daily exercise half-hour. After the first attempt at the latter, he noticed that Gestas rattled as he left his cell; they'd shackled him.

He rolled over on his bunk, his back to the wall and his face towards Bar Abba's cell. He could hear whimpering coming from within, and shook his head. *Impossible*, he thought. *Unless they've not pushed his hatch all the way home either.* He lay very still, listening to the grizzling. It had to compete with Yaakov's cheerful rutting and the woman's high-pitched giggling, but that was severely rhythmical, with predictable pauses. He climbed off his bunk and crouched down, his fingers spread, putting his ear to the floor. He saw rather than heard the origin of the noise. A sliver of light shone along the floor into his cell: there was a crack in the brickwork, extending six or so inches up into the masonry. At the bottom there was a ragged hole, maybe half an inch high. He crawled forward and blew into it, clearing away powdered mortar and making it large enough for him to see part of Bar Abba's bunk and the cell's metal toilet and sink. Bar Abba was kneeling on the floor, clad only in loose trousers, rocking back and forth. His back and presumably his buttocks were scored across with angry red lines. They'd stopped bleeding and were covered with some sort of white salve, but even so it was a dreadful sight. Bar Abba put both hands over his mouth as he rocked. Ben Yusuf recognised the gesture. He was trying to avoid being sick.

'Don't turn towards me,' he said, 'but there's a gap in the wall. We can talk.'

'I know,' Bar Abba answered through his fingers, still rocking, not turning his head. 'I hear you praying through it. I like your prayers.'

'Why was Gestas screaming?'

'They used the *flagellum* on him,' he said, 'not just the rattan.'

'Why?'

'He was rude to them. The medic warned him, but he didn't listen. About half of it was the *flagellum*.'

'Saleh?'

'That was the name on his uniform.'

A glorious, soaring male voice floated along the corridor from the direction of the infirmary. Ben Yusuf and Bar Abba listened as Cassius warmed up his vocal cords, going from low to high and high to low a few times. Lonuobo shouted out a request.

'I can try,' said Cassius, 'but it's high, even if I start lower down.'

He got most of the way through a complex, coruscating melody before stopping and apologising. 'I'd need to climb a stepladder to sing the rest of that. It's a woman's song.'

'Well may you sing,' Ben Yusuf heard Saleh shout, 'but for now, you can both help wheel this poor half-dead thing into his cell. I'll look in on him myself.'

'He spat on you, sir.'

'And you wrote off a set of my fatigues, Cassius, using that bloody *flagellum*.'

'*Ha-Satan* has a beautiful voice to sing,' Bar Abba said softly, 'and hands of stone to flog.'

'They don't know what they're doing is wrong, Bar Abba,' he said. 'Cassius and his jewelled eyes, the kind medic who likes to fornicate, men who move so well while they beat you.'

This time the Zealot—very slowly—did turn his head to face the wall. The expression on his face was not hostile.

'Simon and Yehuda used to talk about what you said,' he started, his voice still soft, even distant. 'Our leaders always said you weren't willing to commit to the struggle. Some even wanted you dead; you were diluting our message, we'd never chase the Roman filth out with people like you around.'

'When you did what you did on Sunday, Bar Abba, did you know it was wrong?'

Bar Abba had two brief but terrible images dance before his eyes: the uncomprehending woman in the lobby who had pointed out to Simon—as one would if teaching a not-quite-bright child—*I'm a hetaera, not a whore*; and the middle-aged man he'd pushed off the roof. Bar Abba had been wearing a black balaclava. The citizen had twisted his head and looked into his eyes. *Very brave*, he said, *keeping your face hidden like that*. Bar Abba had pushed him over the railing then, but the man spread his arms as he went—deliberately, gracefully—like some monstrous bird frustrated only by its failure to fly.

'Yes, I knew it was wrong.'

'Then your sin is greater than that of singing, flogging Cassius of the violet eyes.'

Bar Abba stopped rocking and began to shudder, his body wracked with sobs. Ben Yusuf watched him as he bent forward, still careful of his shredded back. He rested his elbows on the floor, propping his head in his hands.

Cornelius invited Cyler to dine in the Officers' Mess, outlining his trial arguments over a meal and a bottle of wine. He was grateful when the young man showed his shrewdness and insight, making useful suggestions and even spotting an error in his reasoning.

He'd come to the conclusion that Cyler—for all that his tastes outside the law were rather basic—would make an exceptional military lawyer when the time came. He poured both of them a glass and pointed a finger at Cyler's face.

'You are not allowed to fail your Finals, Cyler Lucullus,' he said.

'I won't, sir, I promise. I've got a good average so far, and I've even won some prizes in rhetoric.'

Cyler sat back in his seat, admiring the beauty of the Officers' Mess and appreciating the quality of the food and wine. Life was good right now. He'd spent the night alternating between sleep and sex with a woman who delighted him; his commanding officer valued his legal skills; he was on top of both his coursework and the army's physical requirements. He'd run a sub–six-minute mile yesterday on only seven hours' sleep in the previous 48 hours and been complimented by the X *Fretensis* senior physical trainer.

'I need someone as my instructing clerk for this trial. I can't ask Crispus and even though Viera's back in Jerusalem, he's had nothing at all to do with the matter.'

'I'd love that, sir.'

'Three days without fatigues and guard duty, time to run in the mornings, and time to make yourself clean and gorgeous for your woman at night.'

'Yes, sir, that's right.'

'I appreciate your candour, Lucullus, I really do. You're an educated man, well on the way to becoming better educated, but you're completely frank about what you like.'

'I do like cultural things, sir, but I like sex and wine and food more.'

'A true hedonist, then.' Cornelius winked at him. 'Given a choice between a night at the theatre and sex with your woman, what would you choose?'

Cyler forked a chunk of pastry into his mouth. 'I'm greedy, sir,' he said after swallowing. 'First a night at the theatre, *then* sex with my woman afterwards.'

Cornelius laughed; Cyler *was* primitive, but it was a beautiful, uninhibited primitivism. It perhaps accounted for his fondness for the aviatrix. He didn't care what other people considered attractive or acceptable, instead thinking only of what he found enjoyable. 'Has she taken you up in one yet?'

'Not yet, sir. Now I know I'm clerking for you I might ask her about tonight.'

Cornelius pointed a fork at him this time. 'You realise that clerking means you're basically my personal servant. You're not allowed to lose anything.'

Later, while Cyler was sitting with a book of Cicero's most famous trial speeches held open across his knee, a thought came to him. He waited until Cornelius had finished rehearsing his address and sat down beside him to drink a glass of water.

'Did you ever work out how he knew about you and *Medicus* Saleh?'

'No, I didn't, and it annoys me.'

'Saleh doesn't know?'

'All he said was that some people can read other people, and

Cyler smiled. 'There's a Macedonian in my Cohort who's a bit adventurous,' he said. 'I'll introduce him to you if you like.'

'Would you do that?'

'Don't know what they're missing,' he added. 'You *strix* women should start running your own advertising.'

'Saying what?'

'Best sex in the Empire, that's what,' he said as Julia alighted and walked towards them.

'I'm going to introduce'—he looked at the other aviatrix; she was shorter, darker and shapelier than Julia—'this lady to Eugenides.'

'I'm Apicia,' she said. 'I would like to meet your Eugenides.'

'He's determined to find us all men,' Julia said.

Apicia smiled at her and turned to go, looking at Cyler.

'We don't all want men,' she said, 'but I do.'

'There are nine hundred men in the First Cohort, most of them not spoken for.'

Julia watched Apicia leave and then slid her arms around Cyler's waist, looking up at him. 'I have one confused *strix* now,' she said, pushing her hips into his. 'She's beside herself over you.'

'I thought you said it was only instinct.'

'Love is instinctual, Cyler. She loves you.'

Cyler had always been careful never to let the *amor* word pass his lips; he'd always spoken of *eros* or *cupido* instead, keeping women—who he loved *simpliciter*—at arm's length. This one, though—this one was *something*. He wanted her to have his babies, she made his head go round with lust, and there was a ferocious loyalty there, too. He rucked her skirt up, not caring that they were visible from the ground below, and perhaps more widely across the city.

Te amo, Julia, he said, *te amo.*

We make beautiful things.

PART VII

They leave Omelas, they walk ahead into the darkness, and they do not come back. The place they go towards is a place even less imaginable to most of us than the city of happiness. I cannot describe it at all. It is possible that it does not exist. But they seem to know where they are going, the ones who walk away from Omelas.

—Ursula K. Le Guin

The little group of Zealots walked away from the lake and the town and into the blinding dust. No one paid them any heed. Yehuda had tied Kelil's elbows together behind his back. From time to time he kicked him and the young man fell forward. Sometimes this meant he fell on his face and cut his cheeks. Once he split his lip open. The rest of them waited while he staggered to his feet, blood dribbling down his chin where a tooth had pierced the flesh and come out the other side. No one moved to help him. Yehuda laughed, a high, forced sound.

The rest of the Zealots Yehuda had called in for the 'Rabbi of Capernaum' job were unknown to Saul, and they frightened him. They had close-cropped skulls and black spade beards and boasted of legionaries whose throats they had cut with lengths of wire. Two of them wore drab olive trousers from army disposals while a third wore a closely flecked Persian desert camouflage jacket. Saul found this disturbing, juxtaposed with the Roman trousers on the other two. If they were angry with Kelil they gave no sign, merely looking on as Yehuda made him suffer. Eventually the group stopped in the lee of a low hill, the sun high above them. Saul realised he was very thirsty and had neglected to fill his water canteen before leaving Capernaum.

'Did you warn him?' Yehuda wanted to know.

'I told him I had been sent to kill him,' Kelil said.

Kelil's gaze was defiant without anger. He looked at each of the men around him in turn, making eye contact with them. Saul turned away.

'Why didn't you kill him?'

'Because he belongs to the town, Yehuda, and the townsfolk respect him.'

Saul hung back while the argument went back and forth, as though Yehuda needed to wind himself up first before he could bring himself to kill. Saul was fairly sure that's where it was headed: Kelil would be dumped in a culvert somewhere for a Roman patrol to find, his neck broken.

'You think you have the power to judge,' Kelil was saying, 'but judgment is in God's hands, not yours.'

This, Saul saw, was the trigger they'd wanted, although when it came he'd been expecting Yehuda to push Kelil to his knees and shoot him in the back of the head. Instead, he picked up a rock and threw it. The others hesitated at first and then joined in. One of them handed his heavy coat to Saul and soon he had half-a-dozen of the things draped over his left arm. Kelil did not try to break and run, and in any case they had wandered so far from civilisation it wasn't as though there was anywhere he could go, at least not quickly. Saul had never seen anyone stoned before, and was not familiar with so much blood. His parents may have been Romanised, but even they drew the line at public executions, gladiators and cage fights. He'd seen pictures, of course, or watched highlights packages—always surreptitiously—on screen. He'd also heard the excited babble of his fellow students as they described what they'd seen at this or that festival. The blood looked more orange than he thought it should; his fellow students assured him this was just an effect of the light.

Kelil was on all fours now, trying to protect his head. He curled into the foetal position and Saul closed his eyes. He heard the dull thump of the stones against the young man's body, heard Yehuda's imprecations. At some point Kelil stopped screaming and all he could hear was the grunting and panting of his killers. A Roman pushprop formation went overhead, loud and whiny, and Saul looked up. They were too high to see what was taking place on the ground below. If there'd been a strix, maybe its aviatrix would see, but even then, she'd need to be looking. When Saul looked down again, they were piling rocks on top of Kelil's body, hiding it.

'We need to go to the lake,' Yehuda was saying, 'and wash up. When the Romans find the body, they'll use dogs to track us down.'

THE TRIAL

'Counsel,' Pilate said in Latin, 'may we have appearances?'

He self-consciously adjusted his toga and touched the gold-dipped laurel leaves encircling his head. He was not enamoured of the Empire's formal court dress—in part because he could not drape a toga without help—but long use had habituated him to it. He noticed that Linnaeus seemed to wear his toga with genuine ease, while Cornelius looked oddly overdressed out of uniform.

Horace had seen both counsel when he walked past the robing room to open the court. Cornelius Getorex, he told Pilate, had his arms outstretched like a circling *strix* as a tall, dark young man in dress uniform—his clerk—robed him with the aid of a printed diagram. It was not going well.

'I think I've folded something over when it should have gone under, sir,' he was saying. 'We'll have to start again, sorry.'

'You mean *you'll* have to start again, Cyler Lucullus.'

The *Praetorium* was packed: for the first time in his governorship, the press box was filled to capacity. He even had troops on the doors to check media credentials before permitting entry to the courtroom. Not all interested members of the public could be accommodated, and Pilate had ordered his men to make a rough selection based on relationship to the suspect or witnesses or counsel, leaving them to allocate any spare seats on a discretionary basis. Claudia had broken her own rule about never attending her husband's cases and he seated her in the jury box beside Fotini and thirteen other members of the public. A woman in midwife's robes had been rebuffed despite insisting that she was Cornelius Geto-rex's woman; her response was to approach the lawyer as he emerged from the robing room. His face lit up and the two of them proceeded to kiss passionately while the crowd looked on. The soldier who'd tried to exclude her looked sheepish.

'You must be the only man in the legion who doesn't know who she is,' Cornelius said.

'Sorry, sir. I've just been posted here from Jericho for Pass-over, sir.'

Pilate scanned the public gallery. There were Galilean peasants in rough clothes, looking around with expressions between fear and awe. Beside them were a mixture of Romans and Greeks and Hellenised Jews, mainly civilians but with the odd soldier in their midst. He saw Viera's white head and Saleh beside a pale young woman who was breastfeeding a small baby. Beside them was a dark, striking woman who the young mother seemed to know; she kept looking across at Linnaeus with an anxious expression on her face in between admiring the baby and its parents.

Ben Yusuf sat in the dock in a handsome, dark-maroon gown, his beard trimmed and his head now covered with bristles a little longer than a soldier's. His hands were fold-ed in his lap and his face was blank. He looked presentable and neat and Pilate admired his counsel's attention to detail. Linnaeus's instructing clerk was a young woman from one of the Caesarea firms, Clara something or other. He noticed her gaze straying to the man in the dock, but for the most part she busied herself with ordering Linnaeus's papers, marking rel-evant pages with sticky notes covered in his messy, back-slop-ing handwriting.

Cornelius's papers were already sorted into binders, marked with colour-coded tabs tracing neat diagonal lines down each side. Each binder was numbered on the spine with Greek symbols; he took the one marked α and opened it to the first tab, setting it on the podium. His clerk had very little to do as a consequence, and was reduced to handing his senior officer the occasional drink of water or code citation.

Pilate banged his gavel once after the two lawyers had announced themselves.

'There are some preliminary matters to which I must attend before we commence the trial proper. First, the matter of the gavel. When I bang it twice, like so'—he demonstrated—'you must stand.' He noticed Romans in the room struggling against powerful instincts telling them to leap to their feet. 'When I bang it once, like so'—he demonstrated again—'you must sit immediately, and in silence.' He noticed the Galileans nodding, comprehension coming to them now.

'Members of several media organisations have applied for the right to record trial proceedings. This practice has become increasingly popular in the last five years. It has long been my view that it undermines the dignity of the court and has, on occasion, made trials look like *ludi*. Therefore, I refuse the application. There is a courtroom artist present whose drawings will be available to all members of the press.'

He looked up, catching the young woman's eye. She was behind the bar table, a sketch block across one knee. He suspected she was drawing him. He saw several members of the press pack pull sour faces. His ruling meant that they had to stay for the whole proceeding or risk being scooped by a more attentive reporter who elected to remain.

'You will also notice that the soldiers acting as court orderlies and reporters are unarmed. It is an inflexible rule of Roman procedure that there are to be no firearms in either the Senate House or in courtrooms, for obvious historical reasons.'

Greeks and Romans nodded sagely at this, but Pilate noticed more looks of perplexity on Galilean faces. He resisted the urge to curl his lip.

There is such a thing as history that everyone ought to know.

'The Divine Julius Caesar was shot from the public gallery of the *curia* by a fellow senator. Before that day it had not been the custom to search senators before they entered the chamber.'

Pilate remembered pointing out to a Persian refugee—an abolitionist granted an academic post at *Collegia Roma* on the basis of persecution at home—that Romans preferred not to solve their political problems with violence. The Persian had smiled sadly and said *I thought that was a solution you Romans used rather often.* He'd then held an imaginary rifle to his shoulder and mimed pulling the trigger.

'Now, on to more substantive matters; I must place on the record that counsel for the defence, Don Andreius Linnaeus, and his concubine have been staying in my official residence since Sunday evening. This was necessitated by the destruction of much of the Empire Hotel, where they were staying formerly. During that time, Don Linnaeus and his concubine have dined separately from my wife and me, and we have been careful to avoid discussing the case currently before the court. I am aware—were this a citizen trial—that this could constitute an appeal point. I reveal it now in the interest of candour and the open administration of justice.'

Cynara had been fast asleep—the first good sleep she'd had since Sunday night, in fact—when she'd woken up with a start. Her father was standing beside the bed, his hands clutched across his stomach, fingers from one hand encircling the other wrist.

'Papa?'

'Maybe it's age, Rivkah, but I need moral support today.'

She rolled over and sat up, facing him. She rubbed her eyes.

'I was sleeping. My name is Cynara, now.'

'Please come to court with me.'

His face was ashen; she stood up, pulling her nightclothes around her. She gave thanks that she'd never adopted the Roman habit of sleeping naked.

'It's just court, Papa. It's how Romans solve their problems, when they're not fighting.'

'I have to give evidence, Rivkah. I don't think it will be of much use, but I want to know that at least one person is there for me.'

She did not comprehend her father's involvement with Ben Yusuf but it worried her to see him so distressed. The corners of his eyes were moist.

They caught a taxi to Antonia together and she watched as he went to a special room set aside for witnesses. She pointed him out to one of the guards and the man waved her into court; then she saw Rachel coming out of the toilets, her baby strapped to her chest like a northern woman. She didn't like the thought of being bored rigid by a court case and seeing Rachel outside the courtroom lifted her spirits. Rachel was delirious with joy when she told Cynara that Saleh wanted to adopt Marcus as his son 'in the proper Roman manner' and have two more children with her.

'He is so good, and so gentle,' she said, 'and an officer.'

If anyone deserves a break, Cynara thought, *it's Rachel.* Cynara watched Rachel wrap Marcus, her hands deft as she worked. Saleh joined her and took the boy when she was finished, resting him upright against his shoulder and rubbing his back. Cynara found this soothing to look at; the closely involved young couple and their child distracted her from the courtroom around her.

Cynara had become aware of Rachel's terrible story when Rufus had been part of a team detailed to the Empire Hotel after a man's body was discovered at the bottom of a lift shaft. The death was eventually ruled accidental, but the intervening investigation had allowed Rufus time to establish that Cynara was Jewish and that she might have some idea of what to do with the beautiful girl who'd been staying in the *vicus* with Photis, a comrade's woman, for the last three months. He had approached her shyly, turning his beret over in his hands, outlining his circumstances.

'They shunned her after I rescued her,' he said, miming a fireman's lift, 'because I'd touched her arse, and because she hugged me afterwards... with gratitude. Her parents and brothers are all dead.'

'Oh, God.'

'The Rabbi said the villagers would kill her if I didn't take her away with me. He was ashamed of his own people.'

'So you...?'

'She had some minor burns. I made out they were worse than minor and we brought her to Jerusalem for treatment. The Sepphoris medic had a go at me when we airlifted her out.'

'Why?'

'Nice way to get yourself a pretty fuck, he told me.'

Cynara had wanted to scream at the moon at that point, at the worst of her two cultures rolled into something toxic and foul.

'She doesn't like living with Photis, *Donna* Arimathea,' he went on, 'and now I want her to live with me.'

'Isn't it the Roman way to build your woman a flat in the *vicus* and have her live there? Then she wouldn't have to stay with your friends.'

'Yes, *Donna*, but I haven't made her my woman yet. I mean, I haven't even touched her—and the reason she doesn't like staying with Photis is, ah, because she and Luopo, well, Photis is Syrian—'

Cynara took pity on his discomfort, smiling. 'Whenever

he's there, they fuck nonstop, in every different position, and don't care if Rachel sees them while they're at it, yes?'

The relief on his face was immediate. 'Yes, *Donna*, and with loud music, too. I don't know if seeing that will put her off if I take her as my woman. She seems to like me. She's always pleased to see me. Sometimes when we're alone she strokes my hair. I do want to fuck her, but the Sepphoris medic is wrong.'

Cynara nodded, understanding his awkwardness.

'Build her a flat in the usual way, making sure she sees it and knows that it's for her. When you're finished, take her to your bed; she will not object then. Under Jewish law, once you fuck her, she's your wife.'

'I want her to like it, *Donna*. I want her to like me.'

She smiled. 'Be a patient and gentle teacher, then.'

'You will note,' Pilate was saying now, 'the absence of a jury; non-citizens are tried by judge alone unless they bear the jurors' daily costs privately. This does not substantially alter the procedure, however. First, the State will present its case. It will call witnesses and elucidate evidence from them. The Defence will then question those same witnesses with a view to clarifying, confirming or rebutting that evidence. The same process then obtains in reverse. Once counsel have finished their questions, I ask any questions I deem relevant based on the authority vested in me as Examining Magistrate. My goal, of course, is not to take sides but to find the truth.'

Cynara watched Rachel stare at Saleh as Pilate explained himself. He touched her cheek and smiled.

'Finally, you will note that *Aquilifer* Getorex, the State's counsel, is not in uniform. This is because he appears before the court in his citizen capacity, not as a soldier, abiding by civil and not military law.'

Pilate nodded at Getorex, his face a mask.

'The State's case, *Aquilifer* Getorex,' he said.

Cornelius uncurled his great frame carefully, keeping the folds of his toga pinned to his sides.

Cynara watched Cornelius build the prosecution case. 'At its heart, this is a very simple matter,' he said several times—just often enough to be telling but not so often as to be tedious. 'There are multiple charges here—felony murder, failure to warn, riot, assault—and only the first is capital. To understand that offence, however, one needs to keep all the others in mind. To that end, I am going to turn from law to sculpture and cut you a relief with a narrative sequence, like the panels on a triumphal arch.'

Cynara caught herself nodding at this.

'Before you, Procurator, is a man convinced of his destiny, of his own importance. His story begins in the Galilee, where he first sensed this destiny and acted upon it, gathering followers around him. Two turned out to be terrorists whose murderous activities were known to the Suspect. Instead of reporting them to the authorities, he "forgave" them, a concept that not only takes his own people's law and twists it out of shape but laughs in the face of anything a Roman would consider *clementia*.'

Some of the Galileans in the room were getting lost in his educated prose. Pilate had ordered Lonuobo back to his seat, presumably to keep him fresh for when he was really needed—to translate for witnesses who spoke only Aramaic—and was now conducting the trial wholly in Greek. She saw one or two leave, shaking their heads.

'The Suspect's conviction that he had a destiny to fulfil manifested itself in two incidents, one merely irritating, the other murderous. First, he marched into Jerusalem through the city's Beautiful Gate with all the trappings of a Jewish King. One State witness—an officer in the Third Cohort—will recount this incident, while High Priest Caiaphas will explain what it means and how deliberate a challenge it is in the context of Jewish folklore and history.

'Second—and only a day later—he led his followers into the Jerusalem Temple and incited a major riot. During that riot, Samuel Kohen was killed while struggling with the Suspect. Samuel Kohen was a souvenir seller, not a moneychanger. He wasn't rich or notable. He was just a merchant engaging in the truck and barter that helps to make the Empire rich. He sold postcards, mainly—' Cynara watched as Cornelius's dark clerk handed him two cards, one showing the Court of the Israelites, the other Antonia's spectacular Officer's Mess. He held them up in front of his podium, looking at Pilate. 'He leaves a widow and six children.' Cornelius now held the two cards up in the direction of the press box. Cynara could see various reporters' pens skittering across their notebooks.

Pilate leant forward. 'May I remind you, *Aquilifer* Getorex, that there is no jury and that showing exhibits to the press gallery will have no effect on the outcome of this trial?'

Cornelius bowed slightly, his point made. 'My apologies, Procurator; it won't happen again.'

'Go on, *Aquilifer* Getorex.'

'Some of the witnesses the State calls will adduce evidence for the Suspect's sense of destiny; others will adduce evidence of his wilful dalliance with terrorists and his dances with their doctrines; others again will adduce evidence of his callow disregard for human life. Samuel Kohen, it seems—a man without destiny—could be dispensed with.'

For the first time, something the Prosecutor said reached Ben Yusuf; Cynara watched him curl over and tuck his chin into his chest like he'd been hit. She noticed the Procurator staring at him, his eyes narrowed almost to slits. Pilate dipped his pen in the bench's inkwell and wrote something in the heavy, leather-bound judge's book open before him.

'The State's case, Procurator, will convince you that—while it is possible to argue that none of the individual crimes warrant the death penalty—viewed globally they do. Further, the State submits that a global view is the only reasonable view to take. During the course of preparing the case, one of my subordinate investigating officers made the observation that there is nothing more dangerous than a man who considers himself an instrument in the hands of an angry god. It is the State's submission that the Suspect is just such a dangerous man.'

Cornelius waited for his words to sink in before sitting down; Cynara heard Saleh inhale sharply beside her. Marcus stirred and gurgled in response. Rachel placed her fingers gently over his mouth while Saleh scribbled something on a scrap of paper and passed it to her.

That's my line, he wrote.

'Don Linnaeus,' Pilate was saying now, 'do you wish to raise any preliminary matters, or will you wait to elucidate the Defence case in cross?'

Linnaeus stood up, touching his gold headband and letting his warm, kindly gaze meet Pilate's.

'I will make a few comments, Procurator, by way of clarification if nothing else.'

'Go on, Don Linnaeus.'

'Procurator, it may well be that my client thinks he has some sort of special destiny. It's also entirely possible that he favours light over heavy in the cages and the Reds in the circus.'

There was a ripple of laughter around the courtroom at this; lightly armed fighters tended to get much the worst of it in the arena and the Reds were perpetual wooden-spooners at the races. Cynara caught herself smiling and noticed that Pilate was also chuckling.

'Jokes aside, he probably does hold views that most—if not

all—Romans find disagreeable. I'm his counsel and I've learnt quite a bit about what he thinks over the last week or so. I have to say I think he's in cloud cuckoo land half the time. For his part, he probably thinks me, my lifestyle and my personal habits the embodiment of evil.'

Cynara knew Andreius Linnaeus's brilliant reputation, and for all that the prosecutor was very good, she got the impression this man was operating on a whole other level. Already a couple of the women in the press pack were looking at him with the sort of frank fascination he could no doubt turn to his sexual advantage should he so choose.

'We don't, however, execute people for thinking they should walk hand in hand with Aeneas. We make them the butt of our jokes, but we don't kill them. There may have been two terrorists among his followers, but both men were expert at concealing from him the depths of their depravity. When put to the test by their subterfuges, my client's first instinct was to save lives, not to take them. One terrorist wanted to kill a Roman officer and his Jewish woman; my client went out of his way to warn the couple. Likewise, Procurator, my client was not responsible for poor Samuel Kohen's death— and what a terrible misfortune that was. Rather, there was a break in the chain of causation between my client's activities and the death. In fact, there were two such breaks. Castigate my client all you wish for his potty views and for the events at the Temple, but give him credit, too. He had to be counselled to enter the Temple in the way he did, by a man with known terrorist connections. And a hefty Temple Guard was the proximate cause of Samuel Kohen's death. Indeed, he was a *novus actus interveniens* par excellence.'

Pilate was nodding and writing furiously in his bench book. Linnaeus had thrown the press a few crumbs and won their sympathy, then turned straight to law.

'Do you have anything else you wish to raise, Don Linnaeus?'

'At this moment, no, Procurator.'

'Good. I grant leave to the State to call its first witness.'

The orderly seated beside the jury box stood and strode out of the courtroom. Cynara could hear his bellow echoing outside.

'The State calls Aulius Valerius.'

A stocky *Optio* in dress uniform approached the stand and swore by all the Gods and Goddesses to tell the truth. Cynara loved Roman courtroom oaths; apart from this first line, they were all different. Valerius was a follower of the Rite of Mithras, which necessitated the orderly holding a lit candle before him as he spoke.

'If I speak falsely, may my soul be scattered to the four winds just as my breath blows out this candle,' he said, and blew it out. A blue curlicue of smoke traced its way upwards in front of his face.

The soldier removed his beret, placing it carefully before him on the stand. Cynara saw that the dark shadow on his chin was all of a piece with his shaven head; if it were possible, his hair was even shorter than the length stipulated under Roman military law. He took a sip of his water and looked expectantly at Cornelius, apologising for his lack of Greek. Lonuobo stood up to translate his Latin.

'Please state your full name and rank, and give a brief outline of your service record.'

Valerius did so; when he was finished Cornelius tendered a paper copy of the history.

'That will be Exhibit Two, *Aquilifer* Getorex.'

'Where were you on the morning of the last day of March?'

'I was leading a security detail on the Beautiful Gate, sir.'

'Please describe what you saw, *Optio* Valerius.'

'We'd had advance warning from a patrol outside the city

that there was a big crowd approaching Jerusalem on foot.
The place was already packed with pilgrims making an early
start on Passover. The area around the Beautiful Gate is congested at the best of times, even though the gate itself is nice
and wide. Our observation post is off to one side, overlooking
it and the street below. I was in there.'

'Yes.'

'We'd already had one boy scraped off his bicycle, a punch-
up between two taxi drivers, and a dust storm. Everything was
covered with half an inch of dirt and tempers were starting
to fray. We'd just arrested a man for defecating in the street
when people started stripping palm fronds off trees in the vi-
cinity. Then they started laying them in the street—the palm
fronds, I mean—and if they couldn't lay hands on any palm
fronds, they started using their own clothes instead. Some of
the palms were on private property; the owners weren't happy
and started beating a path to the guardhouse door, demanding I put a stop to it. I'd just detailed two men to chase tres-
passers out of one man's yard when this one'—he pointed at
Ben Yusuf—'arrived with his entourage.'

'What did he look like?'

'He was riding a donkey, sir, but undersized—a colt, I suppose. There were quite a few people who stayed close to him
and that group didn't change over time, but more and more
people kept tagging along around him. They all started singing, then, and you know how Jews sing. It was a cacophony,
the most irritating racket you've ever heard.'

Cynara smiled at this; she remembered when she'd first
heard Romans sing—on a childhood trip to Caesarea that
inadvertently coincided with one of their festivals—and how
she'd put her fingers in her ears at their squalling vocals and
heavy percussion.

'What were they singing?'

'*Hoshana*, sir. Over and over again, *Hoshana*; there may have been something else, but that's what I remember.'

'What happened next?'

'There were people pouring through the gate and from other parts of the city and traffic started to back up; no one could get through. Cabbies were leaning on their horns and haranguing people out the window. There were so many bicycles so close together they started to tangle each other up. Livestock panicked and kicked and crapped as they turned around and around and it sprayed everywhere. A winery cart overturned and the casks rolled down the street into people's legs. And there were chickens. I radioed for mounted assistance but there was no way we could disperse a crowd like that; if anything inserting more troops would only make it worse. In the end all we could do was protect private and civic property from damage and try to encourage people to make their way through the streets rather than staying put. It was made harder because this one'—he indicated Ben Yusuf again—'wanted to talk to the mob.'

'What did you do?'

'I went outside the guardhouse and told him he needed to get everyone to move along.'

'What did the Suspect say?'

'He answered me in Latin, for a start, which damn near floored me. Not the most idiomatic Latin, mind you, but perfectly comprehensible.'

'And?'

'He said he couldn't shut them up. He said if they shut up, the stones in the ground would sing in their stead. Just the thought of that gave me a headache. There was some more singing and carry on after this, and my men had to break up a few scuffles here and there. He rode his donkey onto a patch of higher ground at this stage and pointed out over the city with one hand. Most of the crowd shut up then, which was a relief. I realised he was crying, really crying. I could see tears running down his cheeks into his beard. Next thing, he told all those people their city would be destroyed.'

'Not that the Temple would be destroyed?'

'No, the whole city. I checked with my men afterwards that they'd all heard the same thing. My Greek may not be the best but my Aramaic isn't too bad. I know what he said. He told them that Jerusalem's enemies would swarm in from all sides and... bomb it back to the Stone Age.'

'What, all ten years?' someone asked in a penetrating undertone, in Greek. There were more snickers from Greeks and Romans dotted here and there. Pilate banged his gavel.

'That will be all from the gallery, thank you.'

He waited until the courtroom was silent, then nodded at Cornelius.

'What's your estimation of the crowd numbers?'

'It's hard to say, sir, because the city was already packed. Our intelligence unit examined the photographs and suggested twenty thousand, but it's difficult to know.'

'Thank you, *Optio* Valerius.'

Cornelius looked at Pilate.

'No further questions, Procurator.'

'I'd like those photographs and estimates tendered, *Aquilifer*.'

'Yes, Procurator; I'll get them to you during the luncheon adjournment.'

'Don Linnaeus?'

Linnaeus stood, smiling warmly at the soldier, who eyed him with suspicion.

'*Optio* Valerius, you were sitting in the guardhouse for a good part of this incident, were you not?'

'Yes I was, sir.'

'I am not a ranking officer, *Optio* Valerius.'

'Sorry, ss—' He struggled to avoid using the honorific; the process of doing so made him uncomfortable.

'Isn't that unusual, sitting in the guardhouse for that long in the midst of a developing, ah, situation?'

'It can be.'

'Why were you sitting in the guardhouse, Valerius? I think the court needs to know.'

Valerius scraped his beret off the stand in front of him and held it across his knees. His fingers drummed with nerves.

'I'd got a *Dear Marcus* letter,' he said at length. 'It came that morning and I hadn't opened it. I was saving it.'

Cynara could see the corners of his eyes begin to moisten as he spoke. Linnaeus did not speak, his head to one side, mimicking sympathy, although she knew this was all show.

'Where is she from?'

'From Malta, my home province.'

'Isn't it the Roman custom for soldiers to take a woman only once they're posted?'

The soldier's gaze became fixed on the lawyer's, save the odd sidelong glance towards Cornelius.

'That is the custom, yes. We thought we could make it work.'

'And you learnt of her decision to go with another man less than half an hour before my client's entry through the Beautiful Gate, yes?'

'That is correct, ss—' He shook his head and scratched behind his ear.

'I put it to you, *Optio* Valerius, that this court can't rely on a single thing you've said so far. Your own distress probably made the situation worse. You were upset and distracted. You're blaming my client for a situation you at least co-authored.'

'No, that's not true. I know what I saw, and I know what I did. No one could have handled that situation any differently, not without blood in the streets.'

'Even through your tears?'

Valerius was angry now, and he raised his voice as he made his points. Cynara got the impression he'd been a drill instructor at some point.

'This affected my heart, not my eyeballs or my mind.' He tapped his temple with one finger. 'I love my woman, but my first duty is to the Empire.'

Cynara could see several of the soldiers in the audience nodding at this. They might think Valerius a fool for trying to route around Roman military custom, but they were firmly in his corner when he pulled out the talismanic word *duty*.

'No further questions, Procurator.'

'All right, Don Linnaeus. *Optio* Valerius, to your knowledge, has a Jewish community leader or religious figure ever entered Jerusalem in the same way—through that gate, with a great entourage—and riding on a donkey?'

Valerius mastered himself.

'My understanding is that there have been two, Procurator. After the Ben Yusuf incident, I went back through our provincial records. The earlier instances happened when we took over direct administration from Herod, and nearly forty years ago. They led local revolts and caused terrible loss of life; the Æsculapion hadn't been completed, of course. Unfortunately there are no extant photographic records of events except for mug shots of the two men, both of whom were executed.'

Cynara saw Pilate wince.

'Back then, they'd have been crucified, yes?'

'Yes, Procurator, they were. They were the last in the province to be executed in this way. There were photographs of that, too'—he paused, swallowing—'apparently taken as keepsakes.'

Cynara felt an enveloping chill settle on the courtroom.

The educated and witty Romans in the press gallery were for a fleeting moment ashamed of their ancestors' habits, despite the esteem in which Roman ancestors were held. The fact of crucifixion—their people had tortured and executed tens of thousands in that way—they could accept. The callousness of men who took souvenir photographs of it, however, was another matter.

Cornelius stood up. 'Procurator, the State can tender the relevant documents as an exhibit, if you'd like.'

Pilate shook his head, wincing again. 'No thank you, that won't be necessary.'

'As you wish, Procurator.'

'Well, maybe it did deter,' he said softly, to no one in particular. 'It took forty years for another one to crop up.' He looked at Valerius. 'Thank you; you're free to go.'

'The State calls Tiberius Julius Binyamin Bar Binyamin, Prefect of the Temple Guard.'

Cynara knew that the Temple Guard didn't enjoy much respect from the Roman troops stationed in Judaea, but it was also fair to say Binyamin Bar Binyamin the individual was both well liked and well respected. It was a known fact he'd worked hard to smarten up the Temple Guard, and that they could now march properly and in good order, use their weapons with a reasonable degree of skill, and all look the same on parade was largely due to his efforts. They could even do star jumps in time and pushups without sticking their arses in the air.

He swore on the Torah and removed his heavy bronze ceremonial helmet, revealing a large white kippah on top of a greying Roman army high and tight. He was overweight, although underneath the layer of fat was a massive and muscular man. He placed the helmet at his feet and crossed his

forearms, grasping his thighs, sitting very upright and looking at Cornelius, his demeanour both placid and stolid. He
did not move—save his lips—as he answered Cornelius's
questions, staring hard at the prosecutor, his head and hands
still. She spent the first half an hour of his testimony trying
to place his accent, which while clearly Jewish was not from
within the province. She understood his colloquialisms and
verbal tics with difficulty.

'I know we don't have a very good reputation,' he was saying, 'but only thirty of us are full-time salaried guardsmen.
Everyone else has a job somewhere and gets a day's release a
week from their employer to undertake duties at the Temple.
I have to work within those limitations.' For the first time, he
shifted in his seat. Cynara could see beads of sweat forming
along his hairline.

'But the Friday before last just went wrong from the outset.
We even had a fire start in one of the storerooms in the Court
of the Israelites—'

'Deliberately lit?'

Binyamin smiled, the skin around the corners of his eyes
creasing. For a moment Cynara saw a warm and gentle personality emerge.

'*Ayuh*, I wish I could say yes to that question, *Aquilifer*, but
it was accidental—a gas cylinder for one of the altars with
the valve left open. It's an easy enough mistake to make—I've
done it myself at home. Someone lights a match and the
whole lot goes up.'

Cynara heard low giggles from behind her; a strongly built
middle-aged woman with her curly hair pinned back in Greek-
style silver bands and a young man—broad shouldered, solid
and very much his father's son—were sitting behind her. It
seemed that at least some of Binyamin's family had come to
support him in court.

'Iscariot insisted on travelling with us to the spot where he said Ben Yusuf was hiding out. We were going to approach in mounted formation, but Iscariot couldn't walk and we were sure Ben Yusuf's hangers-on were armed.'

'Where were they?'

'They were in Gethsemane, on the slopes of the Mount of Olives, below the city cemetery. If you don't mind a lot of tombs at your back, it's a beautiful place.'

'I understand Gethsemane is a public park?'

'The land used to belong to the *Kohanim* but they leased it to the city. As far as I know it's still in state hands.'

'Yes,' said Pilate, stirring behind his bench, 'although as you say, the state only takes the benefit. It could be returned to the Temple authorities at any time.'

'By the time we got to Gethsemane, it was dark. The city was in lockdown, there were troops and stray animals everywhere, and it was impossible to get anywhere quickly. *Optio* Macro threatened to call in air support but...' He paused, scratching his head. 'I just couldn't stomach the thought of one of those... *ayuh...* monstrosities tearing people to pieces.'

Cynara caught herself casting around the courtroom looking for blue-uniformed aviatrices. She saw one, lean and fair, two or three rows in front of her and off to one side. She was staring at the prosecutor's dark instructing clerk. At that moment, he turned to face her and beamed. She lifted one hand in front of her breasts and gave him the smallest possible wave with the tips of her fingers.

'You knew who he was by sight?'

Binyamin pulled a face at this.

'Of course I did, and so did my men. Some of your Roman troops probably knew what he looked like, even if they didn't know his name. We needed Iscariot because Ben Yusuf still trusted him. We expected a firefight without him there; we were hoping that Iscariot's presence plus Jewish troops would forestall some or all of any violence.'

'You are aware that the Zealots and *Sicarii* have tended to focus their attacks on Jews they consider collaborators—translators, drivers, women who go with Roman soldiers, community officials, even members of your own Temple Guard?'

'Yes, but that's always been singly or in small groups. We made the judgement call that they wouldn't fire on a large group of Jews. As it turned out, we were wrong, although Iscariot proved invaluable.'

'How so?'

'Ben Yusuf and his confreres had their backs to some of the more impressive olive trees in the Gardens, and had set themselves up in a spot that's easy to protect, especially at night. They had a mixture of arms—Roman carbines and pistols, a Persian RPG and ordinary grenades. When we saw that, we were worried that they'd decided to make some sort of last stand then and there.'

'Can you provide an estimate as to numbers?'

'Anywhere between thirty and fifty, *Aquilifer*; it was dark and hard to tell. The Temple Guard doesn't have any night-vision equipment. I can say there were more of them than just Ben Yusuf and his core group of followers.'

'What did Iscariot do?'

'I'm coming to that, *Aquilifer*. Once he was told of our situation, the *Kohen Gadol* insisted we try to take him alive; Ben Yusuf had entered the city as our prophecies foretold and many on the Sanhedrin were sure that his death in a gun battle would precipitate a full-scale uprising. *Optio* Macro detailed two of the best snipers in X *Fretensis* to join us. I pointed him out to both men. They were armed with tranquilliser darts rather than bullets; the plan was to take down Ben Yusuf and whisk him away to the *Vinculum* until Passover was over and so drain the aggression out of the population.'

'Why not just shoot him and be done with it? If you take the head off, the snake no longer bites.'

Cornelius's question and comment invited laughter, from people in the press box for the most part but also from many in the public gallery. Pilate and Linnaeus were grinning, too. The prosecutor's face was sincere but utterly Roman in its complete absence of pity. Binyamin fidgeted and uncrossed his arms.

'Please understand, *Aquilifer*, I mean no offence by this— I'm a veteran of sixteen years standing, and a Roman citizen— but, *ayuh*, it's the view of many Jews that Romans are too free with killing.'

Cynara found herself warming to Binyamin. Her father had once told her that on the two occasions he could remember the Sanhedrin requesting the death penalty from the Roman administration, the relevant Procurator had simply signed and stamped the legal paperwork without bothering to read it. Joseph was naïve, then, and had asked why. 'Because you Rabbis would take it up the arse with a concrete pole before you sentenced someone to die unjustly.'

'Iscariot insisted he could walk and that he would approach Ben Yusuf directly. I had visions of him getting shot but he struck out towards Ben Yusuf before I could pull him away. He called out to them so they knew who he was and didn't shoot him.'

'How did they respond?'

'The men around Ben Yusuf lowered their weapons and someone shone a torch in his direction. I shouted out as well, identifying us as the Temple Guard. I told them they were surrounded. I heard one of them tell the others not to shoot; and that they shouldn't be killing Jews.'

'How did that go down?'

'Well, no one shot at us. Iscariot was really hobbling and I could see they were concerned. They crowded around Iscariot; they were overjoyed to see him, too—that much was obvious. Some clapped their hands and one idiot fired his weapon into the air. During this, Iscariot kissed Ben Yusuf, full on the lips'—he touched his hand to his face—'like so.'

Cornelius flicked the hem of his toga, his eyebrows knitted together.

'Like a Greek?'

The question embarrassed Binyamin and he flushed under his beard.

'I suppose so, yes, *Aquilifer*.'

'And?'

'As soon as Iscariot drew back, the Roman sniper beside me felled Ben Yusuf with a tranquilliser. They thought we'd killed him and half a dozen rushed us. The second sniper took one of them down with a dart but another fellow covered an enormous amount of ground and got close enough to fire on Malchus, my 2IC.'

'What happened?'

'The man was a rotten shot, and only succeeded in taking his ear off. Malchus went down beside me. At the same time, I heard gunfire from the other side of the gardens and my own men had to respond to being attacked. What I didn't know then was that quite a few of Ben Yusuf's closest people didn't try to fight. They just kept *schtum* and hid in between the tree roots. At least one of them bolted.'

'Did you try take them all into custody?'

'No. The High Priest only wanted Ben Yusuf, and I'd ordered my men only to fire if fired upon. By that stage men from the Second Cohort had turned up, though, and at sight of Roman troops quite a few of Ben Yusuf's hangers-on decided to open fire.'

'So they were more inclined to fire on Romans?'

'It would seem so. We did have a real situation, though. My men couldn't retrieve Ben Yusuf's body, and the Second Cohort felt cheated of a proper battle and were spoiling for a fight.'

Cynara looked towards the press box, wondering if any of the media people understood the point he was making. Roman soldiers did not become frenzied with bloodlust when they fought, but they loved to fight. They were then methodical and destructive, killing efficiently until their commanders either called them off or ordered them to slake their appetites. They were very proud of this characteristic, so much so that it was part of a legionary's military oath. 'We never lose control of our troops,' they would say. 'Instead, we tell them when they are permitted to lose control.' The slaking had been become rarer in recent times, but every soldier kept his ear cocked for the order, 'no quarter'.

'*Optio* Macro arrived and ordered his men to shoot anyone who resisted them, which they did—with some relish, I might add. This process was well underway when I heard him order one of his subordinates to tell the men to search the area and shoot anyone who resisted arrest.'

'Yes.'

'I remonstrated with him over this, pointing out the High Priest wanted Ben Yusuf, and that he and his men had only been despatched as cover for us. He argued with me, saying that anyone in the Garden of Gethsemane that night was obviously a Ben Yusuf hanger-on and that his presence couldn't have an innocent explanation. I pointed out that they were more likely to kill drunks, cottagers, and homeless people as opposed to any real Zealots. To my very great relief he hesitated for a moment and then countermanded the order.'

Cynara was now even more impressed with Binyamin; she knew Marius Macro.

'When the Romans had finished their work and loaded the corpses into one of the big rotary pushprops, I ordered two of my men to retrieve Ben Yusuf and to locate Iscariot.'

'Yes.'

'Fortunately, he was lying not far from Ben Yusuf, who'd woken up—although he was pretty woozy—and they were talking to each other.'

'Can you remember the substance of their conversation?'

'I don't think I'll ever forget it, *Aquilifer*.'

Quite a few of the press people looked up and leant forward in their seats, pens poised. Pilate adjusted his wreath and breathed into his hands, gazing over the top of his reading glasses.

'Iscariot was apologising, just repeating the word "sorry" over and over. Ben Yusuf was bemused. I've never seen a man look so lost.'

'What did he say?'

'"He didn't come," that's what he said. Over and over again, "he didn't come".'

'Was he expecting reinforcements?'

'I don't know, *Aquilifer*. Maybe he was, but from where we'll never know. Ben Yusuf and his people had a picked a good spot, but they finished up firing outwards indiscriminately. If they'd have used their position properly, they'd have still lost, of course, but they could have made it expensive.'

'I didn't think you were in the business of advising Zealots on military strategy, Prefect,' said Pilate, leaning forward. 'It's just as well no one else turned up. I think we can all agree there's been enough carnage this week.'

Binyamin paused again at this point and rubbed his hand across his face. 'Iscariot had started to blubber and *Optio* Macro ordered him taken back to Antonia.'

'Did Ben Yusuf say anything else?' Pilate asked. 'Anything

other than an intimation that he expected outside help?'

'*Ayuh*. He said that God had abandoned him, and that he now had to drink a cup of poison to its dregs.' Binyamin drank from the glass of water on the stand before him. 'It was like someone had reached inside his chest cavity and torn out his heart—'

'A trifle theatrical, perhaps,' said Pilate, 'but then that's common enough when it comes to matters of religion in this province.'

Cynara noticed quite a few heads swivel to face the Procurator, who had been carefully neutral in his comments thus far. He was tapping his pen on the blotter in front of him with one hand and rotating the X *Fretensis* flag on its polished wooden base in the other. He looked grumpy and in need of caffeine.

'—Macro came over and stood beside me, looking down at Ben Yusuf as two of his men loaded him onto a stretcher. He ordered him to the *Vinculum* and walked beside the stretcher, shaking his head. I heard him say to a senior officer in the Second Cohort that Ben Yusuf had picked the wrong battle.'

Cornelius smiled. 'True enough.'

'And then Ben Yusuf said from his stretcher that true power does not come from fighting.'

Most of the Romans in the room—even their dyspeptic Procurator—chuckled at this. Cynara suspected they found it childish and amusing, simply because it contradicted the evidence of their own eyes.

'What did *Optio* Macro say?' Pilate asked.

'Nothing, Procurator. He just shook his head again and then ordered two men into the pushprop with Ben Yusuf.'

'Fair enough,' he said, looking at Cornelius. 'Any further questions, *Aquilifer* Getorex?' he asked, his tone acidic.

'No, Procurator.'

'Don Linnaeus?'

Cynara noticed that Linnaeus had scribbled out notes on

several sheets torn out of a block of yellow legal pad. Cynara suspected from his body language that he, too, was impressed with the Prefect.

'You'll forgive me, Prefect, if I ask you where in the Empire you're from? I've spent your whole testimony trying to place your accent, and have utterly failed.'

The question was sincere but also disarming, and Cynara had to respect the skill of the man asking it. For his part, Binyamin laughed and broke into a dazzling smile. He leant forward and folded his hands together on top of the stand.

'I'm from Alexandria,' he said. 'But I've lived a long time in Jerusalem, and I grew up speaking Hebrew, not Greek or Aramaic. My wife is Alexandrine, however, and we speak a lot of Greek at home. You're not the first person to find my accent entertaining.'

Linnaeus seemed delighted with this titbit and beamed. He turned to the notes in front of him.

'You mentioned during your testimony that you were surprised that the suspect's closest followers did not join in the firefight, yes?'

'Yes, that's right. I'm reasonably sure that the man who shot Malchus's ear off was a member of the inner circle—based on where he was standing when the sniper took Ben Yusuf down—but I can't be certain.'

'So, for the most part, the shooting was coming from people not intimate with the suspect?'

'Yes, but that's because we had Iscariot with us. They trusted him.'

Linnaeus pressed the tips of his fingers together and looked over the top of them, one eyebrow raised.

'That's not the question I asked, Prefect. Please take care to answer my questions, nothing more.'

'Sorry, but—'

Linnaeus cut him off.

'And you heard an order not to fire on Jews, yes?'

'Yes, I did. We all did—ask any of my men.'

'And that order came *after* you'd announced who you were, and that they were surrounded?'

'Yes, it did.'

'And you were only fired upon after Ben Yusuf was shot?'

'Not fatally, though, as I said, it was a dart—'

'But a dart sounds like a bullet, does it not?'

Binyamin realised what Linnaeus was getting at and stroked his beard with one hand before answering.

'The sound is different, like the difference between blanks and normal cartridges. It's easier to spot for the soldier firing—the feeling, the recoil is different—but to an untrained person, they sound the same.'

'Yes, that was my point. So these people only became hostile once they'd been fired on, and after—for all they knew—their leader had been killed?'

'We had Iscariot, though, you must remember that—'

'Please answer the question, Prefect.'

Cornelius stood up.

'Procurator, that's two questions. The State's witness is right to be confused.'

Cynara watched Pilate smile at the prosecutor, perhaps sharing some sort of lawyerly in-joke.

'Yes, *Aquilifer* Getorex, fair point; Don Linnaeus, one question at a time, please.'

Cynara noticed he put a line through each question on the yellow paper as he asked it, and she found herself amazed.

He knows every question he's going to ask in advance...which means he must know the answers, too. How do you do that?

'Is it fair to say that the arrival of Roman troops escalated the situation?'

'Yes, it is; only a few of them were shooting at us until then. When the Second Cohort fronted, most of them started firing.'

'But not his closest associates?'

'No.'

Pilate leant forward, resting his pen against his chin.

'You seem very sure of that, Prefect. How is it you could tell the difference?'

Binyamin shifted uncomfortably in his seat; Cynara suspected he did not want to reveal how it was he knew to draw the distinction.

'I'm Prefect of the Temple Guard, Procurator. I've seen Ben Yusuf and his followers in the Temple precincts, many times. I know most of them by sight, and three or four by name as well. They all came to Passover last year, for example. I remember Ben Yusuf getting into arguments with the *Kohanim*.'

'That's the Sanhedrin, isn't it?'

'Not always, Procurator; it's possible to be a Kohen without being on the Sanhedrin, but the men he was debating were on the Sanhedrin.'

'How would you describe these, ah, debates, Prefect? What sort of tone?'

'Friendly, on the whole, Procurator; I do remember some of the *Kohanim* getting cross simply because it was Passover and they didn't have time to sit around and debate the finer points of the Torah. Ben Yusuf got more doctrinaire and argumentative over time. For the most part, though, there was good will on all sides.'

'Interesting, Prefect,' Pilate said, looking at Linnaeus.

Linnaeus chewed his lip; Cynara suspected he hadn't enjoyed the Procurator interrupting the flow of his questions.

'What did Ben Yusuf's closest associates do, if they weren't firing on the Temple Guard or the Second Cohort?'

'I'm not certain in every case, but I did see three or four of them hide, and one ran away.'

'You're completely certain about that?'

'Yes, I am.'

'Why?'

'He had nothing on, that's why. That tends to show up loud and clear through night-vision binoculars. I borrowed a set from Macro. He thought it was hilarious.'

'Definitely into the Greek,' said a penetrating voice from the public gallery. Titters echoed around the court; Cynara looked over her shoulder at Binyamin's wife and son; both smiled back at her, while the young man shrugged his massive shoulders.

'That'll do,' said Pilate, banging his gavel.

'And just before he was taken into custody, he said he rejected violence?'

'Yes, he did, at least when it comes to securing true power.'

Linnaeus scratched his chin, looking hard at Binyamin. Cynara knew he was what the law students from *Collegia Roma* would describe as an impressive witness. At no stage had the Prefect lost his composure or been diverted. Although called by the State, his transparent honesty meant that bits of his evidence would work for both sides.

'Prefect, I put it to you that Ben Yusuf had conveyed to his closest followers that violence was best avoided.'

'I don't know; I don't think so. They were well armed, they trusted Iscariot, and I'm sure they thought they were going to get help.'

'Likewise, I suggest that the fact that the violence came from people less intimate with Ben Yusuf indicates that he was being misinterpreted, or that individuals were acting on their own and without his knowledge.'

'That leaves aside the man who shot off Malchus's ear.'

'You yourself admitted that it wasn't clear who fired that

shot, yes?'

'That's true.'

'Your experience of Ben Yusuf and his closest followers in the Temple precinct and their debates with members of the Sanhedrin indicates persons capable of discussing and re-solving their differences amicably, yes?'

'That was last year.'

Linnaeus raised his eyebrows at Pilate.

'No further questions, Procurator.'

He sat down heavily; Cynara could see he was unhappy. Cornelius stood up, catching Pilate's eye.

'Before the witness is excused, may I raise one point in re-examination?'

'Yes, *Aquilifer* Getorex, go ahead.'

'Prefect, when Ben Yusuf said "he didn't come", what did you take that to mean?'

'I wasn't sure, to be honest, but thinking about it there are two possibilities. To my mind, he was expecting help from outside, although why he would want to try to attack Jerusa-lem from a park two miles outside the city limits is not some-thing I understand. The other option is that he expected God to help him.'

This clearly caught Cornelius with his trousers down and his face registered shock.

'Ah, could you explain a little more?'

'The *Moshiach* can call on armies of angels if need be, *Aqui-lifer*. Maybe he thought God would come to his aid.'

Cornelius waited for the titters echoing around the court-room to subside before closing the folder on top of the podi-um in front of him.

'The State calls *Kohen Gadol* Kayafa, High Priest of the Jerusalem Temple.'

Pilate looked around the gallery, lingering on the press box.

'With my leave, the High Priest will appear via the Eye. He cannot set foot in Antonia and then administer the Passover Rite; he will be made ritually unclean if he does so. I have granted leave because of his exceptional circumstances. It is not to be taken as a precedent.'

Cynara thought of her father; he had once been careful to observe laws like that, as had she, at least as much as boarding in a Roman school would permit.

'What happened to make you change?' she'd asked him at some point in the last two years.

'The laws were made for man, and not the other way around.'

'Procurator, my clerk will establish the connection and make sure everything works smoothly. In the interval, may I suggest a brief adjournment?'

Cynara looked at Pilate's face as he watched the dark young clerk fiddle with cables and switches and swear softly. He wasn't pleased, but there was little he could do. He banged his gavel twice.

'The court is adjourned for fifteen minutes.'

AGRIPPA

Cynara desperately wanted coffee, but there wasn't time. She drank at the fountain—it was decorated with a handsome stone lion's head; the water flowed out of its mouth—and looked longingly at the soldiers and aviatrices making their way to one of the messes. Some of them returned moments later with cups of coffee balanced in their hands. The area outside the *Praetorium* was soon filled with its rich smell. She sighed, walked across the colonnaded mezzanine and leaned over the guardrail, admiring Antonia's great parade ground from above, imagining matchsticks holding her eyelids open.

'I take it you'd like one of these?'

She spun around to see a man with a familiar chiselled face—clipped and styled light brown hair, bright blue eyes and short but distinguished silver sideburns—offering her a cup. He wore a distinctive loud collar pinned at the front with a *Collegia Roma* chain. She could have kissed him.

'Thank you so very much...'

'Severus Agrippa, *Newshour*.'

'Oh, my, I'm sorry, but you look different, I'm so sorry...'

'Coffee,' he said, handing her the cup. 'Drink up; we are now minus eleven minutes and counting.'

She took it from him gratefully and sipped. He cocked his familiar head to one side and appraised her. She had a sharp vision of him cocking his head in the same way during *Newshour*; the human-interest stories that wound up the broadcast often got the trademark Severus Agrippa head cock. She also caught herself giving thanks that she'd worn one of her smartest robe and cape ensembles—it made less of her breasts—and taken the time to apply make-up.

'And you are...?'

She felt herself caught on the hop again.

'I'm sorry, Don Agrippa, I'm Cynara Arimathea. How do you do?' She extended her hand; he took it.

'Severus, please, Cynara—may I call you Cynara?'

Oh, you Roman seducer, Don Newshour. And do I care? No, I don't care.

He sipped his own coffee; she wanted to know how he'd secured it when she saw one of his aides—a dark young woman she'd spotted in the press gallery—talking to one of the younger Roman officers. She watched the soldier pat her on the backside and then head towards the mess. Agrippa unfolded a sheet of paper and held it out towards her.

'Are you any relation to the Arimathea on this Defence witness list?'

'He's my father,' she said, 'and the reason I came today. I wasn't planning to.'

He put his cup down in the stone alcove beside the water fountain, holding one hand up, the fingers outstretched.

'Your father—he's on the Sanhedrin?'

She thought she'd save him the trouble of drawing information out of her bit by bit, and filled him in on her background. The shock on his face when she got to the Empire Hotel was real. He stepped back, his skin pale under what she suspected was a studio tan.

'Perhaps I chose the wrong young woman to charm,' he said. 'I think I ought to let you be.'

She shook her head. 'Right now I'll take all the charming I can get.'

He nodded and chuckled at this. They both leant against the rail and drank in silence. Cynara saw the young officer return with two more cups of coffee; he handed one to Agrippa's aide. The two of them were standing very close together and giggling. She suspected that there would be an attempt to circumvent the rules against unregistered women in at least one officer's quarters tonight.

'I'm curious about how this Ben Yusuf character is viewed in Judaea, Cynara,' Agrippa said, looking at her. 'There isn't time to discuss it now, but there will be over lunch.'

He smiled again, touching the back of her arm and turning her towards the courtroom door.

Andreius Linnaeus, I do believe I have met your match.

She saw Rachel leaning against the wall with Marcus in her arms; the baby was getting scratchy. Saleh had his hands on either side of her, palms pressed against the wall. He bent his elbows and kissed her.

'Young love,' said Agrippa.

'I'll tell you their story at lunch. It may help you to understand Judaea a little better, if that's what interests you.'

Agrippa inclined his head and left for the press box, his sable gown billowing behind him. Cynara saw Rachel stare at him as he went, her expression goggle-eyed.

'Did he ask you out? The man from *Newshour*?'

'He did.'

'You lucky woman.'

Cynara smiled at her.

'Rachel, he wants information, and he is willing to pay. Severus Agrippa has a wife and a concubine, both very beautiful and very accomplished; I doubt in the extreme his interest in me will last any longer than a single night.'

'So you will fuck him?'

'I think so. If only to see whether that gravity-defying hair keeps its shape.'

Rachel giggled, holding Marcus to her shoulder. Cynara

turned to face her.

'Your good Saleh, Rachel, has he ever told you what his mother does for a living?'

'She's a Priestess of Cybele, and for this reason he doesn't have a father. The temple is his father.'

'Where?'

'In Caesarea.'

Cynara's voice was soft.

'The best teacher I ever had—a woman who helped me to understand Romans almost as well as I understand myself— was your Saleh's mother. If the son is anything like his mother, you're a lucky woman indeed.'

'The prophecy is from Zechariah,' Caiaphas was saying as Cynara took her seat beside Rachel and Marcus. 'It runs as follows:

> Rejoice greatly, O daughter of Zion,
> Shout, O daughter of Jerusalem!
> Behold, thy King cometh unto thee,
> He is just, and having salvation;
> Lowly, and riding upon an ass,
> A colt the foal of an ass.'

Caiaphas looked out from the wall behind the witness box; once again Cynara found herself marvelling at how they did that. The courtroom walls were all hewn stone, marble and cedar, and yet his image seemed to sit flush against the wall itself. She understood the principle: that crystals could both store and transmit information. She even grasped some of the mathematics, but the actual mechanics of construction were beyond her. Caiaphas was in his priestly robes—blue and white, his gold breastplate encrusted with gems—and wearing his turban. She had to admit he looked both serene and commanding.

'How old is this verse, *Kohen Gadol*?' Cornelius wanted to know.

'About five hundred and forty years; many scholars and scribes have tried to determine the exact date, but it has never been fixed with certainty.'

'There's no mention of any particular gate, either,' Cornelius went on, 'or is that in another part of your, ah, oracles?'

Cynara smiled at the prosecutor's awkwardness, noting for the first time that both Romans and Greeks wore perplexed expressions on their faces, while the Galileans understood instinctively. Agrippa made uncomprehending eye contact with her. 'Please explain,' he mouthed in Latin.

'They are not oracles, Procurator, but texts that provide moral guidance and bring us closer to the Lord.'

Cornelius nodded, perhaps out of a desire to be polite.

'That the Beautiful Gate—or Golden Gate, as it is sometimes called—will be the point of entry for the *Moshiach* is part of a long-standing tradition, our version of your *mos maiorum*.'

Cornelius nodded again, this time showing understanding.

'And this *Moshiach* is meant to be a leader of your people?'

'Every Jew—even the lowliest, the least educated, even whores and lepers—knows what a man coming into Jerusalem riding a colt via that gate wants to say. He is making a messianic claim.'

'And this *Moshiach* is meant to reign as a king?'

'Yes.'

'And your king is meant to drive Israel's enemies from the holy land and the holy city?'

'He will make our enemies understand the wrongs they have committed against us. He will be righteous, and he will bring about an end to war.'

'So, we'll know when the *Moshiach* has arrived?'

'He will drive you out of our country.'

Cynara thought he spoke that last line with far too much relish to be safe, but Pilate did not seem perturbed. Cornelius continued with his questions.

'And he will not be a Zealot?'

'He will not kill the innocent.' Caiaphas seemed to shift in his seat—it was out of view—and stroked his beard. 'An important part of our tradition speaks of gathering all the Jewish people from exile and bringing them home. You Romans know that there are Jews in Rome, in Gaul, in Alexandria and Cyprus. There are also many Jews in Persia and even some in the Kushan Kingdom.'

Caiaphas, she suspected, was angry. He went on.

'The moment he came through that gate in that way he made an unsupportable messianic claim and invited his people's destruction at Roman hands.'

Cynara looked at Ben Yusuf or—as the Romans insisted on calling him—'the Suspect'. Apart from his visceral reaction to Cornelius's account of Samuel Kohen's death, he had revealed nothing.

'High Priest, can you tell the court when you first became aware of the Suspect and your impressions of him over time?'

'I saw him interviewed on JTN. As soon as the interview finished, I contacted colleagues I knew in the Galilee—*rabbanim* and heads of *yeshivot*.'

'Yes.'

'My first impression was a positive one, I will say. I agreed with much of what he was saying.'

Cornelius turned to Pilate.

'Procurator, with the court's leave, I'll play that interview now. My clerk has set up the Eye so that the High Priest can see any footage we play here.'

'I grant leave, *Aquilifer*. I must admit I'm curious.'

Cynara watched the clerk feed a solid white rectangle with a pitted surface into a brass device in his hand and wind the handle. He approached the witness box and sat the device on the stand so that it had line of sight to the Eye. He hooked two fingers around the handle and pulled it towards him.

Ben Yusuf—his hair short but not shaven—was standing outside what looked like the Imperial Taxation Office in Sepphoris. 'I am not opposed to taxation,' he was telling a rather insistent young woman from JTN. It was windy and his beard and her hair kept blowing into their respective faces. 'But there have been two separate incidents in the last week in this very city where collectors have beaten people unable to pay.'

The broadcast was in Aramaic, with Greek subtitles.

'Many people in Judaea object to paying Roman taxes in their entirety, *Mar* Ben Yusuf; what's your view of that?'

A shadow crossed Ben Yusuf's face.

'I think I've made it clear that we should pay the Roman government what is due,' he said. 'What I object to is the violence often involved in the collection. This seems to stem from the use of private contractors who are actuated only by the profit motive.'

The camera cut to the green and blue *CreditGallia* wordmark hanging in front of several of the building's columns.

'Are you suggesting that the Romans should collect their own taxes? Would that be any better?'

At that point the camera zoomed out, taking in the buildings on either side of the tax office. A soldier with *Optio* flashes walked out of one of them, hand in hand with a woman in a fitted tunic so short Cynara considered 'hem' a better word for what she was wearing than 'skirt'. Both of them waved cheerfully at the camera as they crossed in front of the tax office and he led her into the barracks; Ben Yusuf and the reporter watched them go.

'And that's another issue,' he said. 'Everywhere their soldiers are stationed, they bring vice.'

The reporter was not to be diverted.

'Would the military collect taxes more justly than the private contractors?'

'I don't know,' he admitted, 'but something has to be done.'

The report cut back to the studio, where Cynara recognised Mary Magdalena. 'Ex-cage fighters with chains,' Mary Magdalena said. 'Of course, they wouldn't do that in Jerusalem or Jericho, now would they? Or am I editorialising?' She smirked; the recording ended. The clerk retrieved the device and Caiaphas's face reappeared.

'You're back in view, High Priest,' said Cornelius. 'Please go on.'

'When I spoke to colleagues in the Galilee, however, the image was more mixed. He routinely attacked them using the most vituperative language—"nest of vipers" is one line I remember—and had among his associates a man who'd attempted to perpetrate an honour killing. Some of his teaching in the Galilee also seemed to be very close to zealotry. I received reports—all of which I've handed over to *Aquilifer* Getorex—from colleagues describing calls to arms, attacks on Roman rule and an assertion that the Temple, or even the whole city of Jerusalem, would be destroyed. At this stage I still didn't know what to make of him and so gave him the benefit of the doubt, but when he began to attract crowds numbering in the thousands rather than the tens or hundreds, I knew we had a problem.'

'How so, High Priest?'

'I'm old enough to remember the last years of Herod and the first years of direct Roman rule here—I was in *yeshiva* then. There were two uprisings in quick succession shortly after Procurator Coponius took over, and they were ugly and violent and many of our people died. They both started in the same way, little meetings turning into something much bigger, and quickly. Men who rode into the city on a donkey—and via the Golden Gate—led both.'

'Did they call themselves Zealots back then, High Priest?'

'Those two rebellions are my first memory of the word being used in that way. Before the uprisings, to be *kanai*—as it is in our language—meant only to be zealous for God.'

'And now it means...?'

'Indiscriminate killing of the innocent—as we saw on Sunday—and the deliberate killing of people who are most valuable to us: teachers, medics, *rabbanim*, linguists and merchants. This killing is done purely on the basis that the individuals in question are willing to work with Rome. Today's Zealots are men who parlay their supposed love of Judaism into... into something savage and bestial.'

Cornelius waited, letting his witness's words sink in. Cynara watched as the courtroom artist added the finishing touches to a portrait of the High Priest. Cynara suspected that the artist had made a judgement call on Caiaphas's importance as a witness by choosing to colour him in.

'Please tell the court about Samuel Kohen, High Priest.'

Caiaphas's voice became thick and strained, as though he had a bad cold.

'Samuel, like me, is a descendent of Aaron, and so from our people's priestly line. However, descent is not enough to guarantee one a priesthood at our Temple. Apart from many years of education and training, one's family must also be pure. Samuel's father—a friend of mine and a very decent man—married a woman whose husband had abandoned her and his children, posted her the *get* and then dishonoured the *ketubah* by refusing to pay her what he'd promised at the wedding.'

Roman faces around the room registered shock. They may not have understood the Jewish terms, but they understood that a contract had been breached in the most egregious way, and that another man had stepped in to remedy the breach.

'Samuel was the child of that union. I promised his parents that although Samuel could never serve in the Temple as a priest, he would always have a place there. He sold souvenirs and took pictures, in the end becoming a successful photographer. Many of the postcards sold in this city feature his pictures.'

'And Samuel's family?'

'The Temple is supporting his widow and educating his children; they're at Jerusalem Academy. The boys will go to *yeshiva* afterwards. I am also trying to find her a husband; it is difficult because all of Samuel's older brothers are married.'

This time the Romans in the room burst into applause. Caiaphas—trapped on the other side of the screen with transducers designed to ensure clear communication only with Pilate and counsel—took time to appreciate that they were applauding him. Cynara could see that Pilate had been wrong-footed; he looked most unhappy.

'Order!' he barked, banging his gavel; the applause refused to die away. His voice was louder the second time around, as was the rap of his gavel. 'I will have *order* in my court, and I will have it *now.*'

Cornelius waited for the gallery to settle, staring at the binder open before him. Cynara caught his expression; like Pilate, he also looked distressed.

'No further questions, Procurator.'

Linnaeus stood. This time he was not smiling.

'*Kohen Gadol,* you mentioned that Zealot is merely the

Greek word for *kanai* in your language, yes?'

'That is correct.'

'And someone who is *kanai* is merely zealous for God?'

'Yes.'

'The term carries no violent overtones?'

'No. Zealotry on behalf of God must never be out of hatred or for personal gain.'

'High Priest, please tell the court the story of Pinehas, the first *kanai*.'

Cynara watched—even on the other side of the glass, as it were—the colour drain from Caiaphas's face. She knew why, too, and looked at Rachel. Rachel was holding Marcus very close to her and her skin was even paler than usual.

'If you are unwilling to tell the tale, High Priest, then I will; please feel free to interrupt me at any point.'

Caiaphas's mouth was working; he bit his lip. 'I will tell it,' he said. He wriggled like a fish on the end of the line, scratching behind his ear.

'Pinehas was a Kohen, the grandson of Aaron,' he said. 'He led our people against a terrible heresy. Our men had begun taking Midianite women, who introduced them to the worship of Baal. As a result, God caused a dreadful plague to break out among the Israelites. Moses forbade the worship of Baal, but Zimri of the Tribe of Simeon ignored his warning, and lay with Cozbi, despite the wailing of his fellow Israelites beside the Tabernacle. In the Tabernacle, Pinehas slew them both.'

'Come come, High Priest, you've missed a bit. What was Cozbi's profession?'

Caiaphas's voice was flat. 'She was a Priestess of Baal.'

'As were many of the Midianite women?'

'Yes.'

'And how did Pinehas kill her and Zimri?'

'He ran them both through with a spear while they were in the midst of the sex act.'

'Thank you, High Priest; non-violent, you say?'

Cynara felt a piece of paper pressed into her hands from beside her. Rachel had written in clear if ungrammatical Latin, *I only see my Saleh's mother. That could have been her.* The young woman seated beside Linnaeus also handed him a note.

'My instructing clerk informs me that there is a Temple to Baal and Astarte in Caesarea. Not looking to encourage any Zealotry there, are you?'

Rachel stood and made her way along the row, excusing herself as she went. Marcus stirred as she reached the aisle and began to wail; Cynara hesitated for a moment, and then followed her out of the courtroom.

When she got outside, Rachel had disappeared, presumably into the toilets. Cynara pushed the door marked with the Venus astrological symbol open and saw that she was changing Marcus's nappy next to one of the sinks. She was crying as she worked.

'Don't cry, Rachel. It's only an old story. It happened a thousand years ago.'

Rachel looked at her, her eyes ablaze.

'They're better than us, why is that? Why would we want to kill my Saleh's mother? What's wrong with us?'

Her distress seemed to transmit itself to Marcus, who was now howling. Rachel leant forward, her hair hanging loose. Cynara could see tears dripping onto Marcus's chest.

'I don't know,' Cynara shouted over the din, 'this whole thing just shows how Romanised you've become.'

'What do you mean?'

'Most Jewish girls would be *thrilled* to think of their

mother-in-law in that position.'

Rachel stared at her, tears smearing her make-up. She leant over her baby again, shaking with both tears and laughter, stroking his downy head. He pulled her nose, making her laugh harder.

'Cynara, that's, that's... I don't know what that is.'

Cynara folded the wet nappy and stored it in the canvas bag at Rachel's feet. Rachel pulled Marcus's tunic over his head and swaddled him.

'I think he would like a swim,' she said.

'Well, let's give him one. I think Caiaphas will be answering the defence lawyer's questions for a while.'

They battled their way through the crowds outside Antonia and made their way into the cool, dark labyrinth of the *vicus*. Rachel stepped lightly; she was spry from making her way up and down its interlocked flights of stairs many times each day. Cynara found herself short of breath.

'You're fit,' she gasped.

'I swim every day,' she said, 'with other women; we all watch each other's babies.' She paused to unlock a door that had been freshly oiled; the cedar gleamed in the soft light. Cynara followed her inside, watching her drop the dirty nappy into a wooden bucket and begin collecting things for the baths. She took in the small kitchen with its rows of gleaming metal pans hung above a gas stove off to one side and the solid table under the window with its two carved chairs. The biggest space was dominated by their bed, which was also finished with carved, polished timber. There was a wooden cot beside it. Set into the far corner was a Roman god-shelf, although instead of the customary portrait of the Emperor behind the bronze *Lares* there was a carved ivory statue of Cybele personified as Roma, and cut flowers on either side of the silver bowl and its sticks of incense. There was a portrait of Rufus in dress uniform, the X *Fretensis* standard and flag behind him.

'Who does the flowers?'

'I do, every morning,' she said, 'it's women's business. They learn flower arranging in the temple. Saleh says I should put pictures of my parents and brothers there, to honour their memory and to talk with them, but I haven't yet.'

Cynara nodded. Rachel knew that—were they alive—her family members would be offended by their placement on a Roman *lararia*. Saleh, by contrast, knew their daughter and sister's failure to honour them in the proper way would offend their *manes*.

Sometimes the things that divide us... really do divide us.

'Now,' Rachel said, 'let's go to the baths and give this boy some exercise.'

Cynara scratched the back of her head, feeling awkward.

'Would I be able to use some of your make-up? It's just... I have lunch and then—'

Rachel cut her off. 'Dinner with Agrippa, and you can't get home first, and you want to look nice. Of course!'

Rachel stepped close to her and examined her face.

'I know,' Cynara said, 'you're a lot paler than I am.'

'Yes, but Photis is dark, and so is Gemma.'

Cynara watched as Rachel skipped out of the door and bounded along the landing, banging with the palm of her hand against two doors in succession. Two women—both dark and curly—greeted her. One had a toddler at her feet, hugging her leg.

'This is my friend Cynara,' Rachel announced, 'Severus Agrippa from *Newshour* has asked her out... so it's our job to make her look lovely for him.'

'I'm Photis,' said the woman with the toddler. 'Rachel used to live with Luopo and me.'

Ah yes, the pair who bang like a barn door in a gale.

'I'm Gemma,' said the other woman. 'My real name is Ruth, but he can't say it, so he calls me Gemma.'

'Did he really ask you out?' Photis wanted to know as she whirled around her flat collecting towels and oils and make-up, 'Don Agrippa from *Newshour*? Is he as handsome in person as he is on screen?'

'Yes, and yes,' said Cynara.

'Well, I will make you lovely with these hands,' she said. 'In Damascus, before I went with Luopo and had his daughter, I was a beautician. I even had my own stall, in the apothecary.'

The four women trooped downstairs to the baths; Gemma carried Photis's daughter Flora on her shoulders; Photis explained that there was one large room in the *vicus* with three screens cut into the walls. They often watched *Newshour* or showed their children educational programs or amused themselves with the endless joyous inanity of Roman cinema re-runs.

Cynara submitted to their ministrations, letting them oil her skin and scrape her clean and wash and style her hair. They frolicked in the water in between times, giggling and splashing each other. Cynara knew that they would care for each other's children when provisions had to be obtained or errands run, breastfeed each other's children when a mother's soldier had leave and the pair wanted some 'sexy time', look out for each other when one was ill or needed help. They would cooperate like worker bees in a vast hive. Photis sat opposite her on towels in the warm air of the *tepidarium*, her tools and brushes at her side. Cynara saw Rachel swimming backwards with Marcus's hands in her own, her movements careful and correct, characteristic of one who has only learnt to swim as an adult. Gemma took similar charge of Flora while Photis lavished attention on Cynara.

'You'll have to report back,' said Photis. 'You know, tell us what positions he likes.'

'And whether he's got a big cock,' Gemma said.

'And if that hair is natural, or if he sticks glue in it or something,' Rachel added.

'And if he's a stud.'

They all giggled, while Cynara felt herself colouring. She hadn't had this sort of conversation since her days at the Hotel School, when—during her first year—she'd 'gone native', living in a manner indistinguishable from her Roman friends. She was on a full scholarship, Judaea was far away, and Roman men found her honey skin and dark-green eyes exotic. *The Adventures of Cynara Arimathea, in which our heroine indulges in copious quantities of sex, drugs, and bloodlust, with a twist of despair*—included a failure to turn up for a morning exam in one of her mathematics courses.

Who in their right mind schedules exams for eight in the morning?

That two Praetorian Guardsmen were pleasuring her at the same time may also have had something to do with it. They'd turned up at her door in dress uniform the night before bearing food and sparkling wine and saying—like automatons—'we are here to please you,' regardless of what she said in response. At one point she shut the door in their faces, only to open it five minutes later, curious and—she had to admit—aroused. They were beautiful young men. She knew intuitively—it was a series of logic gates snapping open to let something pass through—when she had that thought, *they are beautiful*, that her eye had come to see things as a Roman might see them. Both were still there, stock still, barely repressed grins on their faces as she looked at them. She knew both through a friend, one better than the other. The older of the two poured a glass and handed it to her.

'I have an exam first thing tomorrow.'

'We are here to please you.'

'Are you trying to lose me my scholarship?'

'We are here to please you.'

'Oh to buggery with it. Please me.'

Fortunately, her results throughout the year to that point were so good she scraped a pass—retaining her scholarship—although she bade farewell to the prize for the best student in her year.

There were grumbles from the press gallery at the early adjournment; most Roman courts sat through until about two or three in the afternoon and then wound up for the day, leaving people free for the afternoon. It was considered a form of recompense after the very early start.

'My apologies to those more familiar with the usual practice, especially in Caesarea,' Pilate said, 'but we won't get through all the evidence in two days, otherwise, and the court simply cannot sit through Passover. We are also waiting on a crucial witness.'

Claudia joined Fotini outside, also rather piqued at her husband's timetabling.

'The way this is going, we'll be sitting until six this evening,' she said. 'I've met Irenaeus Andrus, the bravest man in the province. If his brains were dynamite, he wouldn't have enough to blow his helmet off. His evidence will want to be good, that's all I can say.'

'I suppose we can leave if we want,' Fotini said, 'although it is interesting. I've never been to a trial. I got called for non-citizen jury service once, in Alexandria—the suspect was some organised crime figure who coughed up for a jury—but I wasn't empanelled. That's the closest I've ever been, just hanging around waiting for my name to be called.'

'I may go home,' Claudia said. 'Antony and Camilla will get up to no good otherwise.'

'Aren't the servants there, though?'

'If you think four moderately educated Greek servants are any match for my daughter, you have another think coming.'

'What will she do?'

Claudia waved her hand distractedly. 'Camilla's version of no good tends to involve alchemy and physics. Demanding academic work and regular sex with Marius keep the worst of the impulse in check—'

'But he's not around much until Sunday, and school is out.'

'Exactly,' Claudia guided her towards the water fountain, avoiding the mass of people spilling through the doors behind them. 'During Passover last year—after three or four days with no Marius, I think—Camilla decided her father's briefing reports needed livening up. Pontius came home from Antonia to be given the gift of a fine nib pen by our daughter, which he immediately took into his study to annotate his reports. At some point he made the mistake of tapping the end of it on his desk, and it exploded. Louder than a firecracker, it was. I thought someone was shooting at the Palace.'

'Wha—'

'Camilla had stuck a lump of calcium metal in there, along with water, of course. In its solid form, calcium metal takes quite a while to react with water, but when it does, the effect is impressive. And my husband is a champion pen tapper. Camilla's always found his tapping irritating.'

It was at this point that Fotini noticed Agrippa and Cynara kissing alongside the railing. Cynara looked especially beautiful, although Fotini had long thought her attractive.

'Well, look here,' she said, 'that lady was my boss at the Empire.'

'Severus Agrippa,' Claudia said. 'He always did move fast.'

'Do you know him?'

'He was in first year when Pontius and I were in final year. He studied rhetoric, like me. He's from a vast and talented family, he's very gifted, and he always gets what he wants.'

'And now he wants Cynara.'

Cynara waited for Agrippa outside the courtroom, confident that she looked fabulous; Photis was an artist. Gemma had curled her hair into shiny ringlets and used one of her own silver headbands to hold it back.

'Look at that lovely high forehead and slender waist,' Photis had said. 'He won't be able to keep his hands off you.'

He led her across to the taxi rank on the other side of the square and directed the driver to The Pit, one of the gaming establishments in the Greek Quarter. The two Greeks on the front counter—both Corinthians, she could hear their accents—treated him with exaggerated deference.

'You'll be back for the Cage tonight, Don Agrippa?'

'Indeed, gentlemen—and that reminds me—reserve a place for Cynara Arimathea.' He curled his arm around her waist; the two men looked first at her, then back at Agrippa, with some envy. She could tell he was pleased by their response.

'Welcome to The Pit, *Donna* Arimathea,' one of them said, inclining his head ostentatiously, his voice oily. 'We hope you enjoy our hospitality.'

The speed with which he set out her evening made her reel. She hadn't been to a cage fight in years—but Agrippa seemed able to master her will without effort. Like Linnaeus, he radiated a slight but thrilling air of danger. He had large, strong hands and used them to move her about. The eagerness with which she found herself complying was disconcerting.

He'd booked a private dining room, something she found excessive until three people stopped him and asked for his autograph on their way in and out of the lift; this he gave, but she could see the relief on his face when he closed the door to their room behind him.

'What happened while I was gone?' she asked, struggling to keep her tone neutral and her mind clear.

He poured both of them a glass, shared out prosciutto and melon and broke bread.

'Andreius Linnaeus is a very good lawyer, as if we didn't know already. Turns out Caiaphas knew one of the Zealots who followed this Ben Yusuf character.'

'Iscariot?'

'Yes.'

'I've met him, in my father's house.'

He looked at her, his eyes alight; for a moment his reporter's instincts dominated those of the urbane man about town.

'Well, it seems Iscariot needed money to support his aged parents, and when Caiaphas offered him enough to pay out their mortgage in exchange for Ben Yusuf in Roman custody, he jumped at the chance.'

Cynara's mouth dropped open; the shock on her face must have been very great, because Agrippa reached across the table and put two fingers under her jaw, closing it gently.

'However—and I assume the rest of this will come out over time—it seems your High Priest has managed to catch a tiger by the tail. The incident in the Temple designed to facilitate Ben Yusuf's arrest got rather out of hand, and Caiaphas did not know it was coming. It seems it was Iscariot's way of giving the man he considered a craven collaborator the finger. Caiaphas got his man, but the price was public humiliation and a friend's death.'

'We'll never really know, I suppose. Iscariot suicided.'

Agrippa went off into gales of laughter. 'He had a meaningful encounter with several flights of stairs, at a guess, or suffered a dose of lead poisoning while trying to escape.'

'He suicided, Severus.'

'You sound very sure of that,' he said, surprise in his voice.

'I trust the man who told me,' she said, 'but I doubt he'd talk to you.'

He shrugged, not pressing the point. Cynara suspected he was willing to be patient. 'Linnaeus was doing his best to make Caiaphas look like some sort of Persian satrap,' he went on, 'but it wasn't working. The Prosecutor—who is a good young lawyer—was able to pull quite a bit of it back.'

'How did Linnaeus get him to admit to bribing a Zealot?'

Agrippa shrugged. 'It seems Iscariot insisted on accompanying the Temple Guard to the place where Ben Yusuf was hiding, and the Zealots do not enjoy warm relations with the Temple Guard. Linnaeus smelt a rat, and chased it down.'

Cynara shook her head, impressed.

'My father says Caiaphas has been a good High Priest. I presume you know Pilate's predecessor went through High Priests like food through a goose.'

'That came up when I had a couple of my staffers go through the archives. I suspect Pilate's rather pissed off that his High Priest has been dealing with Zealots, although it does seem that Caiaphas went to Iscariot because there was no one else. Getorex asked for re-examination and—as I say—dragged quite a bit of it back. My aide felt rather sorry for Caiaphas. He's in a mess of his own making.'

'And Linnaeus is a very good lawyer.'

'Yes, but he'll struggle to win this one, even though he's getting the better of the argument at the moment.'

'Why?'

'After Pilate excused Caiaphas, Getorex wheeled out his CCTV evidence and the Commander of the Second Cohort. Now, I'm not a lawyer, but I've seen plenty of criminal trials and as video evidence goes, it's very strong. Linnaeus couldn't lay a hand on either.'

'I'm not sure I understand what Linnaeus is arguing, Severus. I know what the words mean, but not in a legal sense.'

'He's trying to argue for a break in the chain of causation, something that cuts away Ben Yusuf's responsibility for Kohen's death and lays it elsewhere.'

'Well, he did bounce off that Temple Guard.'

'Yes, but Ben Yusuf went in there *armed*, that's the problem. He must have known that things would go wrong. Of course Getorex held the whip up for the world to see, and we'll be featuring it on *Newshour* tonight, along with some of the footage.'

'I see,' she said, spearing an oyster and lifting it to her lips.

They ate in silence for a while, building a great midden of oyster shells in the bowl beside the silver platter.

'Tell me about the young medic and his pale and pretty wife,' he said at last. 'I'm curious.'

Cynara smiled; he'd forgotten nothing. She outlined Rachel, Rufus and Saleh's story. He watched her intently as she did so.

'So this Saleh has only had her for a few days?'

'Yes, and Rachel is already very fond of him.'

'He seems a good young man, from what you say.'

'He is.'

'There's a name for this system, isn't there? It came up when Caiaphas was on the stand.'

'Levirate marriage,' she said, 'although neither of the examples you've heard about today are true levirate marriage.'

'I do feel a bit sorry for the other chap,' he said at length.

'Rufus? Why?'

'I mean, what if she were ugly? Would he have to take her then?'

Cynara shook her head at him. 'Spoken like a true Roman.'

She watched his face; he was pensive, even sad, as he sipped his wine.

'You know,' he said, 'I've been reading the, whatchama-callit, stories about your God. There's quite a decent Greek translation; I picked it up in Rome before I left, in the *Collegia Roma* bookshop.'

'The *Septuagint*?'

'Yes, that's it.'

He reached down beside his chair into his briefcase and withdrew a neat, fat hardback with a picture of the Temple on the cover, handing it to her. She took it and turned it over in her hands, reading the commentary on the flyleaf.

'Philo is a good scholar,' she said, referring to the man who'd written the introduction. 'He tries to combine Stoicism with Judaism and Platonism. It doesn't really work, but you've got to respect him for making an effort.'

'You should translate this *Septuagint* into Latin—it'll be a best seller, all that senseless violence.' He paused, thinking for a moment. 'Needs a snappier title, though.'

Cynara had watched *Newshour* for years, and while she'd always known that both Severus Agrippa and Arminia Brenna were given to mischief and play in their presentation, they were also careful to retain a mask of public neutrality. Not so in private, it seemed.

'Do you always mock what you do not understand?'

He stroked the back of her hand, describing a circle with his right forefinger. She entwined her hand with his. He ran his thumb along hers, then brought her fingers to his mouth. He licked each one in turn and returned her hand to her. She wanted to challenge him, but she also had a clear mental image of straddling him, his hands on her breasts as she rocked back and forth. It was difficult to disagree with a man who made her head spin.

'I mean, isn't your God a shit?' he said. 'I thought ours were bad enough, demanding maidens be sacrificed in order to ensure fair winds for Troy and whatnot, but I think you've topped us.'

'What do you mean?'

'Joshua taking Jericho comes to mind, Cynara. Here is someone who outdoes Rome at Carthage. Not just men, women and children, but all the animals as well.' He was becoming excited, swigging wine and poking olives into his mouth. 'And you keep doing it over and over, on your God's orders. There's the Midianites... or was it the Moabites? Carthage apart, at least we sold the defeated into slavery and turned a profit out of the whole exercise; your God tells you to go out and burn money in His holy name. And people offering their wives and daughters up for gang rape rather than have their male guests molested, what's with that? What's his name? Lot, that's it. And the business about "whoring with other gods"... who a man worships in his own house is his business, surely? Any Roman confronted with a God like that would have given him the vulgar finger long ago.'

She wanted to be angry, but his blasphemy was so acute it was impossible not to laugh.

'And another thing,' he said, taking his fork in his hand like a murder weapon. 'I do like your use of the word *smite*. Even the mighty Roman Army does not *smite*, and I think it's high time we started to learn.' He stabbed the bread on his plate.

'A knife would work better,' she said.

'You see, you know about smiting,' he said. 'We will have to learn at your knee.'

He continued stabbing his bread with the fork.

'Oh I love it. Smite, smote, smitten, smiting, smiter... it's just fabulous.'

This was very funny; his immaculately styled hair was shaking with the effort he put into his stabbing. She waited until he'd made his point, refilled their glasses, and sipped from hers, once. With effort, she brought her breathing under control.

'CR hasn't reported it, but it's known around the place that your father engaged Andreius Linnaeus as defence counsel and is considered one of Ben Yusuf's followers—' He paused while she registered shock at his knowledge. 'Don't worry, your father's secret is safe with me.'

She exhaled slowly, placing her hands palms down on the table.

'Now, the thought of the High Priest dealing with Zealots is one thing, but what does a member of the Sanhedrin in good standing see in someone like Ben Yusuf? Your father's quite an exceptional *chocolatl* merchant—I extracted his last three or four annual reports from Company & Mutual House in Rome. What's in it for Joseph Arimathea?'

'That's a bit awkward to answer—'

'Off the record, of course.'

'My father was always an observant Jew, Severus. Even though he sent all three of us to Roman schools and insisted that we have the best of Rome and Judaea growing up. I used to think he came to follow Ben Yusuf because he'd never really recovered from Mama's death, but that's too neat. In any case, Mama died when I was small—I don't even remember her very well.'

'Maybe the reaction was delayed?'

'I don't know. It's possible. He still has pictures of her all through the house, and their *ketubah* is framed and hanging in an obvious spot. It's also possible some of it was disappointment, too—with his children. My eldest brother moved to Gaul for business and married a Celtic woman; my next brother moved to Heliopolis and married a Samaritan. Arguably, the second was worse than the first—'

'Jews and Samaritans have history?'

'That's one way of putting it.'

He smiled, touching the back of her hand again.

'I'm the only one who stayed in Jerusalem, but I spent a long time away first.'

'Studying in Rome?'

'Yes, and I almost didn't come home. I came *this* close to marrying an officer in the Praetorian Guard. There are still times when I regret that—he'd have made a wonderful father. Over time, though, I think Papa just became very tired. Keeping the laws didn't seem like *mitzvoth* any more. His observance began to slip, although he always kept the most important commandments, and still does.'

'Where does Ben Yusuf come in?'

'I was living on site at the Empire when Papa started to get serious about Ben Yusuf. I'd sometimes see him written up in the papers or on JTN, and Papa began to call me, telling me when he'd be on screen. He can be very impressive.'

'Ben Yusuf?'

'Yes, very funny and apt. I'll never forget seeing him on JTN tearing strips off a man who kept calling him "good teacher". It was the worst sort of sycophancy, and Ben Yusuf saw straight through it. Eventually his interlocutor realised that flattery was getting him nowhere and he asked, directly, how he might attain eternal life—'

Agrippa shook his head at this. 'Why anyone would *want* eternal life is beyond me, I'm afraid. I'll take my seventy-ish years, and when it stops being enjoyable, I'll just avail myself of the Green Dream.'

Cynara bit her tongue, although she knew this view was common among Romans—Stoics, Epicureans, followers

of most of their rites. People routinely had themselves eu-
thanised when life ceased to be pleasurable.

'—And Ben Yusuf pointed out that surely he knew the
commandments.'

'In Jewish religion?'

'Yes. Of course the fellow said that he'd kept the commandments since childhood.'

Agrippa, she could see, was horribly fascinated by this,
leaning forward over his food towards her, fork in hand.

'What did Ben Yusuf say?'

'He challenged him to sell all his property and give the proceeds to the poor.'

Agrippa was disappointed, and sat back in his chair.

'I don't get it. Maybe my sense of humour gland needs juic-
ing up.'

'And of course, the fellow didn't want to comply. He walked
off the set.'

'Well, why should you give away your hard-earned to
just anyone?'

'Spoken like a Roman,' she said. 'Our version of *philotimia*
is different from yours.'

'You don't say,' he said. 'Giving good things to unworthy
people. If you keep doing that, you know, you'll only encourage them.'

'We think you should help the poor and needy.'

'The best way to do that is sound economic policy, and to
support the family, not free stuff.'

Cynara changed the subject. She'd had this argument time
and again while living in Rome, and had no desire to reani-
mate it.

'At the same time, Papa also warmed towards all his children. We talked about the change among ourselves and
we agreed it was a good thing. Both my brothers and their

families came home for Passover last year—a first for quite a few years—and my father began to enthuse about Ben Yusuf to all of us. Isaac—my brother in Heliopolis—even went to hear Ben Yusuf speak. He asked him Hillel's question at the end.'

'Hillel's question?'

'Hillel was a famous and learned Rabbi; he died about twenty years ago. There was a story going around that he could recite the Torah while standing on one leg, and a Roman visitor to the Temple asked for a demonstration. By that stage, Hillel was an old man; he stood on one leg and told the Roman, "That which is hateful to you, do not do to your fellow. That is the whole Torah; the rest is commentary; go and learn."'

'That's appropriately Delphic. I like the sound of this Hillel. What did Ben Yusuf say to your brother?'

'Something very similar, Severus; he told Isaac that he should do to others what he would want done to himself.'

'That's actually very different,' Agrippa said softly.

'How so? Please, no hairsplitting Greek philosophy. It makes my head hurt.'

'I'm Roman, Cynara, we don't do philosophy; this is simpler than that. Your Rabbi Hillel's injunction is negative, telling people only that they should not interfere with others. Ben Yusuf's is positive, telling people that you should interfere with others, that you should do something to them.'

'But only good things, Severus, that's the point!'

'Whose good, Cynara?'

His eyes sparkled and she suspected he was smiling at his own cleverness.

When they returned to Antonia, sated with good food and fine wine, Agrippa turned to her, kissed her and then rejoined his staff. She watched him go, touching the spot on her bottom lip where he had let his mouth linger, before she noticed Fotini beside her.

'I believe you've still got my identity card,' Fotini said.

'I'm sorry.'

She fished in her handbag until she saw the flash of yellow and handed it to her.

'What's he like?'

'Sex on legs, Fotini.'

'Thought so. Have a great night.'

Three days without bathing or shaving does little for most men, and Gaius Crispus was no exception. He rubbed his bristles with one hand and noted that he now stank so badly he could pass for Galilean. When Pilate had first locked him up, he had stripped off his uniform jacket, boots and socks, draping them over the bottom of his bunk, but all that meant was that while his clothes remained clean; he reeked. One of the cage's previous occupants had pissed in the corner and the cleaning detail hadn't managed to catch it all. The scent was metallic rather than acidic, which suggested a soldier who'd walked into Antonia out of his skull on *Sunshine* and left a fair bit of it on the floor. His busted nose was responsible for part of the stench: it had continued to bleed after *Medicus* Felix had reset it, and his pillow and shirt were stained with blood that smelt of soil. That was when he could still smell. Eventually one of the nurses came in and injected him with a coagulant.

Of course, it also didn't help that the stockade cages abutted the *caldarium* and enjoyed referred heat from its underfloor piping; he was trapped in a permanent summer. He rolled over on his narrow bunk, clawed at the pillow and attempted to doze. He could feel sweat trickling down between his shoulderblades and heard noise from within the baths complex itself: pipes expanding and contracting, splashing water, men scrubbing themselves clean, noisy discussion of post-Passover plans. These tended to involve leave in Damascus or Heliopolis and quantities of sex and drugs.

'On your feet, soldier,' he heard from outside the cage.

The voice was Capito's; he opened one eye and saw the legion's commander standing beside Lonuobo, his arms folded. Crispus hauled himself upright and saluted; Capito did not respond.

'Have you reflected on Monday's conversation about the primacy of elected officials, Crispus?'

'I'd already reflected on it at the time, sir. What I did was reasonable in the circumstances and saved many hundreds of lives.'

'Say that at your court martial and you'll be run out of the legion.'

'Undoubtedly, sir, and straight into the Senate.'

'You're very sure of yourself, Crispus.'

'How else are we supposed to defend the Empire, sir? Harsh language?'

'Not like what we did, sir.'

It was Lonuobo's voice. Crispus had wondered why Capito had brought him along.

'I did it for Tzipi,' Lonuobo said, 'and Tzipi would be ashamed.'

'I did it for the Empire, and I'd do it again. Sometimes you have to fight fire with fire. People like Iscariot do not belong inside the charmed circle marked *humanity*.'

'Going by that logic,' Capito said, 'nor do you.'

Lonuobo saw Crispus's face relax, becoming preternaturally calm.

'No, sir, I don't. The crucial difference is I know this, and have always known it. People like Iscariot have to be taught, by any means necessary.'

He stepped towards the bars, looking at both men in turn. Lonuobo looked away, perhaps from force of habit; Crispus outranked him. Capito continued to meet his gaze. A small muscle in his cheek twitched, but his face was otherwise unmoved. If he hated—or had come to hate—this Consul's son and scion of privilege, he gave no sign.

'If you keep this up, Crispus, you won't just be out on your ear,' Capito went on. 'You'll be unable to walk for a fortnight.'

'I've always expected a flogging, sir. I'll take my licks and stick the scars on a campaign poster if I have to.'

THE PROSELYTE

Esther could hear scratching noises at their front door. She put her matzo balls to one side, directed Naomi to cook them and went to investigate. She hoped it wasn't the soldiers the Procurator had insisted be posted to guard the High Priest's house the previous week. No one had briefed them on proper behaviour, which meant they used the private rooms they enjoyed in the servants' quarters to fuck Greek Quarter women, drink, and play loud music when they were off duty.

Esther had become familiar with the words one of them shouted when he was about to come and the lyrics to half-a-dozen popular cinema tunes. This annoyed her, because she knew Romans were capable of being reserved and polite, at least in public. That said, one of the songs she actually liked; it was slower than the others, and she noticed the noisy one always played it post-coitus. It told of a small hill town under blue skies whose *duumviri* locked people up in the local jail whenever they got a bit too rowdy. In the last verse, the boys all left to join the army and the girls all went to factories in the city, leaving the town under its blue skies with a population consisting entirely of old people.

She opened the door to see her husband standing outside fumbling with his house keys and disdaining assistance from the two soldiers on duty. He was crying.

'Kayafa?'

One of the soldiers—the lusty one, she recognised his voice—turned to face her. He pushed the door the rest of the way open, his fingers flicking hers by accident. She snatched her hands back from him, and his skin flushed.

'He's in a state, *Kyria*,' he said in Greek. 'Please help him.'

The concern on his face was genuine, which shocked her. She did not associate compassion with the Roman military. Caiaphas stepped inside at last, wiping his face. He did not reach for her, holding his hands up in front of him, waiting. She could see the soldier staring at her, uncomprehending.

'I'm not *niddah* now,' she said. 'I've bathed.'

The two soldiers looked at each other, shaking their heads as she and Caiaphas embraced. The lusty one shut the door behind them; as he did so, Esther saw him use his right forefinger to draw a circle around his ear. She led Caiaphas into the kitchen and sat him down at the table, sitting opposite him and holding his hands in hers.

'What is it?'

'I've outsmarted myself, Esther, and Arimathea's clever lawyer caught me doing it.'

She'd asked, that morning, whether he wanted her to join him in his office at the Temple, but he'd shaken his head and told her he needed to face this particular unpleasantness alone. Esther had some awareness of his horsetrading and manoeuvring as High Priest but there were times when it became too labyrinthine even for her, and she appreciated it when he tried to stop the politicking from following him home.

'I should never have paid Iscariot. That man was poison and now he's dead the poison is spreading out everywhere and polluting everything it touches.'

He was shaking his head, a look of despair on his face.

'We were making chicken soup and matzo,' she said. 'Let me get you some.'

'The balls won't be finished for a bit, *Gveret*,' Naomi said, 'they've only just gone in.'

'We'll start with soup; bring us some and then you can go to your quarters.'

Caiaphas took the soup from her with gratitude; his distress subsided as he ladled it into his mouth, his shaking hands slowly steadying. Esther stroked his hair, noticing after a few minutes that Naomi was still hovering in the kitchen.

'You can go, Naomi. Please don't think you have to stay.'

Naomi shook her head and stared at the floor. Esther suspected the soldiers had said something to her. Their desire to bed her was obvious enough, and Esther had heard them make sucking and whistling noises as she went to and from her room in the servants' quarters.

'Is it the soldiers?' Caiaphas asked, looking up.

'Yes, *Kohen Gadol*. They say filthy things to me, all of them—'

'Can you tell them off, Kayafa?'

'I don't care if I can or can't, Esther. I will.'

Naomi stepped towards him, her hands held up in front of her.

'Not Terence,' she said, her face flushing. 'I like Terence.'

Caiaphas rolled his eyes at this. 'Which one is he?'

She looked down again. 'He's on the front door today.'

'Not the one who makes all the racket, surely?' Esther asked, surprised.

'No, *Gveret*, the other one, the quiet one; I like him. He's nice to me.'

'Even though he says filthy things, too?'

She nodded, rubbing her eyes. 'He doesn't mean it like the others. He's not a bad person.'

'I have had Romans and their shit *up to here* today, I really have,' Caiaphas growled. 'I wish they'd all crawl away and *die!*'

Naomi shrank back against the wall, both hands in front of her mouth; Esther put her arms around her shoulders. Caiaphas stood up.

'Leave us to our lives, and we leave them to their vices, yes? Isn't that fair?'

He strode across the room and flung the door open.

'Which one of you is Terence?' he asked in Greek. The taller and darker of the two turned to face him and saluted smartly.

'At your service, sir.'

'He speaks Aramaic, *Kohen Gadol*,' said Naomi. 'The others don't, except cuss words.'

Caiaphas rounded on her, speaking in Aramaic so they both understood him. The lusty one looked away from the three of them, his face immobile.

'If you want to go off with this Terence, that's your business, but I don't approve. It's sluttish. Do your parents know?'

'My father wants his grandchildren to be citizens, *Kohen Gadol*,' she said. 'My brother married a Jewess who is a Roman citizen. My parents had to pay a big bride price for her.'

Esther watched as Caiaphas stomped down the path to the cream and ochre adobe servants' quarters, anger radiating off him. He banged on the doors to the rooms where the soldiers were quartered.

'Fuck off, I'm sleeping,' she heard one of them yell. Caiaphas kept banging and yelling. Eventually the four that guarded the residence at night surfaced, scratching their heads and armpits and crotches and looking sheepish. One of them dangled his carbine at his side with a casualness that frightened her. Two of them were bare chested. The lusty one, she noticed, had hesitated at first and then followed her husband. She remembered Pilate saying he had some sort of minor rank that put him in charge of the other seven men.

'She's Terence's woman, sir,' he was saying to Caiaphas's back. 'I'll make sure they all understand that. Sorry, sir.'

Caiaphas turned and pointed a finger at the man's face while the others looked on. 'You,' he said, 'I'm sick of hearing your music. I'm sick of you bringing whores onto my property. I'm sick of hearing you screw around. There are some parts of the Latin vocabulary I can do without, that my wife can do without, and that my twelve-year-old son can do without. Do you understand?'

'Yes, sir; sorry, sir.'

'That goes for all of you,' he yelled, gesticulating. 'Now,' he said, pointing towards Naomi, 'leave her alone. Stop speaking filth to her, do you hear me?'

Esther felt Hillel take her hand; she thought he'd been reading in his room but then she noticed his hair was wet. Ever since his stay in Caesarea with the Pilates he'd gone for long daily swims in their residence's big *frigidarium*.

'Papa's very angry, isn't he?'

'The soldiers were nasty to Naomi, Hillel.'

'Why does she like kissing one of them, then?'

'Because human beings are very strange, as you'll learn.'

'Antony says you have to step on enlisted men, otherwise they get ideas.'

'Well, your father's doing some stepping, then.'

'Now, where are the other two?' Caiaphas wanted to know.

'On the rear gate, sir,' said the lusty one. 'I can send for them.'

She saw the soldier detail a subordinate to retrieve them, and heard her husband give both a similar dressing-down. One of the two made the mistake of kissing his teeth when he thought Caiaphas wasn't looking.

'Don't do that again, soldier; I know what it means and I *will* tell the Procurator and have your back turned into shredded beef, I promise you. *Intelligis*? Or do I need to repeat it in words of one syllable or less?'

The soldier realised Caiaphas was serious and dropped his head; he apologised and flicked his fingers nervously down the front of his fatigues. Caiaphas threw his hands in the air and marched back up the path to the big house.

'I think they'll behave, now,' he said as he stepped inside.

'I think so, too,' Esther said. 'Now tell me,' she added as neutrally as possible, 'what happened in court today, dear?'

Terence and the lusty one walked back up the path while they talked. Naomi served matzo dumplings and then seemed to vanish; it took a moment for Esther to realise that she'd left the house by one of its other exits. She craned her neck to see where she'd gone, noticing that Terence had paused in the middle of the path, squinting. Naomi walked towards him, and he reached for her hands. She pulled back at first, shyly, but he caught her fingers. He seemed to be apologising to her. The two of them walked towards the servants' quarters. The other soldiers watched in silence, their faces unmoved. They made no noise or ribald comments now.

'It goes back further than that,' Caiaphas was saying. 'When we met him outside Caesarea after that banquet at Pilate's, I should have resolved then and there to have nothing to do with him.'

Once they were in the lee of the building and partly obscured by shadow, Terence and Naomi began kissing. These were gentle little kisses. In time Naomi coiled her arms around his neck and he kissed her harder. She was crying and he rubbed his face against hers, smearing her make-up. Finally, he broke away and she stroked his cheeks with both hands, smiling. Terence turned and made his way back along the path towards the house. Naomi went into her room.

Later that afternoon, after Caiaphas had gone back to the Temple, Esther saw Terence waiting outside the door, nervous.

'*Gveret*,' Terence said as she went to unlock it, 'may I speak with you? Just for a moment?' He spoke in Aramaic—good

Aramaic, she noted—and turned something over in his hands. It took a moment or two for her to realise it was one of Hillel's books, a child's account of Passover, printed on heavy, high quality paper. At that moment, Naomi appeared behind him. He took her hand and they both smiled shyly. The two soldiers on either side of the double doors—one of them the man who had kissed his teeth earlier in the day—were like human statues, giving nothing away.

'All right, Terence, come in. I can only spare a moment, though.'

'I think I ought to return this. Naomi borrowed it from Hillel for me.'

She took the heavy hardcover and watched as the two of them stepped into the residence, Terence marvelling at its undecorated and austere beauty, Naomi standing very close to him and looking up at his face. Her eyes were shining and her cheeks glowed, and Esther suspected they'd just had sexual intercourse. Terence curled his arms around her from behind and rubbed his cheek against her hair, which was wavy and lustrous.

'*Gveret*, how does one become a Jew?'

At that moment Esther found she needed to sit down.

The soldier removed his beret—it bore insignia indicating he was one of their parachutists, so he was exceptionally fit and strong, even by the Roman military's high standards—and was turning it around and over in his hands with nerves. Naomi continued to smile up at him.

'You can start by putting your hat back on,' Esther said, 'you cover your head before God.'

Terence complied, his expression quizzical; he went back to holding Naomi. Esther twisted around and picked up a stack of papers from a shelf in front of a series of photographs of Hillel in his school uniform and various brightly coloured kippot. She began to leaf through them until she found a three-page document. She handed it to Terence.

'Can you read Aramaic, or do you only speak it?'

'I can read it, *Gveret.*'

'Before you even think about becoming one of the *gerim*, you should keep these seven laws for a year. I think you will struggle with laws one and four.'

Terence read through the document in silence; Esther could see his lips moving as he read, his forehead creasing with effort and concentration.

'These are the Noahide Laws,' she said. 'They are for gentiles, so you can be *ger toshav*, a proselyte at the gate. That is the first step along the path.'

'I cannot keep a shrine for Roma and *Lares* and the ancestors?'

'No, you can't. That's idolatry.'

He looked down at Naomi, bending one hand up to stroke her cheek with the tips of his fingers. Esther suspected he wanted to cry—his eyes were very bright—but she couldn't be sure. Romans tended to emotional lability at the best of times.

'Can I keep my grandparents' photograph?'

'Of course you can; but you mustn't worship it.'

'And I cannot go to the field brothel on the frontier or when we go to war?'

'No, you can't. That's adultery.'

'Those are hard rules, *Gveret*. When you're in the field, it's good to know that someone will cut stone for you and remember your face when you're gone; it's nice to feel a warm and lustful body beside yours to remind you that you're alive.'

'Yes, Terence, you will struggle; but God will remember you when you are gone, and your Naomi will always remind you that you're alive.'

'What if I do either and no one knows?'

'God will know.'

He nodded, his expression bewildered, and looked at her. 'The others I already keep, *Gveret*, or at least I think I do.'

'That's very good. I'm impressed.'

'I've never indulged the Greek vice, I don't tell lies and I obey the law; I mean, some of these rules are the same in Roman law. We condemn murder and theft, too.'

'Do you watch the *ludi* or go to the cages?'

'No. My parents are Stoics, and discouraged us from that.'

Esther put Hillel's book down on the shelf in front of his photographs and studied the young Roman before her. She liked Stoics, despite their obsessive concern with valour.

'In a few months, if you can keep these seven laws, you make a formal statement of intent to the Beth Din. If you can still keep them after a year, then come to my husband and talk to him about conversion.'

She turned to Naomi. 'Teach him what he needs to know for the Seder, and I will ask Caiaphas to add his name to yours for the *korbanot*. Pay special attention to the questions'—she paused, looking at Terence, seeing a *cantor* with a beautiful voice—'can you sing? Many Romans sing well.'

'Yes, I sing well, *Gveret*. People say I have the best voice in my Century.'

Without warning, he began to sing *When Marcus Comes Marching Home*. Her first instinct was to stop him, but his soaring vocals were so impressive she found herself struck dumb.

They love their country so much; my God it is terrifying.

'And then teach him our songs,' she said to Naomi when Terence had finished. 'Hillel will help you if need be.'

'Buy your fruit cake here, fruit cake for sale—extra nuts guaranteed—in the Antonia Officer's Mess... fruit cake on special today.'

Cyler placed a metal tray with coffees, fruitcake and a selection of the marzipan animals and crystalline fruits popular for *Megalesia* before Cornelius, Mirella and Julia. Mirella set small plates in front of each of them while Cyler laid out napkins.

'Erk. Who puts milk in their espresso?' Julia wanted to know.

'Ah, that'll be me,' said Cornelius.

'He can't help being British,' said Mirella. 'They put milk in everything.'

Cornelius kissed her cheek and raised his milky coffee to his lips.

'You'll keep,' he said.

'You know, it's nice,' Julia said, biting the leg off a marzipan deer, 'the way they try to make up for everyone's leave being cancelled.'

'You mean, *we* try to make it up. That's enlisted men of the Third in there on kitchen detail at the moment,' said Cyler, 'I copped *Megalesia* in the kitchens last year. It was so bad I couldn't eat marzipan for six months afterwards.'

'What did you do?' Julia asked.

'Failed a drug test,' he said. 'Had too much fun on leave in Heliopolis and hadn't got rid of all of it.'

'You know, this really is exceptionally nutty fruitcake,' said Mirella. 'I'm going to go to work this evening full of nuts.'

'Having spent the day in suitably nutty company,' Cyler said, 'you'll be nutted out.'

The four of them spent a few minutes tittering, drinking their coffee, and sharing sweets. Mirella fed Cornelius one of hers. Cyler and Julia held hands under the long wooden bench like naughty schoolchildren.

'He really is off his trolley, isn't he?' Mirella said at last. 'Even his own people think he's off his trolley.'

'I keep waiting for one of them to say he used to piss on the third rail as a kid,' Cyler said.

'Lucullus, that's a nasty image,' Cornelius said. 'We haven't won yet.'

'His nuttiness is separate from us winning, sir. I mean, I hope we win, but he's bat-shit crazy regardless.'

'You didn't think that when you talked to him in his cell,' said Julia.

'No. He seemed pretty reasonable, actually. Maybe that's why he's nutty. He can hide it, seem normal, fly under the radar. Then when he's got you nice and relaxed, he announces to the world that your forces are going to blow Jerusalem sky high.'

Cornelius nodded and drank, trying to think of a way to make his point.

'You may be right,' he said after a while, 'but for all his craziness, I think he's explicable. Look at it from his perspective: his little country and its funny little religion were doing just fine until we come along. They'd seen off lots of other people with imperial ambitions. They'd even seen off Antiochus. Then they get a major dose of shock and awe courtesy the Imperial Roman Army. We slaughter twelve hundred of them on the Temple Mount after bitter urban warfare. One of our Legates walks into the taboo part of their Temple... am I painting a picture here?'

'You are when you consider that we then gave them Herod as opposed to direct Roman rule, yes,' said Julia.

Cornelius hadn't expected her to agree with him; in his experience aviatrices—partly through being recruited so young—tended to support imperial policy uncritically.

'I keep forgetting Herod,' said Cyler. 'I haven't had a lot to do with many Jews since I've been posted here, but every single one I've spoken to hates him.'

'Despite his beautiful Temple?' Mirella asked. 'I mean, it is spectacular.'

'Despite his beautiful Temple, Mirella,' Cornelius went on. 'He left three quarters of the city unsewered and dependent on wells. He went through wives the way some people go through clothes. He killed three of his own children. And this is only fifty-odd years ago, give or take.'

'And people have long memories,' Mirella said. 'Especially these people.'

Linnaeus crossed the square, ice creams in hand. The breeze caught his toga and it billowed behind him. The sight of a male Roman citizen in full regalia invited more than the usual number of stares; it was common enough to see counsel in robes flocking outside the law courts in Caesarea, and Romans would break out the toga or stola on festival days, but Jerusalem had no Roman festivals. Linnaeus suspected the only place some of the people hovering around the square had seen anyone dressed like him was in the pages of history books, or on screen. Some people stepped aside with exaggerated politeness as he passed, although he also attracted curious children and clouds of beggars: from a little boy who leapt up and touched his gold headband to a woman who stood on one hand and somehow curled her feet over her shoulders from beneath. He made the fatal mistake of passing the latter a one *denarius* note. He was then confronted with the fact that instead of half-a-dozen, he now had upwards of twenty following him, and no free hands. He handed one ice cream to Fotini and another to Clara, his clerk from Caesarea. He turned to face the beggars.

'Will you lot piss off?'

'That won't be very effective,' said Fotini.

'Why?'

'You said it in Greek.'

Fotini repeated the imprecation in Aramaic; Linnaeus watched the beggars at least move backwards.

'Never give them anything,' said Clara, 'or you'll never live it down.'

The three of them withdrew into Antonia's entrance hall and surveyed the scene outside through the barracks security system. Clara shook her head at the massed crowds streaming towards the Temple. Already, the square was choked with pilgrims and their sacrificial animals: lambs, goats, flies, stink.

'I am so getting on that train straight after sentence on Friday,' she said. 'I've got the best costume for *Megalesia*, and my man has some leave at last.'

'Good on you,' said Fotini. 'Remember us here in Jerusalem when you're having a good time.'

Linnaeus was unhappy with his cross-examination of Binyamin, and said so.

'It doesn't really bear on the case,' said Clara. 'All that evidence was a large exercise in guilt by association. It doesn't look great, but it's not relevant to the felony murder charge, or even whether he knew what Iscariot was up to otherwise.'

Fotini licked her ice cream and admired Clara, who she'd already determined to stay in touch with once she'd moved to Rome. Clara was gifted with both robust good sense and a kindly disposition.

'You're just not persuaded by all this Zealotry business, are you?' Linnaeus asked.

'No, Andreius, I'm not.'

'Why's that?' Fotini asked.

'He's not mad enough,' Clara said. 'I was born in Caesarea. I know what Judaean mad looks like.'

'And he isn't it?'

'No, he isn't it.'

Ben David waited on platform two for the train from Sepphoris, holding a sign with *Centurio Irenaeus Andrus* painted on it in large black letters. He'd not expected to keep getting such well-paid work through Linnaeus, but the wily lawyer ensured that he'd had plenty of evidence to retrieve, coffees to buy and persons to ferry about. Ben David caught himself wondering if Andrus would wear his *Corona* on his head, like Pilate did his wreath of office—he'd been decorated with every award for valour worth having in the Roman Army, after all. He tried to remember if he'd ever seen a Roman wear the *Corona* on any occasion other than an official military parade or reception.

He heard a train whistle; he stood up and held his sign in front of his chest. The train was packed solid with pilgrims; he looked down its length towards third class and saw a large contingent sitting on top, their hands clasped around their knees. Several had bedrolls bound up with thin cords while others carried pillows under their arms. They helped each other down from the roof and then retrieved wives and children from within the carriages. They swarmed through the station, paying him no heed as they crowded around and past him. He also looked for Roman uniforms: there were plenty, but all fatigues and body armour. He suspected Andrus would be in dress uniform.

And he was.

He saw a soldier assisting a woman down the steps from one of the first-class carriages. She was hugely pregnant, resting one hand on top of her swollen belly. He'd heard the story that pregnant women were supposed to glow, but he'd long suspected that any glowing was the exception, not the rule. This woman, however, was a glower. She was about twenty-one or twenty-two, with unblemished olive skin and black waist-length hair. Heads all through the station—mostly male, but plenty of women, too—swivelled to look at her. She was like something off the *Ara Pacis* in Rome, or the Temple of Ishtar in Antioch, beautifully expectant and filled with grace. She took the soldier's hands and he helped her onto the platform.

'Our taxi is here,' she said.

The soldier turned to face Ben David, who beheld the strangest eyes he'd ever seen: one emerald green, one dove grey. The soldier was in his late thirties, robust and muscular and with a chiselled, symmetrical face—so symmetrical, in fact, it was as though the gods were playing a joke with the asymmetry of his eyes. He was bare headed, and Ben David could see the worm-like scars from a couple of near misses trace their way through his brown bristles. When he curled a hand around the woman's waist, Ben David noticed the back was covered with crosshatched scars, like something administered in some long-ago initiation ritual.

The soldier retrieved their trunk, picking it up with deceptive ease. He walked towards Ben David, smiling. The woman waited, her loose robe hanging over her belly. Because she was so big, it was shorter at the front.

'We have to go to Antonia,' he said in Greek, handing the trunk over. Ben David led them to his cab, loading the trunk—he wondered for a moment what was inside to make it so heavy—and watching as Andrus took the woman's hands and helped her into the back. She sat down and rested her head on his chest; he enfolded her in his arms, whispering into her hair.

'Does the baby want to come, or are you just tired?'

'Just tired,' she said. 'Hold me.'

Ben David watched them in his rear-view mirror as he nosed his way through masses of people. The distinction between roads and footpaths had gone, and he found himself apologising when a camel tried to poke its head through the driver's side window.

'I should have gone to pee at the station,' he heard the woman say.

'They'll be cleaner at Antonia,' he said. 'Hang on.'

Ben David waited some time for a herd of goats plus goat-herd to make their way around the cab. He suspected the woman had gone to sleep against her husband's chest.

'I read about you in the paper,' he said. 'Do you wear your *Corona*? I mean, I've seen men wear them on parades...'

'Sometimes,' he said, grinning. 'Not a lot of people ask me that.'

'It's very, ah, exalted.'

'Once I wore it round the *castrum* for a whole day for a bet,' he said, 'but then I forgot and walked outside with it on. I wondered why everyone was staring at me.'

Ben David found this funny.

'This one made me take it off'—he pointed to his sleeping woman—'she said it was puffery.'

Ben David laughed. He'd expected someone far more rigid and fierce. He watched as Andrus stroked her hair, his lips and nose resting against the top of her head. One hand stroked her belly; Ben David caught himself counting the fine crosshatches on the back and wondering what could have wounded him like that. In time, low, sweet sounds came from Andrus. It took him a little while to appreciate that he was singing to her as he held her, in dialect. Ben David understood not a single word.

After lunch, Cynara and Agrippa were late into court and arrived just in time to see Andrus swear the traditional soldier's oath by Mars. 'Should I lie, may I be broken as I break the head from this arrow.'

'That's an exceptionally handsome man,' she heard

Agrippa whisper as Andrus took his place on the stand. They watched the court orderly guide Andrus's round wife to a spot where she could watch her husband's testimony without having to stretch her neck. Cynara noticed how Andrus looked on at this with his flinty stare, as though the enlisted man might break her somehow. She rested her hands across the top of her belly.

'*Centurio* Irenaeus Iulius Andrus was called by both State and Defence in this matter,' Pilate said as Agrippa found his seat. 'My usual policy in conflicts like this is to review all relevant statements and assign the witness to the side he seems most likely to support. In the case of this witness's evidence, I have found that he cannot be so assigned. To that end, I will conduct the bulk of the examination.'

Cynara knew this was unusual. She felt for Andrus, alone on the stand as Pilate made his service record an exhibit, for all that the article in yesterday's *Tempus* had made him sound like the bravest man in the Empire.

'*Centurio* Andrus, could you tell the court how you came to know the Suspect?'

'*Procurator*, about three years ago, I heard rumours of an itinerant holy man in the region,' he said in Latin, with Lonuobo translating into Greek, 'but I was only prompted to investigate further when I received a complaint from the Station Master in Sepphoris.'

'Which was?'

'That he and his younger brother, Yacob, were persistent fare evaders, Procurator, who would "ride the rattler" all over the Province.'

This induced a ripple of laughter.

'And?'

'During a patrol in Nazareth I sent a subordinate to speak to the two boys with a view to resolving the problem without recourse to law.'

'Did that work?'

'No, Procurator, it didn't. The Station Master contacted me again later, talking of dozens, sometimes hundreds of people sitting on trains and not paying.' He looked towards the press box. 'You've seen this during Passover, no doubt, and we all let it pass—the transport infrastructure would buckle, otherwise—but this lot were sitting up there when the carriages below were empty. It was some sort of political statement.'

There was more laughter.

'I learned that both the lads had spent several years working on various big projects in Sepphoris, including the Antipater Memorial Theatre and the re-laying of the Forum. When I ran into one of the local construction managers at a function I thought to ask him about the Ben Yusuf boys.'

'What did he say?'

'That they were bright, hardworking and honest, and he had trouble believing that they could be engaging in criminality on such a grand scale.'

Cynara looked at Ben Yusuf. She didn't think it possible for a human being to be utterly impassive, but he was making a fair attempt. She observed him for several minutes, coming to the conclusion that he didn't blink, either.

'Next time I was in Nazareth, I detailed a section to arrest the two brothers, only to discover they'd moved to Capernaum about a fortnight before.' He stopped, as though unsure how to proceed.

'Yes?'

'Well, Procurator, then it gets complicated,' he said at last. 'I didn't see either of them again, even though they were intimately involved in an incident in Capernaum that I investigated.'

'You have plenty of time, *Centurio* Andrus. I'll stop you if anything isn't clear.'

Andrus took a deep breath.

'You need to understand that outside Sepphoris, the Galilee is a strange place, especially to someone from a big city in Italy or Gaul. I'm from rural southern Italy—I'm *Calabrese*—so I have a little understanding, but only a little.'

He indicated this by pinching the thumb and forefingers of one hand together.

'It's like someone took our laws, tore them into small pieces, threw them up in the air, then waited for them to land. Now, some of those laws just happened to land in the same place as ours; many of them didn't.'

'Yes.'

'The Commander of the garrison in Capernaum was *Centurio* Propertius of the Second Century, and a fine officer. Just after I was promoted to Cohort Commander, Propertius took a'—he searched for the word, his eyes turned up—'a *pais*, a *padika* as the Greeks have it. He cleared this with me and moved the boy into his quarters.'

Pilate was inscrutable. Several of the media people were looking at the ceiling, switching off as the afternoon dragged on.

'What made this different—and difficult—was that Propertius's boy came from Capernaum. That is, he was native to the Galilee.'

Cynara noticed the entire press box switch on and sit up.

Pilate looked flummoxed. 'How?'

'Apparently the villagers had known since the boy was small that he preferred male company. His mother, a respected widow, told me that when he was little, he would steal his sister's clothes. He used to sit in the window, she told me, watching our men march down the street; he liked soldiers. At the age when many young Galilean men are betrothed to a village girl, she caught him with magazines and pictures of

Greek love. Often, she saw him using the public *vocale* beside the *agora*. At the time, she didn't understand how he got money to use it; she never gave him any.'

Cynara could feel something cold and stony settling in the pit of her stomach. She saw Agrippa and other civilised city types chuckling at Andrus's coy descriptions, oblivious. 'At some point she had to travel into Sepphoris with two of her sons; she wanted to have them apprenticed to a good trade. Anyway, she told me that she "lost" the younger of the two. She sent his older brother to go looking for him, and then went looking herself. He was in the changing rooms at the baths with Propertius when she found him, and they were in each other's arms, kissing.'

Cynara put her hands over her mouth.

'It became clear over time that Propertius wanted more than just a *cinaedus*, and that the boy would be useless to any woman as a husband. Propertius told me that he wanted the boy to live with him in the barracks. Capernaum's Rabbi also approached me when he was visiting Sepphoris and asked if I could "do something" that would let everyone save face but also preserve the boy's life. The villagers normally stone boys like that—they call them "sodomites", from an ancient Judaean city where the Greek vice was common—but in this case they were afraid of Propertius's anger.'

Cynara listened to his dry, unemotional delivery and watched his small, neat hand gestures. His eyes were very bright as he spoke, but she knew he would not cry on the stand and shame himself.

'Eventually I convened a meeting in the Basiliké Stoà in Capernaum with the Rabbi, the boy, his mother and Propertius. We agreed that the boy should go to Propertius, while the Rabbi promised that he would stop the local lads from harming him, so long as he and Propertius didn't shove what they were in the villagers' faces. Propertius promised the boy's mother she could visit her son whenever she chose.'

Cynara felt she now understood the concept of a 'captive audience'. She saw Galileans pulling sour faces, Romans with their hands in front of their mouths, Greeks scratching the backs of their heads. The stillness was palpable and menacing.

'The Rabbi was true to his word, while Propertius made sure that he never touched the boy when they were in public or visiting his mother. Everyone left everyone else alone.'

Pilate pushed his pen against the blotter so hard the reservoir snapped, staining his fingers. The ink spread, but the blotting paper soaked the worst of it up. He rubbed the back of one hand with the other, smearing blue everywhere. He did not move otherwise.

'Not long after, Zealots became active in the region. I lost three of my men to IEDs. An enlisted man had his woman stoned. The day I came from Nazareth to Capernaum, Zealots saw Propertius with his boy. Perhaps they had become habituated to tolerance, perhaps they had become careless. All the vendors I spoke to told me that Propertius sent the boy back to the barracks with a simple kiss and some kind words. The Zealots must have seen this, because the boy did not get home; that night Propertius returned to an empty bed.'

Cynara made eye contact with Agrippa, who was mouthing something. She could not make it out through her tears.

'I despatched a search party and contacted his mother and Capernaum's Rabbi. Four of my men captured a known Zealot and tortured him into revealing where the boy had been taken. I wasn't sure if he was telling the truth but we had no time. I took about half of the first Century and the Rabbi with me to the nominated place. We found a distressed farmer. He was so crushed he didn't want to speak to any Romans; he hadn't known Zealots were using the caves at the back of his property as their hideout. He led us to one of the fences around his farm. By now it was evening, and he'd cut the boy down and wrapped him in a blanket and given him water to drink. When he found him, he said, the boy looked like a scarecrow. He'd been pinned to the fence with barbed wire. He'd been beaten so badly his body was black.'

Cynara watched as the man from the Athens Broadcasting Service fled the courtroom. She could hear him being sick outside, despite the courtroom's reinforced double doors.

'What did the Rabbi say?' Pilate wanted to know. 'That isn't in your statement.'

'I should have put that in, Procurator. I'm much better at speaking than writing. When I write, I make mistakes.'

Pilate nodded.

'The Rabbi was very, very angry. He seemed angrier than us, and we were very angry. When I could get sense from him, he told me that the Zealots were from outside, not Capernaum, and they had no business trespassing on what he and the villagers had worked out. He said they had a system, and that life was more important than purity.'

Pilate leant back in his chair, rubbing one inky hand with the other.

'I radioed for a pushprop and took him to the Sepphoris Æsculapion. I went with the wounded boy, the Rabbi, and a medic. The rest of my men made their way back to barracks as fast as they could. At the Æsculapion, I learned the boy was bleeding inside, and that while he seemed coherent, he would soon die from the haemorrhaging; his liver had been split in two. The *medica* released him to Propertius with the Green Dream and instructions on how to administer euthanasia so he could die at home with someone he loved. The pushprop took both of them and the Rabbi back to Capernaum.'

Another presser—a woman this time—bolted from the

media box, joining the vomiting Athenian outside.

'I dealt with some mind-numbing administrative work and went to bed. It was that evening the Ben Yusuf boys had chosen for their move to Capernaum. I saw nothing of the events that followed. I thought they were still in Nazareth, as my later actions show.'

Andrus's gestures had become even more confined, and he was now looking at a spot on the courtroom floor.

'Propertius could not bring himself to administer the lethal injection, wheeling the Æsculapion trolley into his bedroom and lying beside it on the bed. He told me that his boy would wake at strange moments, begging to be kissed, or begging for a shot. Propertius would give him a small shot, but never enough to send him across the Styx, never the big phial.'

Even the Galileans in the gallery had their hands in front of their mouths now.

'He consumed an entire bottle of port during the next few hours, becoming very drunk. At some point he left his quarters, wandering around the *castrum*. At some point again, he left the *castrum*, wandering into the *agora*. There he came upon Ben Yusuf and his hangers-on, who'd just arrived. He told me later he'd heard of Ben Yusuf's prodigious powers as a healer in fields that medicine could not cross. Like most of our people he doubted these stories, although when you are out of your mind with grief doubt is never at its strongest.'

Cynara found herself warming to Andrus as she had Binyamin of the Temple Guard. There was something radiant in his doggedness and honesty.

'Propertius was desperate and drunk and heartbroken. He begged Ben Yusuf to make his boy well. Ben Yusuf said that he would come and do so, but Propertius was ashamed; his quarters were decorated with the things a Roman soldier with a fondness for boys likes. He told the holy man that all he had to do was speak the words, and if those words had transforming power, then they would transform. He did not have to step inside his quarters.'

Cynara noticed for the first time that Ben Yusuf's face was no longer impassive, and that tears were streaming down his cheeks.

'Propertius returned to the barracks and lay down on his bed beside the Æsculapion trolley. His boy was asleep. He looked at the big phial and put it aside once more. He awoke nine hours later with a thumping hangover to discover that his boy had climbed out of the trolley and was pleasuring him with his mouth.'

Pilate's voice was almost inaudible.

'And the boy was well?'

'Yes, Procurator. The boy was well.'

There was a tidal wave of movement, noise and chatter around the courtroom at this. Cynara saw press people bolt outside and heard snatches of an order to 'clean up that bloody mess'. Someone dragged the Athenian back inside, summarising Andrus's testimony in a series of staccato bursts. Pilate picked up his gavel, preparing to use it, but then held it loosely in one hand as he stared. He sat there, frozen in place, until Horace stood, turned and shoved a piece of paper under his nose.

'Order!' he yelled. 'I will have order in my court.'

He repeated this process several times until the agitation and noise subsided. He swallowed and rested the back of one hand in the palm of the other in front of his chest, staring at Andrus.

'I know you recounted this in your statement, *Centurio*— which counsel have seen, I might add—but I find it inconceivable. It simply cannot be true. Signs and wonders of this sort have not happened since the rise of science. Gods no longer walk on the earth; we have to do the walking ourselves now.'

'Procurator, I saw the boy just after he'd been beaten, and I saw him a fortnight later, with Propertius, healthy, happy, well—still shaken, of course, the cure did not affect his memory of what the Zealots had done to him—but very much alive. I have no explanation.'

Pilate drummed his inky fingers on the blotter, clearly wondering what to do. Cynara suspected he wanted to pursue the issue further but couldn't see how to do so without distorting the trial process. 'Where is Propertius now?'

'In Britannia, Procurator. After this incident he requested a transfer to another legion in a province as far as possible from Judaea. It is not the custom to send men to a different legion far from their original posting when they've already served eighteen years. In light of the circumstances, however, I supported his application. He and the boy went nearly two years ago.'

Pilate looked towards the press gallery.

'And before any of you make a request, *Centurio* Propertius is protected as a serving military officer. If any of you attempt to locate him and make him news fodder, I *will* make a contempt ruling.'

Cynara noticed Andrus's wife staring at Ben Yusuf; eventually the latter turned in the dock and faced her. They seemed to know each other; both smiled in a relaxed way.

'What was your relationship with the Suspect after that, *Centurio*?'

'I came to know him a little better, Procurator. He was often in Capernaum and Sepphoris and other towns dotted around the Galilee. Of course I spoke to him after the business in Capernaum, but he wasn't very helpful.'

'Deliberately obtuse?'

'No, Procurator. I don't think he had any idea how he did what he did. Word of it got around, of course, especially in the Galilee. More people wanted to watch him speak, but they also wanted him to perform, like a trained animal at the circus. Sometimes he turned up in Sepphoris—alone—seeking sanctuary with me. Sometimes I let him sleep overnight in my quarters.'

For the first time, Cynara saw Pilate fix his gaze on Ben Yusuf; the Procurator took off his reading glasses, holding them to one side of his face.

'My main dealing with him came in Nazareth, though, soon after I took a woman who came from there.'

Cynara saw a decent number of people turn their heads and stare at the gorgeous pregnant woman seated towards the front of the public gallery. At that moment, she beckoned to one of the orderlies, who helped her stand. She walked slowly outside; male stares followed her as she went.

'Her brothers were angry that she'd gone with a Roman soldier and two of them ambushed us in an alley while we were on the way back from the theatre. This they did in the name of honour.' For the first time, Cynara noticed he was becoming voluble. 'They wouldn't know what honour was if it leapt up and bit them on the arse.'

'*Centurio* Andrus,' said Pilate, breaking in, 'are you an expert in Judaean *mores*?'

'No, Procurator.'

'Well, in that case, I'll ask you to stick to the facts.'

Andrus nodded, his eyes flinty. 'I shot both, killing one and wounding the other, Procurator. My woman and I went into the *castrum* straight afterwards.'

He now looked smug.

Where you screwed her arse off to make your point, no doubt.

'The surviving one did not give up. Ben Yusuf had allowed him to join his followers, but I think he lied about his real reasons for wanting to follow.'

'This is Iscariot?'

'Yes, Procurator. At some point when Ben Yusuf was travelling around the countryside Iscariot must have let his plans for us show. This meant we received an unexpected visit.'

'From Ben Yusuf? He visited you and your woman?'

'We were very pleased to see him, and gave him a picture of Propertius and his boy taken somewhere in Britannia's green fields that they'd sent over especially. He took it and thanked us, but I don't think it meant to him what it meant to us. Propertius wrote a letter offering money, too, but as far as I know Ben Yusuf never took it.'

'What was the warning?'

'There's a defile near Sepphoris notorious as a Zealot hold-out. It's almost impossible to police except from the air and I have to admit I'd been content to keep them bottled up, which was probably an error on my part.'

'I vaguely remember reading your report, *Centurio*. We lost a *strix*, if I recall.'

'Yes. She and some ground forces pursued several wanted Zealots into a trap. I lost men and matériel and they shot her down from within the defile.'

There was a collective gasp at this; it was almost impossible to take down a *strix*; they were supremely manoeuvrable, silent and productive of irrational fear in almost everyone who encountered them.

'Fortunately, the aviatrix was able to suicide before they got to her. I think they'd have raped her and then torn her limb from limb.'

'Yes.'

'The Zealots knew the machine's value, managed to overcome their fear and horror of it and dragged it away to a warm, dry cave. They then offered me a trade: three prisoners I was holding for interrogation in the *castrum* in exchange for the *strix* body. I was tempted; those things have an astronomical unit cost, and a quick retrieval would mean rapid healing and fusing with a new learner in Damascus.'

Cynara—and she was not alone in this—was transfixed at hearing intimate details of the *strix* program. She knew it had burst from among the brains trusts at *Collegia Roma* and a government body called—innocuously and uninformative-ly—'Military Projects' more or less fully formed, a bit under twenty years ago. The latter was funded partly by the army, partly by industry and partly by individuals, usually through endowments. It had a charter from the Senate and an exemption from the publication of annual financial reports. It made up for this secrecy by providing all its unclassified research free of charge to every major public library in the Empire— she'd read some of their quantitative management papers in Rome while she was studying—although that still left a great deal of classified material.

'Ben Yusuf warned us that it was a trap, and that Iscariot had a beautiful spot to hide in the walls of the defile, and was going to shoot me from there. Apparently he filled his waking hours with terrible curses, swearing to drown me in my own blood. Then he planned to come for Soraya.'

'Yes.'

'I feigned nonchalance, but the information frightened Soraya, who'd been disowned by her family. I was all she had, and she clung to me. Ben Yusuf was sorry for the effect of his words but couldn't take them back.'

'What did you do?'

'Refused to go in person, Procurator, and—unsurprising-ly—the deal was off.'

Pilate pressed the pads of his fingers together and looked at Linnaeus and Cornelius. 'Counsel?'

Cornelius stood up.

'I wish to raise a matter before the court.'

'Raise it, *Aquilifer* Getorex. There's no jury for me to send out while we engage in legal horsetrading.'

'I seek to have this witness declared hostile.'

Pilate said nothing for several minutes; Cynara could see him contemplating matters in his own mind. He dangled his reading glasses from one hand, swinging them back and forth.

'I can see why you might request such a declaration, *Aquilifer*,' he said at last. 'Ask your questions, then, adhering to the normal rules of cross-examination. I will constrain you, however, should you become too aggressive. *Centurio* Andrus has provided invaluable context in this matter.'

Cornelius turned to face his brother officer.

'Your relationship with the Suspect hasn't always been so cosy, has it?'

'No, it hasn't.'

'And that was to do with the manner in which you acquired your woman, was it not?'

'It was, *Aquilifer*.'

'Did you or did you not engage in marriage by capture?'

'I did.'

There was an audible gasp around the courtroom. Cynara noticed that many of the press people—especially the women—looked horrified. She watched their stares track downwards towards the pregnant woman in the public gallery, who had just returned.

'And how did Ben Yusuf react to that?'

'He accused me of *porneia*, *Aquilifer*.'

'How did you react?'

'I laid him out.'

'Who do you think you are, *Centurio* Andrus? Romulus?'

'*Centurio* Andrus, you don't have to answer that,' Pilate said.

Cornelius rested his hands on the podium. His question

had drawn laughter and Cynara could see that Andrus was waiting for it to subside. His face was flushed and his asymmetric eyes blazed. She had a strong sense he was not a man to cross.

'I will answer, Procurator, if granted leave to explain myself.'

'I grant you leave.'

'My answer is no, *Aquilifer*, and this is why. Soon after I was made an officer—nearly eight years ago now—I began to look for a woman to be my companion and to bear my children. There was a girl who worked in the haberdashery in Sepphoris that handled many of our uniform repairs and requisitions. I saw her quite a lot and I liked her. We all knew that Judaea was more traditional than at home, but I thought that was no real hardship. I am from the rural south; there it is the custom for the man to approach the woman's parents and ask them if he can court their daughter—'

Cynara saw several of the city born and bred Romans smiling condescendingly. She remembered it from her time in Rome; travel outside the cities into the countryside and it was possible to find the ramrod straight Romans of legend. They could still shock with their open physical affection and their frank enjoyment of sex, but they produced armies of healthy, pink-cheeked children and the man a woman first slept with tended to be the man she married shortly thereafter.

'—so I found out where they lived and went to call on her parents in the proper way.'

Cynara felt the cold stone in her stomach settling again.

'What happened?'

'The father spat in my face and the mother said that if their girl went with one of the *Romoi* they would sit *shiva* for her. I found out later what that meant. I tried to explain that I hadn't touched her and that while I wanted to very much, it would only be if she desired me as her husband.'

Cynara could hear her heart beating.

'A few days later, we found a body outside the barracks gates. It was the girl from the haberdasher's. She had been stoned, and there was a leather garrotte around her throat. She was hard to recognise; I remember having to look closely at her hair, and at the silver bands around her wrists.'

Cynara felt—again—the cold, creeping dread of the morning. The courtroom was silent as an owl's wing save the ticking of the clock behind Pilate's bench. Agrippa was looking at her and shaking his head. Andrus's voice was flat and cold with suppressed fury.

'I felt terrible shame at my failure to protect her, that everyone in the barracks had seen her body defiled like that. I despatched a squad to her parents' house. Her brothers admitted that they had carried out the killing, even though the Rabbi had tried to stop them. They were proud of it, they said. I ordered them executed on the spot and their bodies signed and exposed.'

Cynara could see two boys pushed to their knees in the dusty village square, two legionaries barely older than they were at their backs, carbines pointed at the base of the skull. Cornelius's hands hung loosely at his sides. He blinked repeatedly.

'Have you stopped it? This... this killing?' Pilate's voice was high and strained.

'Oh, it's getting a lot rarer, Procurator,' Andrus said softly. 'They fear our wrath.'

'Yes.'

'I waited a long time. I did not want another dead woman.'

'Yes.'

'But I still wanted a wife and children.'

'Yes.'

'When I saw another one I liked—and I'd been watching

her for a while, believe me—I did my best to get clear consent, like our men did with the Sabines. I asked her if she wanted to be a citizen. I asked her if she wanted to be a citizen with me. Soraya's an educated woman, in the best school in Sepphoris, too. She's much smarter than me. She knew that meant she would come with me and bear me three children.'

Cornelius nodded.

'After I took her and then killed her brother, I went to her parents and offered blood money and bride price, for the brother and for her. I had a lot—I'd been saving for eight years—but they weren't interested. I contemplated throwing a bagful of money and valuables over the wall, but in the end decided against it. I suspected they'd throw it back.'

'Yes.'

'I have at all times tried to act with honour, *Aquilifer*.'

'No further questions, Procurator.'

Just as Pilate turned towards Linnaeus, Cynara saw Soraya half stand and half prop forward.

'Oh no!'

She flicked her hands beside her head and buried her fingers in her hair.

'I've made a mess.'

Cynara watched with some relief as a statuesque black woman stood, excused herself to the people sitting beside her and trotted down the aisle.

'Don't worry, your waters have broken,' she said. 'The baby is ready to come, now.'

Several things happened at once. A decent number of Romans started applauding. Pilate told everyone save 'relevant people' to remain seated. Andrus ignored this, planting one hand in front of him and vaulting smoothly over the front of the witness stand. The black woman reached Soraya just before Andrus did, holding her hand and encouraging her to walk into the aisle.

'Who are you?'

The black woman pointed to something sewn into her clothing.

'I'm a midwife. You need to come with me.'

At that moment Andrus tried to pick her up. She swatted him away. 'I want to walk.'

He looked hurt.

'It's better for her to walk, *Centurio* Andrus. She'll feel more comfortable.'

Cynara realised at that moment that the midwife was the prosecutor's woman; he had turned to watch her and was positively glowing with pride. She directed traffic now, dispatching Andrus to call the Æsculapion with his army health insurance number and one of the orderlies to Antonia's infirmary for towels, hot packs and dry clothing.

'We've only got men's things,' he said, faintly horrified.

'Doesn't matter,' the midwife snapped. 'As long as it's big. And you need to report back to me when you've done what I've told you to do. We'll be in the loo.'

This they understood, and bolted for the door.

The midwife and the expectant mother followed them.

'And on that note,' Pilate said, 'I think we'll have an adjournment.'

FAMILIA

Claudia went home before Andrus took the stand. The young legionary detailed to the task drove her up to the residence's main entrance and escorted her to the front door, where he handed her over to two other men—their usual guards, Claudia recognised the one with the big smile—and then took his leave.

She found Jerusalem's security suffocating at the best of times but her husband had become paranoid since Sunday, and the soldiers, armoured cars and MRAPs that filled the streets and squired her about made her feel unpleasantly like some eastern potentate's consort. *All I need now*, she thought, *is a bulletproof limousine.* The battle through the streets—only a mile or so—had taken the best part of an hour, although when the soldier suggested a mounted escort to clear away the mass of people blocking their path she declined, despite the taste of dust in her mouth.

'The local people already think we're satraps. Call in a mounted escort to shove them out of my way and you'll remove all doubt.'

Zoë was clearing away the remains of lunch, dodging around the dog. Claudia asked after Antony and Camilla, bending down to scratch Nero's ears. Antony was kicking a ball around the terrace with Milos, Zoë said, while Camilla was swimming. Nero had been with Antony. 'He fetches for hours,' Zoë added. 'Sometimes, I think his heart will explode.' Claudia poked her head into the baths, watching her daughter shear through the water with long, graceful strokes.

Antony appeared, covered in sweat and flushed from the sun, an equally sweaty Milos at his heels. The latter had his arms full of towels and bathing equipment and had to trot to keep up as the boy made his way into the *tepidarium*.

'Have you had any troubles?' Claudia asked.

'No, *Kyria*, although Camilla is grumpy,' Zoë said. 'She slapped Dana for overcooking the pasta and then locked herself in her room. She started swimming about half an hour ago.'

'Well she hasn't burnt anything down or blown anything up, which is some consolation.'

Claudia found Dana cleaning the master bedroom and making the bed. The floor was wet where she'd mopped it. She'd clearly been crying.

'When you're finished there, I'd like a bath.'

Dana stood up, her cheeks streaked with tears.

'I'm finished now, *Kyria*.'

'Good,' Claudia said cheerfully, 'you can come with me and relax a little before the men come home.'

'Is the trial interesting, *Kyria*?'

'In some ways, yes, although I wouldn't want to make a habit of going to watch them. There's a reason I didn't study law.'

Dana smiled, almost skipping as she collected towels and oils for the baths. Claudia got the impression that she was glad to see the *materfamilias*.

Camilla had finished swimming and disappeared by the time Claudia and Dana arrived in the *frigidarium*. Antony was sitting on the side with his feet in the pool, hair plastered to his head as he contemplated the water.

'Where's your sister?'

Antony shrugged. 'I think she might be drying herself on the terrace.'

Claudia noticed that Antony had the beginnings of a breakout on his chin and a light dusting of hair under his nose.

'Is that a trace of bumfluff I see on that manly lip?'

He shrugged his shoulders self-consciously and pushed his hair back from his forehead; it stuck straight up. He then folded his hands across his lap and leant forward, concealing his crotch and looking away from Dana in particular. The two women smiled as he sprang up and bolted out of the baths.

'He's very sweet,' Dana said, her gaze following him as he went.

Claudia looked at her, her expression severe.

'He's to wait until he's sixteen, Dana.'

Dana nodded, looking into her broken reflection in the water.

'My parents gave my older brother the use of a serving woman when he was thirteen, he was so consumed with lust,' Claudia went on, 'which solved the immediate problem but didn't take into account the possibility that he would fall in love with her.'

'What did your parents do?'

'Sent her to work in a relative's household. My father was a leader in the abolitionist movement. It wouldn't do for his son to be seen to make use of a system that was pervasive under slavery. Roman men always used their slaves. My father was very angry with himself afterwards, admitting his mistake in indulging my brother. If Antony shows he wants you, you are to tell me immediately.'

'Yes, *Kyria*.'

'And if you seduce my son, you'll be dismissed and I'll refuse to provide you with a reference. There are plenty of good-looking young men in X *Fretensis* who would be very glad of female company. Go there if that's what you want.'

Claudia had Dana dry her, lightly oil her skin and help her dress before she went in search of Antony. As she padded down the cool tiled corridor in her bare feet she noticed

Linnaeus and Fotini had returned; Linnaeus was on the *vocale* while Fotini was standing in the middle of the room unbraiding her hair.

'Well, Drusus, he's a decent young chap. I think he can be reasoned with once he comes to the throne,' Linnaeus was saying.

At some point during her sideways glance Claudia noticed that he had their *vocale* switched across to the secure line—the little silver lever was twisted to the side—and was writing *Charter–Parti Populares* in bold orange letters on a large piece of stiffened yellow card beside him. It struck her as irregular—that line was for official business—but she shook her head and thought, simply, *oh, politics.*

Antony had retreated to his room. Claudia could hear furtive noises coming from within; she waited until he'd finished what he was doing and then counted to thirty before knocking on his door and walking in. He was under the covers, curled up on his side and staring straight ahead. She sat down on the edge of his bed.

'Go away,' he said miserably, not moving.

'You want to have sex with Dana, don't you?'

'No, Mama. I want to have sex with Dana, and with Zoë, and with Fotini, and with the woman on your bedroom ceiling, and, yeah, with lots of others. One after the other, preferably.'

She laughed at him, leaning across to stroke his hair off his forehead. He flinched at her touch at first, then visibly relaxed.

'I'm sorry, Mama.'

'Don't be. It's normal. Sex is a gift—'

'—from the Goddess, I know. I do go to school.'

Claudia heard footsteps behind her; she turned and beheld her husband standing in the doorway, Nero at his heels.

'I take it we're having the facts of life talk?'

'Oh, he knows the facts of life well enough. I'm trying to dissuade him from fucking the servants, and the servants from offering themselves to him on a platter.'

Pilate laughed and stepped into the room.

'Go away,' Antony said again, burying himself further under the covers. Only the top of his head was visible now.

'Who do you want to fuck?'

'Dana, mostly.'

Pilate looked at his wife. 'And she's shown an interest?'

'She has.'

Claudia suspected there'd already been fumbling touches and gentle kisses behind bits of statuary and in the niches of the *caldarium*.

'She likes me,' Antony said from beneath the covers, his voice muffled. 'She wants it.'

'No, Antony, there are rules,' Claudia said. 'What important anniversary do we celebrate next month?'

He sounded like a frog in a drain, his voice far away.

'Abolition.'

'Very good, Antony. Do you understand, now?'

He sighed. 'Yes, *Domina*.'

Pilate snorted. Claudia shot her husband a filthy look.

'That's not funny.'

'Sorry, dear, yes it is.'

Antony's voice floated out from under the covers once more. 'What am I supposed to do? This is driving me *nuts*.'

Claudia looked down her nose at her husband. 'One for the *paterfamilias*, I think,' she said, turning on her heel and walking out.

Linnaeus and Fotini had vanished and Aristocles was busy in the kitchen when Claudia returned to the dining room. Camilla had changed and was reading on the sofa in a short tunic and a pair of Marius's camouflage trousers. These were loose on her, sitting on her hips and exposing her stomach where the tunic had ridden up.

'Mind you don't go outside dressed like that,' Claudia said. 'It's unbecoming.'

'I won't, Mama,' she said. 'I just wanted to wear something of his.'

Claudia understood this, and did not press her.

'I heard you hit Dana for bad cooking.'

'Yes, I did.'

'Sometimes discipline is necessary, Camilla, but not for poor food, and never physically.'

'It was inedible, Mama. Really and truly. Even Aristocles was upset with her.'

'That doesn't give you the right to hit her. And Dana doesn't work for you. She works for your father and me. Her discipline is not your concern.'

'I'm sorry, Mama.'

'You need to apologise to Dana.'

Camilla sat up straight, boggling. 'You *can't* be serious!'

'I shall stand over you while you do so if necessary. I've just been discussing abolition with your brother. Should I go through it again for your benefit?'

Camilla realised it was useless to argue the point. 'No, Mama.'

'Well, let's go and find Dana, shall we?'

Pilate stepped into the room, beaming, Nero trotting behind. The dog bounded towards Camilla, perhaps expecting Marius. He leant against her legs, his tail thumping the floor. She smoothed back his ears. 'I'm not Marius,' she said. 'I only smell like him.'

'Well, I think that's been sorted, at least for two or three years. He knows how to keep himself entertained without company. We flog him and fire her—very simple—if need be. If he still fancies her in three years' time he can screw her arse off then with our approval.'

Aristocles rang his little bell, summoning the family to supper. Perhaps out of force of habit, Linnaeus and Fotini also appeared, both of them with wet hair. Pilate dispatched Dana to attend to them on the glassed-in terrace closest to their room in Herod's maze. Claudia noticed the relief on Antony's face when he saw that Dana was not serving him. His gaze ate greedily enough at Zoë, of course, but Zoë was Athenian and conservative and so avoided going to the baths at the same time as anyone else in the household. Claudia remembered— strange, she thought, *how it comes back to you*—Dana leaning over Antony at table to serve, her generous breasts pushing out against her tunic, which was always low cut.

'Where's Dana from?' Claudia asked Pilate in dialect, so Antony and Camilla could not understand her. Pilate shook his head.

'I'm not sure,' he said. 'Not Corinth, her accent's too good. Smyrna, maybe.'

Both children were used to their parents claiming privacy by reverting to Samnite or Oscan. Camilla poured herself a glass of white and looked across at her father. She did not like being cut out like that, and enjoyed it when Marius was present; he understood both languages.

'Was it your case that had the miracle?'

Claudia spun to face her daughter, cutting her husband off mid-sentence. 'What miracle?'

'It was on the news. He brought a soldier's *pais* back to life. The dishy one from *CR* was out in front of Antonia going on about it.'

Pilate sighed. 'Ah, not exactly, Camilla; he stopped him from dying. It would seem the ladies and gentlemen of the press have already commenced their usual round of exaggeration and invention.'

Claudia looked from her husband to her daughter, noticing that even Antony was entranced, leaning forward and ignoring Zoë completely, making it difficult for her to serve up his food.

'You can't be serious, Pontius.'

'Today has been something of an education,' Pilate said. He gave a potted summary of Andrus's testimony, watching Claudia and Antony's eyes grow wide and Camilla's wheels turning.

'There must be an explanation,' Claudia said at last. 'There has to be.'

'Aristotle says that the gods cannot and will not intervene in the natural world,' Camilla said tartly.

'Aristotle says a lot of things,' said Pilate, his eyes slitty and fierce. 'No one has suggested a divine origin for this... event. If I read the evidence right, Ben Yusuf has no idea how he did it, and appears to be afraid of his own talent.'

'You cannot possibly believe this, Pontius. The medics at the Æsculapion must have made a mistake with the diagnosis.'

Pilate nodded. 'There is that possibility, although a ruptured liver is difficult to miss.'

'Papa,' Antony broke in, 'has he done it more than once?'

'Allegedly, Antony, but none of the accounts in his dossier meet the required evidentiary standard for a court of law. This one does. I've got the boy's medical records and a photograph taken when he was admitted to the Æsculapion. I've got an account by two transparently honest serving officers. I've got a recent photograph of the soldier and his *pais*.' He paused at this point; Claudia saw that behind the attempt to clarify things for his son there was a real sense of perplexity.

'I could take it further and drag it up to the criminal

standard of proof by tracking Propertius down and putting him on the stand,' he went on, 'but I don't think that's necessary. It's also irrelevant. Ben Yusuf's on trial for breach of the peace, felony murder, malicious mischief and failure to warn. His other activities—no matter how impressive—have no bearing on those charges.'

'It would be a shame to kill someone who can do that stuff, though, Papa.'

'Maybe, maybe not,' Pilate said, his voice soft. 'I find the idea that he can't control it rather troubling. What if he decides to start blowing things up, or setting wildfires?'

'You're sure he struggles to control it, Papa?' Camilla asked. Pilate could see her thinking, her smooth forehead furrowed. He nodded vigorously, his mouth full.

'That came out in Andrus's evidence, and it's shot through all the other accounts in the dossier. Only part of the incident where Roman troops rescued him from being flung off a cliff arose out of the way Irie Andrus got a wife. Several people—including some of Andrus's own troops—mentioned Ben Yusuf's failure to perform in his home village.'

'There are such things as Æsculapions,' said Claudia, to no one in particular. 'Miracles happen there every day.'

Camilla smiled. 'There is an explanation, then—a mathematical explanation.'

Both Pilate and Claudia looked at their daughter. She was careful, as a general rule, not to humiliate other people with her numerical facility. Marius would spout statistics until the cows came home, which meant people tended to switch off. Camilla's interventions—because rarer—excited admiration and interest. Even Zoë and Aristocles had stopped to listen, plates and cups in hand. 'With a large enough sample size,' Camilla said, 'any outrageous thing is likely to happen.'

'I don't understand you,' said Pilate.

'Think of it this way, Papa. Assume that a given event happens with a probability of 0.1 per cent in one trial. That's a pretty unlikely event. The probability that this unlikely event does *not* happen in a single trial is therefore 99.9 per cent, that is 999 in 1000.'

Pilate struggled to remember his high school statistics while Antony hung on his sister's every word.

'This is for a single trial, yes?'

'Yes, Papa. And for two trials it would be 0.999 and then 0.999 again. If the trials are not connected in some way, overall 0.999 times 0.999. For five trials the overall chance is five 0.999s multiplied together, which comes to about 0.995. For 1000 independent trials, the probability that the event does not happen in any of them is a thousand 0.999s multiplied together, which comes to 0.368 or 36.8 per cent.'

'Because it can still happen in some of them. Yes, I see now.'

Camilla warmed to her theme. 'The probability that the event happens at least once in 1000 trials is thus 1 minus 0.368, which equals 0.632 or 63.2 per cent. This assumes an event with a probability of 0.1 per cent in a single trial.'

Pilate waggled his head from side to side.

'Now, where the numbers get really interesting is when you make them bigger. The probability that the unusual event happens at least once in 10 000 trials is thus 1 minus 0.999 multiplied together ten thousand times, which is equal to 0.99995; that is, 99.995 per cent.'

Pilate shook his head. 'Please repeat that in comprehensible Latin, Camilla.'

'This means that your *unlikely event* has a probability of over 99.9 per cent for 10,000 chances. In other words, *even given a highly unlikely event*, the chance that it *never* happens, given enough tries, is even more unlikely.'

'You're really smart,' said Antony, his voice tinged with awe.

'Obviously we're dealing with something much more unlikely than 0.1 per cent in one trial,' said Claudia.

'Of course,' said Camilla. 'What's the population of the Roman Empire?'

Pilate put his hand over his mouth. 'I don't know, to be honest—I haven't looked at the latest census data—three hundred million? Four hundred million? I know it's growing quickly.'

'Your unlikely event is $1/N$,' Camilla went on, 'where N may be the population of the Roman Empire.' She smiled again. 'Is that not a truly large number?'

'*Touché*,' said Pilate.

'So does that mean it is a miracle?' Antony asked.

'No,' said Camilla, 'just very unlikely.'

PLEDGES

Cyler made his way to the North-West tower via his locker in the *contubernium*. Cirullo was stretched out on his bunk, one arm flung back, snoring. The other beds were empty; everyone else was on duty somewhere in the city. He propped on his heels and opened his locker as quietly as possible, retrieving a heavy gold chain. He let the flat gold links—patterned after fish scales—flow between his fingers before dropping the chain over his head and hiding it inside his uniform.

'Lucullus?'

Cirullo was awake, sitting on the edge of his bunk. Cyler turned to face him. Cirullo smiled; Cyler didn't particularly like the expression.

'Off to see snaky lady?' he asked.

Cyler slammed his locker door and drew himself up to his full height.

'You know, Cirullo, there's a new drink you can get in the mess. It's called Shut The Fuck Up. You should try it.'

Cirullo looked self-conscious and apologised; his tone caught Cyler by surprise. He chewed his bottom lip and stared at the floor.

'I'd like to meet one... one of the snake women. I ain't had nothing but whores since coming to this shithole province.'

Cyler pursed his lips, folding his arms and nodding. He looked down on Cirullo.

'I can introduce you, yes,' he said, 'on two conditions.'

Cirullo's face was desperate.

'Whatever you say, Lucullus.'

'One, you'll ask me the same favour in the mess, in the presence of witnesses. Two, you'll stop calling them snake women. Deal?'

Cirullo looked pissed off.

'You drive a hard bargain, Lucullus.'

'Let me know when your cock wins out over your attitude.'

Cyler turned and walked out. He could hear Cirullo masturbating as he climbed the stairs.

The two aviatrices on duty admitted him with smiles and giggles and comments to the effect that Julia was going to come back to something nice in her bed. He grinned gamely but had to admit he was desperately tired. It was all he could do to lock her door behind him, strip off, hang his dress uniform up to air and crawl into her bed.

Whatever this dream was, it was very pleasant... and he seemed to have voluntary control over bits of it. It involved Magilla Macer—his favourite playback singer—giving him a tender and attentive blowjob and responding to his suggestions as he made them. He'd had dreams like this before, when he was a boy. He remembered his mother telling him to attempt something impossible in the world of the dream, then he would know if it were 'real' or not. He held his hands up in front of his face and tried to poke his right index finger through his left palm.

'You're awake,' Julia said, 'and I'm here.'

She had her headtail coiled around his cock and was licking the head. He was very erect. She slid her hands up his sides and flicked his nipples. He went to pull her along his body.

'Let me kiss you, Julia, please... I've been thinking about kissing you all day.'

She made humming noises as she worked, pushing his hands away from her armpits. He stroked her shoulders and arms instead.

'I want to see what you taste like.'

She sucked him until he came in her mouth, only then letting him sit up and pull her body along his so they could kiss. He got a mouthful of his own in the process and was surprised at how sweet it was.

'You taste like marzipan,' she said. 'I love marzipan.'

He flipped her onto her back and draped her legs over his shoulders, grinning his smouldering grin. 'Now, what do you taste like, I wonder?'

He grazed contentedly until she not only came but also squirted him in the eye. It trickled down his face and into his mouth.

'You're sweet too,' he said.

'Kiss me, Cyler, don't be greedy.'

He felt her headtails coil around his wrists and pull him alongside her; she licked and kissed his face, making small simpering noises. He held her to him with one hand and stroked her head with the other; she coiled her headtails in and around his fingers.

'That was good,' he said, 'in fact, that was amazing.'

'You've got a very long tongue,' she said.

He wriggled his fingers in front of her face. 'It's part of a matched set. Look at these things.'

'I'll be sorry when this trial's over,' she said. 'You'll have fatigues again.'

He cupped her breasts. 'Only for a bit; once I get my *licentia*, then you can come to *my* quarters.'

She stroked his cheeks. 'You really do mean it.'

'Very much.' He paused. 'How old are you, Julia?'

'Twenty-two.'

'Now, from what I've heard, you can't have children until discharge, yes?'

He could see her becoming teary. She rubbed her eyes and snivelled, nodding. 'That's in our contract. I'm sorry.'

'Shh, don't apologise,' he said, 'when is discharge? When can you go?'

'Service is counted from two years after they take us away for training. My sixteen years started at age fourteen. I'll be able to leave around twenty-nine or thirty. I'm not sure of the exact month.'

His face brightened. 'That's all right, then. Mind you, the day you're discharged, you're getting pregnant.'

She giggled. 'I don't doubt you'll make it happen, Cyler.'

'I originally wanted four, but since we have to start a bit later, three looks more realistic, so you can space them out and stay nice and healthy.'

'Well, three gets you the baby bonus,' she said. 'That's quite a bit of money. One for Mater, one for Pater, one for the Empire.'

He laughed, hooking his fingers under the gold chain around his neck. He wriggled it off over his bristles and undid the clasp. 'I don't think it'll fit over your headtails,' he said, 'so you'll have to sit up.'

She sat with her back to him, rolling her headtails into one and coiling it on top of her head as he passed the chain around her neck and fastened it. She touched her fingers to her throat.

'It's beautiful.'

'In consideration of love and affection,' he said. 'I promise to be faithful always.'

She twisted around to face him, putting her fingers to his lips. 'Don't make promises you can't keep. If you need the field brothel on campaign, use it.'

He smiled crookedly, showing his teeth. 'I'll just be imagining your head glued onto her body, anyway.'

'It's easier for me to be faithful,' she said. 'I have you to look forward to.'

Cyler kissed her. 'A Roman woman should be chaste.' He reached out and stroked her headtails. 'Can you, ah, inflict pain with these things?'

She bound them into two thick cords, which shot out and coiled around his upper arms, pinning them to his sides. He couldn't move; it was very impressive.

'You mean like this?'

He inhaled. 'Not quite... more like, ah, like a whip; like giving a beating.' He pointed to his back with one hand and made slapping motions. 'Lash me with them.'

She pulled a face.

'You know, make me your *prey*.'

Now she looked curious and aroused. 'That I understand,' she said, wriggling closer to him. 'That I can do.'

Cornelius went for a long run, the evening crisscrossing him with long fingers of fading yellow light. He could hear popping from the rifle range—the wind was in the wrong direction for it to be any louder—and he turned from the main path, cresting a low knoll that let him gaze out over Jerusalem Academy's deserted playing fields. In the distance he saw a groundsman mowing one of the ovals with a great metal grass-catcher sticking out in front of him as he worked. A woman was walking around the edge of the oval checking irrigation pipes as she went. Cornelius paused at the top of the hill, his face and chest streaked with sweat. He took his pulse at one-minute intervals for five minutes, calculating his recovery rate. He was relieved to discover his fitness was good, although he looked at the obstacle course and wondered how speedily he'd get around it these days.

Well look at this one, ladies, he remembered the Centurion from his Basic bellowing, *this here maggot is going to step over the obstacle he is so fucking tall.*

He turned towards the cross-country course and set off at a steady pace. He was ill at ease and could not put his finger on why, so had reverted to form: long stretches of intense exercise alone with his thoughts.

What disturbed him about this discomfort was that he should be happy. He had found his woman—*oh, have I ever got the one I want*—he was exchanging weekly letters with his daughter at home; his career was flourishing; Bella was happy with the cheque he sent each month for Ciara's school fees and horseriding lessons and art classes. In her last letter she'd told him she used some of the money to buy the girl a deerhound to go with her pony. She included a photograph of his daughter—daubed with mud, her hair pushed back from her forehead and sticking straight up—cradling a hairy puppy in her arms. It was clear the dog was going to be enormous.

He made his way along the course into a clearing and looked up as the stars winked into life. In the Mithraeum under Antonia, there was a glorious fresco of the Precession of the Equinoxes running the length of the room. When he'd first been initiated, as a young recruit—years ago now—the Pater had told him the beautiful stars were indifferent to man, that the world was not made for man. It was up to men, therefore, to read their own meaning into what was before them. Over the years, Cornelius had become good at this reading. He could give plausible explanations for many things other people found perplexing or horrifying or wrong. Word got around the legion, which meant there were decent numbers of young soldiers who thought he was the fount of all wisdom. Cornelius knew better, of course, but the constant flattering deference meant when he genuinely couldn't understand something, he felt like a fraud.

And his problem with the story of Propertius and his Boy was not that he did or did not believe it. His problem was that he couldn't understand it. *Why*, he thought, *did he do that? Why help people he hates? Why pretend to help people he hates?* He assembled mental checklists as he ran. Ben Yusuf admitted to starting a riot in the Temple and the State had miles of footage showing him doing just that, while armed. He had terrorists among his followers. He thought Romans as a class were morally corrupt. He put himself above his own people's priests and scholars. And yet. When given the chance, he had tried to help—or had actually helped, Cornelius couldn't be sure, and wasn't prepared to commit to one view or the other just yet—people wholly unlike himself.

Cornelius found Ben Yusuf's talent for ferreting out information about his subordinates disturbing, but now he was starting to wonder if that were all of a piece with what he'd done in Capernaum. He found himself remembering a play he'd seen years ago about a woman who had visions when she met people who were soon to die. It seemed a useful gift; she warned friends not to catch the 07.18 to Central or to avoid the porcini mushrooms at supper. In time, however, she saw only deaths—of her husband, her sister, her parents—as the visions colonised her mind. She slowly went insane. He found the story apt right now. *Whom the Gods would destroy, they first make mad.* If he really could heal the sick and wounded—even though it seemed to be patchy, as Andrus had detailed on the stand—then Cornelius suspected that whatever enabled it (a god or goddess, a malign spirit, a wild power) was doing to him what it had done to the woman in the play. He began to feel sorry for Ben Yusuf, and shook his head in self-reproach.

Cornelius took one last look at the glittering, indifferent stars above and headed for the barracks through the fragrant night air, his steps light for such a big man.

THE CAGE

The Pit at night was a different proposition from The Pit during the day. At lunch, Cynara had noted the overdone columns and the granite and marble foyer. Doric on the ground floor, Ionic on the second floor, Corinthian on the third. Romans were incapable of true architectural ugliness, but they had a taste for ornamentation that was challenging when one was drunk. She noticed the tiny yellow lights picking out every detail of sculpture and signage, dancers with gilded skin and oiled tresses on a raised dais in the gaming room, pageboys serving cocktails to customers identified by the Corinthians— different Corinthians this time—manning the front counter. One of the boys approached and presented them with glasses full of something bright blue streaked with yellow. She clinked with Agrippa and felt the concoction bite at the back of her throat. She could see people punting a large ball back and forth in the pool and shouting. It was at that point she noticed that whatever it was they were drinking glowed in the dark once it came into contact with human skin. Agrippa's lips were cerulean. She caught a glimpse of herself in the glass frontage of the gaming room as the pageboy led them down a wide spiral staircase. So were hers.

The boy took them to a glassed-in observation area set mid-way up a bank of tiered seats. Agrippa pulled her close to him, his fingers raking her side. She looked out over a compact, steepling well, its central point dominated by a fighting square. Above it, a shining metal cage was suspended on a system of chains and pulleys. She'd known what he was planning, but had no idea that there was a cage on this scale in Jerusalem.

At various points around the stands she saw more glass boxes like theirs, their privileged inhabitants lit up like fireflies thanks to spectral drinks. One woman, she noticed, had a translucent blue-green glow under her chin and in the hollow at the base of her throat. The well—the pit—was smoky and dark, dipped in inky blacks and autumnal browns. The brilliant flashes of light—from flesh, iridescent drinks, glinting metal—stood out against the shadows, a beautiful but disturbing sight. Naked girls—their skin gilded like the dancers upstairs and decorated with what looked like green glittering fish scales—began to bring in finger food and set it down before them. They sashayed to the music—not too loud as yet, but already underpinned by elaborate percussion reverberating up through the floor. Agrippa grinned and fed her a fat black olive. Various acts—singers, mainly—warmed up the crowd as the tiers began to fill. Cynara wondered where all the people were coming from, but then started to recognise faces: her own employees from the Empire, the woman who often served her at the bank, a merchant she knew by sight hand in hand with a *gallus* from the Fleet Fox. People stomped their feet in time to the beat. A boy bearing dainties joined her and Agrippa in their box. He too was naked, his skin silver and decorated with blue scales. Cynara smiled at him and—insatiably curious—reached out and stroked his upper arm. Agrippa looked on, amused.

'Those are attached,' he said. 'The scientists have them manifest as they mature, and fade as they age.'

The boy submitted to her touch, sidling up to her and offering her his throat, which was delicately marked with the blue scales; they were like glistening sequins. Cynara noticed they felt cool and metallic under her fingers, but also smooth and fine. Agrippa reached around her and ran the back of his hand over the skin beneath the boy's ear.

'You're very lovely,' he said.

'You both like me, I see,' the boy said. 'I am available for your pleasure afterwards, should you wish it.'

Cynara withdrew her hand as though she'd touched a hot stovetop. Her friends in Rome had told her this, that the attendants in the glassed-in observation boxes of the rich were on offer. She'd believed them—nothing in the *Caput Mundi* surprised her—but to see it first hand still came as a shock.

'That won't be necessary,' Agrippa told him gently. 'There will still be a generous tip, of course.'

The boy smiled and took his leave, while the two girls appeared with more food; one cut sausage on the table behind their seats and prepared a bowl of fruit, placing it before them.

'Where do those beautiful children come from?' Cynara wanted to know. They looked younger and darker than the attendants she'd seen in Rome.

'Oh, Persia,' he said airily. 'Slavery is still legal there.'

Once again, the baldness of it shocked her.

'I see.'

She looked at the three of them, noticing the girls' small round breasts and slim hips and the boy's shoulders. They were broadening, but still adolescent. She guessed that all three were younger than sixteen, but by how far was difficult to spot. Agrippa speared a piece of melon with his little fork and popped it into Cynara's mouth.

'Come, graze,' he said, his tongue touching her ear. 'I'd like to watch you eat, with those pretty blue lips.'

Cynara chuckled and ordered wine, leaning into him. He kissed her, smoothing back her hair and touching the back of her neck, just below the hairline. She felt a little thrill of pleasure course through her.

You are a very bad man, Severus Agrippa, but you are so much fun.

A man in a billowing grey robe and a black cape picked out with silver stars strode into the fighting square. He carried a heavy staff surmounted with an eagle in one hand and grasped his robes in the other. He stopped under the suspended cage and swept the cape out and around him so it shimmered and shone. He thumped his staff against the ground three times, cutting through the hubbub. He held his arms out and circled slowly.

'Listen all! Listen all! Listen all! Here's the final test, the truth of it, the great mark. Since the days of Homer's heroes, men have reserved the greatest feats and greatest fear for single combat. It's not every day that we bring out the challenger and the challenged, and certainly, in the fine and moral city of Jerusalem, it's not something we can do too often. And yet, just as Nestor contended with the giant Ereuthalion so, too, do the people of Judaea have a great story of challenge and single combat—'

Cynara knew what was coming and repressed a strong, instinctive desire to run down the aisle, leap onto the stage and force-feed the barker his staff.

If this involves a sling, I'm not going to be responsible for my actions.

'—Here, they speak of David and Goliath, where the battle was won by the mighty Jewish champion, Goliath—'

At that moment Cynara collapsed into gales of laughter. She could see Agrippa was pleased she was laughing so hard, but that he had no idea why.

'The giant just flattened the shepherd boy.'

He still didn't get it.

'Think of it as historical revisionism.'

'Of course. David's the Jewish one.'

He joined her, now, and the three children assigned to wait on them watched as they both shuddered with mirth.

'I shouldn't be laughing,' she said. Agrippa dabbed at his cheek with a silk handkerchief, shaking his head at her. His screen make-up had run.

'I should have cleaned this off,' he said.

The barker thumped the floor with his staff again, announcing the fighters. Cynara saw that the mistake went all the way down: 'David' was a big man, heavily muscled and brawny, 'Goliath' was notably leaner, but with a muscular efficiency about him. She doubted he was any younger than his opponent. Both were empty handed, a concession to local sensibilities: there would be no fights to the death in the Holy City. They were oiled and naked, glistening under the banks of lights. They would fight, she knew, using the techniques of the *pankration*, which while unarmed was still conducted with extraordinary violence. Only biting was forbidden.

'I present to you, then, two men with a gutful of ferocity and fear,' the barker was saying now, 'two men, to the death!'

Cynara sat up, shocked as the crowd roared its approval. The cage began to descend slowly around the two fighters as the barker retreated into the gloom, beating his staff against the ground. It was then that she saw that weapons—a metal pole with a vicious curved blade on the end, a pair of wooden truncheons, what looked like an oversized fork—were suspended from various bits of the cage. All were pinned high up, in difficult to reach spots. It was ingenious and nasty.

'That's illegal here,' she said. Agrippa touched the sensitive spot on her neck again; she felt her back begin to arch in response.

'Poor Jerusalem,' he said into her ear, 'so determined that no one's allowed to have any fun. No fighting, no fucking, no dancing, no festivals. I sometimes think the powers that be in this town would be happier if we reproduced by parthenogenesis.'

Cynara didn't want to watch someone die. She'd been to the cages in Rome and was disturbed to find the killing didn't repel her as she thought it might. For the first couple of times, she'd gone with friends and felt like the fifth wheel as they giggled and bonded and enjoyed each other's company. When she went again, it had been with Leon, her lover. To her dismay, not only had she found the experience enjoyable, she'd had passionate, animal sex with him afterwards. Watching now with Agrippa, she felt the same process starting over again.

One of the fish-scale children closed the door to their box, cutting the noise considerably. She approached Agrippa.

'Don Agrippa, there is a call for you from your wife. Will you take it at your table?'

Cynara watched as he frowned and scratched his ear. She felt a momentary pang of guilt, blushed and then sighed.

A Roman high school, a Roman academy, a Roman employer and mostly Roman friends. And I'm still a Jewish square.

'Put her through, yes.'

He was still frowning as the bell chimed and he leaned forward to take the call. Cynara focused on the silver finish on the handset. It was shaped like a trumpet; he rolled it in his fingers beside his ear as he spoke.

'Hello, dear.'

He shifted in his seat and kissed his teeth.

'Was it rape?'

'What's the problem, then? If she wants it, let him give it to her.'

'I know that, but—what is it—he's fifteen now, isn't he?'

Cynara realised soon enough that the boy referred to in their conversation was his son. She tried to remember a profile of him she'd read somewhere. She seemed to recall three children, but wasn't sure if all were by his wife or one by the voluptuous actress who was his concubine.

'Take him and get him chipped, yes, that's a good idea,' he was saying, 'and get her an abortion if she needs one. And tell him to keep his bloody head down. Only in our house, and only at festival time.'

He chatted compatibly into the device for a while. Cynara startled when he ended the call and looked at her, his expressive face earnest.

'It seems my endlessly randy son is at it again,' he said. 'We stopped him last time, because he'd only just turned thirteen, but he's fifteen now. I think he can handle it.'

Curiosity won out over good taste. 'But what about your law?'

'Some parents are stricter than others on the "sixteen rule",' he said, 'depending on the position their families and ancestors took on slavery. Many parents would give their son a slave woman to practise on. It stopped him pestering citizen women and made him a better lover when the time came to start courting.'

It was clear from his expression he liked this particular tradition.

Goliath—the lean one—was nimble at clambering around the inside of the cage, securing one of the wooden truncheons. He belted David with it a couple of times, but the bigger man used his weight and height to step inside the smaller man and deflect him into the base of the metal bars. Goliath sprang up immediately, his weapon still in hand. Fighters of all stripes stuck themselves full of drugs and were bloody hard to kill. The dosages were sold in metered phials, but there was nothing to stop enterprising individuals from buying at several apothecaries one after the other and self-medicating.

They also often came from among the poor, although there were certain better-off types who found the risk addictive and thrilling. She'd even known one of her fellow students—he'd failed his finals—go to a well-known *lanista* as a sort of protracted suicide note. She'd been appalled at the thought of seeing him die in the cage, but his erstwhile friends insisted on watching him whenever he was listed to fight. Leon told her he had dishonoured himself by failing his exams and then compounded the dishonour by going to the *lanista*. His death, however—if done properly—would reclaim that lost honour. She did not grasp this until the day she saw him die, exposing his neck to an opponent's pole-with-a-blade without flinching away. She saw her friends cheering the manner of his death, saw the crowd come to its feet in the smoke-filled pit on the Aventine as his body was borne away.

Even worse, she'd then gone back to the barracks—not her halls of residence, unusual this—afterwards and fucked both Leon and his younger *we-are-here-to-please-you* sidekick until she was unable to walk. 'We're alive,' they'd said to her over and over. 'We live.'

Evil is live backwards, she thought after that, lying between them as they slept.

She noticed they made no attempt to grab each other: their oiled skin kept them upright, stopping the bout from turning into an ugly grapple on the floor. Goliath delivered a vicious low kick to David's thigh, holding the truncheon in front of his face, his chest rising and falling as he gasped for air. The kick seemed to galvanise the latter, and he made a despairing leap for the bladed pole, pulling it down from above into his hands and circling it around his head. The polished steel gleamed in the light. Now they both had weapons the fight was more even, and the bigger man used his reach to slash at Goliath, scoring his shoulders and back. In time they faced each other like two bleeding statues, their movements blurred and imprecise from fatigue. The fight must have been going for nearly half an hour by this point; both men had had chances to land a killing blow, but were too exhausted to strike with effect. Her head was ringing from the noise of the crowd. Lust mixed with disgust, and fascination mixed with fear. She looked at Agrippa, wanting him but also wanting to be ill. He was leaning back in his seat, munching contentedly. From time to time he leaned across and fed her something.

'Surely they'll stop it,' she said. 'They'll both collapse from loss of blood.'

'This is a rare treat in Jerusalem. The crowd will expect to deliver a verdict.'

David hacked with his blade at Goliath's ankles. Both of them slipped around in the blood pooled on the floor, and Cynara half stood as Goliath pitched forward. His Achilles tendon had been cut. David stood over him, dripping, turning his weapon in his hands so that the blade pointed downwards. He swept the crowd with his gaze; the cage slowly lifted and the silver-cloaked barker emerged from the gloom. He banged his staff three times again, standing just clear of a pool of blood.

'Is it time to die?' he bellowed, turning and turning.

To her very great relief, the crowd spared him. She watched, hollow eyed, as attendants hosed down the blood and carried both men away on stretchers. Agrippa touched the back of her neck again, and she felt her resistance yield.

She promised herself, as he led her upstairs, that she would try to avoid comparing the accommodation to what she had at the Empire, but in the end she couldn't help herself. Agrippa's suite took up the entire wing on the top floor, and when he flung open the door she saw that a vast rectangular bath set into the floor stood between them and the largest bed she'd ever seen. She looked at the artwork on the ceiling and walls, a mixture of beautifully executed frescoes and painted reliefs of all the better-known positions and quite a few of the more obscure ones. She realised they were in the bridal suite.

'It's all CR could get at short notice,' he said.

He turned to the bar and offered her a drink. She shook her head and walked towards him, putting her hands on his chest. At that moment she realised the three fish-scale children had followed them. For a moment she thought the worst, but they brought out bathing equipment and towels from various cupboards and—this did impress her—scattered rose petals over the surface of the water.

Must institute that at the Empire when we reopen.

They walked towards Agrippa, who handed each of them significant sums of money. One of the girls went to kneel before him, but he caught her before she made it to ground.

'I'd rather you took our clothes for cleaning,' he said, nodding at Cynara and beginning to strip, 'and brought them back tomorrow morning first thing.' Cynara joined him, feeling—as she always did—self-conscious about undressing in front of strangers. The three took their clothes and headed out, closing the door. Agrippa drew her into his arms.

'Your kisses are like other people's fucks,' he said.

He took her by the hand and led her across the room. She then went ahead of him, down the stairs into the water; rose petals clung to her skin. She was surprised to feel him follow behind her, his hands resting on her hips. She'd become used to Roman men and their rituals; if they sent their woman into the bath, they would often pause to light incense at the nearest shrine before joining her in the water. Her friends had told her it was done to ask the spirits for good sex.

'You need to go to the *Lares*,' she said in between his kisses.

He looked at her, perplexed, doing what she had come to call 'the Roman head shake'. This was not a clear nod of approval or outright rejection, but a brisk waggle from shoulder to shoulder.

'I am an Epicurean,' he said softly, stroking her cheek. 'I have cast religion beneath my feet.'

Cynara slipped out of his arms and dripped her way across the tiled floor to the shrine. *My, Venus, you've let yourself go,* she thought. She then realised the statue was of Juno, goddess of marriage, not the goddess of lust. She shook her hands and collected her thoughts, trying her best to remember. She held one hand over the flame and then lit incense. She remembered sex was chthonic, and came from the earth. She pointed her fingers at the ground, touched her forehead and then turned to face him. He was in the very middle of the bath, smiling at her, the water lapping at his nipples. There was a rose petal stuck in his hair, which was flat and straight. He'd clearly dunked himself.

'That was very beautiful,' he said, 'seeing you do something from my people.'

'I think I've got the wrong goddess, though.'

He shrugged. 'Never mind,' he said.

She joined him again, pouring some astringent into her palm and cleaning his face of make-up. He would try to kiss her fingers every time she went near his mouth. They oiled and washed and massaged each other, touching and giggling in the warm water. In time he reached down and lifted her onto him; she coiled her legs around his waist.

They fucked in the bath, then dried each other off and fucked in the bed; he laughed at himself in the mirrored canopy above as she rode him. He was skilled but forceful, taking an aphrodisiac at one point to let him come at her again. He liked to take her from behind, his hands gripping her shoulders. This was intensely arousing and she caught herself telling him, 'make it like rape; you Romans have taken the city, the women are yours.' This delighted him and he leant over her, pushing her face into the bed and bringing one foot up beside her knee so he could bury himself in her further. She felt his balls slapping against her; at one point he dragged her back towards him with his hands around her hips. She started to whimper and he whacked her backside with his open palms, thrusting harder again. At that point they both came and then collapsed, hyperventilating and sweating as they rolled apart and stared sidelong at each other, exhausted, their faces and necks flushed and stippled. The roots of her hair were drenched; a trail of spittle leaked out of the corner of his mouth. She took one of his hands and rested it on her stomach; he spread his fingers and pressed his palm against her. They lay very still for some time.

'That was so good,' he said at length, reaching across her for another aphrodisiac with a shaking hand. 'Let's do it again.'

She nodded. He passed her one as well and she put it under her tongue. She saw the make as she did so; he used the same as Leon, and they'd always made her voracious. He then indicated he wanted her anally, but she shook her head.

'Not on the first night.'

He smiled at this, commenting that future assignations still left 'certain avenues unexplored'.

'I was thinking you wouldn't want a repeat.'

He kissed her. 'Tomorrow evening? A quiet meal first?'

She thought of returning home in the early hours, if only to present her father with a figleaf of respectability, but then remembered how Roman erotic manuals counselled men not to scarper after sex; the least she could do, she thought, was reciprocate. It was the civilised way to behave. She then had a vision of walking into her father's house buck naked, remembering that the servants had taken their clothes for cleaning. *Ah well, no actual choice, then.* When they'd finally fucked each other out—and this took some time, considering the pharmaceutical assistance they'd had—she curled herself submissively in his arms. He kissed the back of one ear and pulled the red silk sheets over both their heads. She felt his breath on her neck as he slept; she soon joined him.

In the morning, they dressed together—their clean clothes were outside, hanging on the door—and caught a cab to Antonia. They went via Joseph's house in the upmarket bit of the Jewish Quarter to collect some of Cynara's make-up and personal effects.

Confident her father would be well and truly asleep, she led Agrippa inside, sitting him on a sofa in the darkened house. He turned his face up and kissed her, chucking her under the chin as she leant over him. She bustled about, retrieving her things—including a different robe and cape for the next day—only noticing after ten minutes or so that her father was sitting in the kitchen, a cafetière in front of him and four or five empty coffee cups scattered across the table. His arms were crossed and he was red-eyed; he looked at Agrippa, who was dozing, his head thrown back. His voice was soft.

'Where have you been, Rivkah?'

Inhaling, she tried to master her shock and surprise; she stood beside Agrippa, one hand stroking his hair, which had already sprung back up.

'Out,' she said.

Joseph looked at her, his face sorrowful, not angry.

'With who?'

'A man,' she said neutrally.

'I can see that,' he said. Joseph looked towards the sleeping figure on his sofa, realising who he was at last.

'That's a lot of coffee,' she said.

The sun was rising and the room filled with soft grey light cut with yellow stripes through the shutters.

'What were you doing?'

Cynara blushed and looked down.

'Ah,' he said.

'I don't think I'll ever be able to watch *Newshour* in quite the same way again, Papa,' she said in Aramaic.

Joseph failed to smile, his glance bouncing from the reporter's familiar face to his daughter's. Agrippa stirred and slowly stood up, stepping around the sofa and curling one arm around Cynara's waist. She watched as he smiled and extended his hand, introducing himself. Joseph shook the hand limply, still looking at Cynara.

'My crew and I are staying at The Pit, in the Greek Quarter,' Agrippa said.

Cynara suspected Agrippa did not grasp just why her father was padding about the house in the dawn light. She hoped he'd had some sleep, that he hadn't spent the night pacing in a caffeine-fuelled haze of anxiety. She noticed he didn't offer Agrippa coffee. She waited for one of them to speak. Finally, she turned to Agrippa.

'Perhaps you should go on ahead to Antonia,' she said, 'and freshen up. I'll come in later, with Papa.'

Agrippa looked relieved. 'Star idea,' he said. 'Coffee at ten, during the first adjournment?'

She smiled at him. 'Of course.'

Agrippa inclined his head towards her father and took his leave; she heard his footsteps fade away down the front stairs. Joseph looked at her as she heard the taxi's engine cough into life.

'Are you going to marry this Roman?'

'Let me make you some breakfast, Papa, and we'll talk.'

She busied herself in the kitchen, availing herself of some fresh matzo bread and cream. She could feel him watching her as she worked, and it made her nervous.

'Papa, you're staring.'

'I wonder what at,' he said.

She faced him, plates in hand. 'What's that supposed to mean?'

'Am I looking at a harlot?'

'I'll wash your mouth out with something stronger than coffee if you're not careful.'

He avoided eye contact with her and cleared his throat. 'Well, what am I supposed to think? You come back here in the small hours being pawed at by some strange *goy*. You tell me nothing of what you're doing. What happened to the soldier, what's his name, Leon? He loves you, you know. What will it be next? You bring the next one under my roof and fornicate with him?'

She approached the table, setting the plates down. He accepted the food from her, breaking the bread in his hands.

'No, Papa, that's why I didn't bring Agrippa here. Your house, your rules,' she paused. 'As to what you're supposed to think, you might think your thirty-three-year-old daughter is capable of making her own moral choices.'

'But you are a Jew!' he said, his voice rising.

She put her coffee down and looked hard into his eyes. 'As are you, Papa. You, a member of the Sanhedrin, have just made yourself ritually unclean so you can't participate in Passover at the Temple. The busiest time of the year, too, for someone with your responsibilities. I suspect Kayafa's reaction bordered on the unprintable.'

'This is a trial! An innocent man may be executed.'

'And you could have agreed to give evidence through the Eye, but you didn't. You have prioritised your relationship with Ben Yusuf over the law. The nature of my relationship with Agrippa is different, but the principle is identical.'

He sighed and smiled grimly. 'What was your result in

rhetoric again?'

'You should know, Papa, you've still got the certificate.'

He brightened immediately. 'Would you like to see it?'

He bounced up and went into his study. Moments later, he came back with a bulging folio and began to leaf through the pages. She looked on in wonder.

'I didn't know you'd kept so much.'

He had her prize certificates, sorted into years; clippings from local papers; sports ribbons; an award for reciting Homer; a cast photograph from the musical, filled with faces she no longer recognised. Joseph found the rhetoric prize certificate and showed it to her.

'You got ninety-two per cent,' he said. 'The next closest person only got seventy-three.'

'Where does it say that?'

'I just remember; I asked your teacher.'

She laughed, tears prickling behind her eyelids.

'When you came home for Passover that year, you didn't eat a single vegetable or piece of fruit. Your brothers and I worried you were going to get scurvy.'

'Was I that bad?'

'I was proud that you were trying to keep kosher when you didn't have to. It can't have been easy in Caesarea.'

She wiped underneath one eye, thankful that she hadn't applied any make-up yet. She turned the last page; there was a copy of her academic transcript from the Hotel School and a clipping from the local edition of *Tempus* reporting her appointment as manager at the Empire. She turned towards her father.

'This is amazing, Papa. I had no idea.'

She slid the folio towards him and closed it. She noticed that his eyes were very bright.

'You know, there's something I could add to that for you.'

He raised an eyebrow at her. 'Hmm?'

'When I got my citizenship in Rome, they gave me a formal document, on parchment, with beautiful calligraphy. It folds open. Romans hang them on the wall. I could bring it home for you.'

'Thank you, Rivkah. I would like that very much.'

She reached for his hands, taking them in hers. 'I'm sorry I can't behave in the way you want me to. I don't expect you to approve... but if you can't accept it, please tell me, and I'll make alternative arrangements until I go back to the Empire.'

He harrumphed and swatted the suggestion aside one-handed. 'No, Rivkah, don't be silly. Why waste money on rent?'

PART VIII

He is no lawyer who cannot take two sides.

— Charles Lamb

Linnaeus and Clara could hear the racket as they stepped out of the robing room. People stood in little clumps, forming a rough circle around the source of the noise. Their arms were folded and their faces were crossed with expressions ranging from bemused, to amused, to irritated. A woman—Linnaeus could not see her, there were too many people in front of him, including several tall soldiers and Nic Varro—was remonstrating with someone in Aramaic. More people joined the crowd of onlookers. It occurred to him that the crowd had assembled itself with uncommon speed, and he didn't like it. He pushed past a couple of the soldiers while two others— seeing his court dress—stepped out of the way. He pulled Clara into his side and looked at Nic.

'What the fuck is this?'

'Ben Yusuf's mother just showed up.'

At that moment the crowd parted and Linnaeus beheld a solid, dark, middle-aged woman, her brown curly hair streaked with salt and pepper and rather distinguished, her eyebrows pencil thin, pointing her finger and yelling at his client. It took a moment for Linnaeus to notice how well dressed she was, how immaculately made up.

That robe is silk brocade.

For some reason Ben Yusuf's guards were walking him in

through the courtroom's main entrance. Ben Yusuf turned to face his mother while the two of them flanked him, as intrigued by the spectacle as everyone else. One had pushed the courtroom door halfway open and then stopped, his fingers bent back. The woman's face was scarlet. Linnaeus approached his client, hoping that CR and JTN and the other networks hadn't arrived yet. Linnaeus took a deep breath and stepped into the clear, touching her shoulder.

'*Kyria*,' he said, 'my client needs to go into court.'

She rounded on him, her eyes flashing, and he got a sudden sense of why Petros and Mary Magdalena had warned him against interviewing or calling Miriam Bat Amram as a witness.

'*Your* client?' she said in Greek. 'Your client has embarrassed his mother, dishonoured his father and humiliated his family.'

Linnaeus looked towards Nic Varro, who had moved closer to him.

'What's she going on about?' he asked in Latin.

'Don't think you can get away with that,' Miriam spat at him in her accented Latin, 'I speak your language.'

Linnaeus could see a CR crew out of the corner of his eye; the cameraman was using the bulk of his equipment to make his way to the front of the crowd.

Nothing like a bit of dysfunctional family entertainment for Megalesia. Great holiday viewing, folks.

'I'll tell you what's going on,' Miriam said in Greek, 'just so you know.'

She drew herself up and put her hands on her hips, facing him, her feet shoulder-width apart. She addressed the whole crowd, turning her head this way and that.

'First he runs away from home and doesn't stay working for his father like he should. Says he's doing his father's work. When the only father who ever mattered is the one who married me after I'd been chucked by one of you Romans.'

She made eye contact with two or three of the legionaries who were looking on. One of them flushed and looked down; another leered and grabbed his crotch. The whirring camera caught it all.

'This means we had to apprentice Yacob to his father's trade and send Martha and Simeon to the factories in Antioch. Then—I haven't finished, yet, don't you turn away—he gets Yacob into his silly religious fantasies and I'm starting to think my husband won't have anyone to inherit the business. And I'm not giving him my girls, oh no. They're for me, for the dress shop in Sepphoris.'

Ah, she's a dressmaker. Explains the clothes.

'Then when my dear husband dies, having given us the very best of himself all his life, this son of mine won't sit *shiva* for him, doesn't even come to the funeral and then tells me to let the dead bury their own dead.'

Linnaeus looked at Clara.

'Make an application for an adjournment,' he said. 'Twenty minutes or so. I've got to talk to our client.'

Clara nodded, pushed past the two guards flanking Ben Yusuf, and went into the courtroom. She was very pale. Linnaeus took Ben Yusuf by the arm and led him into the defence witness room. Miriam attempted to follow them. Linnaeus turned to face her, standing closer to her than most Judaeans found comfortable. She stepped back.

'*Kyria*, you can't come in here. It's off-limits to the public.'

Miriam made a vulgar gesture in his face and turned away, expectorating. 'Then he tells people that if they're going to follow him, they have to hate their mother and father,' she said to the large group still gathered outside.

Cornelius Getorex and his dark young clerk stepped out of the robing room. Linnaeus had never been so glad to see the other side in his life, especially when Cornelius started telling

people to disperse, ordering his men to begin seating specta-
tors in the public gallery, and upbraiding Ben Yusuf's guards.
Linnaeus closed the door to the defence witness room behind
him, noticing that Arimathea, Nic Varro, Petros and Mary
Magdalena were looking on with some anxiety. He turned to
face Ben Yusuf.

'What in blue blazes are you playing at, not sitting *shiva* for
your adoptive father?'

'I thought you had nothing but contempt for Jewish customs,
Andreius, after the questions you asked Kayafa yesterday.'

Linnaeus was very angry now.

'You don't get what it is that lawyers do, do you? Well, let
me tell you one thing we do. We go in to win the case on our
client's behalf. You do want me to win this case, I presume?'

'Yes, Andreius, I do.'

Linnaeus did not like the expression on Ben Yusuf's face;
it was somewhere in between insouciance and contempt. He
noticed Mary's hands were in front of her mouth and that she
was shaking her head. Nic had his arms folded around her
protectively.

'Did you really tell your mother to let the dead bury their
own dead?'

'Yes, Andreius.'

'What's the fifth commandment, Yeshua?'

'Honour thy father and thy mother, so that you live long in
the Promised Land.'

'Romans and Jews don't match up on many things, but we
do agree on this one. Whatever you say in that courtroom, do
not let it slip that you've been telling people to disrespect their
parents. You will lose every Roman in the room.'

'Yes, Andreius.'

Ben Yusuf looked at the ceiling. Linnaeus caught his beard
and pulled his head down so their gaze met. Ben Yusuf tried

to slap his hand away, but Linnaeus didn't let go.

'Every Roman child lights a candle for his ancestors and brings them wine and cakes at the family tomb each *Parentalia*. Every Roman child makes masks for his parents when they die and puts photographs and statues for their *manes* on the god-shelf. You Jews sit *shiva*. Different custom, same principle.'

'Some things are larger than mere custom, Andreius.'

Linnaeus had the strong sensation that he wasn't getting through. 'Look, you Jews believe things that make my hair stand on end. I think your God's got a complex, that your religion is joyless, vindictive, even absurd. However, leaving all that to one side, how many years have Jews been following this Yahweh character?'

Ben Yusuf flinched at Linnaeus's casual blasphemy.

'Many, Andreius.'

'Have some respect for the wisdom of your ancestors.'

Ben Yusuf turned to Ioanne.

'Go to her and comfort her,' he said.

The young man nodded and left the room. Linnaeus spun sharply and followed him outside, noticing that the crowd had gone. Miriam was seated on one of the wrought-iron benches, sobbing, her head in her hands. Ioanne sat beside her, one arm around her shoulders. Linnaeus walked towards the two of them.

'I'm sorry for your loss, *Kyria*,' he said.

She looked up at him just as Ben Yusuf's two guards emerged from the *Praetorium* and retrieved him from the witness room.

'He's going to get himself killed with all this God business,' she was saying. 'When he should be at home in the workshop supporting his family.'

Linnaeus was at a loss, thinking for a moment that Ben

Yusuf and his mother could have stepped out from the lyrics of a Victor Gerius song. There was the boy who joined the legions, the girl who went to the mill, the young couple at the abortionist's, the village where everyone left for the factories in the next province. One song in particular stayed with him, however, and reminded him of Miriam and Ben Yusuf and civilisation upended. It concerned a girl who told people in her remote Gallic village she wanted each day *to be more like them and less like you.*

'Well, it is unusual,' Pilate was saying, 'to abandon your family like that. He should be grateful to her for his existence and behave accordingly. And his adoptive father seems to have been an outstandingly decent fellow, teaching him a lucrative trade. Men do not like to raise other men's children.'

Pilate handed Horace his stainless steel cup and instructed him to check on the courtroom.

'I want to get this underway. I would like to go home at some point this evening, as would you, no doubt. Oh yes'—he paused—'you're welcome to stay overnight after I've thrashed the whole thing out with you. I'll have a room made up.'

Pilate dismissed Horace, leant back in his seat and read through his morning post and other notices. There was a note written in Cornelius's lovely hand. He opened it and smiled when he read its contents, chuckling at the lawyer's asides.

Soraya Iscariot gave birth to a healthy baby girl, Mira, 7 lb 11 oz at 0314 hours this morning after a twelve-hour labour. Mother swears fluently in three languages. Irie Andrus already twisted around daughter's little finger. Tried to name her after my woman. Everyone very appreciative of yesterday's adjournment.

'Events have rendered this man harmless, Procurator,' Linnaeus was saying, 'and events have also rendered him explicable. For all that he believes some very strange things, any bad things subsequent to those beliefs required instigation by other people, people who are now dead. The Defence will call witnesses making this clear. The Defence will also call witnesses pointing up the gulf between the Suspect and those who would see in him some sort of terrorist or agitator. Some sense of his views on the corruption in the Jerusalem Temple is therefore essential in this respect. You may still find his views objectionable or silly. I do not pretend otherwise. You will not, however, find them murderous or vicious.

'I have no doubt many from outside this province will dine out on its general strangeness: its religion, its itinerant holy men, its vastly powerful Temple, its tendency to get carried away over things we Romans consider trivialities. That sense of superiority is amusing but not helpful. It allows us to condemn that which we do not understand. If the last three hundred years have taught us nothing else, it is that the restless search for understanding is what has made us great, and made the Empire great.'

Cyler watched Linnaeus as he spoke. He wondered what even Linnaeus could achieve with what Cyler suspected was at bottom a weak case. He got the distinct impression that Linnaeus was pounding the table. He picked up a scrap of paper and scribbled away, handing it to Cornelius.

> If you have the facts on your side, pound the facts. If you have the law on your side, pound the law. If you have neither on your side, pound the table.

Cornelius smiled at him and nodded, although the edges of the smile were tinged with sadness.

Claudia had considered following Pilate, Linnaeus and Fotini into Antonia for another day in court, but decided she would spend a couple of hours reviewing a mathematics textbook—making use of Camilla's expertise—before giving herself the afternoon off and attending. She felt it was in Antony's interests that she be present to supervise for at least part of the day; there was little for either Antony or Camilla to do in Jerusalem in the lead up to Passover. It irritated her that both of them missed Caesarea's high-spirited fun at *Megalesia* and had done so every year for the last five years, especially when there was so little to offer in its stead: no theatre, no hunting, no horseriding, no lively social occasions with friends from good backgrounds. Antony, Claudia noticed, was still looking hungrily at Dana over his breakfast.

Claudia made much of her irritation with the law, but from time to time Pilate's legal work had at least intrigued her. She remembered the delicate negotiations involved in the merger of two publishing firms—one of which she'd worked for in days gone by—and some of the colourful characters they'd entertained in Rome and Tuscany: *lanistae*, corporate raiders, underworld figures and loan sharks operating just this side of the law. What her arty pals had in rhetorical flourishes, Pilate's wheeler-dealer clients made up for in sheer effrontery.

This trial, she had to admit, had drawn her in, and the two of them chatted quietly while Camilla checked the equations in Claudia's page proofs. *Whoopsie*, she said at one point. *That should be Σ, not $\int$.* Claudia gave thanks for her daughter's keen eye, but noticed that beyond yesterday's mathematical cleverness, Camilla was uninterested in the trial.

'Not your thing, is it?'

'I don't understand it, I suspect.'

Zoë brought them coffee and fruit, watching them anxiously as they worked. She was a lissom little thing, light and nimble in her movements, although today she kept pausing to fiddle with her clothes, wring her hands, and pat the dog.

'Zoë, you're hovering. What's the matter?'

The girl stood in front of them, her head down. She pushed a few strands of dark, curly hair behind one ear. Nero seemed to sense her distress, and he got under her feet in his attempts to stay close to her. She smoothed back his ears.

'I can't go back to Athens, *Kyria*.'

'I thought you were planning to train as a teacher. Why has that changed?'

'I let one of the soldiers have me,' she said, 'I think I love him. I can't go home.'

'Are you betrothed?'

'Yes, *Kyria*, since I was fifteen.'

'Bloody Athenians,' said Camilla. 'He's probably out freckle punching.'

'Camilla,' Claudia chided, 'that's nasty.'

'I was going to go to Antioch.'

'To the mills?'

'Yes, *Kyria*. The pay is higher. Maybe if I send more money home, my father will still honour me as his daughter.'

Claudia held up her hands. 'Have you ever seen a mill?'

'Only from the outside.'

'You'll sleep twelve to a room. Your wages will be docked if you're ten minutes late. You'll pay for uniforms out of that salary. You'll work from eight until midnight.'

Zoë's eyes grew wide at this. Claudia paused.

'Who is the soldier?'

Zoë looked towards the door, and Claudia had a sudden realisation that the fellow in question was the one Camilla called 'the man with the flip-top head'. Zoë beckoned him into the residence, shyly. His grin—if it were at all possible— was even broader than usual. Zoë smiled at him and flushed.

He took her hands. Claudia looked at him, her expression icy.

'I am not given to playing matchmaker, young man, but I hope you were serious when you talked this young woman into your bed.'

He nodded with enthusiasm.

'Yes, *Domina*, I was. I want her to be my woman. I told her that already.'

'Turn your arm out,' she said. He did so, showing the chip there. Claudia nodded, waving his hand away.

'How long does it have to run?'

'Two years, *Domina*.'

'Good. I don't want her pregnant before she turns twenty-one.'

'See,' he said to Zoë, his voice hushed, grinning again. 'The mistress wants us to have fun, first.'

Zoë blushed scarlet and poked his bicep. Claudia looked at her daughter for a moment, wondering what she should do, and then turned to Zoë.

'Does your father have his letters?'

'Yes, *Kyria*, he does. All of us went to school, too, and had odd jobs around the theatre.'

'Would he accept counsel from the wife of a Roman governor?'

'Yes, *Kyria*, of course he would. It's funny, at home. They let Roman women into the *andronites*, as though you are...' she paused, unable to articulate exactly what she meant.

'...Honorary males,' said Camilla, 'It's ridiculous.'

Claudia glanced sidelong at her daughter, noting her lively, clever face.

'I shall write to your father, Zoë,' said Claudia. 'I'll praise your industry and your choice of man.'

'Thank you, *Kyria*. Thank you so much.'

Claudia looked at the grinning soldier, appraising him. He was young and fit and boisterous, with straight white teeth set in a tanned face. The top third of one of his ears was missing, neatly sheared off, but his skin was otherwise unmarked. The cheeriness seemed real enough; he'd had a sunny disposition for as long as he'd been detailed to the official residence. Zoë gazed up at him with utter adoration. He stroked her hair.

'What's your name, soldier?'

'*Decurio* Caius Corbulo, *Domina*.'

She noticed he pronounced his first name with a hard, sharp click, adding no voice, like a real traditionalist. He was from *Gallia Cisalpina*, she established, and he was twenty-six. His siblings worked in the factories of the north; he was the oldest.

'My son needs to be supervised and entertained for the rest of the day, Corbulo. It will be your job to do so. You can't take him too far thanks to the terrorism.'

'I'll think of something, *Domina*.'

'And I want you armed with more than a pistol, as much for show as anything.'

He held up his rifle, smiling.

Claudia outlined her concerns about Antony and Dana and reminded Zoë that she was now permitted to bring Corbulo into the house at night (*when he doesn't have duty, of course*); the latter grinned hugely at this. She noticed Camilla watching the conversation with some gratitude; she would not have to supervise her brother if Caius and Zoë could be induced to do it instead.

Claudia called for Antony, a ten *denarii* note in her hand.

Nic Varro had just been excused and was stepping out from behind the witness stand when Claudia took her seat beside Fotini in the jury box.

'Where are we at?'

'If the locals didn't despise the Temple administration before, they will now.'

Claudia looked at Nic Varro as he took a seat in the public gallery. He held a folded set of charts and documents in his hands, resting them on his lap.

'That bad, was it?'

'If it weren't religion,' Fotini whispered, 'it'd be organised crime.'

Linnaeus stood up once the hubbub had died away, looking at Pilate. The latter scratched one eyebrow.

'The Jerusalem Temple offers services and sets the prices. If they set those prices in our currency then there would be no problem at all, but they demand scrip and control the exchange rate. That's just another way of setting a high price.'

'Exactly, Procurator.'

'If people don't want to pay that high price, they should worship a god that accepts cheaper offerings. The god market is competitive. Your client's attacking the right of merchants to set prices.'

Claudia repressed a strong desire to giggle. She'd suspected her husband would say something like this when the Temple had first been exposed to public scrutiny in the wake of the riot.

'There aren't a great number of alternatives in Jerusalem, Procurator.'

'Are you suggesting that the Temple is a coercive monopoly, Don Linnaeus?'

'Jews are born to their religion, and the law suppresses alternatives. If they want to make sacrifice, they have to come here.'

'Yes, Don Linnaeus, but that really only holds in Jerusalem itself.'

Linnaeus inclined his head.

'The Defence calls Matthias Levi,' he said, as the orderly left the court to retrieve him.

Matthias was a thin, cadaverous man, almost as tall as Nic Varro. His hair and beard were clipped short and his clothes—a long dark-red robe, almost to the floor, bound around the waist with a heavy grey sash—were expensive and understated. Claudia realised that his dark skin was due more to sun exposure than natural pigmentation. He swore on the Torah, and as he did so, Fotini leaned over and told her that Nic Varro had sworn by the *genius* of the Emperor and the *juno* of the City of Rome. Claudia raised an eyebrow; this was code for someone who believed in nothing but preferred to keep up appearances. Pilate had told her that in all his years as a lawyer, he'd never seen anyone use that form of words.

'I started with *CreditGallia* as soon as I finished school,' Matthias was saying. 'They'd just opened a big branch in Sepphoris and a few of us from the same year got work there, people with a good head for figures.'

'From the same year?'

'In my final year at school, Don Linnaeus,' he said. 'As far as I know, a few of them are still there.'

'Yes.'

'I thought the bank would be a good secure job, and would teach me something useful. I wanted to buy a house, and if you work for the bank, you get a much cheaper loan.'

Claudia heard a few giggles around the courtroom at this; he wasn't the first person to go to work at the bank for that reason.

'When *CreditGallia* won the tax collection contract, I was transferred to Capernaum to work in the office there. I'd been there for a few years when Yeshua first came to the town.'

'Were you happy at the bank?'

'In Sepphoris, yes I was. On the whole, people didn't resent me for my job, and I was able to get ahead.'

'But in Capernaum...?'

'I learnt what it is to be despised.'

Claudia noticed he was sweating along the hairline as he recounted the casual contempt the Galilean villagers directed at him. This ranged from people crossing the street to avoid him to an inability to find a Jewish wife.

'Eventually I contracted with a *hetaera* from Caesarea for three years. I wanted a companion, and I was already so unpopular with the locals that fornicating with a Greek concubine couldn't make it any worse.'

Pilate leaned over his bench, pressing his fingers together. 'Where is she now?'

'Sophie? She went back to the House in Caesarea. She thought about staying for another five years, but she didn't like living in Capernaum, and I wasn't going to get a transfer out of there any time soon.'

Claudia had a sudden and rather vivid image of a cultured Greek woman trying to live anywhere in the Galilee apart from Sepphoris. It couldn't have been pleasant for either of them.

'Over time, the hatred got worse. By then I was 2IC of the Capernaum office. A new head had just been appointed from Caesarea and didn't speak Aramaic. We had the boss and his wife over for a meal. We were having a few quiet drinks on the roof when things started landing on us.'

'You were being rocked?'

'In a big way. I had visions of all of us being tarred and feathered and run out of town on a rail. The boss—'

'This was Victor Lucius?' Pilate asked.

'Yes, Procurator. The rocking got worse, and Victor called Propertius at the barracks. Next thing we knew there was a battle between Roman troops with riot shields and tax protesters throwing turpentine bombs. My front garden was on fire, Victor's wife had bits of carbonised paper in her hair, and Sophia was threatening to go back to Caesarea two years early.'

'Not a good day, then?'

'Ah, no, Procurator, it wasn't.' He rubbed the top of his head and leaned forward. 'It was harder after that riot, too. It got that way that I couldn't walk down the street without being abused, while Sophia would get spat on at least once a day and if she were alone, she was constantly propositioned. Victor kept giving me pay raises but over time it became close to unbearable.'

'Yes.'

'Sophia went back to Caesarea and I spent the next six months in a deep dark hole. It came to a head when a local construction firm went broke and I became Capernaum's repossession man. I suppose I got fed up with taking people's houses off them.'

'And this became particularly bad after a local firm went under?'

Matthias rubbed the top of his head with both hands; Claudia could see he was struggling to convey just how upsetting he found his job. 'Look,' he went on, '*CreditGallia* are one of the better banks around the place when it comes to tax collecting. They're not crooked. They don't skim off the top like the previous lot did. But they're unsympathetic.'

Claudia watched her husband closely; he'd been behind engaging a new taxation contractor, and had chosen the Gallic bank because they had a good reputation for financial probity. Pilate was leaning forward over his desk, his fountain pen dangling from his fingers, listening intently.

'After that firm went under, Victor went postcode hunting through the surrounding district and extracted all the files where people had unpaid taxes or were more than two months in arrears. I had the job of serving processes on people who'd just received severance notices. There were times when people would be standing on the balcony with a notice in one hand and process I'd just served in the other.'

'And after summary judgment?'

'I'd turn up with a couple of legionaries and demand the keys. I've had people on the footpath begging me to stop. Once we took possession when a woman went into the Æsculapion to give birth. They came back and had no house.'

Claudia could hear his voice becoming strained as he spoke.

'I tried to be decent, to talk the bank down when it was being too hard. I tried to treat people with dignity, not as numbers on a spreadsheet. Sometimes that meant I'd get taken for a ride.'

'Such is the nature of commerce,' said Pilate, to no one in particular.

'After a while, I wrote a little speech, which I rehearsed. "I will take your house," I'd say. "Don't be under any illusions that I'm too nice to do it. I've done it before, many times, and I'll do it again. Because that's my job."'

'And you then met the suspect?'

'Yes. *CreditGallia* gave Jewish staff Saturdays off in lieu of Roman festival days. It was just after the mother and baby on the footpath, when I saw Yeshua speaking in the synagogue. He was saying that everyone can have redemption in God's eyes, we just have to repent.'

'And you repented?'

'I went up to him afterwards. I wanted to know if he meant what he said. Folks were inviting him over for supper left and right, you know, and I was having trouble getting close to him—people were stepping on my feet and shoving me back. I hadn't been in synagogue the whole time I was with Sophia, and not too often after that. He was the guest of honour, and people didn't want me anywhere near him.'

'Yes.'

'Anyway, he pointed straight at me and told everyone to

back off. "This is the man I wanted to see," he said, "I need a place to stay and something to eat, Matthias; you better get ready!"'

Matthias's eyes were now very bright.

'This caused consternation, and I appreciated—even more than beforehand—how unpopular I was around town. I was called for everything—the Romans' official bastard, crooked, cheat, thief, liar, man who lives with a whore—you name it.'

'Yes.'

'They went after Yeshua, as well. He was consorting with sinners, according to them—'

Pilate broke in. 'Sinners? You hadn't done anything wrong.'

'I'd done wrong in God's eyes,' Matthias answered. 'Living with Sophie'—Claudia noticed the friendly diminutive, he was clearly still fond of her—'collecting taxes for Rome. Repossessing people's houses and leaving them with nowhere to live—'

'I see. Go on.'

'He came to my house with three of his friends—Petros, Ioanne and Yehuda. Yehuda wouldn't step over my threshold. He just sat outside on the steps for the whole meal, until Yeshua convinced him to sleep in the servants' quarters.'

'That's consistent with everything else we've heard,' Pilate mused.

'But Yeshua, he just made me so warm; I'd never been so... warm in my life. The following morning I called in my servants, paid them out for the rest of the year and released them to the employment agency. I walked out the front door and went into the *agora*, to the *CreditGallia* office. I handed Victor my notice and cleared out my desk. My house was paid for. I owed no debts. I was an outward success... but in reality I had nothing, nothing at all. So I had nothing to lose.'

Pilate touched his golden wreath. He apologised to

Linnaeus for interrupting, his gaze fixed on the witness.

'What did you see in the Suspect? My researches and your history—which I have here in my dossier—reveal a conscientious and competent employee. There have no doubt been crooked tax collectors in Judaea, but you were never one of them.'

Matthias became pensive, speaking as though there were no one else in the room.

'This man respected me and understood me, Procurator, when no one else did. He offered me redemption. Even Sophie... who I wanted so much, wanted her to stay with me... I had to pay her for her company, as a concubine'—he had begun to cry in earnest, now, and shiny trails marked his cheeks and lost themselves in his beard—'it was conditional, always conditional. Yeshua's love was unconditional, and it opened my heart to God.'

'What did Victor say?' Pilate wanted to know.

'Nothing at that stage. He must have been angry, though, because I went to stay with Yeshua's people at Petros's mother-in-law's place... I was in town tying up loose ends when two thugs turned up looking for me.'

Pilate's face drained of colour. 'What?'

'I wasn't there, but they did manage to kick in one of her doors, and told Petros that I should watch my back.'

'Victor Lucius,' Pilate sighed. 'Why does that not surprise me?'

'Touchy temper, Procurator?' said Linnaeus.

'Good at his job, but probably should have joined the army and worked with something, ah, more satisfying.'

There was a ripple of laughter around the courtroom at this; Claudia noticed her husband curl his lip. Matthias used the pause to bring his emotions under control and blow his nose. Clara handed Linnaeus a glass of water and he drank it gratefully.

'What did you do next?'

'I followed Yeshua's teaching. I sold my property in Capernaum, my stock portfolio, my artworks... and deposited the proceeds in an account in Caesarea. We went around Galilee teaching and preaching and helping the poor.'

'How?'

'We fed the hungry. We found shelter for people who had nowhere to live, especially lepers.'

Pilate leaned forward. 'We can cure leprosy,' he said. 'It takes a year or so, but it's not difficult to do.'

'Yes, Procurator,' Matthias said, 'but even after a cure people are left disfigured, with their faces scarred and limbs missing. Lepers—even cured lepers—are seen as unclean. Their families reject them.'

'Yes.'

'Yeshua turned people away from sin, and because he forgave, he gained many more followers—'

Cornelius stood up, his fingers resting on the bar table.

'How is this relevant, Procurator?'

Pilate rubbed his chin.

'Yes, Don Linnaeus, I do think you need to press on.'

Linnaeus nodded.

'Procurator, I did want to convey something of the Suspect's, ah'—he paused, unsure of how to convey his meaning—'*philotimia*.'

Matthias broke in. 'It's not the same, Don Linnaeus. Yeshua always said that we should do good things quietly, without seeking honour like... Romans do.'

Linnaeus was wrong-footed by this, and changed the subject. 'This must have cost considerable sums of money. How did you fund yourselves?'

Matthias smiled, his expression beatific.

'At first we sold our property. After the money from that ran out, we would work in short-term jobs—just enough to look after ourselves, the rest went to the poor—and we encouraged people to give money to our work.'

Claudia felt herself wondering how they lived, and why people would want to give gifts anonymously like that. She leant forward, noticing that Fotini—and nearly every Greek and Roman in the public gallery—was doing likewise.

'Jews have always taken care to help our poor and the weak,' Matthias was saying, 'but Yeshua said we needed to go further, that we'd forgotten what it was supposed to mean.'

'Yes.'

'I'd do people's tax returns for them; Yeshua would do jobs in building and construction; Petros and Andreas crewed fishing trawlers. We'd teach and preach to the people we worked with. Yeshua chose more close followers, until there were twelve of us who went everywhere with him.'

'Yes.'

'He came to Jerusalem for Passover each year and debated with our leading *Rabbanim* and members of the Sanhedrin. He said they needed to wake up, to appreciate that our laws were being fulfilled by rote, not with love and justice.'

'Where did you stay while in Jerusalem?'

'With Mary and Nic, usually, although Nic fell out with Simon and Yehuda after the first year and refused to let them into his property.'

'Where did they go?'

'To their Zealot friends in Gehenna, I think. This last year, Petros and Ioanne rented a flat in the Jewish Quarter, because Nic didn't like Sam in his house.'

'Who is Sam?' Pilate asked.

'Petros's son, Procurator,' Matthias said. 'He is disfigured, and you Romans do not like the disfigured.'

'What happened this last Passover?' Linnaeus cut in, beating Pilate to the punch.

'I realised how much Yehuda hated the financial goings-on in the Temple. Yes, we'd all complained about it—everyone does, I think—and as you'd know by now, every Jew has an opinion on how the Lord should be worshipped.'

'We've noticed, yes.'

'Yeshua had argued with the priests about exploiting the poor before, and last Passover I know it got pretty heated, with him accusing the Sanhedrin of stealing food out of children's mouths and some Rabbis calling him an economic illiterate.'

'Yes.'

'Somehow, Yehuda convinced Yeshua that the animal merchants and moneychangers had to be driven from the Temple by force. Simon backed him at every turn, and even Petros and Ioanne were saying how irritated they were with your markets and trading infecting even the highest places of our worship.' He paused. 'We don't want to be like you; we want to be like ourselves.'

Claudia saw her husband's face colour at this suggestion. He'd wrapped his fist around his pen and was driving the nib into the blotter on his desk. *Don't know what's good for them*, he'd say at home when some village in the Galilee objected to the railway or compulsory vaccination.

'What did the Suspect say?'

'He was angry, of course, but he was reluctant. He said that attacking people in the Temple would come back on all of us.'

'What made him change his mind?'

'I don't know, Don Linnaeus. We'd had too much to drink and got a bit grandiose and silly. We thought if we cleansed the Temple, we could... cleanse Jerusalem. Instead of being the guardians of the *corban*, the Sanhedrin have been milking it like a cow, gambling on the Roman stockmarket and profiteering in commodities and agribusiness.'

Linnaeus cocked his head, managing to look uncomprehending. 'The *corban*?'

'The pension fund set aside in the Temple for care of the elderly and indigent. Last year's annual report showed them investing in everything from pharmaceuticals, to entertainment, to arms. They've even got bond holdings in the firm behind the Fleet Fox. We're paying to help you conceal your idolatry.'

Claudia could see her husband struggling to avoid bursting into laughter. He bit his top lip and curled one hand around his chin.

Ah, Don SINDEX, *and here's us thinking Jews aren't any good with money.*

'We know it's a Temple of Cybele,' Matthias went on, 'you know it's a Temple of Cybele. Let's drop the pretense.'

Galileans and Jews gasped and began to talk among themselves in agitated tones; Romans and Greeks looked at the floor. The nature of the Fleet Fox was a poorly kept secret among the local aristocracy and Roman officials, but Claudia knew the average Jerusalemite took the Roman undertaking not to build religious edifices in the Holy City seriously.

Media people bolted outside to file as the noise grew louder. Pilate banged his gavel and bellowed for order; none came. One Galilean, his hair streaming and his clothes awry, stood and pointed towards Pilate like a Sibyl laying down a curse; for a moment Claudia thought he was pointing directly at her husband, but she realised soon enough that the finger was levelled at the S.P.Q.R. and Rome's *fasces* behind his head. 'Filthy idolaters!' he yelled. 'God will rain sulphur on your heads for defiling his Holy City!'

'Order! I will have order in my court!'

The Galilean repeated his imprecation; Pilate pointed at

two orderlies armed with electroshock weapons.

'Get him out of here.'

The soldiers made their way lightly down the aisle and between the rows, their movements fluid and coordinated. The shouting man dropped limply into his seat the moment they touched him; they ferried him outside, one holding him under the armpits, the other by the legs. Pilate dropped his gavel when the sound had finally died away and pressed his fingertips together in front of his mouth; he looked at the dossier in front of him, turning a stapled bunch of papers face down.

'Counsel,' he said at length, looking at Linnaeus, 'some of this is rather incendiary, as you can see. Would you like an opportunity to confer with your witness in private?'

Linnaeus raised an eyebrow, leaning forward. He smiled.

'No, Procurator, these are things about which reasonable disagreement is possible. As I mentioned, many Romans consider complaints like this trivialities, but they matter to people in this province, including the Suspect. That two terrorists could magnify their importance among others unaware of their intentions should be unsurprising.'

'May I remind both you and your witness to keep it *relevant*.'

Matthias nodded. 'I'm sorry, Procurator.'

'Were there any objections to the projected violence?' Linnaeus asked.

'Yes. Ioanne was very much against, and when it looked like we were going to carry it through, Andreas backed Ioanne to the hilt.'

'What about your hosts?'

'Mary was upstairs, fighting with Nic. I went outside for a joint at one point and I could hear them arguing. Nic has never liked Yeshua, although the dislike's been stronger in the last year or so.'

'So you all joined in?'

'Yes, Don Linnaeus, the following afternoon. We marched on the Court of the Gentiles, right past the Temple Guard. Seeing the crowds assembling for Passover, the priests with their gold and silver vessels, the animals ready to be sacrificed, the blood draining away through carved channels, the poor reduced to buying overpriced doves, the baying and bartering and negotiation... men in little booths exchanging Roman money for Tyrian shekels, Roman troops on the perimeter wall looking down on us... it was just too much. It's an abattoir, Don Linnaeus... a great overpriced abattoir.'

Pilate shook his head, nonplussed once more. 'Sacrifice is a fine way to honour the gods. You come together. You mingle with your friends and neighbours. You eat and drink...'

Matthias was in reverie, now, and looked up as he spoke.

'...and we had to do something.'

Claudia watched Matthias describe the riot, visualising the stampeding animals, fleeing pilgrims slipping in piles of sheep shit and pools of blood, Ben Yusuf plying his whip, the fights between people fed up at being overcharged and people doing the overcharging, the delayed reaction from both the Temple Guard and the 2nd Cohort. Heat. Temper. Flies. Stench. Claudia looked around the courtroom. Many of the fresh-washed Galileans were nodding in agreement. She leaned back against the padded upholstery and stared at the ceiling, such that she didn't notice that Cornelius Getorex had begun his cross-examination.

Matthias sized up the handsome, ginger lawyer as he stood, a sheaf of papers in hand. He took the chance to drink from the glass of water before him with one hand, gripping the witness stand with the other, inhaling slowly, trying to slow his beating heart and control his fear. The soldier-lawyer frightened him—*there, I've admitted it*—and not only because he was tall and menacing. The man was stolid, calm, emotionless. Matthias could see him marching through streets lined with cheering crowds, carrying the Standard at the head of ranks of singing men while young women threw rose petals over him. For some reason Matthias noticed his hands: the fingers were long and tapered. They did not look like torturer's hands. The dark young man beside the ginger handed him something before he spoke. Cornelius took the papers, nodded and leaned over the podium, his expression neutral.

'*Kyrios* Levi,' he began, 'when Simon and Iscariot set about convincing the Suspect to attack the Temple, were you aware that either or both had Zealot connections?'

'I knew something about Yehuda, *Aquilifer* Getorex. Both of them hated Rome, but you must be aware that many people in this province hate you.'

Matthias noticed that this did not divert the lawyer for a moment.

'You knew nothing about Simon?'

'No, *Aquilifer*; Simon had less to say. Yehuda was always full of bombast, going on about how he was going to blow up this building or shoot that Roman soldier. He said stuff like that so often it just went in one ear and out the other, at least for me.'

'Yet he often went to Gehenna?'

'Yes, *Aquilifer*, but then, we all did.'

'Why?'

'To minister to the people who live there, to feed their children and help them rebuild their houses when you Romans bulldozed them.'

'And you were unaware that both Simon and Iscariot were Zealots or had Zealot connections?'

'As I said, Yehuda I sort of knew about, but not Simon.'

'And you never met any Zealots while you were, ah, ministering to the tip people of Gehenna?'

'No, I didn't.'

'Never ever?'

'No, *Aquilifer*.'

Matthias noticed that Cornelius let this last response hang in the air, looking at Pilate, one eyebrow raised. He turned a page in the fat binder before him.

'How did Iscariot and Simon treat you?'

'They didn't like me, *Aquilifer*.'

'Why?'

'I'd worked for Rome. I'd kept a Greek concubine. I'd never followed Jewish law.'

'And this dislike was mutual?'

'I tried to keep away from them as much as possible.'

'And yet you stayed?'

'For Yeshua, yes, *Aquilifer*. He was above all our petty squabbles and disagreements. He had a place in his heart for both the tax collector and the Zealot.'

'Which is why you all followed him?

'Yes, *Aquilifer*, very much so.'

Cornelius was less subtle than Linnaeus, and Matthias got the distinct impression he was about to spring a trap.

'He must have been a most remarkable leader, then.'

Linnaeus stood up.

'I object to that, Procurator, it's not a question.'

Pilate smiled; his eyes seemed to sparkle as he removed his reading glasses.

'Yes, fair point, Don Linnaeus; I'll sustain your objection. *Kyrios* Levi, you don't have to respond to that.'

Matthias watched Cornelius rub the top of his bristled head. He was smiling.

'If you were all following *him*, how on earth did you all convince him to lead an attack on the Temple?'

Matthias could feel sweat trickling down between his

shoulderblades. A wave of nausea passed over him.

'I didn't do any convincing, *Aquilifer*. Simon and Yehuda did.'

'Well, how did they?'

'I don't know, *Aquilifer*. Ask them.'

Cornelius's eyes narrowed to slits and his fair skin flushed.

'Procurator, I think we're dealing with an uncooperative witness here.'

'Yes, *Aquilifer* Getorex, that's also a fair point. The witness is directed to answer the question.'

Matthias turned so that he could see Pilate; the Procurator's face was impassive and unreadable.

'Everyone was very angry... outraged, even.'

'Over what, exactly?'

'The abuse of the *corban*, *Aquilifer*; the thievery in the Court of the Gentiles; how Rome is so sure its way is the only way.'

'You are aware that this *corban* is a fully funded pension scheme?'

This question caught Matthias by surprise; he hadn't expected a military lawyer to sound like an accountant. He was reminded—almost painfully—of Linnaeus's warning while they'd been sitting in Ben David's cab and chatting on the darkened Mount of Olives. *Do not underestimate Cornelius Getorex, Matthias.*

'Yes, *Aquilifer*.'

'And that a wide spread of investments is considered financially prudent?'

Matthias could feel irritation rising in him. 'I was an accountant for eleven years, *Aquilifer*.'

Cornelius pursed his lips.

'I presume you're also aware that in a *fideicommissum* arrangement like that, it is the duty of those holding the property to act in the best interests of the beneficiaries?'

Matthias bit his lip; he did know this, but the exact

formulation was at the outer limits of his experience at the bank.

It's a long time since I looked at funds management, and it shows.

'Yes.'

'Which means that the Sanhedrin members managing the fund have to exercise their investment power so that it yields the best return by way of income and capital appreciation, judged in relation to the risks of the investments being considered?'

'Yes.'

'And that this would be so regardless of Sanhedrin members' personal views or their moral reservations on the choice of the most suitable investments?'

Matthias had sometimes had disagreements like this with Sophie: always gentle disagreements, of course; he loved her too much to take serious issue with how she invested her money or her taste in entertainment. The conversations would go on for hours and go nowhere, or would end with her hauling him into bed and telling him to fuck away his frustrations.

'But the Fleet Fox, *Aquilifer...* you do know what they do in there?'

Matthias watched as Cornelius grinned lopsidedly and raised his eyebrows.

He's not rich enough to be a patron, but I wouldn't mind betting that he's used their... facilities.

Linnaeus was looking sidelong at his opposite number and attempting to stifle laughter. Cornelius, Matthias noted, avoided the more senior lawyer's pointed glance.

'And the beneficiaries are elderly and indigent Jews?'

'Yes, *Aquilifer.*'

Cornelius turned a page in the binder before him.

'*Kyrios* Levi, I put it to you that the Suspect led the attack on the Jerusalem Temple, and that you are attempting to exculpate him using the behaviour of two individuals who are no longer alive for questioning.'

Linnaeus had warned him about this part, where the prosecutor would put his case. *Disagree*, he'd said, *but don't remonstrate or give details, or he'll trap you in your own words.*

'No, *Aquilifer*, that's not true.'

'I also put it to you that you were well aware that Gehenna was a Zealot stronghold, and encountered terrorists there regularly.'

'I knew it was a Zealot stronghold, yes—their murals are everywhere—but I never saw any Zealots there.'

'Finally, I put it to you that your criticism of the Sanhedrin's management of the *corban* is borne of deliberate obtuseness, not ethics.'

'So you say, *Aquilifer*.'

Cornelius looked at Pilate.

'No further questions, Procurator.'

Matthias went to step out from behind the witness stand.

'Not so fast, *Kyrios* Levi,' Pilate rumbled from behind him. 'I have some questions of my own.'

Matthias returned to his seat, eyeing Pilate warily.

'You mentioned earlier that you would raise money from people for your work in places like Gehenna, or for the lepers.'

'Yes, Procurator.'

'How?'

'As I said, by working at casual day labour, or by asking for gifts.'

'It's the latter I'm interested in, *Kyrios* Levi, because it sounds highly irregular. Both your own people and we Romans have a developed system of *philotimia*. There are differences of detail but the two regimes are broadly similar. The Priests of Mars and Initiates of Mithras, for example, have funds for wounded veterans based on a contributions scheme, like your *corban*.

Employers and Guilds and Temples have pension funds, as does the military. The examples are endless.'

Matthias scratched the back of his neck, looking at the Procurator's curious and lively face. *This is hard to explain.*

'The people we were helping had never contributed to anything, Procurator. Sometimes they'd never worked.'

'In which case they have recourse to the *corban*, as you yourself explained; among Romans it is the responsibility of family members to care for the poor.'

Matthias felt his irritation rising again.

'And when the old get too burdensome, they bring the "Green Dream" home from the Æsculapion or cut their wrists in the bath.'

There was a white line around Pilate's lips; he was obviously furious but was also doing his best to tamp it down.

'It is give and take, *Kyrios* Levi, and most people make just arrangements. If you think Roman children assassinate their aged parents willy-nilly, maybe I need to remind you of our parricide laws.'

Matthias closed his eyes and inhaled: they'd stopped tying parricides up in a sackful of snakes and chucking them in the Tiber, but the prohibition was still immensely strong. He swallowed.

'I do appreciate that, Procurator.'

'Did you make any attempt to draft articles of association and form a *collegium*?'

'No, Procurator; that would have wasted money we could have given to the poor.'

'This means you stood on street corners like common beggars.'

Matthias wasn't sure what he'd said, but somehow he'd managed to annoy not only the ginger prosecutor—which he'd expected to do—but the Procurator as well. He looked across at Ben Yusuf, who was—as usual—utterly passive and inscrutable.

'Yeshua never tells lies, Procurator.'

Pilate snorted. 'I have visions of a man on a street corner holding a bucket with "pay my mortgage" written on it, for all that people knew where their money was going.'

'We helped people who could not help themselves, Procurator.'

'Did you make any attempt to establish their bona fides?'

'What do you mean?'

'Did you try to find out if they deserved help, like Stoics do?'

'No, Procurator.'

'You've met every conman in the province, then.'

'No, Procurator, I haven't.'

'You are aware—you must be aware—of the legal obligations on those entrusted with managing the *corban*. If priests on the Sanhedrin fail to honour them, the beneficiaries can quite properly apply to have them removed from the board.'

'I know that, Procurator.'

'And yet you and your confreres attempted to change the Sanhedrin's investment decisions with violence. You tried to undermine the rule of law.'

'The law of God is above the law of Rome.'

There was a collective gasp around the courtroom followed by a series of low mutters. Several of the press people stood up and strode outside. Pilate did not bang his gavel, waiting instead for the noise to subside. The Procurator's eyes had narrowed to slits.

'When your god arrives,' Pilate said, struggling to keep his voice even, 'we can argue about jurisdiction, but until then, this province is under Roman law.'

Pilate leaned back in his seat, tapping his blotter with the fingers of one hand. His face had coloured during the exchange and Matthias watched as the blood drained out from under his dark skin.

'There's another thing that's been concerning me about your testimony, *Kyrios* Levi,' he said after a pause. 'It's your attitude to the Fleet Fox and places like it. You admitted that you made use of the House system, with...' he paused and looked at the ceiling, unable to recall for a moment.

'Her name was Sophie, Procurator,' Matthias broke in. 'From the House of Gaia, in Caesarea.'

'Women who combine both intellectual skills and physical charms like that are often trained in the Houses. You made use of one of them, but you condemn it now.'

'I was wrong to live as I did, Procurator.'

'Does Sophie know this is now your view?'

'I went to her and asked her to repent, but she refused. She preferred to continue in her sin.'

This produced laughter, and Pilate snorted again. 'I shouldn't wonder,' he said.

Matthias could feel tears pricking behind his eyelids; they always did when talk turned to Sophie.

He'd gone to Caesarea with Ioanne, and as soon as he set foot in the worldly city he could feel the old ways returning. He went to the baths and washed and shaved, had his hair cropped at the barber's and bought a fashionable linen shirt and patterned Celtic trews. He told Ioanne he wanted to convince her to repent and to turn away from sin, just as Yeshua had managed to do with some of the whores who pleasured Roman troops from the barracks in Sepphoris. Ioanne had been dubious, doubting Matthias's powers of persuasion but nonetheless leaving him to it.

Sophie had been delighted when he'd called on her, setting aside an afternoon and meeting him in the forum. She was

Spartan by descent, lithe and quick like many of her people, her straight brown hair spilling over her shoulders. When he saw her—smiling, the wind blowing her hair off her face, dark eyes sparkling—he felt the muscles in his chest contract. She gave him a chaste peck on the cheek and sat down opposite him. They chatted over creamy coffee and he made his case, finally offering to marry her. She took his hands in hers and shook her head sadly.

'Matthias, you were an interesting and clever man, and I loved you for that, but somehow this Ben Yusuf has lobotomised you. If neither of us has work, what are we supposed to live on? What are our children supposed to live on?'

'Both of us can find work that isn't immoral,' he'd said.

'Yes, but not nearly so well paid, Matthias, and, in any case, I don't think either my current job or your old job are immoral. Someone has to collect the taxes and repossess the houses. Someone has to deal with the fact that there's a mismatch between men and women when it comes to sexual supply and demand.'

'That's only because Greeks and Romans don't think a man needs to be faithful.'

'Not all of them, Matthias. Stoics aren't like that; nor are Pythagoreans.'

He'd started to cry, then, tears dripping into his coffee. She stepped around their table, pulled him upright and then into her arms, kissing him. He let her take his hand and lead him along the *cardo* to Gaia's House and its ornate marble frontage. They stopped outside and she kissed him again. He'd been amazed—as he always was, over and over—at how her body seemed to fit into his. He hugged her closer; she kissed away his tears.

'Come inside,' she said.

Burning with guilt and lust, he'd followed her up to her

rooms overlooking the Temple of Concord on the *decumanus*. He noticed—once again—the fresco of a young man weighing his outsized cock in a set of grocer's scales. It had been freshly repainted, and the eyes seemed to follow him as he climbed the stairs.

'I can't do this, Sophie. It's wrong.'

She rolled him into her bed, throwing her leg across him, unbuttoning his trousers and lifting his shirt. He reached for her breasts. She took the chance to turn his left arm out; seeing there was no chip, she reached across him for a condom, tearing the wrapper open with her teeth. He tried to push it away.

'He says we should be open to life, to the possibility of life.'

'Not if you want to fuck me,' she said. He wilted in her hand, then, and she held him across her palm, perplexed. The wrapper was still between her teeth. She flicked it onto the floor.

'I'm sorry, Sophie,' he whispered. 'I'm so sorry.'

'You need to stop worrying about things you can't control,' she said, 'and start worrying about things you can.'

She masturbated him for a few minutes and pulled her silk shift off over her head, giving him the best possible view. Oh God, he wanted her so much; he drew her to him and began to kiss her face.

'I'm a sinner,' he said, 'I can't stop sinning in the eyes of God.'

She shook her head, disbelieving, sitting upright with her hands on his chest. Her fingers splayed through his chest hair. She reached in between her legs and cupped his cock and balls. It was a bag of kittens down there.

'You know, your god is a pervert,' she said. 'He shouldn't be watching what people do in their bedrooms. None of our gods do, unless they want a piece of the action.'

He tried to remonstrate, but nothing came out. She leant forward again so he could kiss her. He sobbed in between his kisses. He noticed she was crying as well.

'Thank you, *Kyrios* Levi,' said Pilate, looking at Linnaeus and feeling deeply sorry for Matthias. 'The witness is excused.'

Pilate adjourned the court for twenty minutes and despatched Horace to fetch him coffee.

While he waited, he rummaged through the paperwork in his desk drawers, finally rustling up a business card with Victor Lucius's name and the *CreditGallia: Capernaum vocale* sequence on it. He dialled, establishing from the woman who had taken over Matthias's position that Victor had taken leave over *Megalesia* and was currently visiting his estranged wife and children in Italy. As he spoke to the operator, Horace returned with espresso and biscotti. The chime sounded for a long time before anyone answered. The voice that picked up—at length—was a child's: Pilate guessed about eight or nine, but could not divine the sex. The child hadn't been taught proper *vocale* manners and didn't give a name.

'So you want to speak to Papa?'

'Yes, I do. Can you fetch him for me?'

'Um, that's kind of hard right now.'

'Why is that?'

'Mama and Papa went out last night, and they're still asleep.'

Pilate sighed. 'Do you have an older brother or sister I can speak with?'

'I have a big sister and a big brother.'

'Can you fetch one of them?'

'Yes.'

Without waiting for him to respond, the child dropped the receiver. Pilate heard it clunk against the desktop. He waited for several minutes before the piping voice returned.

'I can't find him. I think he went out.'

Pilate exhaled audibly and reminded himself to stay calm.

'What about your big sister?'

'She's helping to paint a festival float at school.'

'I see.'

The receiver thudded against the desk again; Pilate heard a man's voice chastise the child, calling it Creon. *Ah, a boy, then.*

'Who is this?'

Pilate gave his name, listening as a great rush of air gushed from Victor's mouth.

'What's happened, Procurator? Do I have to come back?'

Pilate was aware his voice had an edge to it, but he didn't stop being angry.

'What are you doing now?'

'At this very moment, Procurator? If you must know, trying to save my marriage.'

Victor's voice also had an edge to it, and now Pilate could hear a woman's voice in the background, talking soothingly to the little boy.

'As you may or may not know, I'm currently trying a matter where one of your erstwhile employees is an important witness. Matthias Levi, remember him?'

'Yes, Procurator.'

'I'm concerned about reports I've heard to the effect that you sent a couple of cage fighters with chains to his house after he handed in his notice. Are these reports accurate?'

Victor was drumming his fingers on the table. The woman was kissing her husband now, Pilate presumed on the neck. He could hear her giggling and telling him to come back to bed.

'They're accurate.'

'I went to some trouble to give *Aquila* Finance the boot over crap like that and you go right on with the same shit. Why hasn't *CreditGallia* sacked you?'

Victor laughed; the sound was high and bitter.

'I'm irreplaceable, Procurator. No one in his right mind wants to live and work in Tartarus, not for any amount of money.'

'That doesn't excuse what you did, Victor. If you want the sack badly enough, I'm sure it can be arranged.'

Pilate could hear Victor cluck his tongue; his wife was still speaking to him in the background.

'Look, Procurator, I'm with my family right now. Matthias left us in the lurch at the busiest time of year. I sent cage fighters after him because I was too busy cleaning up his messes to give him the shitkicking he deserved myself. If you've got a problem with that, take it up with Head Office in Nemausus.'

Pilate looked at the fire alarm in his ceiling, trying to work out if he had time to remove it and smoke at least part of a cigar. Victor's voice buzzed into the receiver.

He's at wit's end.

'You know what would be really useful,' Victor was saying now, 'is if we remodelled the coastline. I'm serious. Ring Judaea with explosives and drop the whole province into the Med. We've got the technology to reclaim land. Let's reclaim some ocean.'

Pilate listened to the man vent for another minute or so, exchanged pleasantries and hung up. He then stood on his desk and unscrewed the fire alarm.

'The Defence calls Mary Magdalena.'

Cynara watched male Roman heads snap around to stare as the orderly led her into the courtroom, their eyes tracking her as she stood in the witness stand to take her oath. She declined to swear on the Torah; the orderly looked confused, glancing first at Pilate and then at Lonuobo and Horace. The

latter went to the witness stand and opened the little book
with its collection of courtroom oaths. Cynara grew wide-
eyed as she watched Mary affirm, one hand held up beside
her head, the elbow bent, like a Senator before the Statue of
Victory in the *Curia*. This discomforted Romans and Greeks
alike, while Jews were simply flummoxed. Cynara looked over
towards Agrippa, who smiled at her serenely. Nic Varro—he
had plonked himself directly in front of the press box—was
nodding, perhaps wishing he'd had the courage to do as his
wife had done.

Even though everyone in the room knew her—at least
by reputation—Linnaeus took Mary through her career at
JTN and her experience as a journalist reporting all over the
province. Cynara could see the media experience showing as
Mary answered Linnaeus's questions. She sat very still, pausing before answering, measuring her words with great care.
She kept her gestures to a minimum and smiled from time
to time.

'When did you first encounter the suspect?'

'Personally, or via media reports?'

'In person, *Kyria*.'

'There'd been a report in one of the local Galilee papers
of a near-riot in Nazareth where Roman troops had rescued
a man described as a 'healer' or 'spiritual leader'. I dismissed
it at first but then reports began to filter through of what had
happened to *Centurio* Propertius's *pais*. I couldn't interview
Propertius—Irie Andrus almost always refuses to give re-
leases to interview serving military personnel—but I figured
I could interview Yeshua Ben Yusuf and other people in the
area, so I assembled a crew.'

'What did you learn?'

'That there was a *very* wide range of views about the Suspect, from outright hatred to extraordinary devotion, and all

shades in between.'

'Can you give the court a sample?'

'Many people in the area objected to him because of the circumstances of his birth. He wasn't a *mamzer*, but his mother had coupled with a Roman soldier before her marriage to a local tradesman. In many Galilean minds, this is something only prostitutes do, so he was called "Miriam's son", a euphemism for "bastard". Galileans are usually referred to by their patronymic, not their matronymic, unless the mother is high born.'

'I see.'

'Other people did not care about his birth, and were impressed by his teaching. I made contact with some of them and secured an interview.'

'Yes.'

'He refused to discuss the incident in Capernaum, but he spoke freely about the Roman rescue in Nazareth and his relationship with the Cohort Commander and the people of Nazareth.'

'Hadn't Irie Andrus just hit him?'

'Yes, over Irie's relationship with Soraya. When I first met Yeshua, he had the most spectacular black eye I've ever seen.'

'So, in a sense, the violence was partly the fallout over Irie Andrus's unusual way of acquiring a wife?'

'That was the proximate cause, Don Linnaeus, yes. Andrus—like so many Roman men—wanted a woman and made no bones about claiming one from among the subject population. I know that is your way and you see no harm in it, but in the Galilee it leads to problems. Honour killings, but also things like young women who are rendered unmarriageable or worse, pregnant.'

'It is very different here, yes.'

'Yeshua tried to teach Galileans that blaming the woman

was wrong and counterproductive. It drove young women who wanted more from life into the arms of not only Roman legionaries but also Roman civilian administrators and businessmen. Those women loved their high status, that they had their own money, and that their men did not tell them what to do, but hated that their husbands did not value the marriage bond, using field brothels and *hetaerae* and so on.'

'That is very common among Roman men,' said Pilate.

'He also tried to teach Romans that what they did was *porneia*, that it devalued marriage and women and made them the slaves of their lusts.'

'I understood this led to several incidents in North Galilee...'

'Yes, Don Linnaeus. Local Zealots who wanted to make Yeshua look bad would routinely bring him women who had gone with Roman soldiers or officials and say they should be stoned for adultery or fornication. He would try to talk them out of it, but it didn't always work, and sometimes there were unintended consequences.'

Pilate drummed his fingers on his blotter.

'We once had laws like that—not so harsh, of course, and never fatal, but still punitive. We learnt that they led to murder and mayhem. Men beat their wives. Women poisoned their husbands. Better the quotidian anguish of a marriage that fails and the payment of agreed sums under a contract than people killed in their beds.'

Cynara watched Mary stare at the Procurator; her expression revealed her fear that she'd prejudiced Ben Yusuf's chances. Linnaeus had spotted the same thing.

'What else did the Suspect teach?'

'He was adamant that people throughout the province—Roman, Greek and Jew alike—had a misapprehension of religion: what it was for, what it could do.'

'Which meant?'

'That people are not by nature unclean. That what you eat does not make you unclean; rather, it is what you do in your life. That people should be judged on their character, not the circumstances of their birth.'

'And this aspect was attractive to you?'

'I had made myself unclean simply by going with a Roman man. I wasn't a Jew any more, and yet I wasn't Roman.'

Cynara looked towards Nic Varro; he was chewing his bottom lip and did not look happy.

'How did the Suspect's, ah, philosophy assist you?'

'He taught me that I am intrinsically loveable. That...' she paused, looking down, uncomfortable. Cynara knew enough about Ben Yusuf's message to guess something of what she wanted to say.

'These are fine sentiments, Don Linnaeus,' said Pilate, his tone still tetchy, 'but really incidental to the matter at hand. You need to press on.'

'Yes, Procurator, I will.'

Cynara had the feeling that the defence had lost the Procurator. She suspected it stemmed from Ben Yusuf's high-minded sexual morality. She leant back in her seat and stared up at the elaborately moulded ceiling. *Why am I not surprised?*

Linnaeus was going through his paperwork, looking for something. His end of the bar table was always messier than the prosecutor's, and his rummaging was now making it messier still. Eventually, his instructing clerk handed him a sheaf of papers. He plonked them on the podium and lifted his eyes.

'What was your relationship like with the Suspect's other followers?'

'It varied,' she said. 'I got on best with Ioanne, Joseph Arimathea and Andreas Bar Yonah. I often fought with Yehuda and Simon. I sometimes disagreed with Petros Bar Yonah and

Markos, but also often agreed with them.'

'What made you disagree with some and not others?' asked Linnaeus.

'Yehuda and Simon forgot Yeshua's teaching about judging people based on what they do, rather than on what they were or are, and treated my husband very badly. They despised me for showing my face on screen, and regarded me as a whore. They were then shocked when Nic refused to allow them into our house.'

'And Petros?'

'He had the Galilean distrust of a woman in authority, Don Linnaeus, so he did not know what to do with me. To his credit, he did try.'

Cynara found herself warming to Mary Magdalena the witness. What was most impressive was not so much her doggedness and honesty, but that her personality didn't change on the stand. Her voice wasn't strained, and she wasn't sweating or nervous. She seemed at ease.

'What about Matthias?'

'Like me, he was trying to forgive himself for his past. We got on well, although he was very conflicted inside. He often considered himself unworthy of Yeshua's love.'

'How much did you know about other followers' backgrounds?'

'You mean Yehuda and Simon? Very little, to be honest, except that they were unlike me in almost every way. I was still working at JTN; I didn't get to see the rest of the group as often as I might. Petros was in a similar position, with a young family.'

'So you didn't think to give your job away, as others did?'

'No, I didn't, apart from moving into production, which I did in an attempt to cool Yehuda and Simon's hatred for me.'

'Did it work?'

'They just focused all their hatred on Niccy.'

'Did the Suspect share any of those attitudes?'

'Not that I ever saw, Don Linnaeus. He could be critical, but he was never a hater.'

Cynara noticed that Nic was now smiling. He was an emotional barometer of the most revealing sort.

'But Yehuda and Simon's hatred continued during the lead up to this year's Passover festival?'

'Yes. Everyone save Petros and his young family asked for hospitality with us. We have a six-bedroom apartment, but accommodating all of them is difficult. Niccy refused to admit Simon and Yehuda to the complex, which meant none of them could get in; it was raining; they were all standing together outside the gate; everyone's tempers were getting rather frayed. Eventually Nic remembered that he had an eight-man tent from army disposals stored away somewhere. He, Ioanne and Andreas sloshed about and put it up beside the complex swimming pool, while the rest of them stood out of the wet.'

'Did you speak to any of them after they'd all decamped to the tent?'

'Off and on, yes, although only in snatches. Ioanne, Andreas and Markos didn't stay in the tent all night, either; there were too many of them for that. They came upstairs and stayed in our spare rooms. In the meantime our servants prepared food for everyone and we took it downstairs in shifts. I spoke to people then.'

'What transpired after that?'

'At one point I saw Yeshua and Yehuda arguing, but I didn't stay around to find out what they were arguing about. It was pouring down, the last big storm of spring. Nic and I were both saturated through to our underwear. We also argued over giving Andreas a spare set of keys; I won the argument but Nic loaded a shotgun and insisted on changing the locks the next day.'

Cynara found herself joining in the general laughter at this classic image of the Roman *paterfamilias*.

'I told the three who wanted to stay upstairs to let themselves in when they were ready for some sleep. By the time they did, Niccy and I had gone to bed. I don't think I even heard them come up the stairs.'

'So you were unprepared for the riot in the Temple precinct next day?'

'Completely, Don Linnaeus; I dispatched a crew to cover it, of course, and interviewed the High Priest. I'm not sure if it is my place to say this, but he was unprepared as well. I don't know the details of the arrangement he had with Yehuda, but whatever it was, I don't think it included wrecking the Court of the Gentiles.'

'You'll need to stop your witness speculating, Don Linnaeus.'

Linnaeus nodded and turned to Mary. 'You need to confine yourself to what you saw and heard, *Kyria*.'

'I'm sorry, Don Linnaeus. I should know better.'

'One final question, *Kyria*,' Linnaeus said. 'What was your view of the attack on the Temple?'

'I thought resorting to violence was stupid, Don Linnaeus, but I can see why they did what they did. Even Nic thought the Temple was... administered corruptly.'

Linnaeus swept his toga around him, clasping some of its copious folds to his stomach with one hand.

'Thank you, *Kyria*. No further questions.'

Cornelius watched Mary, perplexed as to how he was to cross-examine her effectively. She was beautiful, serene and poised—not to mention a local celebrity—and to attack her would be counterproductive in the extreme. Cyler slid a piece of paper across the bar table about halfway through her examination-in-chief. ALL THE MEN IN THIS ROOM AND HALF THE WOMEN WANT TO BONK HER, he'd scrawled in messy all-caps. ADMIT IT, SIR, YOU DO TOO. Cornelius wondered how he could turn that fact to his advantage.

He opened his second ring binder—this one marked ß—and stood.

'*Kyria*, I'll try to keep this short, since it's clear from your testimony that you weren't in a position to know about the planned attack on the Temple.'

She smiled at him; he noticed from the corner of his eye that Cyler had doodled a set of parted legs in the margins of his yellow legal pad. Cornelius suspected it was unconscious.

'Thank you, *Aquilifer*.'

'You spoke in your testimony of the Suspect's ability to prevent honour killings.'

'Yes, *Aquilifer*.'

'We have enough trouble preventing that sort of thing with six thousand men under arms. How does an unarmed Galilean tradesman do what we cannot?'

'I only saw it once. A young woman, who had been married against her will to a man from outside Nazareth, was friendly with one of the soldiers Irie Andrus brought with him when he claimed Soraya Iscariot. She knew the Roman from previous patrols in the district, perhaps even over two or three years. He saw her by the well and told her that he had registered her name in the *vicus* in Sepphoris and that she was now free to go with him. He didn't realise that she'd been married in the interval, and she rebuffed him, in fear for her life. He returned to the well the next day with the official forms—all stamped and filled in and showing her name—as a token of his good faith. This persuaded her, and her husband and brother—wondering at her delay—surprised the two of them hidden in the long grass. The soldier was naked and distracted and her husband hit him over the head with a rock, dragging his wife into the town square.'

Cornelius suspected he was shaking his head; he'd only ever heard tell of incidents like this. He'd managed to avoid the Galilee since his posting to Judaea.

'I was there with my crew when the two of them appeared, hauling her behind them. Nazareth has no Rabbi—there aren't enough people there for that—so the Zealots and brigands who pass for religious authorities in places like that were already picking up stones. The *castrum* in Nazareth is set back from the town, so there were no troops present.'

Cornelius watched as Pilate destroyed his fountain pen, staining his hands. Horace stood, turned and passed him a roll of blotting paper and another pen.

'One of my crew started filming, but local men tore the camera out of his hands and removed the cartridge, smashing it into the ground. They started to threaten me, calling me the usual insults—variations on "you are a whore for showing your face on screen".'

Cornelius could feel a horrible fascination rising inside him. He leaned forward.

'What happened next?'

'My crew stood in a circle around me, the cameraman pointing out that if they killed me, the Romans would order their village wiped off the map. I remember him saying *they will send the* striges, *and you will all die*.'

Cornelius nodded. Cyler had told him of the irrational fear most provincials had of the *striges*. Zealots told each other that the Romans had opened a portal to Tartarus and started releasing what was trapped in there, a notion the Air Force made no attempt to dispel.

'I have no idea whether what he said was true, but the

villagers left us alone. A couple of them had already started to throw stones at the woman and she was bleeding from just above the eye. Then—once again, this all happened so fast— they stopped and went looking for Yeshua. He was dragged into the square as well—'

'Were they going to stone him too?'

'They forced him to sit down and told him to make a religious ruling. I can't remember the exact details, but it was to the effect that they'd caught her in "the very act" with one of the idolaters. When the husband said he'd killed the idolater, the woman shrieked with the most terrifying grief. Yeshua waited until she'd stopped and looked at the husband—'

'Did the Suspect seem worried... that the villagers would turn on him, or that he was being expected to kill someone without benefit of law?'

'No, *Aquilifer*. He seemed... diffident.'

Cornelius nodded. If nothing else, Ben Yusuf had a good grasp of human psychology.

'He told the husband that he was a murderer, and had committed a worse sin than his wife.'

Cornelius thought it was a good answer, but one more likely to work on a Greek or Roman or Hellenised Jew, not on a Galilean peasant who'd just caught his wife *in flagrante*.

'The husband flung his rock down in disgust, but one of the other men standing there threw a stone at her.'

'Did that open the floodgates?'

'No. Yeshua caught it. He held it in his hand for a moment, then let it drop. I saw his palm bleeding into the dust.'

'Yes.'

'Then he pointed at each of the ringleaders, like this—' She lifted her hand towards the ceiling, her right index finger sticking out. 'He asked them if they'd gone through life without sin; if they had, then they could kill her.'

'So he shamed them?'

'A lot of Zealots have bad backgrounds—they're petty criminals, or they've used prostitutes, or they've even killed—so it stung.'

'Did they all leave?

'Within minutes. Yeshua and the woman were soon all alone. She pulled her rags around her; she was bleeding badly into one eye. She kept repeating that she needed to go to the Æsculapion, and she had to burn her Roman soldier, her Lucas.'

'Yes.'

'Then—from the direction of the well—Lucas appeared. He was shirtless, wearing boots and the bottom half of his fatigues, with his jacket in one hand and his rifle in the other. He'd put on his helmet but not bothered to do up the chin-strap. I was glad he didn't encounter a square full of people, because I think he may have started shooting.'

'No, *Kyria*,' Cornelius said. 'He would only have *potestas* against his woman's killers, and no one was dead.'

Mary paused. Cornelius realised that he hadn't moved for several minutes, and that he was becoming stiff. He twisted around and knocked a block of yellow legal pad onto the stone floor. Cyler bent over and picked it up.

'She ran to him and started kissing his face. He hugged her, his rifle still in one hand. He was bleeding from one ear, but seemed to be coherent. He took her hand and walked with her to Yeshua, thanking him.'

'Can you remember what transpired?'

'Yes, *Aquilifer*.'

'Can you tell the court?'

'Yeshua asked the woman if this man was now her hus-band, and she said yes. He asked her if she would be faithful to him, and she said yes. He said "good" and then asked Lucas if she was to be his wife. Lucas started to fish the registration documents out of his pocket. Yeshua waved them away, saying he didn't care what the law said. "Do you consider her your wife?" he asked. Lucas said that he did. "Will you be faithful to her, soldier of Rome?" Yeshua asked next, and Lucas did the thing Romans do when they don't want to say "yes" or "no"—'

Cornelius couldn't stop himself from grinning. 'You mean this?' he asked, waggling his head smoothly from shoulder to shoulder, 'at the same time as saying, "it's a little difficult"?'

'Yes, *Aquilifer*, exactly.'

There was laughter—tension-relieving laughter—all around the courtroom at this. Romans could be supremely blunt about some things, but every Jew and Greek in the room knew the Roman talent for nodding when they meant only 'I hear you' not 'I agree' or the affectionate but non-committal headshake.

'Yeshua looked at Lucas and demanded a straight answer. He said "don't wriggle your head at me" and asked again if he would be faithful to her. To my surprise, Lucas said yes, without any trace of dissembling. He even called Yeshua *sir*.'

Cornelius could see Mary's eyes shining; if anything it made her even more beautiful. He suspected she was in love with Ben Yusuf. She reminded him of a couple of the Stoic academics who'd taught him in Londinium: clear eyed and upstanding and fearless. He turned a page in his binder and looked up.

'It was then that I knew this man was remarkable,' Mary was saying, 'that he could make us whole again, and gloriously alive...'

'To do what he did must have taken charisma and courage, *Kyria*.'

'Yes, it did, *Aquilifer*.'

Cornelius made his move.

'I put it to you, *Kyria*, that an unarmed man able to take on a primitive village—and *shame* them into not killing a woman who had been caught *in flagrante delicto*—is incapable of being "talked into" criminal damage, riot and felony murder. He decided to use violence all on his own.'

Mary looked stricken, and shook her head. He felt nauseous as he watched her panicked and pained reaction.

'No, *Aquilifer*,' she said at last, 'that's not true.'

Cornelius looked at Pilate.

'No further questions, Procurator.'

He sat down. He was not proud of what he'd done. Pilate looked at Mary.

'I have no questions either, *Kyria*. You're free to go.'

Cynara took the chance to disappear outside; she noticed Mirella, Saleh, and Rachel were waiting, the latter breastfeeding her baby. Cynara sat on the wrought-iron bench facing the courtroom, her handbag on her lap. She watched the double doors swing open; Mary stumbled out of them, tears streaking her face. The Roman orderly touched her shoulder, asking her if she needed an infirmary pass. She pushed his hand away, sitting beside Cynara and sobbing. Cynara watched as the orderly walked across to the witness room and called Petros Bar Yonah in stentorian tones.

'I let that redhead trick me,' Mary said at last, her voice uneven. 'He's a tricky shit.'

'He's trying to win the case,' said Cynara.

Mary blew her nose and dabbed at her eyes. Her breathing—rapid and shallow—began to slow.

'They're going to kill him, Cynara,' she said, 'because of stupid Yehuda and Simon.'

Cynara did not speak, folding her arm around Mary's shoulders. She suspected Mary was right, but didn't say anything.

'You don't care. Romans can do no wrong as far as you're

concerned.'

Cynara kept holding her. She smoothed back Mary's hair. 'I'm sorry, Mary.'

Mary rested her head on Cynara's shoulder. Cynara continued to rub her neck and back.

'Do you want coffee?'

Mary nodded. Cynara stood and went in search of the junior officer who'd proven so helpful on the coffee front. He'd been left in charge of the witness room. She suspected that minding even very distinguished witnesses—like her father or Nic Varro or Mary—was beneath his rank, but he wasn't complaining.

'Good duty for Passover?' Cynara asked him in Latin.

'Oh yes, *Donna*,' he said, 'much better than stomping around in the heat and dust.' He leaned closer to her, his expression conspiratorial. 'And I snuck that lady reporter into my quarters last night and we fucked like bunnies. It was nice.' He winked. 'She says *Don* Agrippa's nice, too.'

Cynara inhaled, taken aback, reminded sharply that Jerusalem's citizen population was both small and talkative. For some reason she also remembered that a man of his rank shared his quarters with another junior officer, and that both only had single beds. Presumably the other fellow did not mind.

'Well, since you're feeling so lively, would you be good enough to fetch us some coffee?'

'Whatever you like, *Donna*. I've got to be seen to be doing something, or they'll have me out supervising the sheep shaggers in the Temple.'

Cynara returned to her spot beside Mary and waited for the soldier to come back. Mary folded her hands across her knees. Cynara curled her arm around her shoulders again.

'What do you see in him?' Cynara asked at length. 'You're

right, I don't get it—none of it makes much sense to me.'

This admission wasn't strictly true, but a great deal of Ben Yusuf's support and popularity confused her. Mary sat still, not answering. The amused young officer brought both of them coffee. He reminded Mary that she was no longer permitted in the witness room. Cynara waited until he'd made himself scarce before repeating her question.

'He allowed me to say no to Niccy,' Mary said. 'It's the first time I've ever been able to say no to Niccy—on anything.'

'What do you mean?'

Mary recounted—in brief but telling detail—her decision to refuse Nic sex until he agreed to marry her formally. Cynara gasped.

'Did he threaten to leave you?'

'He could have divorced me; we're married under Roman law.'

'Did he threaten to divorce you?'

'I was sure he would, but he never even raised it as a possibility. He always just insisted we were married and that was that.'

'Take it from me, that means a Roman man is head over heels in love with you.'

'He was adulterous, Cynara, but then you know the Roman custom if a woman does not give her man enough sex. I wasn't giving him any, so I didn't quibble when he went to the Greek Quarter. He never brought women home.'

Cynara wasn't sure how to frame the question she wanted to ask. She sipped her coffee.

'Why would you want to say no to Nic?'

Mary didn't recoil from the question as Cynara had expected.

'Until I met Yeshua, I'd spent my life just falling into things. I fell into a spot at Jerusalem Academy. I fell into my job at JTN and then—surprise, surprise—I fell into Niccy's bed.'

Cynara was struggling to read the tone of Mary's voice. It wasn't bitter, but it was... *aggrieved.*

'Did he force himself on you?'

Mary shook her head.

'Niccy would consider force a stain on his character as an Etruscan charmer. He was seductive, attentive... and very bloody persistent.'

'You do love him, don't you?'

'I don't think he understands how much I love him. I don't think *I* understand how much I love him. It's like a monster inside me.'

'So why did you need to say no to him?'

Mary chewed her lip; Cynara suspected that she hadn't quite worked out a reason for what she'd done.

'I've always gone along with whatever Niccy wanted, even when it made me feel... unclean. Sometimes it was just little things—where to eat, what to wear in the studio or out to a concert. He had a thing for floor-length red silk gowns cut up to the waist.'

Cynara giggled.

'Other times it was larger. Pork and more pork without ever asking me what I thought. Once he took me to the Temple of Baal and Astarte in Damascus... with his friends. Romans are so damn persuasive—they manage to get you to do things you don't want to do, and then you enjoy them... blood and sex, the empire of the senses. It's like they found the most primitive part of the human brain and built a high-speed rail link straight to it.'

Cynara patted her hand and felt ineffectual.

'I was in tears for a week afterwards. Even Niccy noticed, and we never did anything like that again. He couldn't understand why I was so upset, though. I remember him saying, "but you liked it while you were doing it". It was Yeshua who taught me to trust my conscience. If something felt bad—even while it felt nice—it probably was bad. And that meant I shouldn't do it.'

'Including marriage to Nic?'

'I didn't feel married to Niccy. Maybe it's from being raised Jewish, but just moving in like that and marking off the year of cohabitation with a big black X on the calendar didn't seem like marriage to me. When I moved in with him—and don't get me wrong, I liked that, liked that I could choose, it was daring and bold—the whole street was watching us load my things into the cab through the shutters. His hands were everywhere, and then he pushed me up against the cab and started lifting my skirt—'

'Like he wanted to provoke them.'

'He thought it was funny.'

'So you still wanted to be married to Nic?'

'Of course. But I wanted it to be a deliberate decision, not just something we fell into. I was sick of falling into things. And it was important enough for me to risk him saying no.'

'That's some risk, Mary.'

'Yeshua says that God wants us to risk the right thing. I believe him.'

The courtroom doors swung open; it was Nic. He strode towards them and sat beside Mary. Mary put her cup down at her feet; the two of them held each other close. Cynara stood aside, not wanting to intrude. Nic rubbed Mary's back and whispered something into her ear. She nodded. The young soldier came and stood beside Cynara, retrieving the cups. Nic looked up at both of them.

'Thank you for looking after her,' he said. 'I should have come straight outside, but I let myself get distracted with Petros's testimony.'

Cynara nodded; the soldier smiled and took his leave. Nic

bent his head forward and looked into Mary's eyes.

'We can go home, go back inside, go into work... whatever you want to do.'

She nodded, her arms around his neck. Cynara could see him fiddling with the fine brocade pouch at his waist. He retrieved a small box and held it up in front of Mary's face, balanced on his palm. He took her left hand in his and then fitted the largest gemstone Cynara had ever seen in a ring on her finger. Rubies surrounded the central diamond; it cast a shadow over her knuckle. Mary put her right hand over her mouth and looked at it with shock.

'Niccy...'

'I know you didn't ask, but I wanted to give.'

Cynara left them to it, making her way down the stairs, out through security and into the square in front of Antonia. She squinted up at the sun, feeling her pupils contract.

Cynara spent most of her lunch with Agrippa—this time in a sunlit Greek restaurant on top of one of the more upmarket Houses—rolling the conversation with Mary around in her head. As she sat working her way through meze and swordfish and salad—pausing sometimes to feed Agrippa olives, and to be fed in her turn—she wondered if the Romans had built one of their high-speed rail links to her hindbrain. Agrippa was looking at her with frank lust and she was reciprocating.

'Apparently this Ben Yusuf is celibate,' he said. 'After seeing her on the stand, I have difficulty believing that.'

'Nic Varro would have his testicles on a silver charger if that happened, believe me.'

Cynara kept ruminating on Mary while answering his questions. At one point she noticed he had stretched his legs out under the table, rather pointedly putting them in between her feet. She felt sorry for Mary—for her awkwardness with

Nic's public displays of affection and his dislike for Ben Yusuf—but she also knew that in the same position she would have acted very differently. *I would fuck Nic Varro every night and twice on Saturdays*, she thought, *if he were my husband.*

The waiter cleared away their plates and refilled their glasses with sweet retsina. Agrippa waited until the man had gone and leaned towards her, speaking in Latin.

'Fancy a quickie?'

'Um, *where?*'

'I'm sure they've got a spare room down below,' he said.

'Severus, you've got a hide,' she said, feeling her ears redden. 'Only if you organise it, and only if the sheets are spotless.'

He kissed her nose as he stood up and, glass in hand, made for the door. He returned ten minutes later with an empty glass and a key. 'I've paid the bill,' he said. 'Apparently it's a common request.'

She drained her own glass and followed him, taking his hand and shaking her head. *About that high-speed rail link...*

By the time they'd finished and she'd effected running repairs to her make-up they were very late catching a cab. Cynara insisted they walk a hundred yards down the street from the House before leaning out from the cobbled kerb and waving their arms.

'You were happy to be dropped off in front of a House,' he said, 'and that's one of the best restaurants in Jerusalem.'

'You didn't have my warm plum lipstick all over you at that point, Severus. I don't wish to be thought a whore. It may not fool anyone but I feel obliged to try.'

He waggled his head.

'You know the saying, Cynara,' he said, 'a Roman man wants a chaste woman in the house but a whore in the bedroom.'

'I know the saying. Now clean your face, please.'

He spent most of the trip back trying to get her dark lipstick off his neck and cheeks; eventually he had to resort to using one of her emollient tissues.

'Now I smell like I've just walked through the perfumery section at Agricola's.'

'We both also smell like a brothel. I can imagine what the soldiers on Antonia's security detail will think of us.'

In front of the courtroom, Agrippa showed his press pass. The orderly waved both of them into the press box. Cynara had just enough time to notice that there were still no spare seats in the public gallery.

'I was the only one who fired a shot,' Petros Bar Yonah was saying, with stubborn solidity. 'All these other people followed us from the Temple precinct out to Gethsemane, and a lot of them had weapons. I had a .454, and Simon had stashed some gear away in the garden, but no one else among the inner circle had weapons of their own.'

Petros Bar Yonah was a solid man, scrubbed very clean. His grey hair spilled over his collar—long by Roman standards, but still tidy enough—and his *payot* were neatly curled and oiled in front of his ears. Likewise, his clothing was simple, but clean and pressed: a heavy cotton shirt over the top of a long tan robe. He rested his hands on his knees and looked at Cornelius, unafraid. Cynara suspected he was most of the way through his cross-examination, and that *Aquilifer* Getorex had chosen to focus on the incident in the Garden of Gethsemane. She rummaged in her handbag for a scrap of paper and scribbled a question on it.

Agrippa wrote underneath her words. *The violence in the Garden undermines his credit as a witness. Or it would if there were a jury.*

'So Simon started handing out weapons?' Cornelius asked.

'Yes, *Aquilifer*; he must have been hiding stuff away in there for weeks.'

Petros's basic naïveté showed with this last comment, she thought; Roman patrols conducted regular sweeps with metal and mine detectors through Jerusalem's parks and gardens. Simon had accumulated his little stockpile in no more than a day or two, hiding ammunition boxes in between tree roots and rifles in long grass.

'What possessed you to bring a .454 to the Temple?'

'I carry it most places, *Aquilifer*. I have a permit for it.'

He fished in his robes and laid the licensing paperwork on the witness stand.

'I'm a fisherman. I used to have two decent-sized boats on Lake Galilee and a fifty per cent interest in an ocean-going trawler. I had a boat burnt on me five years ago and I've also had rival crews try to pinch my catch. A weapon is a necessity.'

Cynara became aware of the scarred state of Petros's hands, hands that had spent many years feeding nets through them and scaling, gutting and boning fish. Pilate pointed at the witness stand.

'I'd like that documentation exhibited, Don Linnaeus.'

The defence counsel stood, nodding his head. 'Of course, Procurator; you'll have it by close of business today.'

Cornelius turned to Petros once more. 'And you shot because you were sure the Suspect had been killed?'

'Yes *Aquilifer*, and because I thought between them the Temple Guard and the Second Cohort were going to shoot the lot of us.'

'You weren't planning some sort of last stand?'

'No, *Aquilifer*. As I said, the weapons were Simon's. We didn't want to fight. I didn't want to fight. I don't think the Temple Guard wanted to fight, either,' he paused. 'Romans always want to fight.'

Petros was looking down at his hands, massaging his

knuckles with nerves. Cornelius waited for the laughter induced by Petros's last comment to die down.

'But Simon wanted a fight?'

'Yes, he did, and so did some of the people who'd followed
us over from the Temple.' He paused, his expression pinched
and grumpy. 'Look, *Aquilifer*, if there'd been more of us armed
and willing to fight, you'd have had a major gun battle on your
hands. To the extent that there was a gun battle, it was thanks
to trigger-happy Romans.'

Cornelius ignored the assertion.

'Did you know any of them, the ones who wanted to fight?'

Petros looked uncomfortable, and fidgeted.

'By sight if not by name, *Aquilifer*; Yeshua has a lot of
followers.'

'Has he ever made any attempt to regularise this
arrangement?'

Petros shook his head, his expression quizzical. 'I don't understand you, I'm sorry.'

'You know, find a cave somewhere; buy some land; build a,
ah, compound.'

Petros laughed. 'If we wanted to be Essenes, we'd join one
of their communities. They escape the world; we live in it at
the same time as rejecting much of it.'

'And you had no inkling that Iscariot was in the High
Priest's pocket?' Cornelius was asking now.

'No, *Aquilifer*, none at all. He'd always been the one who
hated the financial dealings in the Temple more than any of
us... and that goes back years. When he wanted to get personal
about it, none of us were surprised. That was part of Iscariot's,
ah, thing.'

'He must have been very persuasive?'

Petros laughed bitterly. 'We didn't take a lot of persuading,
Aquilifer.'

'But you all knew Iscariot was trouble?'

'Not in any great detail, *Aquilifer*. We knew about his sister, but we also knew Yeshua's view of that, that Iscariot and his brother had brought things on themselves, going up to the *castrum* and interfering with the Roman's woman.'

'And you weren't expecting reinforcements, from Iscariot's Zealot confreres or... elsewhere?'

'No, *Aquilifer*, we weren't.'

'So you have no view on the Suspect's comment to both Iscariot and Prefect Binyamin Bar Binyamin that "he didn't come"?'

Petros looked flummoxed.

'I didn't hear him say that,' he said.

'I'm sure you didn't,' Cornelius said, one eyebrow raised and glancing in Pilate's direction.

As Cornelius began to put his case—going so far as to accuse Petros of dissembling over expected Zealot reinforcements—Cynara felt Agrippa press something into her hands. It was a note, written on a folded piece of his personalised *Newshour* letterhead, and likely written when he'd organised the room for their lunchtime assignation. The paper was watermarked, lovely and creamy. She opened it while he watched.

I have Parti Optimates *business to do*, it ran, *but I will be back in plenty of time to file my report and collect you for the very pleasant evening I've got planned for us. If by any chance I'm late, go to The Pit and wait for me there.*

Yours, Severus.

A FUNERAL

Mage Daria Saleh—through sheer coincidence—met the priest of Mars on the way to the dining carriage. Like her, he was in full regalia, although he was still in the process of pinning his cape around his throat. She hailed him—two senior officers of the Roman civil religion both on the way to Jerusalem had to be going for the same purpose.

'Son of Mars.'

'Daughter of Cybele.'

'Rufus Vero's funeral?'

'Did he follow your rite?'

'No,' she said. 'My son has taken his widow and child in the proper manner.'

The priest smiled and nodded, inviting her to sit opposite him and ordering some simple food—olives, cheese, bread, oil and a pitcher of wine—for both of them. He introduced himself—he was an Alexandro, and when he said it, she could hear his Hispanic accent—and paid for their meal. They shared and talked quietly as the scenery rolled by outside.

Alexandro—who, on the army's behalf, had to officiate at the funeral—knew more about the arrangements. There would be an armoured vehicle waiting at the station, he told her, to prevent any complications arising from walking through Jerusalem in their official robes, and the army had kept Rufus's body stored for two days longer than usual in order to allow his parents time to reach Judaea from Italy. The young widow was to deliver the *laudatio*.

'They'll probably be on this train, then,' she said. 'Although

I haven't seen a man in a white toga anywhere.'

'He may be dressing in his compartment,' he countered. 'I hope the widow will be able to manage the *laudatio*. She's not one of us.'

'My son has helped her,' she said. 'She'll be all right.'

She told him a little of Rachel's background as relayed to her by her son, watching the priest's eyes widen when she got to the death of the family in the Galilee, and her subsequent rescue by Rufus. He nodded, impressed.

'What a fine man,' he said. 'A credit to the legion; I hope he was a good and faithful husband to her.'

Daria detected—as soon as he used the word *faithful*—that Alexandro was a Stoic. His upright bearing, missing left ear and mass of fine scars on the same side of his neck indicated that he was ex-military, and although she'd met him once or twice before at official functions, she didn't know what he'd done since his retirement.

'My son and he were blood brothers; Rufus nominated him as guardian for his little boy. My son speaks very highly of him.'

Alexandro fished in his robes for a few minutes, pulling out a folded piece of paper.

'Knew I had it somewhere,' he said, smoothing it out on the table. 'His family is from Lucca. He's the oldest of five. His parents are Sirius Vero and Anca Felicia. They've brought their youngest daughter with them; apparently she's too small to leave with the nanny.'

'They're rich?'

The priest waggled his head. 'I'm not sure. Father's a successful apothecary; mother has a name indicating servile origins. In the middle somewhere, I'd say.'

When their train pulled into the station, Rachel and Saleh—dressed for a funeral—were waiting on the platform.

Daria and Alexandro walked directly towards them, finding themselves joined by a middle-aged man gone completely bald—his scalp was shaven clean—and his wife, who was leading a little girl by the hand. All were dressed in white, the man in a toga, the woman in a stola, the little girl in a white tunic. Both adults had been crying; the little girl seemed bemused by events, and was staring and pointing.

Daria and Alexandro stood to one side as Rachel showed Rufus's parents their grandson. The two of them were delighted with Marcus, complimenting Rachel on having produced such a *fat* baby. Daria and Alexandro stepped forward only once Rachel had introduced Saleh to them. He exchanged kisses on each cheek with Anca and then knelt before Sirius, his head bowed. The *paterfamilias* clasped his hands and pulled him upright, and they, too, exchanged cheek kisses.

'There's a closed armoured vehicle outside,' Saleh said. 'We're going straight to the Roman cemetery at the *colonia* and then back to Antonia for the wake.'

Sirius nodded, looking around him at the massed pilgrims as they went down the stairs to the MRAP, Daria and Alexandro bringing up the rear. He noticed that there was a second vehicle in the convoy, and that its side windows had been carefully blacked out. That, he knew, contained his son's body.

Rachel nestled herself into Saleh's arms as the vehicle ground its way through masses of people in the city and then out towards the *colonia*. She tried to avoid staring at Sirius; she could see Rufus's face refracted in his older features. She'd long known that Rufus resembled his father—that much was obvious just from the photographs in their flat—but seeing the same smile and gestures, even down to the way Rufus would stick his little finger in his ear and wriggle it about when the ear itched, was almost too much to bear. She caught herself remembering how Rufus made love to her—he would often start by wriggling down under the covers and kissing the small of her back—and began to cry. She clutched the text of the *laudatio* in one hand and looked at Saleh.

'I'm going to mess this up.'

'No you're not,' he said mildly, holding her to him.

She'd been worried, too, at how Rufus's parents would react to Saleh, that it would look like she'd taken another man with indecent haste, but he'd shaken his head and—most important—explained.

'Back in the day, a widow was expected to take another husband, the sooner the better,' he told her, 'especially a young widow. The old Romans thought a widow had the chance to give another man pleasure and children, and to enjoy her life. Why should she be locked away?'

'It's, it's... very different,' she said.

'So what you've done is entirely right and proper, as you'll see.'

When they reached the *colonia*, she saw that the other seven men in Rufus's *contubernium* had built the pyre and were standing around it, waiting. The decurion approached Rufus's parents and—as Saleh had done—kissed his mother and knelt before his father. When Sirius had pulled him upright, he motioned to two of his men. They came forward, holding something wrapped in oilcloth between them. They handed it to Anca, who balanced it in her hands as Sirius lifted the corners of the material.

It was a death mask—intricately carved from some scented wood—and a very fair likeness. Rachel and Saleh went to look at it, while Daria and Alexandro walked towards the second vehicle. Saleh then joined the seven men lifting the board under Rufus's body—clad in his dress uniform, drenched in oil, covered with saffron, his hands crossed at the wrists—and bearing it towards the pyre. Alexandro began to sing; the others soon joined him. One of the soldiers played the same air on a fife, guiding them all as they sang. The tune was surprisingly joyous. Rachel stood beside Sirius, and he took her hand. Anca slid her arm around her waist.

'It's happy music,' she said at last, not able to think of anything else to say.

'He lived well,' said Sirius. 'He loved life. He served the Empire with distinction. He made love to a beautiful woman. He fathered a handsome son. This is good.'

When Alexandro and the soldiers had finished singing, the priest motioned to her. One of the soldiers picked up Rufus's little sister and bounced her up and down in his arms; she giggled and squinted into the sun. Rachel handed Marcus to Anca, stood in front of the pyre and unfolded the *laudatio* as the men slid the wooden base on which Rufus's body rested onto the top. She'd originally wanted to start with an apology: she knew little of their customs and did not want to mock them with her lack of skill. Saleh had shaken his head, and for the first time, she saw him become emphatic.

'You're doing something honourable. You're remembering your husband. Hold your head up. Now is not the time for the *humble humble humble* routine people in this province seem to like.'

He'd helped her write it, of course, polishing up her Latin grammar and making sure it sounded right, but the substance was hers. She told of her rescue, of how Rufus had always treated her with honour, of his gentle courtship, of his delight when Marcus was born. She also told of the manner of his death, 'defending civilisation' as Romans always put it. When she finished, she began to wail, but was relieved to note that she wasn't alone. Anca and Saleh and the decurion were all making a fair old racket. Alexandro then walked around the pyre, chanting his prayers and flicking scented oil over the wood.

'Do not seek for this warrior, this son of Mars, in any one place, for if one drinks water he is in it somewhere; if one breathes air, he is in it everywhere.'

She noticed that the crossed timber pieces were nearly his head height. One of the soldiers passed him a flaming torch; he then waved everyone back. The pyre took with a great whoosh of wind and fire; Rachel returned to Anca and Sirius and retrieved her son. The whole group stood and watched it burn for half an hour or so, the flames reflected in their pupils, throwing wine onto the timber; the camphor and sandalwood spread through the pyre filled the air with perfume.

'Tomorrow, we return to claim his ashes,' Alexandro said to her.

'What do I have to do?'

'I'll lead you around the remains of the pyre,' he said, 'and show you what to collect. You place them in an urn his comrades have prepared and then deposit the urn in the military tomb over there.' He pointed.

'I can't keep them?'

The priest's kindly face showed a momentary flash of horror.

'You mustn't bring his ashes back to your house,' he said, 'you don't want *manes* in your house. They're supposed to stay in the cemetery, where they belong.'

She nodded.

The whole group made their way down the low rise towards the MRAP and piled inside, one of Rufus's comrades taking the steering wheel. She sat in between Saleh and Anca; Marcus was scratchy again—she was sure he was teething—and insisted on playing with her breast before attaching himself to it. Anca smiled.

'Rufus used to do that,' she said.

Men from the 3rd Cohort had prepared a room in Antonia for the wake; there were pitchers of water and wine and various cakes, savouries and sweets. Rufus's comrades set about serving the rest of them. Rachel could feel herself getting tipsy as the afternoon wore on, and was conscious at one point that her hair smelt like sandalwood. Sirius did get drunk, listening to Rufus's comrades regale him with stories of his son's talent for high jinks and humour. He started to list noticeably and the decurion procured two comrades to help him and Anca and their little girl to their room in the north-west tower.

'You're just down the corridor from the aviatrices,' the decurion said to Anca. 'But they won't disturb you. They keep to themselves for the most part.'

'Except when they're bonking fellows from the First Cohort,' said one of the other men.

Daria and Alexandro stood in front of Rachel and Saleh once Rufus's parents had left. Daria took her son's hands.

'Sirius wants Marcus to stay in his family line,' she said. 'And to that end, he's asked me if he can adopt you as his son.'

Saleh was taken aback; he hadn't expected to make that big an impression.

'I told him it was up to you. I think he's a good man and yes, he does remind me of my patron. He's the best of Roman manhood: an excellent father, a loyal husband and a bold and shrewd businessman. Sleep on it and talk to him in the morning.'

Saleh nodded at his mother and stood up. They embraced. Alexandro looked at Rachel.

'Meet me in the Antonia entrance hall at first light tomorrow,' he said, 'and we'll attend to the ashes.'

Under the dispensation accorded relatives after funerals, Saleh brought both Rachel and Marcus into his quarters overnight. He took out his bedroll and set up a makeshift cot for Marcus on the floor while Rachel knelt beside his bed and changed the child's nappy. She admired his neat quarters as she worked: the shelves of medical textbooks, his official *licentia* hanging on the wall along with his awards and citations. When she'd finished and Marcus had settled, Saleh propped on his heels in front of her, his jacket undone. She could see his Alexandria Academy chain tangling with his identity disc. He took her hands in his.

'I will understand if you say no,' he said, 'but I would like a great deal to make love to you now.'

She stood, kissing him and sliding her hands under his open jacket and around his waist. She wanted him very much. She shivered as he undressed her, his fingers brushing against her skin. She suspected he could tell as he took her that she was responding to him as a lover for the first time.

Today, Antony decided, had been a good day. Corbulo and Zoë were both young enough to remember what children enjoyed, so he'd had a trip to the cinema to see *The Riddle*—Sarius Roscius Junior's first film in five years—and an extended run playing Corinth Game in one of the shinier parlours. He'd done well enough at the latter to win back the cost of both their lunch and cinema tickets and then some, which tickled Corbulo no end.

'Look at this, Zoë,' he said as they went next door to trade Antony's prize token for cash. 'We're going to go back to the mistress with a profit.'

Zoë was perplexed as they went through a dark tunnel and emerged in a tiny, grimy office.

'Why can't he claim his prize in the parlour?' she asked. 'In Athens, you just go to the counter and get your money.'

'Gambling for cash is illegal in Jerusalem,' Corbulo said,

'by order of the Sanhedrin. So they give these out instead'—
Antony held up the painted wooden seagull that stood for his
winnings while Corbulo pointed at it—'and you come here to
get your money.'

Zoë glanced at the bored-looking man behind the counter.
He was clean enough, but the glass in front of him was clearly
bulletproof and his hair was lank and greasy. Corbulo bade
Antony drop his wooden token into the security drawer. The
man yanked the drawer inside, retrieved the token and counted out a decent number of coins. He dropped them into the
drawer and shoved it back towards Antony, who retrieved the
contents gratefully.

'I think I should buy both of you ice creams,' he said, 'at the
gelateria outside Antonia.'

'That's expensive,' Zoë said, 'all the tourists go there.'

'If I go back to Mater with a full ten *denarii*, she'll think you
just stuck me under a tree somewhere and went off and spent
the day bonking each other.'

Zoë went scarlet. They had sloped off in the middle of the
movie; she thought Antony hadn't noticed. Corbulo smiled
indulgently and winked at him.

'Getting anywhere's a real trial just now,' he said. 'I say we
walk to Antonia and take in the sights.'

'While avoiding the sheep shit,' Antony said.

'I do believe your balls have dropped,' Corbulo said. 'Pull
your head in. You're not a man, yet.'

Antony complied; Corbulo was a stocky, broad-shoul-
dered man, and Antony still young enough to be bent over
his knee and thrashed. The walk, while slow, was pleasant
enough, and Corbulo's relentless cheeriness was a tonic of
sorts. Antony took in the fire-eaters, buskers and beggars with
real interest, taking turns to hold first Zoë and then Corbulo's
hand. At one point he walked in between them while they

made moony faces at each other over his head. He noticed
Jews staring at this, disgusted expressions on their faces. He'd
once asked Hillel about what he called the 'no hand-holding'
rule, but hadn't been able to make much sense of the other
boy's response.

'Boys aren't supposed to hold hands,' Hillel had said.

'But I hold hands with my father,' Antony protested, 'and
we still get stared at.'

'No boys,' Hillel repeated. Antony had shrugged, not pressing the point.

They waited to be served at one of the stone tables outside the *gelateria*. Sitting down for table service tripled the
price but since Antony was paying, Zoë made no complaint,
enjoying the balmy weather and watching contractors keep
the square free of sheep shit and rubbish. A young woman
took their orders, scooting away to another table as soon as
possible. The *gelateria* was busy. The square was relatively
free of stench. There was also the good smell that came from
sacrifices wafting over the Temple walls, which Antony knew
would get stronger tomorrow.

He looked at Corbulo and his rictus grin, noticing that
while the soldier clasped Zoë's hand and talked with her, his
gaze never stopped roving over the square, quartering it, sizing
it up, an all-corners watch. Antony saw that his eye paused on
the wide walkway on top of the Temple's outer wall surrounding the court of the Gentiles. Roman troops in helmets and
full-body armour were stationed at intervals along it, looking
down into the mass of humanity and animals below. As the
boy watched, Corbulo laid his rifle across his lap and pulled a
multi-tool from his pocket. He began detaching the sight.

'What are you doing?' Antony asked.

'Unscrewing my scope.'

'Why?'

'Because if I look through it while it's still attached, they'll think I'm lining people in the square.' He paused, smiling. 'Use your head, Antony.'

Corbulo held the sight to his eye, balancing it neatly between his ring and middle fingers, looking at some of the soldiers on the wall. Zoë leaned close to him, one hand on his shoulder. He touched her fingers gently and then held the sight in front of her face.

'Get a load of this.'

There was a moment of complex wriggling as the two of them adjusted themselves so she could see what he had seen. Antony leant forward, noticing that some of the troops on the wall were moving a great deal more than Roman troops on perimeter duty usually did. He squinted.

'Oh, my,' Zoë said, blushing scarlet again. 'What idiots.'

Corbulo handed Antony the sight.

'At your two o'clock,' he said.

Antony balanced the weight of the beautifully machined instrument in his hand, copying what Corbulo had done with his fingers. Dancing around the crosshairs were several Roman troops—no, more, there were seven—with their backs turned. They'd dropped their trousers as a group and were waggling their naked buttocks at the pilgrims and merchants in the Court below. People were starting to notice, and Antony saw pilgrims pointing at the wall and moving towards the site of the offence. Something sailed through the air—a stone, or perhaps some spoiled food—and landed near one of the mooners. Antony handed the sight back to Corbulo.

'I think we'd better go home, now,' Antony said. Zoë was nodding, her eyes wide and the skin around her lips pale.

'I think you're right,' Corbulo said, reattaching the scope with controlled haste. He was no longer smiling. 'Let's get out of here.'

He slung the weapon across his chest, took Zoë with his
right hand and Antony with his left and strode towards the
taxi rank, jumping the queue and earning some glaring hos-
tility. Antony chanced to turn just as Corbulo shoved both
him and Zoë into the cab. The gelateria had emptied. The
proprietor was rolling the shutters down while the man who
sold pizza slices in the middle of the square had closed his
van and barricaded himself inside. People streamed into the
square from everywhere. The soldiers stationed in front of
Antonia had gone down on one knee, and there were more
of them than usual. A *strix* circled over the Temple. Bottles
and junk flew through the air. One bottle was burning from a
rag stuffed into the neck. An officer screamed into his radio.
People climbed over each other's backs in an attempt to scale
the section of wall where the seven soldiers were standing.
The men had dressed themselves and turned to face what was
a developing riot, their rifles levelled. The people climbing towards them did not seem to care that they were looking down
the barrel. Just before the cab pulled into a side street, Antony
saw the telltale puff of crenellated white smoke that indicated
the presence of tear gas.

Cynara felt like an impostor, sitting in the press box in Agrippa's
absence, even though he'd invited her to join him. The feeling
had been at its strongest when her father was sworn. He'd
scanned the public gallery for her, and when he didn't spot
her she could see his face fall. It was only as he sat down that
he'd chanced to look into the press gallery and seen her. His
eyes lit up, but there was a troubled cast to his mouth as he
looked at her and saw the empty seat beside her. She cursed
the fact that nothing could be done about the Empire Hotel
until after Passover; she would be glad of her rooms there
when the time came. She would be glad, too, when Agrippa

returned to Rome and she could put her dalliance with him to one side. He tickled her in ways very different from Leon, which she did not like because it made her regret her decision to refuse Leon's proposal. Leon, she thought, had cured her of a taste for predatory Roman men, turning her toward 'the other sort'; the devoted fathers and protective husbands.

She folded her hands in her lap, watching her father answer the questions the lawyers put to him, detailing his role on the Sanhedrin and that body's relationship with not only Ben Yusuf but also the various religious communities scattered throughout the province.

'It seems there are a range of views on Ben Yusuf within the Sanhedrin,' Linnaeus said.

'Yes,' Joseph responded. 'We are conscious of our differences, but also of our similarities. You need to understand that the *Kohen Gadol* is one of my relatives, and his current wife is cousin to my late wife. We disagreed over Yeshua's teachings, but we have agreed on other things in the past and will no doubt agree in the future.'

'Were you aware of the *Kohen Gadol's* dealings with Iscariot?'

'No, Don Linnaeus, and I have to say I disagreed with the forgiveness Yeshua extended to Iscariot and to Simon.'

Pilate held up his hand, halting Linnaeus mid-sentence. He pulled a single sheet of paper from his dossier and read out a succinct paragraph outlining the distinction between forgiveness and *clementia*. Cynara was surprised at its accuracy and incisiveness; she suspected that someone rather expert in matters of religion had drafted it on Pilate's behalf.

'You thought they were too dangerous to forgive?' Linnaeus asked when the Procurator had finished.

'At that stage my distaste for them was more personal. Simon insulted my daughter.'

LEON

Cynara closed her eyes, remembering the time her father had managed to corral Ben Yusuf and his closest followers together at his residence. He'd brought in caterers and invited his children to meet the new religious leader. Isaac and his Samaritan wife had made their way down from Syria, which meant her father called Cynara every hour at work, trying to convince her to put in an appearance. She held him off until he backed her into a corner, asking her if she were avoiding the family home on purpose.

'Papa, Leon is visiting.'

'Bring him with you, if that's what stopping you from coming.'

She'd gasped, trying to imagine what her father would make of the Deputy Prefect of the Praetorian Guard, a man who had a concubine but would much prefer Cynara to marry him. For her part, she'd talked to Leon after the conversation with her father.

'I'd like to meet one of your holy men, Cynara,' he said. 'It would be good to learn what makes them tick.'

'This is my father's house, Leon,' she said, 'not an opportunity to gather intelligence.'

'I'll be very discreet,' he said, winking at her.

Leon wore dress uniform—including a long red robe with gold piping that reached to the middle of his calves, restricted to the Praetorian Guard—and a red and black boat cloak over his buttoned jacket. She watched as he clipped the gold chain symbolising his authority around his neck, pressing the links flat under his collar with its profile of the Emperor. She dressed conservatively, in a concealing fuchsia *chiton* with a cream silk veil pinned to the hair piled on top of her head. He offered her his black-gloved hand as they made their way downstairs.

'You drive me wild when you dress like that,' he said.

'Leon, my father isn't a naïf, but if you make it Roman-obvious, he'll be very annoyed.'

Leon nodded; he understood. He had impeccable manners and knew how to showcase them to good effect.

To start with, the evening had gone well. Joseph Arimathea was a skilled host and the food and wine were excellent. Several of Ben Yusuf's followers had professional backgrounds and she noticed Leon and Matthias chatting amiably in a corner, brandy snifters in hand. Everyone had washed and gone to some trouble to dress in clean, albeit often plain clothes.

Ben Yusuf was socially adept and literate, with a clear, resonant voice. Petros's wife was gentle but authoritative, instructing the servants on the care of her disfigured eldest son with calm efficiency. Petros was genial and good-natured, even when trapped into giving advice on the best local fishing spots. Ioanne showed he could speak the purest Attic Greek—even better than Nic, which the latter acknowledged. Mary interrupted them in the middle of what looked like a competition to see who could quote the most of the *Symposium* from memory. Nic had extricated himself from the conversation with some difficulty and told Cynara *sotto voce* that if he were 'that way inclined,' he'd have difficulty keeping his hands off the young man. Cynara noticed, too, that Iscariot and Simon avoided Nic and Leon, pointedly staying on the other side of the banqueting hall.

The difficulties came when the group reclined to dine. Some of Ben Yusuf's followers were uncomfortable with what they considered to be an imported, Hellenistic custom and most of them struggled with where they ought to put their arms and how to prop themselves up comfortably. Only Matthias and

Ioanne were genuinely at ease, and only Petros and Rebekah were willing to learn by example, copying Nic and Mary. Leon made the mistake of explaining what to do to Simon, of all people. The latter's head whipped around. His tone was icy.

'Content yourself with turning one of our women into a whore, *Romoi*, and leave me alone.'

'*Romoi* is the plural form,' Leon said, almost by reflex. Cynara resisted the temptation to smack her forehead.

'*Leon*,' she hissed. 'Ignore him, please. He hates you.'

Simon spoke very little Latin, but seemed to understand what she'd said. He stared at her.

'Do you hate yourself?' he asked in Greek. She had no idea what he was getting at; only that he was hostile.

'What do you mean, Simon?'

'When he puts his hands on you at night and you think he loves you and you think you love him, do you hate yourself?'

The conversation around the room ebbed away; she could hear Leon controlling his breathing only with considerable effort. She had seen Praetorian Guardsmen use unarmed combat techniques with each other, at the barracks in Rome, playfully. That had frightened her enough. She didn't doubt for a moment Leon's ability to kill everyone in the room.

'You went to their country, yes? Went to the kingdom of the wicked and learnt what they have to teach, yes? Became one with them, yes? Then you came back home, but they make you hate yourself, so you have to change.' He pointed at her head. 'Your hairstyle is like theirs. You dress like them. You speak like them. You watch their bloodthirsty amusements. You rut with one of them, or perhaps two or three all at once, thinking that you have been set free. You tear the hair out of every part of your body except your head, because that's what they like, yes?'

'Simon, all those things are my choice. Nobody makes me do them.'

'And instead of a husband and children, you run a palace of fornication and profiteering on their behalf, yes? You must hate yourself, working for these sick fucking people.'

The idea of the Empire Hotel being a palace of fornication and profiteering amused her, and she had to restrain herself from bursting into laughter. She could feel a low buzzing behind her eyes—too much to drink, she suspected—and Leon's hand on the small of her back, supportive.

'Simon, that's enough.'

It was Ben Yusuf's voice, low and penetrating. He was glaring at the Zealot, his eyes narrowed. Leon looked first at Simon and then at Ben Yusuf.

'You might want to reconsider the company you keep,' he said. He turned back to Simon. 'As for you, did your father not beat some manners into you?'

Cynara looked across at her own father; his mouth was moving but nothing came out. Petros was looking down; Rebekah covered her mouth with one hand. The stunned faces above striped banqueting rests turned slowly. She knew that the whole incident took no more than a minute or two, but time seemed stretched and distorted.

'I don't need to hear manners lessons from *kufer* filth,' Simon said, emphasising the vulgarity. At this, Leon stood up and began unbuttoning his jacket. Some of the outside caterers were Greek, and knew what was coming. Joseph finally spoke, his voice a strangled squeak.

'I'll not have you fight in my house.'

'I wasn't intending to fight in your house, *Kyrios*,' Leon responded, inclining his head to the *paterfamilias*, his fingers still working, revealing a cream tunic and barrel chest. 'I was intending to invite this reprobate to step outside and settle his differences like a man, instead of insulting my woman and your daughter.'

Simon also stood up. Cynara wanted to be sick, now. Leon's eyes were hard and cold, like chips of blue tile, shallow, as though he'd drained all that was good and kind in him out of his mind and locked it away somewhere for safekeeping. She had only seen that look once or twice in all the years she'd known him.

'Sit down, Simon.' It was Ben Yusuf again; his voice low and clear. 'He will kill you, and there will be no comeback. He will tell his commanders a lippy Jew insulted his woman and that he got a little too enthusiastic when repaying the insult.'

'I didn't insult her,' he said. 'I told the truth.'

At that Leon—his arm a blur of movement, coordinated and sharp—backhanded Simon across the face. The latter sprawled backwards, collapsing onto his dining couch. His eyes rolled back in his head momentarily, before he recovered and struggled to a sitting position, clutching at his neck. Iscariot scurried to his friend's side and crouched down, his face concerned. Cynara wanted the ground to open beneath her. She knew what Leon's gesture meant: he could have punched Simon, and knocked him out cold. He had a huge reach and fists of stone. A punch, however, passed only between equals. The backhander was a Roman's way of saying, *you are my inferior*. Even worse, Leon was left-handed. Joseph looked at Leon. His voice took on a pleading tone.

'Please, not in my house.'

Leon glanced at Ben Yusuf and Joseph, then lowered his eyes. 'I'm sorry, *Kyrios*. That was too much. With your and Cynara's permission, I will leave now. I lost my temper and failed to restrain myself.'

He began to re-button his jacket, looking around for a servant to bring him his boat cloak.

'No, Leon, please stay,' Joseph said. 'I want you to stay.'

Simon rubbed his reddened cheek, staring at Leon in real

fury and struggling to stand. Leon's fingers paused on the last button, one just below his imperial collar insignia. He was clearly stunned at Joseph's request. Cynara took the chance to grasp his free hand, guiding him to the place beside her.

'Papa has asked you to stay,' she said. 'I also want you to stay.' He nodded, putting his arm around her shoulders. She leant close to him, speaking softly in Latin. 'Thank you for defending my honour.'

'You are very keen to judge, Simon,' Ben Yusuf said, his tone still even and controlled. 'And you forget that judging is hard work, even for people much wiser than you.'

To Cynara's wonderment, Simon also apologised.

'And he somehow defused the makings of a very nasty fight?' Linnaeus was asking now, dragging her back to the present and his evidence. The effect was something like seasickness, and most unpleasant.

'Yes, Don Linnaeus. I really did think that Simon would stand up and keep pushing and that Leon would wind up killing him.'

'Even after he'd been hit once?'

'You could have cut the air with a knife. I don't think I'd have been so frightened if a gang of thieves had broken into my house.'

Cynara looked around the press gallery, self-conscious; the journalists from the *caput mundi* knew who Leon was; some of them may even have met him in person. The Athenian reporter smiled at her.

'You're a regular Penelope,' he said, 'lots of high-class suitors. Is there an Odysseus we're not hearing about?'

Linnaeus wound up his examination-in-chief with her father's view of the Sanhedrin's business dealings and a discussion of the *corban*. Joseph pointed out that Ben Yusuf couldn't be expected to know how to administer a pension fund. When Linnaeus expressed surprise, Joseph defended the purity of his motives.

'You need to remember, Don Linnaeus, that in every society save your own, making money from money like that is seen as disreputable, like making something out of nothing.' He paused. 'Yeshua—and many others, including me—grew up in a tradition that finds Roman commerciality deeply troubling. His views on the *corban* may be ignorant, but they are not born of malice.'

Cynara looked towards the dock, to see if there were a break in Ben Yusuf's extraordinary impassivity. She thought there was. He had unfolded his hands and was gripping the sides of his carved teak chair while staring straight ahead. *He knows Papa just called him stupid*, she thought. She looked at her father, filled with respect for his gentle sagacity. *Somehow he managed to call him stupid without... insulting him.* Linnaeus turned towards Pilate, bowing slightly.

'No further questions, Procurator.'

Pilate stirred from behind his bench, looking at Cornelius, his glasses dangling from one hand. '*Aquilifer?*'

'I do have a few questions, Procurator. I will try to be brief.'

Cynara understood why; the afternoon was drawing on, and Pilate still had to question the Suspect in his capacity as Examining Magistrate. She turned towards Agrippa's empty seat, hoping he would put in an appearance sooner rather than later. She wondered what business the *Parti Optimates* could possibly have in Jerusalem.

'Rabbi Arimathea,' Cornelius began, 'are you aware of any other links between the Sanhedrin and organised Zealotry apart from those between the High Priest and Iscariot?'

'No, *Aquilifer*, and even learning of that single act of bribery has been a shock to me.'

'So there has never been, to your knowledge, any other contact between members of the Sanhedrin and terrorists?'

'To my knowledge, no.'

'When you had the Suspect and his followers to dine at your residence, were you aware that Iscariot was a terrorist?'

Cynara leant forward, one hand in front of her mouth.

Papanonononopleaseno!

Cynara and Leon had arrived early, and while Leon was on the roof taking in the twinkling city sights with her brother and sister-in-law, Joseph had pulled her aside, avoiding the servants, standing beside one of the burbling fountains in the residence's baths so they could not be overheard. 'I don't know what to do,' he'd said, 'but remember that shooting, the medic—'

'The abortion clinic?'

'Yes, that one.'

'Why?

'That was Iscariot, one of the Teacher's followers. He'll be here later tonight.'

She remembered her terror and alarm, her desire to protect her father mingling with anger and something else harder to identify.

'You can't have him in your house, Papa. For God's sake, you are *paterfamilias* in your own house... you'll have to tell Ben Yusuf this Iscariot isn't welcome.'

'It's too late for that. They're on their way here.'

She'd been furious; she took her father's hands in her own and tried to hold her voice steady.

'Listen to me, Papa, please. I'm no lawyer, but I know Romans. If you know he committed this terrible crime and you then shield him from the law, you make yourself complicit in that crime. You must not have him in your house! Please.'

'No, *Aquilifer*, I wasn't aware of any terrorism, although I learned soon enough that he hated Romans. I became aware over time of the situation with his sister, but also that the Roman officer in question had no desire to pursue the matter further.'

Cynara struggled to keep her face a mask, revealing nothing. She leaned back in her seat, looking up. The Athenian reporter was watching her closely; she could see him out of the corner of her eye. She found herself wanting Agrippa, wanting him beside her at least, although that soon blurred into memories of Leon wrapping his strong arms around her after the to-do over supper. They'd climbed the stairs onto the roof after Ben Yusuf and his entourage had left, sitting on wicker chairs along with Isaac and his Samaritan wife, drinking sweet dessert wine as the moon rose. When Leon was in the loo both of them drew her aside.

'You should marry this Leon,' Isaac said, 'he's a good man.'

'He loves you,' her sister-in-law added, 'as much as Romans can be said to love. He's honourable. He's successful. He's gorgeous.'

'If I marry him, I have to go to Rome and leave Papa alone.'

She heard Leon's booted feet thump their way up the stairs from below. He'd donned his boat cloak; the night was cool. He'd taken her in his arms, then, and wiped away her tears, wrapping his cloak around her. The silk lining slid over her skin as she rested her head on his chest.

'I will wait for you, Cynara Arimathea,' he'd told her in Caesarea, before he left. 'One day, you will be ready.'

'I do not agree with everything he says, and I think resorting to violence in the Temple was an act of singular stupidity,' Joseph Arimathea was saying, 'but I do think there is much to what he says.'

'Such as his criticism of the *corban*?'

'No, not that. There is much in his criticism of the currency exchange and sacrifice system in the Court of the Gentiles. It is almost as though it is calculated to exploit the poor, and if you have learnt nothing else of Judaism in your time here, *Aquilifer*, you will know that, among Jews, care for the poor and indigent is of central importance.'

Cornelius inclined his head; Cynara thought she saw the flicker of a smile at the corners of his mouth as he turned.

'Surely, Rabbi, if the Temple is rich—whether from its investments or the activities of its merchants—it can afford to be more generous to the poor?'

'By taking money from them now only to pay it back in the future, *Aquilifer*? You of all people should know that's bad economics.'

Cynara listened—only at the most superficial level—as Cornelius put his case. Hovering at the edge of her consciousness was the knowledge that her father had perjured himself and God rained down lightning upon liars. *And he had to*, another part of her mind answered. She closed her eyes again, wondering at the buzzing sound that seemed to have settled in behind her eye sockets.

The courtroom door flew open and a Centurion in full battle dress—she could see his rank—charged through it, running towards the bench. While the door swung back into place she became aware that the buzzing was coming from outside Antonia, and it was very loud. The soldier handed something to Horace, who spun on the spot and then shoved it with a distinct lack of formality under Pilate's nose. Cynara watched him read. He leaned forward, closing his bench book and putting his fountain pen to one side. The skin around his lips was white. He banged his gavel.

'Ladies and Gentlemen, I am adjourning the court for an indeterminate period. Rabbi Arimathea, you're free to go, I have no questions for you. I must now inform everyone here that there is rioting in front of both Antonia and the Court of the Gentiles. While I cannot prevent members of the press from doing their jobs, the situation outside is very danger-ous. Tear gas and riot control armour have been deployed, as have both the *Vigiles* and the Temple Guard. I assure you all, however, that if you remain within the fortress—in fact, if you remain seated in this courtroom—you will be safe.'

He looked at the legionary in battle dress. 'Sound the alarm, soldier, if Capito hasn't ordered it be sounded already.'

As he stood, a siren began to wail. Cynara looked at the empty seat beside her. Claudia Procula, she noticed, had fol-lowed her husband, pushing past a court orderly.

'They did *what*?' Pilate bellowed as he strode down the corridor towards his office, the Centurion trotting to keep up with him.

'Mooned the pilgrims, Procurator.'

'From the top of the Temple perimeter wall?'

Pilate barged into the War Room just as Horace unlocked it for him. Lonuobo followed Horace, turning on the lights and two of the screens.

'It's only on JTN at this stage, Procurator.'

'Thank the Goddess for that,' he turned to Lonuobo. 'Do they have footage of members of the Imperial Roman Army doing the bum dance? I bloody hope not.'

'I'll watch and see, Procurator.'

'I want those arseholes up on charges... and the men.'

Pilate looked at the screen, watching as Roman troops and *Vigiles* with rectangular riot shields and metal barriers tried to corral the demonstrators away from the steps of Antonia and the Temple's Sheep Gate, which was choked with bleating ani-mals and terrified pilgrims. He could see burning bottles flying through the air, clouds of tear gas and rioters burning home-made versions of the X *Fretensis* banner with its wild boar and the Emperor's personal Standard with its bundled *fasces*.

'Giant papier-mâché effigies in three, two, one...' the Centurion snickered.

Pilate rounded on him just as Capito and Claudia arrived in the War Room. 'This isn't funny,' he said, his tone low and menacing. 'Look behind all the rioters and their oil bombs lighting up the screen. Look at the outside wall of the Temple. Do you see that big dark pyramid shape?'

'Yes, Procurator.'

'That, I'll have you know, is bodies. People who were trying to climb over the top of each other and then had a tear-gas canister dropped on them from above. The JTN crew isn't game to get any closer to it because of all the smoke and fire going in the main square, but that's where the deaths will be.'

Pilate remembered his first major *iniuria* matter, when he was three or four years out of law school. The crowd at a provincial amphitheatre had rioted over a ticketing cock-up and had pushed in large numbers against the riot-proof fences at one end of the arena. Before the whole thing finally collapsed into the sand below, fifty-odd people had been crushed to death. He remembered sitting in his office looking at the big glossy black and whites of the dead, laid out on stretchers outside the amphitheatre. Nothing had prepared him for those images.

'Procurator,' said Capito, breaking in, 'all available forces have been deployed to contain the riot. I have ordered the seven men responsible detained and they're currently in the Stockade.'

Pilate gazed at the old soldier; for the first time in his experience, he thought Capito looked very tired. '*What* possessed them, Capito? This is... such a deliberate provocation.'

'Er, hmm, well, they were actually coming from Rufus Vero's

funeral, Procurator, and they'd all had too much to drink. And weren't feeling too happy about being here or about the local populace, either.'

Pilate touched his fingers to his temple, awareness stealing up on him. 'That explains the number... they were the other men in his *contubernium*, yes?'

'Yes, sir.'

'And what genius decided to rotate them onto Temple perimeter duty straight after a comrade's funeral?'

'There was no decision as such, Procurator. We don't have the troops during Passover to relieve any more than one or two men after a funeral. *Medicus* Saleh, Rufus Vero's blood brother and his son's guardian, was relieved for the afternoon.'

'Saleh's a good officer.'

'Yes, Procurator, that he is.'

'What is the problem with enlisted men in Judaea, Capito?' Pilate asked, his voice almost plaintive. 'Does the army lobotomise them before sending them here? Or only send the ones who come in the bottom third of the General Intelligence Assessment?'

Capito was wary. He looked down momentarily before making eye contact again. 'No, Procurator, but they can't get laid here and it tends to prey on their minds.'

It was a rhetorical question, Capito, but thank you anyway.

'Pontius.'

It was Claudia's voice, high and strained.

'Yes, Claudia.'

'I sent Antony into the city with Zoë and *Decurio* Corbulo for the day. I don't know where they are.'

Pilate sat down behind his desk, his head in his hands.

Camilla looked down at Aristocles, at his sweet face, clasping a handful of the kiss-curls on either side of his head as she ground against him with her hips, noting where the silver filigree headband above his eyebrows pinned some of the soft down flat against his scalp. *He really is very pretty*, she thought. Myron, her last servant, he'd had a beautiful sculpted body, but she always had to visualise Marius's handsome, hatchet-faced head attached to his shoulders in order to come. *Very silly girl you were with Myron*, she thought in a lucid moment, leaning forward so Aristocles could fondle her breasts. *You were indiscreet, and Pater caught you.* He pinched her nipples and she began to moan. She spread her fingers over his smooth chest, contrasting it with Marius's dark thatch. On balance, she preferred the thatch, but the Greek fondness for male hairlessness was delightful on a semi-regular basis. Aristocles began to stroke her flanks and backside and she moaned again.

Sex hadn't occurred to her when her mother had left for court and Antony had left with his two minders. She'd done a weights circuit, swum a mile, bathed and eaten before retiring to her laboratory to paint her most recently completed model aeroplane. She had seen Aristocles in the *tepidarium* and not-ed how handsome he was, but in an abstract way. He winked at her and she smiled back, but thought nothing more of it. She'd been leaning over her models desk, painting yellow tips onto the scimitar-shaped propfan blades of her *CPI Falco 70*. She straightened up and noticed Aristocles standing in the doorway. This time she did see his beauty in a sexual way. She poured water into the airbrush tank to blow the nozzle clean and then wiped her hands on her cotton tunic.

He clearly thinks I'm hot when I'm dressed in a smock covered in paint and smell like a bunch of different reagents. Interesting. Oh well, de gustibus non est disputandum.

He was smiling; he'd been watching her for some time.

'You're very good at that, *Domina*.'

She cocked her head to one side, aware that his use of an

honorific from the time before abolition meant *I wish to be treated as you would have treated me in the days of slavery.* She pressed against it, just a little, just to be sure. 'Household servants don't have to use that title in the *familia Pilata*, Aristocles.'

'But I want to use that title to address you, *Domina*,' he said, 'while the others are away.'

She stepped closer to him; he wore only a linen wrap from waist to knee, showing off his fine torso. She ran a fingernail down the neat cleft between the two masses of pectoral muscle, pausing at the solar plexus. He stepped forward to kiss her, but she held up her hand and rested her fingers on his lips. 'No kissing, Aristocles; the kiss is for Marius.'

'Yes, *Domina*, I understand.'

He writhed under her now, his head back, throwing his arms out to the side, showing the chip in his left forearm. *He's got lovely control*, she thought, *I'm very tight and he hasn't lost it yet.* She was close to coming herself. She traced the chip's outline with a fingernail and let go the restraint that had kept her sliding up and down his cock at a steady pace for the last twenty minutes. *Thank you contraception*, she thought as she bounced, the bed shaking with the violence of her movements. *Thank you science. Thank you medicine... Thank you MEN!* She collapsed forward, over him, her hair framing his face. She could feel him unloading inside her. He kissed her cheek and she flinched away from him.

'Just your cheek,' he panted, 'please.'

She turned her head and felt his lips and tongue caress the other cheek. He smelt of mint and coriander, rosemary and thyme; good, healthy food smells. She stroked his hair.

'That was lovely, Aristocles. Thank you.'

'Yes, *Domina*. Thank *you*.'

A tear-gas canister had exploded against the windscreen

on the way from Antonia and they'd worn a deal of it as it swirled around the cab. Once they'd reached the sanctuary of home, Corbulo had cut Antony's favourite blue tunic off his body with scissors while Zoë threw his socks and underpants straight into the rubbish. The tunic followed them, Corbulo keeping it well away from his face and eyes.

'Is it ruined?'

'More than ruined,' Zoë said. 'It's poison now. We're lucky we only got the edge of it.'

Corbulo insisted they all bathe; Antony was glad of the warm water in the *tepidarium* and submitted to Zoë's gentle touch as she cleaned his skin and looked into his eyes, holding him under the fountain and flushing them out. At one point Dana joined her. Antony kept his expression neutral.

'I didn't know tear gas was so nasty,' he said.

'Your eyes are still red,' Zoë said, turning from Antony to Corbulo. 'Will he be all right? I know it's worse for children but I didn't realise how much worse.'

'He should be. I wouldn't want to take anyone outside right now, not even to go to Æsculapion. They'd have to be at death's door. I'm sorry we couldn't let the cabbie into the residence. He looked like death warmed up after we paid the fare, even with that tip. Stupid bloody security protocols.'

'He was still in the street when we came upstairs,' Antony said. 'I saw. I think he means to wait it out, or at least wait until he can see properly.'

The troops detailed to protect the residence—there were more of them than Antony realised—stationed themselves at vantage points throughout and around the palace. He watched as they rolled solid protective screens in front of exposed bits of colonnade and over windows and then armed the electric wire that ran around the top of the walls. In the background, he heard the hum of the palace's generator, a fallback in case the electricity grid failed.

When he realised that Zoë and Corbulo had no plans to leave the baths, Antony hauled himself out of the water—his fingers had gone all pruney—and went in search of his sister, Nero following at his heels. He figured he had quite a story to tell, and wanted to show his rabbit-red eyes to her before the effect wore off.

Antony stood outside Camilla's bedroom, Nero at his feet. The dog snuffled at the bottom of the door, and his tail thumped against the floor. Antony knocked, but his sister didn't answer; loud music and sounds of sexual pleasure came from within. He shrugged; perhaps Marius had slipped away from Antonia for a couple of hours. It was the kind of thing he'd do, at least in Caesarea, and maybe Jerusalem as well.

Dana had dressed him in a soft linen wrap; he drew this around his shoulders and tucked the longest piece around his waist while he waited for Camilla to finish. The man's voice, he realised, did not belong to Marius, but to the boyishly handsome cook from Antioch. His sister was using Aristocles for release, as she'd once used Myron the trainer and as he wanted to use Dana. He waited until he heard them both shout, counted to sixty and then pushed the door open. Camilla whirled around to face him.

'Antony, fuck off! My room is off-limits, you know that.'

She leaned across to the side and shut the music off. Aristocles propped himself up against the bedhead, his legs spread, while Camilla seated herself in between them. He curled his hands around her; she clasped them in her own and held them across her belly, pulling the covers up to her waist. They were both slick and shiny with sweat and very flushed. Nero shot around Antony's legs and launched himself onto the bed, standing in front of Camilla and licking her face.

'Nero! Not now!'

Aristocles chuckled at this and patted the bed beside him. Nero stepped over his leg, turned towards the foot of the bed and settled, resting his head against his thigh. His tail thumped against the bedhead as Aristocles scratched his back. Antony took in the artwork in his sister's room—he didn't see it very often—artwork that resembled what he knew his parents had ordered for his room in Caesarea. The walls depicted—panel by panel—an imaginative seduction decorated with mythological *trompe-l'œil* motifs in each corner: Pan playing pipes and dancing over the skirting, a nymph trying to climb out of an acanthus border, a snake so rendered as to seem to be crawling from one panel to the next over a pillar. In many of the images, the young couple depicted looked out, making eye contact as though seeking approval from the people who used the bedroom.

'Why are you here?'

'I thought Marius should know that there's a riot going on in town... but I see he's not around.'

Antony's tone was arch.

'Yes,' she said, 'He's in the barracks, and I had an itch. Aristocles was kind enough to scratch it for me.'

'I could tell Pater,' Antony said.

'I could torture you to death, too.'

'The rules are different for women, once you're spoken for.'

'You could tell Pater, yes,' she mused, an odd little half smile on her face. 'But I don't think you will, because I think you want something.'

Antony flushed almost as bright as Camilla at this suggestion. She was, he realised, speaking to him as an adult for the first time. He was reminded—painfully—that Camilla was considered one of the cleverest young women in the Empire.

'I want Dana,' he said at length.

Aristocles spoke up. 'And she wants you, Antony.'

'That is your price, Antony?' Camilla asked.

'Yes. If you don't tell Pater or Mater about me, I won't tell Mater or Pater about you.'

Camilla cackled at this, vastly amused.

'Oh ho ho, you are a treat, Antony. Our father the lawyer is in there, but he doesn't yet know how to bargain. I will need Aristocles to scratch my itch on an occasional basis. Each scratching now invites the most unpleasant possibility of discovery, thanks to you. Presumably, you want Dana more than once, yes?'

'Yes, I do.'

'That's very simple, then. We trade fuck for fuck. You are now in credit, and owe Dana a thorough porking. I shall see that she knows of your obligations to her. I'm sure she'll be delighted.'

Antony stumbled backwards towards the corridor, twisted and went to pull the door to behind him. He heard Camilla's voice, clear and ringing.

'Do remember, Antony dear, I'm not promising that you won't be discovered... just that I won't tell.'

'You're fucking with me, big sister.'

'No, Antony, we are fucking with each other.'

Cynara asked the orderly's permission for her and her father to step outside, which he gave, smiling. The two of them walked across the mezzanine in silence, arm in arm. They came to the railing and looked out over the parade ground.

'I thought that would be worse,' he said at last.

'You did well, Papa.'

His voice was low and strained.

'I lied, Rivkah. And I have never lied in my life, not since I was small, before my bar mitzvah.'

'I know, Papa.'

'We despise the Romans for many things, but they are an

honest people. I have lied in one of their courts. I am ashamed.'

She threw her arms around him, hugging him fiercely. She did not know what she could say to him. She told him she loved him and continued to hold him as he sobbed.

'And the lie came so easily,' he said. 'I thought my tongue would stick to the roof of my mouth and I would humiliate myself. But oh no, out it came, so smooth.'

The young *Optio* in charge of the defence witness room— free now the last witness had been excused—approached them. Cynara could see the concern on his face.

'Can I get you anything, Rabbi?' he asked.

'Some water for him, soldier, please.'

He nodded and strode away, putting a clean cup underneath the stone lion water fountain and then bringing it to them.

'I was ordered to report to my Century as soon as the last witness came out of court,' he said.

Cynara nodded, watching him walk away. At that point— his hair uncharacteristically messy and his clothes rumpled—Agrippa appeared in her field of vision. When he saw her and her father he began to slow, stopping about six feet away, waiting. She felt relief wash over her, some of which must have transferred to Joseph, who relaxed a little in her arms. Agrippa approached them, his expression uncertain.

'I'm sorry to interrupt, but you probably don't know that there's been a serious riot outside. People are dead, there's been looting and the Archives and Registry Office is still burning—'

'Pilate made an announcement in court,' Joseph said. 'How did it *start*? That's what I want to know.'

Cynara could see Agrippa's shame as he related the incident on the Temple wall. He stopped, waiting for one or the other of them to speak. He reached out and touched the back of Cynara's hand.

'It's no consolation, I know, but I'm sorry. My people have behaved very badly.'

Both of them nodded; she felt her father squeeze her hand.

'The worst of it's over now,' he went on, 'but the army and *vigiles* have ordered all cabs except those with an official court pass out of the city. You'll have to walk home, either now or after the Procurator examines the Suspect. I wouldn't wish that on anyone. The streets are full of looters.'

'I think I'll cope,' said Joseph, although Cynara could tell he didn't relish the prospect. Her father was seventy-two and had a dodgy hip.

'*CR Judaea* has an official media vehicle that seats eight. I'm happy to use it to get you home, either now or after the hearing is over. One of our local stringers will drive you.'

Cynara watched her father's face, seeing gratitude mix with perplexity.

'The only thing is, if you prefer to wait, you'll be sharing with me and the rest of my crew... and your daughter, of course.'

'I'll wait,' he said, standing slowly, 'and thank you.'

Linnaeus borrowed Cyler from Cornelius and headed down the dedicated stairwell to the cells at the back of the court, Clara the clerk at his heels. He was grateful for the dark young man's guidance; without it he'd be hopelessly lost. Cyler led both of them to Ben Yusuf's cell, opened the door and stepped back.

'I can't come in,' he said.

'You're the other side, yes. How do we contact you when we want to get out? The cells are soundproof.'

'I'll put you in an interview room. Then you just press the panic button under the desk and it'll come through to me in the monitor room.'

Cyler led the three of them to one of the interview rooms

along the corridor and left, closing the door behind him.

He could see Linnaeus and Clara talking urgently to Ben Yusuf through the glass in the top of the door. He liked the look of Clara. She'd opted for a mid-calf powder-blue robe that buttoned up the side and hugged her figure, revealing a high, round backside. Even better, he'd grabbed a handful of that backside on the way downstairs and she'd placed her hand over his and held it in place. He went to the monitor room, rummaged through the stack of *Milesian Tales* in the corner, chose one he liked and sat behind the desk with it. 'And you read them on the train,' he remembered a Jewish whore he'd seen in Heliopolis telling him. 'I don't shock easy, but when I went to Rome on holiday and I saw all these nice well-dressed people sitting on the train going to work, reading those filthy picture books... well, I was shocked.'

He smiled at the memory and kept reading, admiring the line art, thinking of Julia.

'If we get this right,' Linnaeus was saying, 'you'll go inside for a decent stretch, but you won't die. Your exercise in the Temple grounds killed one person, injured several and did a fair bit of property damage. I'm not excusing what you did... but as you no doubt heard during the commotion upstairs, Roman troops have managed to top you in the stupidity stakes. At least a dozen dead, hundreds injured and millions in damage.'

'Insurance companies already charge a higher Jerusalem premium,' Clara said. 'That's about to go up.'

'What will happen to the men who started... this riot?' Ben Yusuf asked.

'They'll be flogged, and the Decurion may be relieved of his rank, but they won't be executed, which is part of my point. Much as I hate to say it, the riot will have focused the Procurator's mind on the real issues.'

Ben Yusuf looked at the two of them, watching as Clara scribbled notes on a block of yellow legal pad while Linnaeus spoke. They were efficient, these lawyers; he admired their professional thoroughness and equanimity. At one point Clara leaned close to Linnaeus and said something into his ear. He nodded.

'Now, when the Procurator examines you, he's likely to have already formed a strong view when it comes to sentence. I know Pilate pretty well, however, and he is capable of shifts on the basis of a personal examination.'

'Yes.'

'One thing he doesn't like is people with tickets on themselves, which is one reason why he's made some rather tart comments to our witnesses. He'll probably do the same to you. He'll be trying to work out if you're just lippy, or if there's something else in there.'

Ben Yusuf understood Romans and their dislike of people they thought 'full of lip'.

'Lip,' his mother told him, when he was small, 'well, Romans think you have to earn the right to give lip. They won't respect you for you; you have to earn their respect. You have to *do* something first.'

'Trust is given,' he remembered a legionary telling him sometime, somewhere, 'but respect is earned.'

'So answer truthfully; but if he asks you something and you don't know the answer, admit you don't know.'

Ben Yusuf watched as Clara sounded the buzzer, summoning Cyler to the door. The young man let them out, smiling, slightly awkward because he was using his left index finger as a bookmark. He ordered another legionary to take Linnaeus and Clara back upstairs and locked Ben Yusuf in his cell. The latter watched through the open sliver in his hatch as Cyler trotted along the corridor, book in hand. He turned left into the monitor room and passed out of sight. Ben Yusuf went and stretched out on his bunk, being careful of his good court clothes, folding the fine material underneath him.

Cyler wanted to finish his *Milesian Tale*—he'd forgotten how good it was. It was one he'd first read a year or more ago, as much for the line art as for the story. He wasn't totally convinced by the modern trend to have the first dozen or so pages in colour—it looked like bad fresco when printed—but the majority of the pages were black and white just as they'd always been, and fabulous. He folded one of the corners over and looked at the ceiling, avoiding the bank of screens on the wall. He wanted the court day to end. Then he could run a couple of miles, bathe and retire to Julia's quarters and await her return from duty. He looked towards the open door, glancing down the corridor with its sick-making artificial light. There were some things you just couldn't make beautiful, no matter how hard you tried. He stood up, book in hand, and stepped outside, walking slowly. He stopped in front of Ben Yusuf's cell, running his fingers over the hatch, seeing for the first time the narrow opening with a heel of hard bread jammed into the runner at the bottom. His hand went to his chin and he smiled.

'So that's how you've been doing it,' he said.

Ben Yusuf's visage swam up out of the dark; both men could see a strip of the other's face and part of one eye. Ben Yusuf's was dark brown and flecked with yellow, Cyler's hazel and flecked with green.

'Doing what, sir?'

'Finding out about people. About *Medicus* Saleh. About *Aquilifer* Getorex.'

The knowledge that Ben Yusuf's knowledge depended—at least to a degree—on something of a cheat was oddly reassuring.

'What do you want?'

Cyler focused through the slit on Ben Yusuf's single visible eye, feeling the hair on the back of his neck stand up.

He's mad as a cut snake, but sort of interesting, too... like a cut snake.

'I'm not supposed to be talking to you,' he said. 'Technically, I'm the other side. Worse if the *Aquilifer* was doing it, of course, but even so.'

'Then why are you standing outside my cell?'

'It's not your cell; it's the Roman army's cell.'

Cyler was rather pleased with that line; one thing studying law had taught him to work on was coming up with witticisms in a timely fashion, before the moment had passed.

'And you're not supposed to be outside it?'

'No, I'm not.'

'What do you want, Cyler Lucullus?'

Cyler started at the use of his name.

'I don't know,' he said, finally adding, 'I think you're mental.'

'Why do you think that?'

'All the god business you go on with. That's mental.'

'Then you're saying that everyone in Judaea is, ah, mental.'

'Not in the same way. You're extra mental. You're a *loony*.'

'Maybe.'

Cyler wanted to kick himself. Once again, he'd felt drawn to speak with Ben Yusuf and the man had snared him in lengthy conversation. He waggled his head from side to side. Ben Yusuf was smiling at him; he could see the muscles around his eye crinkling.

'Are you happy, Cyler Lucullus?'

'That's a strange question.'

'It's a simple question.'

Cyler could feel irritation rising in him. Stoics and Epicureans and Hedonists had been arguing over the substantive content of 'happiness' since Saturn had devoured his children. Cornelius mocked his simple tastes, but Cyler read philosophy in his spare time. After all his reading, he was pretty sure that pleasure was an end in itself, but not much more than that.

'It's a simple question,' Ben Yusuf repeated.

'No, it's not, not in an abstract sense.'

'You know how you feel, surely?'

'Of course I do.'

'Well, are you happy?'

Cyler pulled at the base of his dress jacket, making sure it sat neatly over his hips, flicking his fingers across the shiny gold buttons.

'Happiness isn't a continuous state,' he said. 'It's fleeting. You don't get to keep it.'

'What is it that makes you happy?'

Cyler didn't like where this was heading; it was personal—even intimate—and he knew if Cornelius caught him talking to the Suspect he'd be in a world of pain. He also knew—from his classes in rhetoric—how dangerous it was to let someone else get into a pattern where he asked the questions and you were stuck with answering them.

'I think I'd better go, now,' he said. 'I really shouldn't be talking to you.'

'So you think you should follow the rules?'

Cyler stared at him, seeing the clever segue from abstract theory to personal application. It was a cheat, but he still answered.

'I think that's important.'

'Do you really?'

'Look, I've got to go—'

'You have a choice, Cyler Lucullus, about rules.'

Now Cyler was pissed off. He had forgotten more about rules than this reprobate with two murdering terrorists among his fellowship had ever known. He watched Ben Yusuf's dark eye.

'Enlighten me.'

'Do you want to protect civilisation?'

'Yes,' Cyler said, baffled, 'that's why I joined the army.'

'Rome has trained you to be a wolf, but if you're going to protect, you need to be a sheepdog.'

Cyler saw, in his mind's eye, the great sand-coated sheepdogs of Latium, coming down from the hills with snow in their coats, at farmers' heels. They held off wolves and bears, sometimes even fighting them to the death.

'You can run with the wolves or run with the hounds, Cyler Lucullus, but you can't run with both.'

Cyler peered through the slit in the hatch; like every Roman child, he'd grown up with stories of wolves, with the she-wolf who suckled Romulus and Remus and so helped found the City of the Seven Hills.

'You trespassin',' he breathed, annoyed that—in the grip of anger—he had reverted to dialect, half Etruscan and half Latin. Cyler resisted the temptation to force the hatch further so he could see all of Ben Yusuf's face. He closed his eyes and entered the meditative state he'd learned during his basic, sublimating his emotions as they flowed through him.

'Your people may once have been led by a wolf, Cyler Lucullus, but you're with the hounds, now.'

Cyler turned on his heel and walked away, his hands shaking. He nearly dropped the *Milesian Tale* as he turned, propping himself against the monitor room door until his mind cleared. He forced himself to sit quietly at the desk, facing the winking screens, holding the book open in front of him.

It was almost dark when court resumed. Horace prepared coffee, while Pilate felt lassitude steal over him as he sat behind his desk in his toga, wearing his uncomfortable bloody wreath. The torpor, he knew, came from panicking about his son only to learn that Antony was unharmed and safe at home less than an hour later. He'd have much preferred that Antony spend the day at home roistering with as many servants as he liked rather than give his father a dose of dread that left runnels of cold sweat trickling down his spine. Claudia, he suspected, would disagree.

'The final act begins,' he told Horace as he drank. 'I will try to be brief.'

'Counsel seemed happy with the request to make their closing submissions in writing, Procurator.'

'I'd have *ordered* them handed up in writing, Horace. I want to go home. I want to bathe, to eat, to make love to my wife, to sleep. I dislike being an appendage of my occupation, a tool of the law.'

He suspected Horace was listening only out of politeness; at the same age, he'd been willing to sleep at work in order to steal a march on the cohort of—mostly—young men who'd started at Valens in the same year.

'What did we used to call our slaves, Horace?'

He watched the young man's eyebrows shoot up.

'*Instrumentum vocale*, Procurator,' he said.

'I am not a tool that speaks. Nor are you.'

Pilate swept his toga behind him as he strode down the passageway towards the Praetorium, Horace trotting ahead to open the door. The courtroom was still packed; only the press gallery was partly unfilled—it was likely most of them thought the riot bigger news than the trial. He took his place at the bench, watching Horace slide in beside Lonuobo.

'Present the Suspect for examination, Don Linnaeus.'

He watched as Linnaeus moved towards the dock and instructed Ben Yusuf to stand. He whispered something to him;

Ben Yusuf nodded and Linnaeus returned to his seat. Pilate appraised the man before him, resting the tips of his fingers together in front of his face. Ben Yusuf made eye contact with him and did not flinch away; Linnaeus had no doubt told him the Jewish tendency to drop the head as a sign of respect had a counterproductive effect on Romans.

What shall I do with you, holy man?

'I am going to ask you some questions in my role as Examining Magistrate. You may answer all of them, some of them or none of them. Whatever you choose to do, there will be no penalty laid on you for your answers or lack of answers. While the court can use any information you divulge against other persons, it cannot use any information so divulged against you. You are protected from self-incrimination. Do you understand me?'

'Yes, Procurator, I understand.'

Pilate pulled a sheet of paper from within his dossier. If Cornelius and Linnaeus were watching closely, he was sure they would notice it was a sheet of yellow paper, and that it was marked at the top of each page with the Triton that was part of the Valens wordmark, a tribute to their involvement in the development of Roman maritime law.

Yes, I'm still using my old firm stationery. This is very sad.

'When you and your entourage made such a dramatic entry to the city, were you making a Messianic claim?'

Pilate waited; he could hear the clock ticking behind him. He counted to thirty, *one–tiber–two–tiber–three–tiber...* until he was satisfied that he would receive no reply.

'You have caused great dissention among your own people. Do you know why?'

'Some of them find what I say unpalatable, Procurator.'

'Do you know why that might be?'

'I think it's wrong when rich men do nothing to help the

poor. The rich in this city know who they are.'

Pilate wanted to return to the Messiah point, but couldn't see how to do it smoothly.

'Why did your followers attack the Temple Guard in Gethsemane?'

'They didn't, except for Petros, and then he only did that because we were fired upon.'

'So that incident did not represent an attempt to make yourself Messiah by force of arms?'

'If that had been the intent, Procurator, there would have been a lot more of us, we'd have all been armed, and we'd have won.'

Pilate felt blood pumping at the back of his skull. He glanced towards Linnaeus and Clara; both were glaring at Ben Yusuf. That sort of thing sounded reasonable coming from Caiaphas. In Ben Yusuf's less educated voice, it seemed arrogant, even thuggish.

'So you didn't intend to be Messiah, but you could have been one?'

This produced a flash in Ben Yusuf's eyes.

'You don't understand, Procurator. My country suffers under a great weight of poverty and corruption. Is it wrong to want to change that?'

'What do you hope to achieve?'

'My life is dedicated to confronting people with the truth. If you know what truth is, then what I say will make sense. If not, then not.'

Pilate had hoped for some sort of practical program for dealing with Judaea's 'poverty and corruption'. Instead, he was getting vague *pablum*. Well, two could play that game.

'What is truth?'

He listened once again to the ticking clock, not expecting an answer and feeling a trifle ashamed at presenting a tradesman from the Galilee with a poser for the ages. He looked over towards the jury box, making eye contact with Claudia. She smiled at him.

'If you had the power to fix this poverty and corruption, what would you do?'

'Make the rich give up their wealth. Let the poor worship God without the costly intercession of the Temple. Raise up the downtrodden.'

'You realise poverty and corruption in this province have lessened since the commencement of direct Roman rule?'

Now Ben Yusuf's eyes fairly blazed. Pilate thought, *about time.* Linnaeus was looking at his client and chewing his lip. Clara was looking at the fine decorative ceiling. Cornelius and Cyler were passing notes to each other.

'You think that by pulling on the levers of power, you can make anything happen. What did one of your scientists say? Give me a lever and a place to stand and I'll move the world?'

'Well, Archimedes was Greek, but yes, you get the idea.'

'It's not like that, and one day you'll learn it's not like that. God has granted you your great power, and God can take it away.'

Pilate resisted the temptation to make further smart remarks. He looked at Linnaeus.

'I've finished my examination, Don Linnaeus.'

Linnaeus stood and then gestured towards Ben Yusuf, indicating he should be seated. Pilate looked across at Cornelius.

'Do you have anything to add in response to that? Bear in mind I have your closing submissions already.'

Cornelius stood; he looked tired, dark circles under his eyes standing out against the pale skin.

'No, Procurator. The State rests.'

Pilate turned towards Linnaeus.

'And the Defence?'

Linnaeus stood. He didn't look anything like as exhausted as his opposite number, but then, Cornelius Getorex had other duties to the legion besides lawyering.

'The Defence rests, Procurator.'

Pilate scanned the packed public gallery; the press box had refilled for the most part, as journalists had wandered back in after filing.

'I will pass sentence tomorrow at zero eight hundred hours,' he said, glancing at Horace. 'Clerk, adjourn the court and collect the exhibits.'

PART IX

Tu regere imperio populos, Romane, memento
(Hae tibi erunt artes), pacique imponere morem,
Parcere subjectis et debellare superbos.

Roman, you are to rule the Empire's peoples: remember
These shall be your skills: to bring peace, impose the law,
To spare the beaten and to beat the proud.

—Virgil

Saul curses Roman thoroughness as he wields his pick, trying to dig into the road surface. He finally manages to prise out a lump of concrete, only to note he still hasn't broken through to the dirt; there's a layer of what looks like herringbone-patterned bricks underneath. Concrete has flowed into the interstices, binding them together. He swears again.

'What is it, Saul?' It's Elias, the older Zealot from Jerusalem who's been assigned as his supervisor.

'Fuck them for Roman bastards,' Saul says. 'They overbuild everything to buggery. How far does this fucking concrete go? All the way to Serica? Wouldn't bloody surprise me.'

The older man clambers up the shoulder and stands beside him, his greying hair and beard picked out in the moonlight. Saul wields the pick again; his forearms are rubbery with effort, and he drops it.

'Let me have a go, Saul.'

Saul sits down beside the depression—he's reluctant to dignify it with the word 'hole'—his hands clasped around his knees. He can

feel blisters forming in the hollow between his thumb and forefin-
ger. Elias works steadily, deepening the ditch. As Saul watches he
takes a tape measure out of his pocket and measures the depth.

'Halfway there,' he says. 'You made a good start.'

Saul nods, grateful in some ways to have dispensed with the two
Samaritans. The old man he found faintly ghoulish, with his silence
and refusal to bathe, while as far as Saul was concerned the woman
was a Roman's whore. They'd collected Elias in the village after the
rain had washed it clean, rills of water cutting through damp dirt
in the streets—and deposited Saul and Elias and the bomb on one
of the lonelier stretches of the Jerusalem–Jericho road under cover
of darkness. When the old man and the young woman turned their
cart away and headed back towards the town, Saul spat. Elias, he
noticed, was unmoved.

'He young and good looking,' she had told him when he asked her
why. 'He take me to Cyprus next month. That be nice, you know.'

'You're supposed to be fighting them.'

'We is, Saul, but different ways fighting to you Jews. The Ro-
mans, they run things nice, you know. We just want to run Samaria
ourselves, but we still run it their way. We don't need no Romans to
do it now, we learnt. When they go, I still let Clodius put his cock
in me, but he don't be ruling my people. We be ruling our people.'

Saul nodded, not pressing, suspecting Samaritan perfidy.

'We've got to get off the road,' Saul says.

Headlights bear down on them from the north, and both men
roll part way down the hill, pulling drab cloaks over their heads
and hoping the metal pick they've abandoned doesn't reflect any
light. The vehicle roars past: a refrigeration truck with advertising
painted on the sides. Saul suspects it's supplies for the Vinculum,
the Roman prison. The two men wait until the engine noise fades
away completely.

'Your turn again,' says Elias.

Saul takes the pick and resumes his work, Elias standing by with a shovel to remove the dirt and rubble in the hole. He breaks through the brickwork at last and starts to worry at the looser mixture of gravel and cement underneath. Elias takes out his tape measure again, checking the depth.

'Almost there,' he says.

'So you saw the start of it?' Pilate asked when Corbulo described unscrewing his scope in front of the gelateria.

'Yes, Procurator; it was a bit bizarre at first, and didn't really hit home. I think it took me about a minute or so to realise that we had to get out.'

'You two did well,' said Claudia. 'I'm very relieved.'

'I'll ensure your excellent handling of this incident goes on your service record, Corbulo,' Pilate added.

Zoë and Corbulo were standing before the *familia Pilata*. They—plus Horace—were gathered around the small dining table reserved for informal occasions like this. Nero was stretched out beside Pilate—he'd palmed the animal several pieces of cheese to keep him quiet. Events in the city meant he'd missed out on his usual run with a couple of men from the garrison, and he was frisky. Aristocles and Dana served up the family's supper, stepping around the dog, while Pilate poured out more wine for everyone, even Antony. He directed Dana to provide a glass each to Zoë and Corbulo.

'We were very lucky no media organisation got footage of the mooning incident. It's one of those things that's funny in a bad way.'

The hammer beside the little silver bell on Pilate's house *vocale* in the next room began to strike. He directed Milos to answer it and leaned forward, pouring a small libation into the table's central hollow. Nero bounced up, wagging his tail, staring at the bottle in Pilate's hand. Pilate reminded himself he needed to talk to Linnaeus about Nero's sudden fondness for Tuscan red.

'Well,' Pilate said, 'Horace and I will have some liqueur chocolates and dessert wine after our meal and try to come up with the right sentence—'

Milos reappeared, his face ashen.

'Procurator, it is *Legatus* Vitellius, and he is very angry.'

Pilate looked at the rest of the group.

'Oh dear,' he said. 'I wonder what I've done now.'

Claudia watched her husband leave, glancing from Antony to Horace to Camilla. She could hear Pilate's voice becoming agitated in the next room, but not what he said. When it became clear that he would be out of the room for some time, she dismissed Zoë and Corbulo. The two of them retreated into the corridor, glasses in hand, smiling and giggling.

'Go make babies,' Camilla said archly, once they were out of earshot.

Claudia heard Pilate hang up with some force.

'Fuck,' he said. 'I think you'd better see this.'

He sounded very strained. Claudia could hear the faint burr of a screen in the background. It was most unlike her husband to interrupt a meal for *anything* on screen, and she and Horace—then Antony and Camilla—walked out of the small dining area in single file, Nero at Camilla's heels.

'I thought you said there was no footage of the mooning business.'

'I was wrong,' he said, 'and I have just been told how wrong by our esteemed Legate.'

'JTN?' asked Camilla.

'I wish. It's CR. Empire-wide. This is rapidly turning into the worst week of my life.'

'It's two nights before the *Megalesia* parade,' Claudia said.

'Anyone at home watching screen right now is a *bona fide* hopeless case.'

'Well, the Legate was watching.'

Claudia paused; she noticed Pilate had taken his food with him and was scarfing it down while he watched replays. Nero gazed up at him, drooling. A little puddle had collected on the marble floor.

'Don't eat in front of the screen, Pontius. It's common. How many ways can you watch seven men drop their trousers?'

Camilla snorted. 'Maybe they're hoping to identify them from the close-ups.'

Claudia turned it off and shooed her family back into the small dining room. Pilate made dark comments about Vitellius's desire to drop ordnance on every transmitter in the Empire.

'The story is out now, and what happens, happens. Enjoy your meal, do your judging, then'—she leaned close to him and spoke in dialect so that Antony and Camilla could not understand—'make love to me.'

He nodded, sipping his wine.

Claudia looked through the leadlight in the top half of the door into the residence's main study. She could see both of them—oddly distorted, their hair crinkled and their heads misshapen thanks to irregularities in the glass—sitting in padded armchairs, smoking, drinking and gesticulating. Pilate's feet were hidden behind piles of law textbooks. Horace had a copy of the Criminal Code open on his lap and was leafing through it. She reached out and touched the fine spray of flowers picked out in one section of the glass: neither of the two men seemed to notice her presence.

She turned, then, running her fingers along the austere vegetative mosaic that decorated the wall, before climbing the stairs to their room. She could hear the servants—and one or two enlisted men—clearing away downstairs. Her feet oriented her without benefit of light, finding the edge of the Persian carpet and thence the enormous bed she'd insisted on purchasing when Pilate was first appointed. *I will not sleep in Herod's bed.* She undressed and rested on top of the bedclothes, staring into the black and listening. The city was quiet with the curfew, bereft of human voices but alive with the bleating of sheep and goats. She heard an air force pushprop formation go over, low and loud, reminding the locals just who was in charge. *Probably from Syria*, she thought, *Vitellius letting us know he's our superior as well.* She began to feel a slight chill and rolled into the brushed cotton, worrying for her husband and wondering if he regretted his appointment to this benighted province.

THE DREAM

'It's cruel,' her father said, 'that's why you can't watch.'

It must have been before her parents divorced, because he was still at home and both her brothers were there. She seemed to be about fifteen. She had just come from the baths, and was twisting her damp hair up on her head. The light was limpid and butter yellow, and her future stretched out before her, glowing. Her parents had been arguing: her mother wanted to let the three of them go, but Lucius said it would not do for the children of a prominent abolitionist to be seen gawping at the last crucifixion in Capua. It was ghoulish enough, he said, that local merchants were making a festive occasion out of it, selling little models made of pipe-cleaners and carvings on decorative glass. There'd also been a series of stomach-churning black and whites in the local paper—a retrospective of sorts—that inspired her father to pen one of his very best 'Outraged of Capua' letters.

'We need to see it, Papa,' Claudia said at length, 'so we don't forget.'

Her father snorted. 'You want to feed the eye, don't you?' he said to his children, pointing at one of his own, 'to let it have its fill of the lovely spectacle.'

'I've never seen one,' Claudia's older brother said. 'I suppose I am curious.'

'The world does not exist for your entertainment,' her father went on. 'People are not tools or playthings.'

He stared at her brothers. Both were fidgeting and looking at the ground. Her mother was aloof, her arms folded.

'You've won the abolition argument, Lucius, and you're about to win the crucifixion argument. Give it a rest.'

Husband and wife looked at each other, storm clouds gathering. Claudia knew there would be a tremendous row, just as there had been less than a week earlier when her mother had taken the three of them to the *ludi* without telling her father. Claudia liked the *ludi*, even though she agreed with her father intellectually about their wrongness. She liked the drama and excitement, and—truth be told—she found some of the fighters downright sexy. She knew a fair few final years at her school that felt the same way. One had even acted on it, which was daring in the extreme; gladiators were low rent. Even among the most extreme Epicureans and Hedonists, fornicating with one of them was considered *stuprum*.

'We can't put a stop to cruelty in one area only to have it break out somewhere else, my dear,' he said. 'Slavery is cruel and degrading; so are the *ludi*; so is this sort of vicious public punishment.'

'Stop with this *we* business, Lucius,' her mother said. 'Harsh punishments *deter*.'

In the end, the three siblings slipped away while their parents argued. Claudia led the way to the spot outside the city limits where the killing would take place, her brothers in tow. Much of the population was streaming along the *Cardo*: parents, children, local dignitaries, a press photographer with his camera and tripod in hand. Claudia saw beggars rubbing shoulders with town councillors, saw a man open a car door for one of the *Duumviri*. Crowds of little children stood around the Grey Ghost, admiring it as the driver guided it through the throng and away from the execution ground. The *Duumvir*— he had approved the method of execution, duck diving for the line in time to beat the Senate's cut-off date—was extemporising to anyone who would listen about bloody Stoics and how there were too many of them in the government these days.

Claudia smiled inwardly—she was proud of her father and his abolitionism. People in Capua remembered Spartacus and his supporters laying their hands on the town's armoury and arming local slaves with upwards of 200 breech-loading rifles and a good quantity of gunpowder, lead shot and pikes. There was an engraving in the town library of the forum obscured under a pall of smoke as the rebelling slaves shot down anyone and anything that moved. She had always been distressed at the fate of a legionary's horse in the foreground: it thrashed on its back, the whites of its eyes showing, a soldier—the rider, she presumed—beside it with half of his head missing.

Claudia crested the hill, feeling one brother take her hand. The first man was already nailed up and writhing, and both his agony and the rich, coppery smell of his blood shocked her. The three crosses were irregularly shaped, closer to a Y than the Greek *Tau* familiar from drawings and photographs. Blood covered the white stones below him and she saw one of the *Vigiles* wipe his cheek with distaste: he'd been dripped on. The blood left maroon streaks on his dark-green uniform.

'I think we'd better go now.'

The voice was her little brother's; the whites of his eyes were showing like the horse's in the engraving as he turned his head to look behind him at the crowd. It had taken on a frenzied, festive atmosphere. The second man was screaming as the *Vigiles* dragged him towards one of the crosses.

'It's not the best in us, no,' she said.

Claudia looked at the three condemned; they were noncitizens, of course, and one of them was begging for mercy in accented Greek. She could see he was asking to be shot. One of the *Vigiles*—he was carrying a placard with the word *raptio* painted on it—threw his hands up in the air; another made a vulgar gesture at the crowd. The whole thing had become performance, and she felt queasy. Her brother's voice was more insistent now.

'We have to go, or I'm going to be sick.'

Just as she went to turn away, she saw the third man hauled across the stones to his fate. In one of the peculiarities of large, public events, he glanced up and made eye contact with her, a pleading look on his face.

It was Ben Yusuf. She sat upright in bed and screamed.

'That's my wife,' Pilate said, looking up from *Intention in the Law*.

Horace could hear the wail floating along the passageway and butting up against the study's outside wall. He fumbled as Pilate shoved his brandy snifter at him and barrelled out the door, his footsteps echoing along the stone floor. He stood and followed the Procurator—slowly at first, then faster—both glasses in hand.

Claudia was still rigid, her eyes open and staring. Pilate crawled across the bed and enfolded her in his arms, wrapping the covers around her shoulders. At first she spoke gibberish and did not seem to recognise him; Horace appeared in the doorway, silhouetted by the light.

'Give me one of those,' Pilate said, snapping his fingers behind him. Horace handed him a glass, and he raised it to her lips.

'Drink this,' he said. 'We could hear you shouting from the study.'

She came back to herself and relaxed into his chest, taking the brandy from him gratefully, gulping. He touched her face, noticing that her cheeks were wet.

'What was it?'

'Ben Yusuf,' she said. 'It was a dream. Somehow he got into one of my childhood memories.'

'Wha—how?'

'When the three of us went to see the last crucifixion in Capua, and Mama and Papa were on the downward spiral to divorce.'

Pilate nodded; she'd told him the story several times.

'He'd turned into one of the condemned men,' she said, 'and he looked at *me*. Right at me, as though I could stop what was happening to him.'

She drained the rest of the glass and put it on the bedside table, then crawled back into his embrace.

'He has no business being in there,' she said, emphatic. 'Those are *my* memories; that's *my* past.'

Pilate turned his head to face Horace, still holding Claudia.

'I think we'll call it quits for tonight. I've got a fair idea of what I'll do tomorrow. Go to your rooms; breakfast is at six.'

Horace nodded and took his leave, closing the door behind him. Pilate turned to Claudia; she was sobbing again. He held her, rocking gently back and forth, rubbing her back and kissing the top of her head.

'Can you spare him?' she asked.

'From what?'

'The death penalty.'

'Why?'

'The man in my dream—no, no, the man from when I was a girl—he was crucified for rape, but it wasn't rape. I went to school with the girl who used him. He was one of their servants. She liked him and liked the sex, but of course it was improper, a wealthy citizen woman with a non-citizen man. Her father was progressive; he didn't care about the sex, as long as it was only sex. Then she fell pregnant and tried to elope with the boy. Her father caught her and used his *patria potestas* to compel her to have an abortion. He had the serving boy charged with rape.'

'She was under sixteen?'

'Yes.'

'I'm glad that custom has fallen into disuse,' he said.

'Camilla uses servants from time to time, Pontius. You must know this.'

'I sacked Myron when that was going too far, and gave Camilla a piece of my mind. She's chaste now, and Marius supervises her ritual obligations.'

Claudia inhaled; he knew nothing of the dalliance with Aristocles.

He paused. 'Even when we were young, setting someone up on a false charge was poor form. A call to the nearest munitions plant or mill would have solved the problem; the boy may have even appreciated a job there.'

Claudia rubbed her eyes.

'The serving boy was innocent. Maybe Ben Yusuf is, too. Maybe that's what the dream means.'

'I thought you were the rational one,' he said. 'Remember what you said about Propertius's *pais*?'

Her voice was small and distant.

'Yes. I thought that there must have been a misdiagnosis.'

'Have you changed your mind?'

She clung to him then, and he rolled onto his back, pulling her on top of him. She rested her head on his chest.

'I don't know, Pontius. Watching him sit there with his face so still it could be cut from stone... and not being able to make head nor tail of what he stands for.'

'Yes,' he said, 'that's been on my mind, Judaeans and their God and religion and whatnot.'

'You need a little of it, Pontius, it's useful.'

He kissed her and felt her start to respond to him.

'I wonder if that's true sometimes, I really do.'

She drew her head up and away from his at this; he could

just make out her eyes and lips in the dark.

'People need order, and religion gives us order,' she said. 'Imagine what Romans would be like without order. We'd be ungovernable.'

He reached over and turned on the droplights in the ceiling, bringing up Gratus's immense erotic marquetry while he stroked her bare back. He waved one hand around the room, smiling.

'Right now, these are my orders, and you need to tell me which ones you plan to make.'

SENTENCE

To Pilate's surprise, the public gallery was packed. He smoothed out the wrinkled sheets of yellow legal pad he'd written his remarks on and scanned the room. Cynara was sitting beside Agrippa in the press box, and they were holding hands unselfconsciously. Joseph Arimathea was beside them, talking quietly with Agrippa, who laughed at something Arimathea said. He could see Saleh and his woman and baby, although Cornelius Getorex's midwife was absent. An aviatrix with her rippling silver hair was seated as close as officially permissible to Cornelius's instructing clerk, watching him with the curving smile one saw in Etruscan sculpture crossing her lips. Occasionally he turned to face her, mirroring her smile and unconsciously mimicking the position of her hands and feet. Cornelius pressed his fingertips together in front of his face and stared into the distance, his face inscrutable. Fotini was in her usual spot in the jury box, although the seat beside her was empty; over the morning crossword, Claudia had decided that she would stay at home for the day and write some long neglected ad copy.

Linnaeus and Clara had prepared submissions on sentence— Pilate could see pages of scribbled notes, and a copy of *Criminal Sentencing and Procedure* open but face-down on the bar table. *Shouldn't do that, you two: way to break the spine.* Pilate looked up from their scribblings, scanned the room and touched his wreath, feeling the golden leaves prick his fingers. He looked at Lonuobo, motioning the translator to stand.

'First, I turn to some preliminary matters. On Tuesday a military tribunal, convened on orders from *Legatus* Vitellius and headed by *Advocatus* Lucretius Viera of X *Fretensis*, convicted three individuals of murder *dolus directus* and rape. Those individuals are known by the names Bar Gestas, Yaakov Dismas and Yeshua Bar Abba. They were captured on CCTV, and in one case by the news media, committing the crimes in question during Sunday's attacks on various Jerusalem landmarks. This footage has been made available on my orders to members of the press. Please see the senior court orderly after I've passed sentence in the instant matter if you wish to obtain copies.'

Pilate paused; his mouth was dry and tasted of ashes. He could see local Romans and not a few Greeks smiling, although members of the press looked shocked. *Ah, military tribunals, we love them. Can't have too much justice getting around the outposts of Empire, now can we?*

'*Advocatus* Viera sentenced them to be flogged and executed. The flogging has already been carried out. It falls to me to confirm the death penalty, which I now do. The three condemned will be conveyed from the Porta Antonia to Golgotha and there be executed by firing squad drawn at random from members of the First Cohort. The execution is to be carried out forthwith.'

Pilate paused while one of the orderlies stood, saluted and strode out of the courtroom to convey his orders to Marius Macro, who would select the firing squad by lot. Pilate suspected that this had already been done, and the orderly was only present for appearances' sake; it was traditional.

'I now turn to the matter at hand. Stand up, Yeshua Ben Yusuf.'

Pilate took a sip of his water.

'You have been charged with one count of criminal

damage, one count of felony murder *dolus indirectus* or in the alternative *dolus eventualis*, two counts of failure to warn, one count of riot and fifteen counts of aggravated assault. With the exception of the failures to warn, these alleged offences took place on a single day, during an attack you led on the Court of the Gentiles in the Jerusalem Temple. I have had cause to read and consider the evidence placed before me, including the very clear video evidence obtained through the Temple security system. For your benefit and for the benefit of the many people present today, I will make a few remarks before stating my findings.'

Pilate paused and took another sip of his water.

'I do not think you are a bad man, but I do think you are a stupid man. I do not mean to say you are intellectually stupid, because it is plain you are not. I do think, however, that you have not the faintest idea what to do with the gifts you have, and this is coupled with a tendency to violence. This has led you into innumerable cul-de-sacs and blinded you to malevolence among your own followers. It has also become increasingly clear to me that while you represent no direct challenge to Rome, you do represent a very considerable threat to the peace, order, and good government of this province. This threat is chiefly because you believe two things. The first is your repeated contention that your spiritual ideas should override those already developed by your own people after a considerable period of trial and error. The second is that, in furtherance of your attempts to undermine your own people's practices, you are willing to place yourself above the law. No one is above the law, not even the Emperor. Romans are not much given to philosophy, but Aristotle was surely right when he argued that the best government is a government of laws, not of men. Much of this foolishness is occasioned by your ignorance. There is a reason why we do not reckon carpenters jurists, or jurists, carpenters.'

Pilate looked at Cornelius, and then at Linnaeus. Both men's faces were masks, revealing nothing.

'I find you culpable *dolus eventualis* for the death of Samuel Kohen, not culpable for the first count of failure to warn and culpable for the counts of criminal damage, riot and assault. I find that the second count of failure to warn is not proven on the evidence before me.'

He turned to Horace, who was waiting for his signal.

'Call on the prisoner.'

Horace nodded, staring at Ben Yusuf as he stood up, a printed card in his hand.

'Yeshua Ben Yusuf, you are convicted by the Procurator of Judaea of one count of felony murder without the presence of intent, one count of criminal damage, one count of riot and fifteen counts of aggravated assault. Do you have anything to say as to why sentence should not be passed upon you according to law?'

'Yes, Procurator, I do.'

Pilate arched his eyebrows. *You would, wouldn't you?*

'Well?'

'It's not that you Romans are evil, it's just that you have no idea what you do.'

Pilate waited for a full minute, counting down the seconds.

'Is that all?'

'Yes, Procurator.'

'Sit down, please, Yeshua Ben Yusuf.'

Pilate lowered his gaze, making eye contact with both Linnaeus and Cornelius.

'Counsel, I invite submissions on sentence. *Aquilifer* Getorex for the State?'

Cornelius stood. Cyler passed him a tabbed folder, taking the time to smile at his silver-headed woman as he did so.

Pilate noticed that Cornelius's case for the death penalty was not as enthusiastic as it might otherwise have been, while his argument for a hefty prison term and physical chastisement was clearer and more persuasive. Pilate was not fond of flogging, although he thought it worked well on people—especially young men—who destroyed public or private property or otherwise made a nuisance of themselves.

Linnaeus emphasised Ben Yusuf's lack of criminal antecedents and gave a brief précis of the Stoic argument against flogging: that in so degrading the criminal, the State degraded the man who carried out punishment on its behalf and coarsened any members of the public who watched. Pilate had heard so many submissions on sentence in his time that he found he was listening with only one ear. He saw Linnaeus sitting down out of the corner of one eye.

'Thank you, Don Linnaeus, that was very helpful.'

He gathered the exhibited references from Ben Yusuf's previous employers, all glowing, and patted them into a neat stack, opened his ring-bound sentencing manual to the correct page and then looked at the prisoner.

'I came very close to ordering your execution, Yeshua Ben Yusuf, but in the end thought better of it. I think you are more likely to learn the error of your ways if given a lengthy period of time to think about what you did. To that end, I sentence you to ten years' imprisonment for the death of Samuel Kohen, four years' imprisonment for the riot and criminal damage counts and three years' imprisonment for the assault counts. The first two sentences are to be served consecutively; the latter is to be concurrent. I also order physical chastisement as a global punishment, forty strokes.' He pointed at two of the orderlies. 'Take him down.'

Pilate was unprepared for the spontaneous outpouring of joy this engendered; in the midst of the cheers, hugs and applause he saw people—mainly Galileans—praying and standing up in their seats. Even Cornelius and Cyler were smiling, while Linnaeus and Clara slapped each other on the back. Greeks and Romans quietly took their leave for the most part, while media people disappeared off to file, often at a brisk trot. He couldn't remember such a positive reaction to any judicial ruling he'd made previously.

Pilate had Horace adjourn the court; he chanced to turn and look towards Ben Yusuf as he left. The man was still utterly impassive, lifting his feet mechanically as the soldiers shackled him. He made eye contact with Pilate, his gaze level and unblinking and somehow *knowing*.

What's that about, I wonder?

Pilate stood on his desk and unscrewed the fire alarm, all the while instructing Horace to fetch some good wine, olives, cheese, cigars and the form guide.

'I know the sun isn't over the yardarm yet, but I've earned a bloody drink after this week!'

Pilate disappeared into Gratus's over-decorated bathroom at the back of his office and washed his face and hands. Sentencing always made him feel dirty, and he took some care to be thorough, smoothing down his eyebrows and cleaning under his fingernails. When he returned, Horace was waiting with cigars, olives and wine, but no form guide.

'It's *Megalesia*, Procurator, so there's no racing.'

'Of course, I forgot. Oh, and invite counsel into chambers.'

Pilate perched his wreath on the nearest bust of Caesar; Horace swept it up in a single, well-rehearsed movement and hung it on the wall where it belonged, then handed Linnaeus and Cornelius wine and cigars. Linnaeus helped himself to bread and oil while Cornelius lit up, blowing smoke rings.

The three of them stood at Pilate's big window and watched the firing squad assemble in the parade ground, talking.

'Your clerk bolted,' Cornelius said. 'Women don't usually run that fast.'

'Oh yes,' Linnaeus said, 'I think she's on the train already. There's a lusty young officer waiting to impale her at the other end.'

'Bit like *my* clerk, then,' Cornelius said. 'I hope he wasn't being too obvious. He's in love as well as lust, and it's doing his head in.'

Pilate chortled and faced the two men, turning his back on the execution detail below. Someone had thought to play a selection of popular film music over the barracks PA system as Marius Macro bellowed orders, pointing and gesticulating, and it made its way fitfully into the room. *There is nothing*, Pilate thought, *like the Imperial Roman Army for sheer bloody crassness.*

'I suppose that was a bit of a draw, gentlemen,' he said.

'I'm glad it's over,' said Cornelius. 'I've got two weddings to organise.'

'Romans don't do bigamy,' Linnaeus said. 'What's your excuse?'

Pilate grinned. 'I believe it's known as the phenomenon of the circling mothers-in-law,' he said. 'One in Londinium, one in Carthage, yes?'

Cornelius nodded.

'And there's a priority dispute, yes?'

Linnaeus grasped the situation and chuckled.

'In that case, have you decided which half of the Empire you're never to set foot in again?'

'Ah, no. That's the problem.'

The three of them grinned as Horace brought more wine and nibbles.

'Well, you got more than you bargained for, am I right?'
Cornelius said, looking at Linnaeus and swallowing an olive.
'Come to Judaea, get a woman. That's not the usual story.'

Linnaeus laughed, the beautiful relaxed laughter Pilate
knew was thanks to Fotini.

'The way things are going,' Pilate added, 'you'll be apply-
ing to the Senate asking to marry her.'

Linnaeus flushed. 'Maybe,' he said.

Pilate turned again and looked into the parade ground.
The popular music had stopped, to be replaced with the som-
bre drumbeats that presaged an execution. The firing squad
was in the process of marching out through the Porta Antonia, the three prisoners chained together in an open-topped
armoured vehicle at the foot of the steps. The three lawyers
stood in silence as the parade ground emptied and the drumming faded away. Off to one side, in a colonnaded shadow,
Pilate saw his future son-in-law in close conversation with a
lean, muscular man stripped to the waist. He squinted, trying
to make out the lean man's face.

'Who is that?'

Linnaeus belched. 'What?'

'Not you,' Pilate snapped. '*Aquilifer* Getorex, is that who I
think it is?'

Cornelius stood beside the Procurator, his eyes narrowing,
not out of a desire to see any better, but with anger. Linnaeus
stepped aside as Cornelius leaned against the glass, one arm
above his head. 'Gaius Crispus,' he hissed, 'you should be in the
bloody stockade.'

The two men were laughing about something now. The
conversation continued for a few moments, then they shook
hands. Marius detailed two men to stand on either side of
Crispus, stepping backwards, his hands behind his back. He
was holding *Parti Optimates* paperwork; Cornelius could see

the wordmark. As they marched Crispus across the parade ground towards the stockade, Marius turned for a moment, looking skyward and grinning hugely. Cornelius watched him grin, the hair on the back of his neck prickling with alarm.

Cyler wasn't pleased when Cornelius detailed him to accompany Ben Yusuf to the *Vinculum*. He'd been looking forward to putting the rest of the morning to more productive uses before circumstances reverted to their usual pattern and he would be unable to see Julia each day. He trotted downstairs and changed into battle dress; while he was fitting his body armour, one of the men in his *contubernium* wandered in and asked him who he was. Cyler gave him the finger and told him to fuck off.

'You'll pay for that,' the man said. He was dusty and sullen and bronzed from the sun. 'Three days' nice inside work.'

'I can see it already,' Cyler said amiably. 'A short-sheeted bed with raisins in it, a used condom in the helmet.'

'Don't give us ideas.'

Cyler made his way through the underground tunnel to the basement holding area where Antonia's vehicles were parked. Most of the bays were empty; they were on duty somewhere in the city. He leaned up against the wall where the prison van always pulled in and fiddled with a magazine, removing some of the bullets and then reinserting them again. The temperature down in the bowels of the fortress didn't change much from one season to the next, and the stone behind him was cool to the touch. He flattened his palms against it while he waited. Above him, he knew, were the *Camera* and the infirmary and the monitor room and the cells; beside him was the engine room. He could hear its faint hum. He looked up when he heard approaching footsteps and the clank of chains. He saw Cassius's peculiar eyes in the dark before he saw the rest of him, and made the fig sign behind his back.

Cassius and Enneconis had Ben Yusuf between them, supporting him lest he fall. Their movements were not gentle, and Cyler suspected they'd contrived to administer the flogging themselves. Floggers were supposed to be drawn from the whole cohort by lot, like executioners, but there had always been a degree of tolerance extended to men who liked both jobs and volunteered. The two soldiers shoved Ben Yusuf towards Cyler; he collapsed onto his hands and knees and then looked up, his eyes huge and pleading. His prison garb was spattered with blood. Cyler could see he'd received medical treatment, but his back was shredded. There was also blood drying above his hairline, and Cyler wondered what the two had done to him.

'Did you use the *flagellum*?'

'Only ten strokes, sir,' said Cassius. 'Five each for the men in our *contubernium* killed outside the Fleet Fox.'

Floggers had a fair bit of freedom to scale up, although the general rule was that the *flagellum* only came out if the prisoner remonstrated with his captors or was in some way ill mannered. Cyler bent at the knees and helped Ben Yusuf to stand.

'What's wrong with his head?'

Cassius fidgeted and looked sidelong at Enneconis, who stared at the ground. Cyler held Ben Yusuf upright, running his fingers over what looked like puncture marks around his hairline. They had pissed blood; scalp wounds always did. His beard was matted with it.

'He's a Jewish king,' said Enneconis, 'so I made him a crown—'

'—out of razor wire,' said Cassius, interrupting. He was smirking. Cyler wanted to hit him. He was training as *immunis*—so he had authority over the two of them—but no real leverage beyond the fact that he was marked out as a future officer. Cassius and Enneconis knew it, and both continued to grin. Cyler ordered Enneconis to fetch a first-aid kit and set about rubbing antiseptic cream into the puncture wounds.

'You two are sick fucks,' he said as he worked on Ben Yusuf's head, having to use all his strength to stop the man from collapsing on the floor. Cassius and Enneconis looked on, unmoved.

'I could be skullfucking my woman,' he growled in Latin, 'but no, instead I get to clean up your messes.'

Cassius grinned wider, but Enneconis stared at the floor, ashamed. Cyler thought about taking Ben Yusuf to the infirmary, but was diverted when the boxy prison van with square blacked out windows pulled into its designated spot beside them. It was marked down the sides with the Capital Correctional Management wordmark. Ben Yusuf rested his hands on Cyler's shoulders in an effort to stay upright. Cyler leaned close to him, noticing that Cassius had wandered over towards the van. Enneconis spoke very little Greek, so he took his chance.

'Sorry about them. They're still with the wolves.'

Ben Yusuf started at this. 'You remembered.'

Cyler could see the driver and his offsider in their green and black uniforms up front. The offsider—baby faced, he looked no more than seventeen—made his way around the back and opened the big double doors to admit the four men.

'There's a press pack outside,' he said in his strong *Puglie* accent. 'They tried to take pictures of us when we came in.'

'They're allowed to,' said Cyler, going to help Ben Yusuf clamber into the back of the vehicle. Cassius and Enneconis hung back, watching him struggle in his shackles.

'Move, you useless tubs of lard,' Cyler bellowed at them, 'you half killed him, so you can stop him dying now.'

Enneconis and Cassius stood on either side of Ben Yusuf while Cyler clambered into the van. Between them they half pulled, half shoved Ben Yusuf inside. Cassius and Enneconis sat on either side of their prisoner while Cyler sat opposite, waiting while the prison guard closed the van's rear doors. They made a heavy and satisfying clunk; Cyler ran his fingers over the seal. If nothing else, it showed that the people who supplied prison equipment had been paying attention to the question of security. Cassius banged his fist on the metal behind him.

'Solid,' he said.

'I hope so,' said Enneconis. 'I hear bad things about the Jerusalem–Jericho Road.'

'Bloodiest twenty miles in the Empire,' said Cyler. 'Well, so they say.'

The driver—an older man, his head a black-and-grey thatch—guided the van out from under the fortress and into the crowded sunshine of Passover. The young guard rolled down his window and cocked his elbow out of it, admitting sheep and food smells. There was a grille in between the cab and the van body. The teenager turned and poked his face into it, smiling at them.

'This'll take a while,' he said, 'getting out of Jerusalem. What do you want to hear?'

'What have you got?'

The young man began flicking through a box of rectangular cartridges, holding them up in front of his eyes and reading off the labels.

'Victor Gerius; Gaia Polla; Magilla Macer—'

Cyler wasn't in the mood for Victor Gerius's introspection and he thought Gaia Polla's voice overrated, so he cut the guard off and exercised authority's privilege, demanding Magilla Macer.

'She sings good stuff for *Megalesia*,' he said. 'Stick some of that on.'

The guard grinned and complied; Magilla Macer was uni-
versally acclaimed, partly because she could sing traditional music as well as her own material. Soon, the van echoed
with her soaring, coruscating vocals and intricate percussion.
Cassius sang along with some of it, but her voice was often
too high for him and he sang a harmony instead. Sometimes
Cyler and Enneconis joined in, and Cyler could see the two
men at the front of the van singing as well. They were all getting rather carried away—clapping, foot stomping and trill-
ing—when Cyler happened to look at Ben Yusuf, who had his
hands over his ears. Cyler craned his neck towards him and
clasped his shoulder.

'Do you need water?' he asked in Greek. Ben Yusuf nodded; he really did look miserable.

'Is it too loud?'

Ben Yusuf nodded again, putting his hands over his ears
once more. Cassius stopped singing and clapping and glanced
first at Ben Yusuf, then at Cyler.

'Is he sick?'

'Not very well,' Cyler shouted, 'not after your stunt this
morning.'

Cassius kissed his teeth, taking care not to direct the gesture at Cyler. Cyler thought about chipping him, and then
thought better of it, instead sharing some of his water with
Ben Yusuf. Standing up, he lifted Ben Yusuf's shirt and looked
over his back, noting the spot in his shoulder where he'd been
given an antibiotic injection. He was chopped up, all right, but
the wounds had already started to seal and would heal well.
Cyler unhooked the keys to Ben Yusuf's shackles from around
his wrist and released him, humming along with the song, his
voice fine and clear, although not as spectacular as Cassius's.
Ben Yusuf smiled at him and rubbed his ankles while Cyler
looped the shackles around the bench the three men were

sitting on. It was bolted to the floor.

'It's festival time for us,' he said at length, 'and our festivals are, ah, different from yours.'

'Yes,' said Ben Yusuf, 'sex and death.'

This comment fell in the silence between two songs, so all of them heard it. Cassius and Enneconis went off into gales of laughter. Cyler restrained himself, keeping his hand on Ben Yusuf's shoulder and looking into his eyes.

'And honour and victory and prosperity,' he said, 'those too.'

Cyler watched though the darkened windows as the van made its way through the crush of pilgrims outside. Some of them pulled faces at the Roman music pouring out through the cab's open windows, while others smiled. There was the occasional metallic *thock* against the van—especially in more open spaces—as children threw stones at it. Cyler could hear the two prison guards arguing over preferred racing stables. 'They change managers more often than they change their underwear,' he heard, as well as, 'Yeah, the bloody Blues missed the transfer window on him, didn't they?'

Cyler zoned out, ignoring their bickering. It was hard to keep up with Roman sport in Judaea, although Julia was a proper racing addict and—wonder of wonders—supported the Greens, like he did. This was a good thing. He'd heard of divorces over sporting differences. He leaned against the wall, his hands clasped between his thighs, dozing for a bit. He supposed a bit of sleep just now would be a good idea; Julia had been *very* affectionate last night and he was tired. When he woke, Cassius and Enneconis were playing scissors, paper, rock and speaking animatedly in Vasco, Ben Yusuf was fast asleep between them and the countryside was racing past outside as Magilla Macer climbed into the very top of her range. The two guards in the cab were still arguing over charioteers.

Saul waits as the two young Zealots from Jericho take their positions on either side of him, piling up loose stones from an abandoned and partly demolished Antiochan pillbox that gives a good view of the Jerusalem–Jericho road. 'It won't take a direct mortar hit,' Elias says, 'but it'll provide cover.'

Saul nods and looks over the two young men. He doesn't know how much use they'll be, but they've got good new Persian rifles: bolt action, still, but long barrelled and, he hopes, accurate. Romans are always armed to the teeth with Capuas and Ravennas, both with muzzle velocity so quick you could be hit before you heard the first bullet. One of the young men smiles at him; he smiles back and looks down at the mass of blood blisters on his hands. Even if he wanted to, he doubts he could hold a rifle in his current state.

Elias has been grouchy since shortly after they finished burying the bomb. Less than two hours later, in the dawn light, a busload of women in short dresses and frilly knickers along with a few pretty boys—all of them in heavy make-up, their eyes picked out in brilliant greens and blues—had made its way past their position. HOUSE OF THE SPIRITS was painted on the side in bold letters, along with the blue and gold Guild wordmark and contact, JSM 3414, underneath. PROUDLY SUPPORTING THE MILITARY SINCE A.U.C 710 ran a line in smaller print around the wordmark. Elias had wanted to detonate then and there, but Saul refused. Elias was furious with him, and the two of them rolled around in the dust behind the pillbox for some time until Saul managed to wrench the transmitter out of Elias's hands, screaming at him. He saw Kelil's serious young face as he did so, and felt nauseous. Elias had spat at him afterwards—as the bus disappeared from view—but Saul shook his head.

'I'll do a lot,' he said, 'but not that.'

'Roman filth, Saul.'

'Greeks and Syrians, not Romans.'

'You're Roman too, PAUL.'

That frightened him, and he had a sudden panicked urge to dump the transmitter and run as fast as he could back to Damascus. He fought it down, thinking he'd make this job his last.

'Whatever comes next,' Elias said, his tone menacing, 'it goes up. Seems we picked a shit time; there's nothing on the roads.'

When a prison van crests the hill, Saul knows there will likely be a Jewish prisoner or prisoners inside, and he's disappointed, but he also knows there will be two guards up front and maybe one or two legionaries as escorts. He visualises the filthy turn their minds have taken, the military contractors inviting their enlisted brothers in arms to fuck around in the prison for a bit, knowing that the soldiers are feeling hard done by. As the van draws closer, he hears the unmistakable sound of the smutty music Romans like to play at this time of year, percussion like a train pulling fast out of the station and a woman moaning like she's about to come. He can see the two contractors up front, the driver tapping the steering wheel and singing.

He raises the transmitter, steadying himself against a slab of concrete, sending the signal home.

Cyler could smell shit. He felt something wet clinging to his face and went to push it away; it took a moment for him to realise it was a length of intestine. He pondered this for a moment and hoped—in a detached, academic sense—that it wasn't his own. He closed his eyes, wriggling bits of his body to see if they were still there. His toes and fingers checked in, and he could still turn his head. A spare tyre was in his lap. He looked at it for a moment or two and then pushed it off. There were more intestines there as well, along with a clump of black, curly hair stuck to the roof, which he could see out of the corner of his eye. He wrinkled his nose, trying to deal with the stench. Even the Roman army's surpassingly thorough training failed to prepare its men for the extent to which battle smelt like shit. The van—what there was left of it—seemed to be on its side and twisted in the middle. He turned his head, realising that the intestines belonged to the young guard in the front of the van. The force of the blast had managed to feed him through the open grille between the cab and the sealed hull. In its way, this was very impressive.

He listened for dripping fuel and scrabbled around in the dusty dark for his rifle. He located it under a mixed pile of rubble and twisted metal, checking the magazine was free of blood and dirt. He lay on his back for a few minutes, cleaning it, then sat up slowly, avoiding the window above him. As he sat up, something sharp and metallic drove into his gut. He looked down; half-a-dozen metal fragments had perforated his body armour and he could see the green paint used on the van's exterior on some of them. At least one piece had gone all the way through. He lay back very carefully and began to strip the armour off, pulling shards out as he went. He unbuttoned his jacket and ran his fingers over his stomach, feeling for injuries. There was one deep puncture just above the floating rib on his left side. He felt under what was left of a bench for the first-aid kit, opened it and cleaned the wound, packed it with gauze and then sprayed it with a hemostatic agent to stop the bleeding.

The van's hull was still mostly intact, although the two guards in the cab were in many pieces. Enneconis was already upright and awake behind him, seated with his rifle in hand. He had pushed himself up against the wall and drawn his knees up. His knuckles were white, his eyes fixed on a point in the middle distance. His lips were moving but he made no sound. He was unharmed and remarkably clean. Cyler reached up and waved his hand in front of his eyes.

'Base to Enneconis, come in Enneconis.'

'I'm here, sir,' he said softly.

'First combat?'

'Yes, sir.'

Cyler thumped him on the shoulder.

'You're about to lose your virginity.'

The young man grimaced and began to look for Cassius.

They found Cassius and Ben Yusuf tangled together on the other side of the narrow twist, which they wriggled through on their bellies. It was very dark and cramped and smelt of soil and blood. Enneconis picked up a black helmet from beside his feet, knocking it with his knuckles. Ben Yusuf was out cold but unharmed, while Cassius was covered in blood from a long gash—from shoulder to elbow—down one arm. He was in the process of binding it up, holding the end of the bandage in his teeth.

'Did you pass out?'

Cassius shook his head, finishing the binding before he spoke.

'You two have been out for about twenty minutes.'

'Have they fired on us?'

'Twice after the bomb went off, but nothing since.'

'Can you get back through there with that arm? There's more room to move, and we can use the side window up top to get our Zealot friends to show themselves.'

Cassius smiled; Cyler suspected the sniper had divined his plan.

'Bring that helmet,' he told Enneconis, 'and bring the prisoner. I don't want him dead.'

They struggled their way through the twisted chassis, Cyler leading the way, Enneconis dragging Ben Yusuf and Cassius grunting and swearing as he made his way through the gap while trying to avoid tearing the fresh bandage off his arm.

'I should go underneath,' Cyler said.

'No you shouldn't, sir,' said Cassius. 'You couldn't hit the side of a barn with a handful of peas.'

Cassius's violet eyes fairly blazed in the dark, red coming to dominate the purple. They really were extraordinary. Cyler smiled at the witticism; he was a good sportsman and very bright, but an excellent shot he was not.

Cyler smashed out the remains of the metal grille with his rifle butt, widening the hole, then removed the human remains from around it. Cassius stripped off his body armour and wriggled his lean frame through, while Enneconis cleaned his long-barrelled Capua 28-4. He handed the rifle, body armour and bipod to Cassius once he'd made his way through into the wrecked cab. They listened as he dropped himself through the hole in the floor and set up underneath the hull, the different components clicking together with satisfying efficiency.

'Can they see him, sir?'

'I don't know. Give me that helmet.'

Cyler took a multi-tool from one of his pockets and began removing the window, slowly, carefully. Eventually it popped out in his hands; he dropped it at his feet and perched the helmet on the end of his rifle, raising it through the opening.

The mutilated van is partly on its side, surrounded by satisfying quantities of Roman blood. Saul can see an arm, still clad in its green and black uniform, sawed off neatly at the shoulder. There's a helmet, too. He and Elias and the two younger Zealots watch for what seems like hours for any further movement.

'I think they must all be dead,' Saul says. Elias shakes his head, looking through the binoculars.

'I saw it wriggle. There's one man in there alive, at least.'

'Why didn't it all blow up?'

'Sometimes they don't,' Elias says. 'They harden the fuel tanks and put flame retardants in there.' He points. 'The fuel tank will be

in the best-protected part of the vehicle.'

Just as Saul makes to comment, a helmeted head begins to raise itself through the side window in what is now the 'roof'. Before Elias has time to intervene, one of the young men beside him fires on it, giving a little whoop. The helmeted head withdraws, quickly.

'Idiot!' Elias yells, just as they come under fire—close, accurate fire.

Saul has never fought before, but he realises the Roman still alive in the van now knows their position, and that he's a very good shot. Elias wriggles towards the young Zealot on his belly, telling him to get his bloody head down. The man is spooked now, and he stands up and begins to run towards the wreckage, firing wildly. As Saul and Elias watch, two Roman bullets smack into his chest. Saul expects him to drop, but he keeps running—albeit crookedly—until a third bullet takes the top off his head. His legs piston up and down for a few seconds; he finally drops to the ground, twitching.

'The sniper's under the wreck,' says the other young Zealot. 'I saw the light on his gun barrel.'

Elias turns to face him.

'Good,' he says, 'You've got something between your ears, even if your friend never did.'

Cyler could feel sweat running down his arse crack as he balanced the helmet above him; it was hot inside the wreck, even with the window open. He grinned at the enemy's stupidity as he flicked the helmet off the end of his rifle and pulled it inside. He flopped against the wall of the van, listening as Cassius put one of the Zealots away. It was very satisfying when simple plans came off like that.

The close firing had stirred Ben Yusuf into wakefulness, and Cyler ordered Enneconis to give him water.

'What happened?' Ben Yusuf asked in Greek, massaging the side of his head.

'IED,' said Cyler, 'and now they're trying to pick us off.'

'Zealots?'

'Nah, the Persians have invaded.'

Cyler snickered as he saw the horrified expression on Ben Yusuf's face.

'Only kidding,' he added, patting the other man's cheek and grinning. 'It's just Zealots trying to shit up *Megalesia* on us.'

Ben Yusuf formed a fist and bit his fingers to keep from crying out as gunshots began to ping against the wreck, creeping closer to Cassius's hiding spot underneath it with each pass. Cyler and Enneconis wriggled back through the narrow gap, leaving him alone.

'We won't do any good in here,' Cyler was saying, raising his rifle and shooting the locks off the rear doors. 'And I'm not planning to die cooped up in a tin can.'

Enneconis kicked the doors open and the two men dropped onto the road shoulder, running to take positions at either end of the wreck. They came under fire, but their movements were liquid and skillful and they evaded harm, at least temporarily.

Ben Yusuf watched through a slit-like gap in the floor as Cassius and Enneconis fought and protected each other. He presumed Cyler was involved as well, but he couldn't see him, only hear his voice from time to time. Enneconis, he could see, was afraid but bold in spite of his fear. Cassius spoke to him, his tone low and calm. Once he rested his hand on the young man's neck, a gentle, solicitous gesture.

'I'll defend you,' he said more than once. 'I'll keep you safe.'

Ben Yusuf crawled into what seemed the least damaged part of the van, hugging his knees to his chest, his teeth chattering. The battle went on for what seemed like hours, long periods of silence interspersed with sporadic gunfire. Enneconis secured his first kill and he heard both Cyler and Cassius congratulate him on it. There was a joyful lip-smacking sound at that point and he realised that Cassius and Enneconis had kissed. Ben Yusuf wanted to pull the rear doors closed—leaving them open, so the wrecked van was filled with light and he could see the stinking and bloody mess, terrified him—but he found himself too frightened to move.

Cyler thought they'd been doing well, until more Zealots turned up and they came under fire from the other side of the road. The blast had lifted that side of the van further from the ground, and there was less cover. Worse, they only realised they were being attacked when Cassius took a bullet in the leg from behind, where he was stretched out underneath the chassis. He rolled over, screaming and swearing, his hands clamping down on the inside of his thigh. Once again—in a detached way—the jetting arterial blood impressed Cyler. Enneconis leant over Cassius and tried to apply a compression bandage, but there was so much blood. The two of them dragged the sniper further underneath the chassis, trying to shield him, while Enneconis manhandled his Capua 28-4 around to face the other way.

'There's too many of them,' said Cyler. 'Use the Ravenna.'

As he spoke, Cassius took another hit in the shoulder of his already wounded arm, driving him sideways, exposing him. He howled and his hands flicked and wriggled at his sides, his coordination sloppy. He pointed at Enneconis.

'Give it to me. I'm not going to give them the pleasure.'

Without demurring, Enneconis's hands went to his lover's side and he gave Cassius his service pistol. Cassius steadied himself, struggling for a moment, trying to lodge the barrel in his mouth while Cyler laid down covering fire. Cyler heard but did not see the pistol discharge, suspecting that the younger man had used the heel of his palm to guide the weapon home.

Enneconis then joined him—he was a good shot, for which Cyler was grateful—and the two of them prepared to make a final stand.

'We kill as many as we can,' Cyler said, 'and then—'

Enneconis cut him off. 'Death before dishonour, sir.'

Cyler could see tears in the corners of his eyes.

Ben Yusuf heard the characteristic light *pop* of a pistol and knew that one of the Romans had suicided. He put his eye to the crack in the floor, watching as Cyler and Enneconis did their best to defend an impossible position. Cassius's booted foot was stretched out beside Cyler as the latter worked his weapon. It was very still. Ben Yusuf found that he did not mind Cassius's death, even though it was Enneconis who had encircled his head with razor wire halfway through a particularly brutal flogging. That he did not mind did not please him, but there it was. He made his way towards the open doors at the back of the van, wriggling through the narrow twist in the middle and dropping to the ground as he had seen the Romans do. He ducked underneath the vehicle, crawling towards the two men. He did not come under fire. Cyler spun his head to face him, then went back to shooting.

'Get back inside, you stupid fuck,' he shouted, all the while firing in short, controlled bursts. 'They won't kill *you*.'

'Out of ammo,' said Enneconis. Cyler reached down and tossed him a magazine. The young man plucked it out of the air.

'The ammo situation is not good,' Cyler added, his tone amused, 'so make it count.'

Ben Yusuf smiled grimly at this. *They value their ammunition, these Romans; they even collect 'bullet fees' from the families of executed criminals.*

'Some air cover would be nice about now,' said Enneconis, squinting upwards.

'Fuck, I got one,' Cyler said, a rictus grin on his face. He took careful aim again; Ben Yusuf watched him compress the trigger. 'And another one; practice makes perfect.'

The volume of fire from the latest group of Zealot attackers dropped away, and Enneconis turned again to the mounted sniper rifle, squinting into the scope and picking off another Zealot, twice in the chest, *boom boom*, once in the head, *booooom*. The Zealots stopped firing; Ben Yusuf could see two figures moving in the far distance. Cyler rolled over and pushed himself back as far as possible into the wreck, sitting up and drinking from his canteen, his rifle propped between his legs.

'When we're dead, you need to stand up with your hands above your head,' he said. 'Nice and high, too, so they can see what you're doing.'

Ben Yusuf looked at the young man's filthy, smouldering face, marvelling at his utter indifference to death.

'Stay there like that for five minutes or so, no matter how much your shoulders hurt. If no one shoots you, walk away from the vehicle at right angles, still with your hands—'

The shots came from behind, close, too, cutting him off. Ben Yusuf watched as Enneconis's neck seemed to shatter and Cyler jerked against the metal supporting him. Cyler looked down at the expanding exit wound in the bottom of his chest, trying to cover it with one hand. Ben Yusuf saw him look at his palm with detachment, holding it up in front of his face. The wound was larger than his hand, and full of black blood.

'Oh shit,' he said, 'this is it.'

Julia and Tisiphone soared over the city, swooping once to pick up speed and then flying in a line straighter than the Roman road towards Jericho and the prison. The distress signal in the van had gone to the prison governor's office, and he'd relayed its position—after considerable delay—to Antonia. Julia did not find this sequence of events particularly impressive, and she added it to the growing file of 'incompetence stories' emanating from the prison. Apparently, he'd locked himself in his quarters with two whores, several bottles of good red and quantities of food and did not respond to repeated bangs on his door. Eventually one of the few guards still sober and on duty borrowed a prisoner—inside for half-a-dozen break and enters—to jemmy the lock. With a fire axe. Only then had the governor stumbled into his office and attended to his duties.

She spotted the wounded vehicle and radioed the push-prop that Vitellius had scrambled in Damascus, then she began to circle. If there had been fighting, it was long since over; there were half-a-dozen dead Zealots—or what looked like Zealots, they had Persian small arms and were not in proper uniforms—scattered at a distance from the van, and several dead Romans. She saw one legionary sprawled on the ground, half underneath the wreck, his service pistol beside his head. It had clearly been in his mouth. There was also a black military contractor's helmet beside the cab, and what looked like an arm, swelling in the heat. The carrion excited Tisiphone, and it was all she could do to keep the *strix* under control.

Saul can see the monstrosity circling, and knows for all that having a dozen of their confreres turn up unannounced was a good thing— got the sniper, we did—they will now be at the Romans' mercy. Elias hunkers down beside Saul.

'Got the other two,' he says, tossing his rifle into the ditch and then joining it. 'Didn't even know what hit them.'

He then looks up and sees the strix.

'I fucking hate those things.'

His tone is one of hatred mixed with raw fear. Saul nods, but shows no fear himself, doing his best to keep the science he knows uppermost in his mind.

'They're genetic constructs,' he says, 'dreamed up by Roman and Greek scientists who get a kick out of playing God.'

'Some of the parts come from abortion, don't they?' Elias asks. Saul nods. This isn't strictly true, but it's too much like hard work to disabuse the older man of his notions.

'Whatever you do, don't move,' he says. 'They respond to motion. If you need to piss, do it in your pants.'

They watch the strix *track down the four remaining Zealots on the other side of the wreck one by one, shooting them and burning them and then—most terrifying of all—skewering them and tearing the corpses into pieces. Men flee from her, but the woman guiding the* strix *takes delight in their fear, using the fierce claws and beak of her machine to rip them up.*

Julia landed and let Tisiphone feed, quartering the area and magnifying anything suspicious while she waited. She destroyed a couple of entirely innocent olive trees to eliminate possible cover and then hopped Tisiphone closer to the wrecked vehicle. The air was still and shimmering with heat; blood surrounding the van had already blackened and hardened. She doubted there would be anyone to rescue, and cursed the prison governor. She flicked a switch above her head and spoke into her earpiece.

'Gentlemen, your ride's here... the emergency special to Jerusalem is now boarding on platform one. All aboard, please.'

There was movement underneath the wreck; she could see what she thought was a Roman soldier dragging a man behind him. The soldier's back was turned and both men were covered in blood. Slowly, the soldier stood upright and turned to face her, removing his helmet and looking stunned, as though he'd been hit in the temple with a mallet. She leant forward, peering at him.

It can't be.

She recognised him properly only when he smiled his crooked smile. She fought down an almost overwhelming urge to abandon Tisiphone and run to him.

Cyler knew this was going to take some very fast and smooth talking, even with his woman as interlocutor.

'I was dead,' he said, 'I was liver shot and bleeding black. He saved me.'

Julia shook her head, not comprehending what he was saying. Cyler had Ben Yusuf draped over his shoulders in a fireman's lift, and was clearly expecting her to take both of them back to Antonia. He was without body armour and drenched with dark blood. She shook her head slowly again, indicating that he should dump the body on the ground and join her.

'He saved me,' Cyler repeated. 'I can't leave him.'

She was angry, and it showed.

'So you want me to bring a dead prisoner back to Antonia and leave the bodies of two brave Roman legionaries to be desecrated?'

'He's not dead,' he said.

'Let me touch him,' she said.

Cyler moved closer and gave her Ben Yusuf's hand. It was white and clammy. She squinted at Ben Yusuf and held the hand, using the diagnostic equipment in her fleshy helmet, her one visible eye slitty with concentration.

'He's already going cold, Cyler. He's dead.'

Cyler shook his head.

'He can't be. *I* was dead. I was gut-shot. I was bleeding to death.'

He moved swiftly up into the *strix*, dumping Ben Yusuf beside the empty navigator's seat and crouching in front of Julia.

He began to remove his jacket. It was stiff with blood, as was his shirt. He dropped both garments on the seat, reached over and took her hand, putting it on his right lower chest. His skin was caked with blood, but there was no wound. He could feel her fingers searching underneath the gore, exploring gently.

'It was there. It was *right there*. I was dying. He told me to hold his hand, and I did, and I lived.'

Saul watches as the Roman soldier walks towards the strix, *Ben Yusuf draped over his shoulders.*

'You didn't kill that one,' he says to Elias. The older Zealot is shaking his head, disbelieving.

'Yes I did. Got him in the back, I did.'

Elias makes no attempt to move or fire, even though the aviatrix has opened the machine's shining eye in order to talk to the soldier, making herself vulnerable. The two of them speak for some time, until the soldier climbs up and dumps Ben Yusuf's body inside. She closes the eye but does not fly off. Saul rubs his face, listening to Elias's breathing become laboured.

'He should be dead or crawling on the ground,' Elias says.

'Yes,' says Saul, 'but he isn't.'

TAILPIECE

Pilate read through *Medicus* Saleh's report again, aware he was shaking his head as he did so. He was fuzzy brained from drinking before lunch but even so, he was sure that he'd taken it all in.

> ...I am no closer to resolving this matter after autopsy than I was before, except to say that Ben Yusuf has experienced blood loss consistent with an untreated high velocity gunshot wound to the liver and was thus hemodynamically unstable. Similarly, Cyler Lucullus's MRI scans reveal scarring consistent with a surgically treated high-velocity gunshot wound. Surgery appears to have been undertaken approximately six months ago, however, there is no record of this in his medical history. It appears that an experienced surgeon has undertaken resectional debridement or lobectomy and has isolated the liver by using clamps on the suprahepatic inferior vena cava, suprarenal cava, and the porta hepatis. The surgeon also gained control of the bleeding with uncommon speed. There is also no sign of the foreign bodies commonly seen with gunshot wounds, e.g. wadding or clothing blown into the liver by the blast...

Pilate leaned forward, buzzing for Horace. The young man was—like Pilate—tipsy but still reasonably sharp. He stood in front of Pilate's desk, blinking.

'I take it you read this,' Pilate said.

'Yes, Procurator, I did. If I shouldn't have—'

'You're my clerk, Horace. For all intents and purposes, you *are* me.'

Pilate leaned back in his chair, his hands clasped behind his head. *What does Camilla say? That's very unlikely.*

'Release the body to Joseph and Cynara Arimathea, as requested,' he said, 'and inform the army medical staff.'

PRINCIPAL CHARACTERS

Familia Pilata

Pontius Pilate: Procurator of Judaea.

Claudia Procula: Pilate's wife.

Camilla: the older of Pilate and Claudia's two children.

Antony: Pilate and Claudia's younger child.

Marius Macro of *Legio* X *Fretensis*: Camilla's fiancé.

Aristocles, Zoe, Corbulo, Dana: household servants, Corbulo on loan from *Legio* X *Fretensis*.

The Sanhedrin

Kayafa: *Kohen Gadol* ('High Priest') of Jerusalem, called **Caiaphas** by Greeks and Romans.

Esther: Caiaphas's wife.

Hillel: Caiaphas's and Esther's son.

Joseph Arimathea: A senior member of the Sanhedrin; related to Caiaphas.

Rivkah Arimathea: Joseph Arimathea's daughter, called **Cynara** by Greeks and Romans; manager of the Empire Hotel.

Naomi: a servant in Caiaphas's household.

Legio X Fretensis

Cornelius Getorex: *Aquilifer* ('Standard Bearer') and military prosecutor.

Mirella Tanita: midwife at the Jerusalem Æsculapion, and Cornelius's woman.

Tullius Capito: *Primus Pilus* ('First File') of *Legio* X *Fretensis*; answers directly to Pilate.

Irenaeus Iulius Andrus, also called **Irie:** Cohort Commander of the Galilee garrison.

Cyler Lucullus: enlisted man marked out as a future officer; studying military law.

Rufus Vero: comrade of Cyler Lucullus; Rachel's rescuer.

Aristotle Eugenides: comrade of Cyler Lucullus.

Marcus Lonuobo: translator and cryptanalyst.

Darius Saleh: medic.

Gaius Crispus: a military prosecutor and prominent senator's son.

Julia Procula: an aviatrix (military pilot).

Yeshua Ben Yusuf and his Companions

Yeshua Ben Yusuf: holy man.

Ioanne and **Andreas:** fishermen, Ben Yusuf's followers.

Matthias Levi: a regional bank manager and tax collector.

Mary Magdalena: a newsreader for the Jerusalem Television Network and local celebrity.

Petros Bar Yonah: fisherman and Ben Yusuf's most senior follower.

Simon: called 'The Zealot'.

Yehuda Iscariot: a senior Zealot.

Zealots

Saul: also called **Paul**, a disaffected Roman citizen.

Elias: a Zealot in Jericho.

Kelil: also known as **Stephanos**.

Yaakov: a fifteen-year-old boy.

Other characters

Andreius Linnaeus: Pilate's closest friend from law school, and Yeshua Ben Yusuf's defence counsel.

Fotini Kallenike: A *hetaera* at the Empire Hotel, later Andreius Linnaeus's concubine.

Nic Varro, owner of the Jerusalem Television Network and successful local businessman, husband to Mary Magdalena.

Soraya Iscariot: also called **Sarah**, sister to Yehuda Iscariot and wife to Irie Andrus of *Legio* X *Fretensis*.

Horace: Pilate's law clerk.

Severus Agrippa: a prominent news anchor from Rome.

Vitellius: Governor of Syria, Pilate's immediate superior.

Zipporah: also called **Tzipi**, wife to Marcus Lonuobo.

GLOSSARY

Ab urbe condita: from the founding of the city (of Rome), traditionally dated to 753 BC, which is thus a.u.c. I. As in our system, there is no 'year zero'.

Advocatus/a: lawyer, advisor.

Aquilifer: standard-bearer, a position of considerable honour.

Andronites: men's quarters in a traditional Athenian household.

Architectus: military engineer (either sapper or civil).

Avunculus: Uncle.

Basiliké Stoà: town hall.

Bingium: Modern Bingen am Rhein.

Britunculus: An unpleasant diminutive for a person from Britain.

Caldarium: the 'hot room' in a Roman baths complex.

Cardo: main street *or* high street.

Cinaedus: rent boy.

Coleones: balls (slang).

Collegium (sing.): the Roman law version of a limited liability corporation with a separate legal personality.

Contubernium: squad or section in the Roman army; comprised of eight men.

Corona: the Roman Victoria Cross or Congressional Medal of Honour.

Culpa: guilt, blame.

Curo! Terra minae: 'Caution: Land Mines!'

Decumanus: secondary main street; it always intersects with the *cardo*.

De gustibus non est disputandum: 'There's no accounting for taste.'

Delict: the Roman law of torts (civil wrongs) against property.

De sua pecunia fecit: 'Built with his/her own money'.

Divi Filius: son of a god.

Divide et impera: 'divide and rule'.

Dolus directus: murder with intent.

Dolus indirectus: murder without intent, but where death is seen as inevitable.

Dolus eventualis: murder without intent, but where death is seen as probable.

Dominus/a: Master/Mistress; *Domine* is the masculine vocative form (the 'calling' case).

Duumvir: mayor, always elected as one of a pair by a system of census suffrage (voting qualification based on property, not gender).

Erastes/Eromenos: 'official' names for the older man/younger man in a Greek homosexual relationship.

Feria: Festival, usually somewhat bloody.

Fideicommissa: the Roman law equivalent of a trust.

Fretensis: 'Of the Straights'; indicates originally formed as marines.

Frigidarium: the cold bath in a set of Roman baths; often large, even swimming pool sized.

Gallus: ladyboy. The plural is *galli*.

Gveret (Hebrew): Madam.

Haruspex: An individual who practises divination based on the dissection of livers.

Hetaera (Greek): a highly educated courtesan.

Infames, infamia: having no reputation to defend, and so barred from bringing a claim in defamation.

Immunis: a soldier with a skill; if a professional (lawyer, medic), something akin to a staff officer, but among subordinate ranks corresponds roughly with 'specialist.'

Iniuria: the Roman law of torts (civil wrongs) against the person.

Instrumentum vocale: 'The tool that speaks'.

Ita, recte: yes, indeed.

Kohanim (Hebrew): priests at the Jerusalem Temple, tasked with management and organising animal sacrifices; always descendents of Aaron.

Kohen Gadol (Hebrew): High Priest.

Kyrios/Kyria (Greek): Sir, Madam.

Lanista: a trainer or manager of gladiators and cage fighters; considered a low-status occupation, although many of them are very rich.

Lararia: god-shelf, similar to Japanese *kamidana.*

Lares: household gods, gods of place; similar to Japanese *kami.*

Laudatio: eulogy.

Legatus: General.

Leno/a: pimp/madam.

Libellus conventionis: indictment.

Licentia: trade or professional qualification.

Limes: border.

Ludi: games, entertainment (plural).

Magister/Magistra: teacher, used as a title, much like 'Sensei' in Japanese.

Magna Mater: the Great Mother, mother of the gods (*mater deum*); used of Cybele.

Manes: the ancestral spirits.

Materfamilias: mother of the household, but only ever used of a woman who has, in fact, borne children.

Medicus: doctor, usually in the military.

Megalesia: The Roman Festival of the *Magna Mater* (the Great Mother, Cybele).

Mezzadri: sharecroppers.

Mitzvah (Hebrew): blessing.

Mogontiacum: Mainz.

Mos maiorum: 'way of the ancestors'; the plural is *mores*.

MRAP: Mine Resistant Ambush Protected armoured vehicle; has a distinctive v-shaped hull, making it difficult to destroy with IEDs.

Niddah (Hebrew): period during and following menstruation when a woman is ritually unclean.

Novus actus interveniens: 'New intervening event'; break in the chain of causation.

Optio: the second in command of a legionary century, although Marius, as *Optio* of the first century, first cohort is a senior officer.

Optimates: Tories.

Pais, padika (Greek): 'boy lover'.

Palaestra: gymnasium.

Parrilla: 'barbecue'.

Paterfamilias: father of the household. His duties extend beyond those in the nuclear family, taking in servants, colleagues of lower status, friends down on their luck and—occasionally—children-in-law. Considered honourable, something to aspire to; commands considerable moral authority.

Payot: earlocks.

Perplexae: complex, intricate and beautiful pattern.

Pietas: filial piety (in a sense similar to that expounded in Confucianism).

Philotimia: private philanthropy for the good of the *civitas* or *polis*; it is always *for* something (education, entertainment, construction, commerce).

Populares: Whigs.

Potestas: power, especially derived from respect or rank, not violent display.

Praetorium: courtroom, especially in the provinces.

Primus Pilus: 'First File'; equivalent to a senior colonel.

Publicani: private firms contracted to exercise the tax collecting power by the Roman state.

Rhenus: the Roman name for the River Rhine.

Scientia est potestas: 'Knowledge is Power'.

Senatus consultum de re publica defendenda: emergency edict, 'state of emergency'.

Septuagint: A Greek translation of key Jewish scriptures popular in antiquity.

Seriatim: one after the other.

Shabbat goy: a non-Jew who runs errands or completes tasks for a Jew on the Sabbath.

Shiva: Judaism's traditional period of mourning.

Sicarii: 'knife men', used of an extreme faction of the Zealots; they particularly target those they consider collaborators with the Roman occupation.

Simpliciter: without qualification or condition.

Sine manu: literally, 'without the hand'; form of Roman marriage where the husband and wife's property interests were kept entirely separate. The most common form of marriage, it ensured a husband had no control over his wife's property, and that he could not interfere with her income or investments. It also forbade joint bank accounts and wives standing surety for their husbands in a real property transaction.

S.P.Q.R. (Senatus Populusque Romanus): The Senate and People of Rome.

Stuprum: general term for sexual immorality, often of a quite sensational sort.

Tabula recta: Alphabet tables, used in cryptography.

Tamesis: the Roman name for the River Thames.

Tauroctony: Mithras slaying the bull; principle cult image of the Mithraic Mysteries.

Tekton: carpenter or stonemason.

Tepidarium: the 'warm' room in a Roman baths complex.

Tribus: Roman constituency; originally geographical, the system was diluted over time until characterised by rotten boroughs and disproportionate electorate sizes and populations.

Vasco: Basque.

Vexilla/um: flag.

Vigiles: fire brigade, and in some cities, the police as well.

Yeshivot: Rabbinical schools. The singular is *yeshiva*.

ACKNOWLEDGEMENTS

No book this large and complex gets written without a great deal of help. The following institutions and people made *Kingdom of the Wicked* possible: the Institute for Humane Studies, whose three fellowships allowed me not only to pursue studies at the Universities of Oxford and Edinburgh but also bought me time to write; the law faculties at both Oxford and Edinburgh, which supported my studies and allowed me to engage in careful deliberation in the areas of jurisprudence and comparative law; Mel Richards, who taught me about the Religious Society of Friends and made me think about the relationship between religion and modernity; James Worthern, who introduced me to a wealth of classical sources, many of them obscure, all of them fascinating, and then helped with translation; Katy Barnett, who was a brilliant and attentive first reader; Sinclair Davidson, who clarified many obscurities in economic theory and provided one of the best lines of dialogue in the book; Paul du Plessis, my Roman law tutor at Edinburgh; Lorenzo Warby, who discussed the intersection of slavery and technological progress with me; Carlo Kopp, who brought his knowledge of military culture and technology to bear on many points in the story; Dave Bath, who introduced me to ancient medical literature and helped me understand how a different medical tradition might develop; Susan Prior, who was an astonishingly sharp-eyed editor, and Justice Peter Dutney, who was an extraordinary and insightful pupil-master.

Any errors, infelicities, and disagreements are my responsibility.

Oxford, Edinburgh, Sydney, London

Helen Dale is a Queenslander by birth and a Londoner by choice. She read law at Oxford (where she was at Brasenose) and has previously worked as a lawyer, political staffer, and advertising copywriter (among other things). She became the youngest winner of Australia's Miles Franklin Award with her first novel, *The Hand that Signed the Paper*, leaving the country shortly after it caused a storm of controversy. Her second novel, *Kingdom of the Wicked*, is published in two volumes by Ligature.

Terry Rodgers is a Scottish graphic artist and photographer who has spent many years designing material for the Fringe, especially Skeptics on the Fringe. He lives in Edinburgh.

COPYRIGHT

ligature*fi*rst